The
LOST
HEIRESS

LADIES OF
THE MANOR

The

LOST
HEIRESS

ROSEANNA M. WHITE

BETHANYHOUSE
a division of Baker Publishing Group
Minneapolis, Minnesota

© 2015 by Roseanna M. White

Published by Bethany House Publishers
11400 Hampshire Avenue South
Bloomington, Minnesota 55438
www.bethanyhouse.com

Bethany House Publishers is a division of
Baker Publishing Group, Grand Rapids, Michigan

Printed in the United States of America

Library of Congress Cataloging-in-Publication Data
White, Roseanna M.
   The lost heiress / Roseanna M. White.
      pages ; cm. — (Ladies of the Manor)
      Summary: "In 1910 Edwardian England, a British-born young heiress raised
   in the palace of Monaco comes to Yorkshire, where mystery and tragedy
   threaten her very existence"— Provided by publisher.
      ISBN 978-0-7642-1350-2 (pbk.)
      I. Title.
   PS3623.H578785L67 2015
   813'.6—dc23   2015009360

Scripture quotations are from the King James Version of the Bible.

This is a work of historical reconstruction; the appearances of certain historical figures are therefore inevitable. All other characters, however, are products of the author's imagination, and any resemblance to actual persons, living or dead, is coincidental.

Cover design by Jennifer Parker
Cover photography by Mike Habermann Photography, LLC

Author represented by The Steve Laube Agency

15 16 17 18 19 20 21   7 6 5 4 3 2 1

To Pappap was my dedication when I
first penned this novel at age thirteen.
After I finished my first rewrite at fourteen,
it said, *In loving memory of Pappap.*
Your life taught me to laugh in every possible moment;
your death taught me to trust Him with all my might.
You helped make me who I am,
and I'll always love you.

CWM

Character List

Brook's Family

Brook Eden	The lost Eden heiress. Full name Elizabeth Brook Eden. Also called Baroness of Berkeley and Lady Berkeley (title inherited from mother).
The Earl of Whitby	Brook's father. Given name of Ambrose Eden, but called Whitby or Lord Whitby, nicknamed Whit.
The Countess of Whitby	Brook's mother, deceased; the previous Baroness of Berkeley. Given name of Elizabeth Brook, but called Lady Berkeley before her marriage and Lady Whitby afterward.
Mary, Lady Ramsey	Brook's aunt, Whitby's sister. Brook calls her Aunt Mary but everyone else calls her Lady Ramsey.
Lady Regan	Brook's first cousin, the elder of Lady Ramsey's daughters.
Lady Melissa	Brook's first cousin, the younger of Lady Ramsey's daughters.
The Marquess of Ramsey	Brook's step-cousin, Lady Ramsey's stepson and her daughters' half brother. Called Ram.
Lady Catherine Rushworth	Brook's second cousin on her mother's side, called Lady Catherine formally, Kitty by her friends.
Lord Rushworth	Brook's second cousin on her mother's side, Lady Catherine's brother and guardian. Given name of Crispin, called Lord Rushworth or Rush.
Lord (John) Rushworth	Brook's mother's first cousin, deceased; the previous Lord Rushworth and father of Lady Catherine and Rush.
Major Henry Rushworth	Brook's mother's first cousin, brother of John Rushworth, uncle of Lady Catherine and Rush.

Justin's Family

Justin Wildon   Brook's childhood friend in Monaco. Also called Lord Harlow or Harlow. Upon his father's death, becomes Marquess of Abingdon, sometimes called Bing. Upon his grandfather's death becomes Duke of Stafford.

The Duke of Stafford
(with subsidiary titles of Marquess of Abingdon and Earl of Harlow)   Justin's paternal grandfather. Given name of Samuel Wildon but called Stafford or Duke.

William Wildon   Justin's father. Called Lord William. He inherited the courtesy title of Marquess of Abingdon after his older brother's death but refused to use it.

Georgiana Wildon   Justin's mother, deceased.

Edward Wildon   Justin's uncle, deceased; the oldest son of the Duke of Stafford, so the Marquess of Abingdon until his death.

Caroline, Lady Abingdon   Justin's aunt, Edward's widow, Georgiana's sister. Justin calls her Aunt Caro but everyone else calls her Lady Abingdon.

Susan, Lady Cayton   Justin's aunt, daughter of the Duke of Stafford, mother of Lord Cayton; Justin calls her Aunt Susan, everyone else calls her Lady Cayton.

The Earl of Cayton   Justin's first cousin, Susan's son. Called Cayton, though Justin occasionally calls him James.

Other Characters

Deirdre O'Malley   Lady's maid to Brook.

Earl Thate   Justin's best friend, called Lord Thate or Thate.

Viscount Pratt   Neighbor to Brook and Whitby, very distant cousin to Whitby on his mother's side. Called Lord Pratt or Pratt.

The Marquess of Worthing   Brook's friend. Given name of Brice Myerston, son and heir of the Duke of Nottingham. Called Lord Worthing, Worthing, and occasionally Brice.

Lady Ella Myerston   Brook's friend, Worthing's younger sister. Called Lady Ella or Ella by her friends.

One

Temptation sat before her, compelling as the sea. Gleaming silver, green leather, the nearly silent rumble of engine . . .

Brook trailed a gloved hand along the door, cast one glance over her shoulder, and let herself in. She couldn't stop the grin as she gripped the wheel of the Rolls-Royce. And why should she? Only a fool would leave such a car running right outside her door and not expect her to do something about it.

"Don't even think it."

His voice brought laughter to her lips, and she looked up to find her dearest friend at the opposite door—her first sight of him in five months. The warm Riviera wind had tousled his hair, making her wonder where his hat had gone today. "Teach me to drive it, Justin."

He glared at her with an intensity to match the Mediterranean sun. All manner of men flooded Monaco in pursuit of its casino, and none could glower like the British. Well, perhaps the Russians, but theirs were more scowls than proper glowers.

9

Though, if he expected her to be cowed by the look, he had taken leave of his senses.

He leveled an accusatory finger at her nose. "I'm happy to take you for a drive in my new car, *mon amie*, but *I* will be behind the wheel."

"Come, Justin." She said his name as it was meant to be said. In French. Soft J and long U, emphasis on the second syllable, the N silent—as she knew no one in his native country did. "Your gift will soon be back in England. We mustn't waste a moment of its time in Monaco. Get in and teach me."

"A moment of *its* time?" But he laughed and slid into the left side of the car, shaking his head. The sun caught his hair and burnished it gold, caught the angles of his face and made it all the stronger. "The prince will have my head for this."

Brook grinned at him. Once upon a time, she had dreamed that they would fall in love and live happily ever after—before she realized a future duke could never be more than friends with a nobody without a past. Before she came to understand Prince Albert wasn't really her grandfather. "He will be jealous, you mean. He must always have a chauffeur behind the wheel." Brook gripped the wheel tighter, until she could feel the thrum of the 40/50 engine in every cell. "Perhaps I will borrow one of the chauffeur's jackets and surprise him one day—after you've taught me."

Justin pressed a hand to his brow, dark blond hair falling over his fingers. "Heaven help me. I'll be executed. My poor grandfather will expire from the shock of it, the dukedom will go extinct, and it will be all your fault. All because you grin at me and I can't say no."

She grinned all the brighter now. "I don't intend to race in Grand-père's road rally—I only want to learn the basics." She made herself comfortable on the seat, positioning her feet on the pedals on either side of the steering column. She had read books and articles about the advances of the automobile, but the pages hadn't come close to conveying the power that came coursing through the floorboard. It was almost as heady a feeling as having a spirited horse under her. Almost.

Justin slid closer, casting her a sideways look she couldn't read—making fear knot in her chest. She'd been waiting months for him to return, had begun to worry he never would, that his family would succeed in keeping him forever in the Cotswolds of England, and he would forget his promises to investigate the seal on the old, yellowed envelope she had pressed to his palm five months ago.

She cleared her throat. "Did you learn anything? In England, I mean?"

Justin adjusted the position of her hands on the wheel. "Of course I did. Literature and mathematics—"

"Justin Wildon."

"—philosophy and science." He ducked his head as if to make sure her feet were where they ought to be. Or to avoid her gaze. "I came across the papers of a German not long ago. Fellow by the name of Albert Einstein, a physics professor. Have you read him? He has interesting theories—"

"Lord Harlow." She narrowed her eyes at him, but he still didn't look up.

"—about Newtonian physics and something called *special relativity*, which I know you'd find interesting." He straightened, focus still on her feet. "There are pedals for clutch, brake, and accelerator. Throttle is on the steering column. You must press upon brake and clutch to begin."

"I know." She pushed them without taking her eyes off his strong profile. "And *you* know well what I mean."

He finally swung his face her way again, jaw set. "We can either talk about that or you can learn to drive. Choose one, for I don't intend to open such a conversation with you behind the wheel of my very new, very expensive automobile."

"Bad as all that, is it?" She prayed again she could live with the answers she'd asked him to find. For eight years now she had known only who she *wasn't*—not the illegitimate daughter of opera star Collette Sabatini and Prince Louis Grimaldi, heir to the throne of Monaco. Not the *petite-fille* of the reigning Prince Albert, as his wife, Princess Alice, had shouted for all the palace to hear before she left him. So if not a daughter or granddaughter to the only family she knew . . . then who?

"Release the hand brake, first of all. There by the wheel, on your right."

Drawing in a long breath, she gripped the wooden handle and moved it as she had seen their drivers do, then checked for carriages or cars in the street. Seeing none, she mimicked the pedal work she had observed, moving her foot from the brake and aiming it at the accelerator.

"Brook!"

"*Quoi?*" She jammed her foot back on the brake.

Justin ran a hand over his face. "*Attends!* Please—wait for my instruction."

Another grin tickled her lips and pushed away the phantoms of the unknown. "When have I *ever* awaited instruction? But did I not let my first arrow fly with admirable accuracy? Am I not a better shot with a pistol than you? Can I not out-fence any young lord?"

At last a breath of laughter relaxed his shoulders. Then he caught her gaze and held it, his eyes as deep as the ocean. "You think I don't know the thoughts rampaging through your mind? But I assure you, you've nothing to worry about. The news I bring is good." He gave her fingers a reassuring squeeze. "But it will change everything. You shouldn't try to digest it when behind the wheel of a car."

She nodded and pushed the questions aside. For now. "Now I check the street *again* and transfer my foot from brake to accelerator while easing off the clutch."

"A statement rather than a question, I see." His fingers left hers as he turned around to look at the street. "All clear. Angle the wheel hard to the left and gently—*gently*—press that foot to the accelerator."

She obeyed, reveling in the increased thrum of the engine. Easing the car forward, a laugh slipped from her lips. She straightened the wheel and headed for the opera house. She could get the hang of this, given a bit more practice. Perhaps she could even convince Grand-père to let her drive one of theirs.

Assuming she remained in Monaco. Risking a glance toward Justin, she barely kept from taking one hand off the wheel to play with the two pearls dangling from the gold filigree of her necklace. "You did verify I'm English, then?"

He shot a look at the fingers she had nearly lifted. As if he knew exactly what habit she'd nearly indulged. "We already knew that."

She sighed and let off the accelerator when they came upon a slow-moving barouche. "We knew Maman said so, but she was hardly in her right mind those last weeks." And for so many years, Brook had hoped and prayed that *that* had been the lie, as Grand-père so often assured her.

"It was right enough. You are indeed English. Which, assuming you've looked in a mirror now and again, oughtn't to surprise you."

Right on cue, the wind cast a tendril of her pale hair before her eyes. She certainly had nothing in common with the rest of the Grimaldis. How many times had she wished for their rich dark hair and fathomless brown eyes? The skin that the sun could kiss yet not burn? A delicate snort was all the response she could manage.

Justin loosed a sigh nearly lost under the purr of the engine. "The story she told seems to be true—she was in York with the opera at the time but did *not* have a child of her own."

Had Brook been anywhere else, she would have let her eyes slide closed so that she could summon the image of beautiful Maman, try to conjure the sound of her sterling soprano. But the memory had faded over the years, until now it was little more than a crystal echo.

"So Prince Louis was right to keep me always at a distance—I am not his daughter." At least she wasn't another cause for scandal in the Grimaldi line. But it also meant Maman was not her mother. And Grand-père . . . He hadn't wanted her to ask these questions. She was, he had said, the only member of his family who acted like family, and what would he have if she left?

But she had to. She couldn't live her life as a pretender. The people were already shouting against him, how much worse would it be if he continued to support her when she had no real claim to him, other than a bone-deep love?

The barouche they followed turned down a side road, and Brook pressed on the accelerator. "What am I, then? A farmer's daughter? An abandoned waif?"

His chuckle helped ease the band around her chest. "*Mais non*. It is as we imagined—you are a nymph from the fairy world."

"A naiad you mean, ruling over a—"

"—a brook. How could I have forgotten?" He captured the curl that obscured her vision and gave it a playful tug. "One of my favorites of our recent stories—'Brook of the Brook.' And where is my fairy princess taking us?"

She smiled, but even the thought of the stories they created and picnics atop the ramparts overlooking Port Fontvieille couldn't erase the questions. "The theater. I have a ballet lesson. I keep threatening to join the Ballet Russes—Sergei says I am as talented as his Russian dancers."

"An imp more than a naiad, surely." He tugged again on her

14

curl and tucked it behind her ear. "I can only imagine how mad that drives the prince."

"It hardly matters what I do." She slowed as her turn approached and prepared to wrestle the wheel around. Her heart thudded, but she drew in a deep breath. If she slipped, Justin would catch the wheel, would keep them from harm.

"You will not take the stage." Justin sounded far harsher than Grand-père had. Perhaps her tone had been too blasé.

Still, she could hardly resist teasing him—and fishing for more information. "Excuse me, your lordship, but why not? My mother was on the stage."

"Collette would have been the first to tell you not to follow her example. And she was not your mother."

"Quite right—I am an orphan, an unknown. Lizette Brook— a nobody."

"You most certainly are *not*."

"Who am I, then?" She glanced his way, brows arched.

"Eyes on the road!"

Hopefully he saw only that she turned her face square to the windscreen and not that she rolled those eyes in the process. "Was I right about the envelope? The seal?"

Maman had left her with boxes upon boxes of correspondence, faded letters from faded loves. But one box of them had been different—they were in English. The tone was different too—not at all what amorous patrons had usually sent to Collette. And more, as she'd searched through the letters in the flat she'd shared with Maman before moving to the palace after her death, Brook had seen a variation of her own name on the ones on the top of the stack. *Give Little Liz a kiss from her papa.* But it had been signed only with *Yours Forever*, and the one envelope with the seal upon it had no address.

Yet again she had to resist the urge to touch her necklace. The necklace Maman had confessed with her last breath had belonged to Brook's true mother. The woman killed in the carriage accident from which Collette had rescued Brook. The *my love* those English letters were written to?

"The seal was helpful. Brook." He sighed again and rested a hand on her shoulder. "It led me to your mother. I saw a portrait of her, and it might as well have been you in a bustle. We found her. We found *you*."

Her fingers curled around the wheel so tightly she feared she'd leave an impression in the wood. "Who, then? Who am I?"

"We're nearly to the theater—pull over here. Foot off the gas, press the brake and then the clutch. Turn, turn." His fingers covered hers as he helped her guide the Rolls-Royce into an open spot nearer the casino than the theater. The moment the car halted, he reached over her to engage the hand brake and then switched off the magneto. The absence of the engine's noise barely made a difference with all the chatter from the street.

But Brook didn't look at the gaily clad aristocrats making their way into the Casino Monte Carlo—she looked at the muscle gone tense in his jaw. "Justin." Her voice came out in a whisper so soft she couldn't be sure he heard her. "Tell me."

He leaned against the green leather of the seat, elbow atop it, and rested his hand on her shoulder again. "You are a baroness."

"A . . . *what*?" She knew the title—one couldn't be the friend of a duke's grandson without getting lessons in the British peerage. Which was why she knew she shouldn't have such a title unless by marriage. "How could I be a baroness?"

The wind tried to toss that curl into her face again, but he caught it and tucked it away once more. "From your mother, who was a baroness in her own right. Passed from her mother, and her mother before her. You are Elizabeth Brook Eden, Baroness of Berkeley—one of only a handful of peeresses whose

16

title is by right and not courtesy. And the heiress to a large estate."

Little Liz. Maman had kept her name, just made it more French—Lizette Brook. Choosing to go by her middle name after Collette's death had been one of Brook's many small rebellions. Her eyes slid shut, her fingers found the warm pearls dangling from her necklace. Her mother's necklace. Her mother. "What was her name?"

"Elizabeth as well, born with the surname Brook, which is where your middle name came from. Countess of Whitby."

"Countess?" Her eyes flew open again. "My father was an earl?"

Justin's free hand found hers, and he linked their fingers together. "*Is* an earl, Brooklet."

Had she been standing, she would have had to sit. "My father . . ."

"Is very eager to meet you." He squeezed her hand and ran his thumb over hers. "It's time to come home, Lady Berkeley."

Brook drew in a long breath seasoned with fruit from the markets, the spice of Italian cooking, and the salty tang of the Mediterranean Sea.

All her life, all her memory, this had been home. All the world she'd needed. "I . . . I must absorb all this."

"Of course you must." He lifted her hand and kissed her knuckles as he had done ever since they played knight and damsel as children, back when she had dreamed it was real. But his eyes remained locked on hers now. "I know you have been praying about this as much as I have been. This is the answer to those prayers, *mon amie.* This is where the Lord wants you. And I will be with you every step of the way."

No doubt he was right. And no doubt when her thoughts stopped crashing like waves in a tempest, the peace of the Lord would descend. But right this moment . . . "I must go. *Au revoir,*

Justin." She leaned over, kissed him on either cheek, and let herself out of the car.

A warm breeze gusted up the street. Brook touched her hat to make sure it was secure, then let her fingers fall to her necklace. A baroness, daughter of an earl. Of all the scenarios she had entertained, that had never been one of them.

Two

Justin was probably the only man in all of Monaco who dreaded crossing the threshold of the famed Casino Monte Carlo. He'd done so enough that the opulence had no effect. The reliefs didn't turn his head, the paintings didn't draw his eye, and the crystal chandeliers were nothing but light for his feet.

He could be thankful they had made their home here in Monte Carlo, because of Brook. But still he wished his father would find a different life.

Perhaps if he lost more, he would. But no, Father had made a fortune at the tables over the years. It was hard to convince a successful gambler to turn over a new leaf when he could turn up a new card instead.

Justin paused at the doorway of the baccarat room. Yes, there he was. A debonair smile upon his face, an impeccable suit on his lean figure, a pretty girl beside him.

Drawing in a long breath, Justin closed his eyes for a moment. Prayed, for the millionth time that day alone, for the strength to have the needed conversation. Again. Prayed that this time Father would hear him.

When he opened his eyes, he saw his father toss back the

contents of his snifter—cognac, no doubt—and stand. He wobbled a bit as he straightened his jacket, but he was smiling. *Blast*. It may have been easier to convince him to return to England had he been fresh from a loss rather than a win.

Father's smile grew when he spotted Justin, and he shook off the woman who had tried to tuck her hand into his arm. "There you are, Justin. Have you been out enjoying your birthday gift? Your Brook saw it the other week when it arrived and assured me it would suit you."

How could he help but grin? Not just at the thought of his new Rolls-Royce, but at the man who had given it. Father had his faults—and twice the charm to offset them. "It is a magnificent car. Thank you."

"Good, good." When near enough, his father clapped a hand to Justin's shoulder and steered him toward one of the washrooms. "I considered one designed by that Bugatti chap but knew you would appreciate the English touch."

"Indeed." And it was as good an opening as any. "Speaking of things English—"

"Save your breath, my son. I'm not going back."

A footman bowed as he opened the washroom door for them. "Good evening, Lord William."

"Pierre."

While Father moved to the mirror, Justin sighed and sat on a plush chair. "Your refusal to come home doesn't change facts. Uncle Edward has been dead for twelve years—you are not Lord William anymore. You are the Marquess of Abingdon, the heir, and will be the next Duke of Stafford."

"And facts don't change reality." Father undid his tie and started the knot afresh. "I have no interest in the duchy. When the old man kicks off, the title may come to me by law, but you'll manage the estate perfectly well without my help."

Justin passed a hand over his hair—what had he done with his hat? He must have left it at the palace when he called on Prince Albert earlier. "He wants to see you. He isn't well, Father—it's time to make your peace."

Father's reflected eyes met his in the mirror. One more tug on the tie and it was in a perfect bow. He turned, faced Justin. "There is no peace to be made."

"But if you only—"

"Don't ask it." Father sighed, and his face softened. "It's for the best. You will make the better duke, be the better overseer of the estate. If I tried to put my hand to it, I would foul it up."

Justin stood again. "Nonsense. If you hadn't an innate sense of how to manage things, you wouldn't do so well here." Though he had to admit he was glad he took after his uncle Edward—and not so glad his cousin, Cayton, his father's sister's son, seemed to take after Father.

Chuckling, the marquess headed toward the casino floor once again, then shifted tack and made for the front doors. "Knowing when to fold a hand and when to bet is a far cry from dealing with tenants and whatnot. As you ought to know, being excellent at the latter but an absolute dunce at cards."

One corner of Justin's mouth tugged up, even as he fought down the desire to claim he *could* be good, if he tried. An experiment he had sworn to himself he would never perform. "Call it lack of interest."

Though his smile remained bright, a shadow flitted through Father's eyes. "I suppose I ought to be glad I scared you onto the straight and narrow. But there are worse lives than the one I have chosen. You ought to toss responsibility to the wind and indulge yourself for once. Set up your singer's daughter as your mistress and—"

"Oh, for—I will not make a mistress of Brook. Or anyone else." And why must they have this conversation? In public, no less?

21

Another footman opened the main doors and handed Father's hat to him—obviously the employees knew the man's comings and goings far better than Justin did. With a shake of his head, he stepped out into the warmth of the evening. The sun was setting behind the mountains to the west, dusting the city with gold.

Mischief had entered Father's eyes again. "Why must you always be so pious? I've seen how you've begun looking at her, and it's no wonder—she's grown into a beautiful young thing. But you can't wed her—one so set on doing right by his ducal grandfather would never disgrace the family name by marrying a performer's daughter."

Justin tried clenching his jaw to keep from rising to Father's bait. But he couldn't stop himself. "She is more than that. Though—"

"Well, she is no princess. She looks no more like Prince Louis than she did her mother."

He followed when Father turned to the right. "Collette wasn't her mother. Brook is English. A baroness, as it happens."

That brought Father's feet to a halt and his brows up. "Really. Well then, I suppose you *can* wed her. Do it here, will you, before you leave again? I don't fancy having to travel through the dratted English rain for your wedding."

There was no reasoning with him. Why did he try? Justin shook his head as they started forward again. "Who said anything about marrying her?"

"Well, you can't make a mistress of her—she's a baroness."

A snort of laughter slipped out. "Where are you going? Shall we have a meal together?"

"Not tonight, I'm afraid, though I wish you had made it home for your birthday—I had a regular gala planned out." Father tipped his hat to a couple strolling toward the casino. "Five and twenty now. Your grandfather must be hounding you

22

to marry soon and be about the business of heirs, chanting nonsense about duty."

"Mm." Regardless of his denial a moment ago, only one face ever came to mind when he considered a wife—but she never looked at him as anything but an old friend. Besides, Brook would have many changes to work through in the near future. "But he knows I have my hands full with learning the estates. And I will have to see Brook settled with the Earl of Whitby besides."

"Here we are." Father halted before a gleaming roadster and rested his hand on the bonnet—apparently he had bought a car by "that Bugatti chap" after all. "The Earl of Whitby, you say?"

Justin couldn't help but take a moment to admire the artistry of the lines. "Indeed. Do you know him?"

"I used to." Father's voice went musing. "I heard he got rather eccentric after the death of his wife and the disappearance of his . . . Wait. Your Brook is his missing daughter? How the devil did she end up with Collette Sabatini, and here of all places?"

"Collette was in Yorkshire at the time. She came upon the carriage accident. Though why she brought her here is a mystery." Justin frowned when Father got into the car. "Surely you don't mean to drive when you've been drinking. A car isn't a horse—it can't find its own way when you keel over in a stupor."

Yet he tossed his hat to the seat and put on goggles and a cap. "You are my son, Justin, not my nursemaid. I am fine—and going to France to keep a dinner engagement. Your bed ought to be made up in the flat, and Fitzroy knows not to expect me."

"Father—"

"I will be home by luncheon tomorrow." He flashed a smile, all gleaming white teeth and charming irresponsibility. "Go and find yourself some trouble—it'll do you a world of good."

Once more Justin had to shake his head. "One of these days

we're going to finish a conversation without you riding off on some new lark."

"Anything's possible, I suppose." The engine sprang to life with a roar and a rattle, and Father gave him a jaunty wave before backing out into the street without even looking behind him.

Justin pressed a hand to his temple. He ought to go fetch his hat . . . after he walked off his hope and frustration.

Grand-père found her on the ramparts. Brook's muscles were still warm and fluid from her ballet lesson, making her feel that if she stretched high enough, she could touch the clouds scuttling over the sky, or reach out and skim her hands through the warm waters. She grinned at him, but the prince's returning smile was small and tight. In his hands he clutched a worn leather book.

Her chest went tight, her relaxation vanished. Her fingers pressed into the warm white stone. "You've spoken to Justin."

"Before he found you." Grand-père didn't stop until he had pulled her tight to his chest and wrapped his arms around her. He smelled of security—ink and paper and a whiff of cologne. "I asked you to let it drop, *ma fifille*. To be content here, with me."

She squeezed her eyes shut against the familiar worsted wool of his favorite jacket. "Grand-père . . . if it were only us, I would. You know that. I love you more than anyone else in the world. But with the people rioting—"

"That had nothing to do with you. They want a constitution—that's all."

It wasn't all. They all knew it wasn't all. She held him tighter. "Prince Louis was right all along. I'm not his. Charlotte clearly is—she is where your hope lies. Adopt her to keep the Grimaldi line going. Get to know her. Love her."

Brook had never even met Charlotte—the illegitimate daughter with another performer, the daughter Prince Louis actually claimed as his own. But for a few years after the girl's birth—before Collette's deathbed confession—Brook had believed the child was her half sister.

"You should never have taken me in after Maman—"

"Hush." He pressed his lips to the top of her head. "You are my *petite-fille*. Whatever your blood, that will not change. And I wish you would stay."

"Grand-père—"

"*Je sais*. I know you will go, you are too headstrong to listen to your old grandfather when you have made up your mind." He pulled away, revealing a sad, proud smile. Touching a finger under her chin with one hand, he held up the book in his other. "You should have this, then. I promised Collette I would destroy it so you would never find it, but I couldn't. I think I always knew you would not be happy here forever—not when there were questions out there in need of answers. It is her journal."

Brook's brows knit. "Whose? Maman's or . . . or my real mother's?"

"Collette's." Though he pressed the journal to her hands, he held it still, held it shut. "Whatever answers it has, she thought they would hurt you. There must be a reason for that. Don't open this until you're ready to know what that reason is."

Mutely, she nodded. Her fingers registered the worn leather, tried to feel what secrets might lie within. Part of her wanted to open it immediately, heedless of the warning, and learn what truth she could. But then she glanced up into Grand-père's troubled dark eyes and lowered the book to her side. She couldn't hurt him like that. It would be tantamount to shouting that all he'd given her, all he'd given up for her, meant nothing. "I will wait, Grand-père."

Relief softened his eyes, and he nodded. "Come inside, *ma*

25

fifille. Dress for dinner and then play for me. Let me hear you sing again before you leave me."

Tucking her arm into the crook of his elbow, Brook let him lead her from the ramparts. Secrets could wait.

An hour turned to two. Justin let the warm breeze soothe him, let the mixed scents of sweet and spice remind him of a childhood spent racing through these very streets. He had found trouble aplenty, adventure and happiness too. And Brook. He had found Brook on one of those unsupervised sprees. She had been but a sprite of a girl then, only five to his twelve, but the mischief in her eyes had intrigued him.

Thate said it was strange that he had found such a steadfast friend in a girl seven years his junior. But it had never seemed so. At first she had simply amused him, and he had fancied her a sister to replace the one he'd barely known. Then it had been entertaining to teach her all the sport he shouldn't have. And now . . . now they had thirteen years of shared history.

The guards let him pass with no more than a nod, and the footman merely pointed him toward the prince's private library. Once he reached the room, the sweet voice spilling out in an Italian aria brought him to a halt.

Odd how much like Collette she sounded, though they shared no blood. Her maman had trained her well. He leaned into the doorway and saw Brook at the piano, accompanying herself as she sang, while Prince Albert lounged in his favorite chair. Her flaxen curls were twisted into some sort of chignon, an embellished band setting it off. As always, she wore the gold and pearl necklace Collette had said was her mother's. Its twin strands of links and pearls met at the filigree in the center, from which two dangling pearls drew attention downward.

Justin forced a swallow. She had grown into a young lady

too beautiful for his peace of mind. The notion of courting her had begun to niggle in the last few months. But he knew well she didn't look at him like he had begun to look at her. He would have to convince her. Win her. After she settled with her father at Whitby Park, after she had come to terms with being Baroness of Berkeley. After he was better grounded in his duties in Gloucestershire . . . then he would try to make her see that they could have so much more than friendship.

When she finished the song with a flourish, Justin joined his applause to the prince's. She stood with one of those heart-stopping smiles of hers aimed his way. "Justin!"

As always, the greeting made him smile. Only his closest family ever used his given name in England, and they never attempted the proper French pronunciation. "*Bon soir, mon amie.* Your Highness."

The prince smiled, but Justin scarcely had time to note it, given that Brook came his way with her hands extended. He took them in his and leaned down to exchange the customary cheek kissing. And grinned at the thought of how her English family might react to the French ritual. "You look lovely tonight, Brook."

An understatement, but it nevertheless brought a pretty blush to her ivory cheeks. "*Merci.* It is the new dress." She released his hands and did a pirouette worthy of the stage. "From Paris. Grand-père had it commissioned."

"I told her she would be the envy of all the ladies in England." Prince Albert stood with an indulgent smile. Justin didn't miss the sorrow around its edges.

"Indeed." Yet it wasn't the gown that would set her apart—it was her spirit. No other lady he'd met in England laughed with such abandon, moved with such grace, put such passion into her every pursuit.

He prayed that spirit, and the faith beneath it, would be enough to sustain her through the transition ahead.

As if the same thought had possessed her, her smile dimmed, as did the diamond gleam in her emerald eyes. "You'll join us for dinner, *oui*?"

"I would be delighted." For now, he led her to the settee and took the cushion beside her. "Has it sunk in yet?"

Her fingers toyed with the dual pearls dangling from her necklace. If there were a surer sign of her perplexity . . . "What if I am not this baroness? What if they turn me away?"

The prince huffed. "That is simple. Then you will come home." He came to them and sat on the settee, resting a hand on Brook's shoulders. He had fought for her, fought to move her into the palace after Collette's death, though the rest of the family thought it a mistake. Because by then Brook had already been his *fifille*—his little girl. Prince Albert would always be her grandfather.

Although even if she were not the baroness, Justin had no intentions of bringing her back to Monaco. He would convince her to stay, somehow or another. The thought of not seeing her for years wasn't to be borne. "We are not mistaken, Brooklet. Had I not been sure about this, I never would have said anything."

"But—"

"There is no reason to doubt, and every reason to believe this is who you are." He held out his hand until she put hers in it, then covered her slender fingers with his. "You have a father eager to love you. An aunt to usher you into society. Cousins near you in age waiting to become your friends. The Lord has prepared your place. There is no need to fear."

He could see the trust returning to her eyes, the sparkle that brought light to the flecks of amber around her pupils, to the rings of sapphire around the emerald.

His chest went tight. What would it be like to gaze into her eyes every day? To hear her laugh, her voice, to share stories whenever they pleased? To have the right to draw her into his arms and see if her lips were as soft as they looked?

Maybe he wouldn't wait to declare himself. Maybe he could win her heart now and deliver her to Whitby as his fiancée—and use the wedding to lure Father home.

Hurried footsteps intruded, startling enough to warrant the frown on the prince's face. When a footman charged into the room, the look of horror he wore brought Justin to his feet, Brook along with him. If some crisis of state were about to be announced—and with the revolt of a few months ago still fresh in their memories, he wouldn't discount it—he would take his leave so the prince could attend to business.

But the servant looked to *him*. "*Excusez-moi*, Lord Harlow. Forgive me for bringing such news, my lord, but . . . your father. There has been an accident on the mountain road."

His fingers went lax within Brook's tightened grip. Clouds gathered before his eyes. "What kind of accident?"

Three

Deirdre O'Malley held the fresh sheets to her chest and sent an amused look toward the housekeeper. How much longer could his lordship's sister keep pacing the halls like a caged beast? Lady Ramsey had intercepted Deirdre nearly half an hour past to keep her from carrying out Lord Whitby's command to ready the Blue Room, but she had yet to decide which one ought to be prepared in its stead.

Though Mrs. Doyle pressed her lips tight to suppress a smile, she sent Deirdre a wide-eyed, cautionary look. "The Rose Room, my lady? Is that one far enough from Lady Regan and Lady Melissa?"

The marchioness sighed and pressed a hand to her brow. "It is *too* far. If we put the girl in there, my brother will know exactly what we're about. I don't want her *near* my daughters, but we can't put her at the opposite end of the wing."

"It would show her plain as day what we think of her," Deirdre murmured into the sheets, though she knew she ought to keep the thought to herself.

But her ladyship smiled and let her jet-clad wrist fall to her side again. "Ah, but my brother is convinced this one is real."

"As he hoped the last three times." Mrs. Doyle started back toward the end of the hall nearer the stairs. "We all know how those ended."

That they did—in each pretender being kicked to the drive. And with the earl becoming more a recluse than ever.

"What about the Green Room?" Mrs. Doyle opened a door halfway down the hall.

Lady Ramsey peered in. "It is awfully grand."

The way the housekeeper's spine snapped even straighter than usual would have been more amusing had Deirdre not caught a glimpse of the clock on the chamber's mantel. Her half-day off duty would begin in another fifteen minutes, but she could hardly leave in the middle of a task without getting a scolding. Though, if she didn't make it into the village by two . . .

"My lady, of course it is grand—they all are. This is Whitby Park, after all."

"So I am aware." Her ladyship chuckled and touched a hand briefly to Mrs. Doyle's arm. "Very well, then—the Green Room it is. I will let my brother know I have changed his arrangements."

Much as she liked Lady Ramsey, Deirdre breathed more easily once the lady had gone back down the stairs. She followed Mrs. Doyle into the bedchamber and set the sheets down. When she turned, the older woman was pulling off the coverlet. "Oh, you needn't trouble yourself, ma'am!"

Mrs. Doyle didn't so much as pause. "Nonsense, Deirdre. Beatrix is putting the drawing room to rights, and making the bed yourself would take too long. With the earl's nieces here, you must be back from the village in time for the dressing gong."

"Then I thank you." She unfolded the first of the sheets and handed one side to the housekeeper. "He swore after the last one that he wouldn't entertain any more pretenders."

A long sigh accompanied her superior's brisk movements. "This one comes on the recommendation of Lord Harlow, a future duke. It is hard *not* to make an exception, given that." She tucked a corner with precision Deirdre had learned from her years ago. "Wish as we may that his lordship wouldn't have to go through this again, it is already set. The girl is coming. All we can do now is pray she leaves the earl's heart intact when she is dismissed."

"Aye." They worked in silence for a moment, but Deirdre met the woman's eye again when they shook out the top sheet. "I have always wondered why his lordship didn't just remarry and hope for a son."

A wistful smile settled on Mrs. Doyle's lips. "You would understand had you seen him with Lady Whitby. He'll mourn her for the rest of his life."

"I suppose it's never easy, losing one's spouse."

Mrs. Doyle fluffed a pillow and put it in place. "How is your mother faring these days?"

"Getting on." As best as to be expected, anyway. Mum couldn't move past Da any more than the earl could his long-gone countess. She helped pull the coverlet back up, smooth it out, position the decorative pillows. "There we are."

"And off you go. Remember—back by the dressing gong."

Not wasting time on anything more than a curtsy and a smile, Deirdre hurried out and up the back stairs, untying her apron as she went. The sparse room she shared with Beatrix was silent and empty, so Deirdre laid the white apron carefully upon her bed and took up her coat, hat, and handbag. Inside the last she'd already tucked the letters she needed to post— one for Uncle Seamus in India and another for Mum and her siblings, including the pound notes.

Half past one already. Heavens, but she had better hurry. Praying she didn't meet with Mrs. Doyle or Mr. Graham, the butler, to be scolded for her too-quick step, she flew belowstairs and headed for the back door.

"Deirdre, wait! I'll walk with you to the village."

She oughtn't to have to stifle a groan, not over Hiram. And any other day she would welcome the company of the second footman. Just not today.

Still, she paused a step away from escape. Noise from the kitchen filled her ears, and its scents reminded her that she would miss tea—and she hadn't put aside any of her pay for frivolities like a biscuit from the baker in town, not this month. It would all head to Kilkeel. Little Molly would need a new coat for the coming winter, Mum had said.

Hiram tugged a hat onto his head as he joined her. "Shall we, then?"

"Aye." Though as soon as they were out in the cool air, she reached up to straighten his hat for him. "Much better."

He laughed and skewed it again. "Stop your fussing, Dee. I'm not expected to look as polished as the silver when on my own time in the village."

"Mr. Graham would disagree." A grin tugged at her lips.

"I don't see him about, do you?" He checked over each shoulder to be sure, though, as they headed around the drive. "Safe and free. Have you any big plans this afternoon?"

Her fingers tightened around the frayed strap of her handbag. "Letters to post, a bit of this and that by way of errands. You?"

"As it happens, my cousin is on his way through the area, and we're grabbing a bite at the pub."

Praise be to heaven—he'd be paying no mind to her, then. "Oh, won't that be a treat for you."

"Aye." Hiram shot her a grin that faded to a comfortable silence. He took up a whistle as the long drive went round a bend.

His ditty proved lighter than the sunshine flitting in and out of the clouds, warmer than the autumn air. She fussed with her jacket's buttons and tried not to sigh. How did he do it? Stay so bright and cheerful all the time, as if his parents were still alive, as if his brothers hadn't all been scattered, as if he hadn't been passed over for first footman when Mr. Graham's nephew arrived?

As if life were fair?

But she couldn't recall ever seeing Hiram frown for more than a minute, and they had both been working at Whitby Park for nigh onto seven years now. Made her wonder if there weren't a screw loose somewhere in that pleasant-looking head of his.

His whistle came to a halt. "Hold up a moment, Dee. I've a lace untied here."

She let her feet carry her a step farther while he bent down, let her eyes sweep across the moors that had never felt quite like home. Maybe one of these days she'd be able to return to Ireland. Settle down with a farmer or merchant who wouldn't mind that her best years had been spent in a lord's house in England, see that Mum passed her later years without working her fingers to the very bone.

Assuming she could ever get ahead of the debt Da had taken on when the crops failed back in 1902. It wouldn't happen on a maid's salary, for sure and certain, though the extra she made as head housemaid certainly helped.

"Dee!"

The panic in Hiram's tone snapped her back to the present. Hooves thundered—and she had wandered into the crossroads. She hadn't any time to realize where the horses were coming from before she was yanked backward. Her feet tangled with Hiram's, and they both tumbled into the ditch. Pain shot through her bottom as she landed.

At the loud whinny directly before her, she looked up to see that the two horses had reined in and one of the riders had dismounted.

Hiram muttered something unintelligible and helped her to her feet as the rider strode their way. A mere glance showed her why her friend had been so quick to pull her up—Deirdre dropped into a wobbly curtsy. "Lord Cayton, my apologies."

The young earl frowned and halted a few steps away. "We are the ones who must apologize for such a careless race. Are you injured?"

"I am well, my lord." Deirdre smoothed her grey skirt and directed her gaze to the ground. No doubt Lord Cayton wouldn't recognize her from the times he'd come to Whitby Park, but it would take no great logic to realize from where they'd come. And his lordship may decide later it was their fault rather than his.

"And you, man?"

Hiram cleared his throat. "No worse for the wear, my lord."

"Leave them to their outing, Cayton, and let's be on our way."

The second voice brought Deirdre's gaze up, but only for a moment. A moment was sufficient to reveal the chiseled features and ebon hair that matched the smooth baritone.

"Coming, Pratt. You're both certain you are well?"

Deirdre nodded along with Hiram as Lord Cayton remounted his horse. They held their place until the riders had continued past and then stepped back onto the road toward Eden Dale.

Hiram let out a whisper of breath and brushed something from Deirdre's shoulder. "Are you hurt, DeeDee?"

"Nothing that hasn't passed already." She grinned to let him know she meant it. "And you?"

"Fine." But he sent a rare frown after the gentlemen before he shook himself and smiled again. "We have an adventure to tell now. And some folks claim village life is too quiet."

She had little choice but to laugh.

The rest of the walk into town was uneventful, and they

parted ways at the pub. Deirdre first posted her letters and then paused outside for a fortifying breath. A look around proved no one paid her any undue mind, so she headed for the church.

Silence embraced her inside the sanctuary, and light slanted in with all the colors of the stained glass. It ought to have brought peace, reverence, but instead her pulse picked up as she slid into the next-to-last pew. Only then did she check her watch—two minutes to spare.

No footsteps sounded, but she felt it when he came in, and she held her breath until he slipped into the pew behind her. Held it until, as always, he leaned forward and pressed a kiss to her jaw. "You nearly frightened me to death back there in the lane."

Her eyes slid shut. "Nothing frightens you, Lord Pratt." Least of all the thought of her being harmed.

"You think me such an ogre?"

"I think you . . . too far above me to be disturbed by my stumbling." She slid away a few inches and turned to see his profile. The first time he had approached her, she had been struck dumb by his beauty. But it was the beauty of a dark angel—that she had learned quickly enough.

His chuckle made no pretense of mirth. Much like the fingers he trailed down her neck never pretended they wouldn't as soon strangle as caress. "Tell me, my lovely Deirdre—how is it you know Lord Cayton?"

Though she wanted to swallow, she didn't dare. Those fingers would note it and mark it against her. "He . . . he came to Whitby Park with his cousin last month. Lord Harlow. About the girl."

"And that is the only time you've seen him? He hasn't come another time to call on Whitby's nieces?" He lifted a brow, his black gaze promising to know if she lied.

"He came to dine once since. But he seemed more taken with Lady Melissa than Lady Regan."

"Good. Good." Lord Pratt rested his arm on the back of the pew. "And Lady Regan—of whom has she been speaking lately?"

Not him, though she wished she didn't have to admit that. "Her preference isn't clear, my lord. Though her sister teases her most about Lord Worthing."

"Hmm." No one else she had ever met could pack so much displeasure into a hum. "You, of course, put in a word wherever you can."

"Of course."

"And Whitby—I heard he succeeded in breaking the entail on the estate."

That, at least, should appease him. "Aye. With no possible heir through paternal lineage, they granted it. The estate will go wherever he wills it, and the title will go extinct when he passes on."

She wasn't sure why so distant a maternal cousin as Pratt had any thought his lordship might name him heir—but then, he knew it was unlikely. That was why he was so determined to court Lady Regan.

Lord Pratt leaned in until their noses all but touched. "And where will he will the estate?"

"I . . . Mr. Graham thinks it certain Lady Regan will inherit, but Lord Whitby never speaks of such things in my presence."

"Of course not." His smile did nothing to soften the steel in his eyes. "But he speaks of it to someone, and someone else overhears. Then that someone no doubt bandies it about in the kitchen later. I ask only that you keep your ears open, my sweet."

Her nod was slight, lest it put her face any closer to his. "I do."

"I know you do. After all, you realize my funds are not unlimited. I cannot keep supporting your family forever, not without—"

"I know." She squeezed her eyes shut.

"Unless, of course, you are willing to—"

"Please. I understand."

He laughed. "Very well, my lovely, cling to your so-called respectability a bit longer." The crinkling of paper drew her eyes open again, and she saw a banknote dangling before her.

Eyes wide, she looked past the note and to him. "Why is it more than we agreed?"

"Incentive." He reached over the pew back and slid it into the handbag she'd set at her side.

There was nothing she could do but say thank-you. Even though she knew the devil never made a gift without demanding something in return.

Four

Rain pelted the window, and the wind howled about the railway carriage. Brook pulled her coat tighter and wished for a blanket.

Across from her, Justin pressed his lips together, but a smile still winked. "Cold, Brooklet?"

Perhaps she ought not to have teased him so mercilessly over the years about his inability to adjust to the Mediterranean heat in the summers. Turnabout was fair play, after all. She crossed her arms and dug up a grin. "It is invigorating."

As he laughed, Brook looked toward the door at the end of the car. Their companions would be back any moment—his valet, Peters, and her governess-turned-chaperone, Mademoiselle Ragusa. Perhaps Brook should have requested some coffee to warm her.

She decided to settle for a body to block the chill from the window and so moved to Justin's side.

Her book thudded to the floor, and he leaned down to pick it up. Then laughed again. "*Dracula?*"

Lifting her chin, she snatched it away and set it beside her.

"It has a portion that takes place in the town of Whitby. How was I to pass it up?"

Though he shook his head, his eyes gleamed. A beautiful sight—for the week they remained in Monaco making arrangements for his father's funeral, he had been so silent she feared he would turn to marble.

"Not exactly scientific research on your new hometown, *mon amie.*"

"Well, it was the best I could find in the meager ten minutes you afforded me in the book shop yesterday." And the thought of her "new home" made her every bit as anxious as the red-eyed stranger had made Harker in the first chapter.

Justin studied her for a long moment, seeming as usual to divine her thoughts from her innocuous words. With a crooked half smile, he took her hand in his. And set the world to rights. "Look." He nodded toward the window.

No new rain pattered the pane, though a few stubborn drops still clung and slipped along. Beyond them, sunshine broke through the clouds and painted the landscape with gold.

Brook drew in a long breath. She had read of the English moors, and Justin had done his best to describe them to her. But nothing had prepared her for the sheer expanse. The land seemed to roll on forever, hardly touched by man. Heather blossomed purple and shone green as far as the eye could see. "It's beautiful. So . . . big. You could fit all of Monaco in that one valley." It made her itch to find a horse and let it have its head, to fly through the countryside until she lost herself in its grandeur.

A new chill swept up her spine. Perhaps she didn't want to lose herself quite yet—not until she knew she had been found.

"Another minute and you'll be able to see the North Sea. That should help you feel more at home."

She kept her gaze fastened on the moors, not arguing when

he slid closer to the window and pulled her along with him. She drew in a deep breath. "How do you survive in the Cotswolds without an ocean nearby? I don't know that I could."

"Whenever it becomes unbearable, I simply go to Monaco." As he said that last word, the mirth faded from his eyes, and his tone went from cheerful to a low throb. His thumb stroked over her knuckle. "I suppose I have no reason to return there now."

Her heart twisted at the pain in his voice. "It has only been a week. Give yourself time to take it in."

Now he gripped her fingers so tightly they pulsed along with the memories. His face contorted for a fraction of a moment before he battled it back into a smooth, handsome mask over the agony. "I tried to warn him. He'd had too much to drink, he ought not to have—but he wouldn't listen. He would never listen, not about anything."

Covering his hand with her other one, she prayed the gentle pressure she applied would steady him. "His choices were his own."

"I know. But I . . ." He touched his head briefly to hers. "I'm sorry. I shouldn't prattle on about my loss when you've a reunion before you."

"Please. Prattle." She tried to grin, though it felt unconvincing.

For a moment he simply stared at her, the sapphire of his eyes going deeper with contemplation. Then he leaned over and kissed her forehead. "You have nothing to fear, *mon amie*. They will welcome you."

She longed to believe him. But the heather outside stretched on and on, no civilization in sight. Everywhere she looked was green and soft purple instead of white and terra-cotta. Lovely, but not *home*. What if her family—assuming they *were* her family—were the same?

The breath she drew in quavered. "And if not?"

His fingers squeezed hers again. "Then you pay a visit to the Cotswolds. There is no ocean there, but there will always be a friend."

Yes, better to focus on the unchanging. No matter what, Justin would always be there. Even if *there* was still too far away. Wishing she didn't feel like a lost child, she clung tight to his hand. "But you will stay in Yorkshire a little while, *oui*? At least until we are sure that I . . . that they . . ."

"Until you are well and truly settled." His smile was his own now, not the shadow it had been the last week. "My cousin Cayton has a house an hour's drive from Whitby. I can stay with him as long as necessary."

An hour's drive—in Monaco, that would take one into France, most of the way to Italy. Odd how it now kept one within the same neighborhood. She nodded and directed her gaze to the window again.

Just in time. The train crested a little knoll, and there, out in the distance, beckoned the unmistakable sparkle of sun on a placid sea. Slate grey rather than emerald and azure, but that was no matter. It was the ocean, capable of raging and calm, of peace and war, of beauty and destruction.

Her lips tugged up. Justin was right—wherever there was a sea, she could find her place.

Mademoiselle Ragusa and Peters returned a moment later, the latter handing a cup of steaming coffee to Justin. The smell brought her to alert—though at the look on Justin's face when he sipped, she couldn't help but laugh. "Not to your liking, my lord?"

"In some things I will always be Monegasque." Justin took another drink but then shook his head and handed the cup back to Peters. "Coffee, if not strong enough to wake a man from a coma, is not truly coffee."

"Hear, hear." Brook raised an invisible cup of *caffe espresso* in salute.

His valet chuckled and settled into his seat across the aisle. "Rest easy, my lord. Soon enough you'll be back at Ralin, where Mrs. Moore knows exactly how you like it—even though no visitor can stand the stuff."

They could be sure at least one visitor would enjoy it, when Brook finally made her way to his home. All her life she had heard his stories of Ralin Castle, of its burgeoning flower gardens and centuries of lore, of the charming Cotswolds region with its thatched-roof stone cottages. A fairy-tale setting—with Justin as the brave prince atop his stately white horse.

"There is Whitby." Justin nodded toward the window, where roofs and chimneys came into view abutting the sea. And atop a hill, a striking, crumbling old church. "And Whitby Abbey there. Your father's home is ten miles farther on. He'll have sent a carriage or a car, I should think, to meet us at the station."

Brook clasped her hands together to keep them from shaking. The knots tied themselves tighter in her stomach as the train slowed.

"We shall call this story 'The Beginning of the Baroness,'" Justin whispered into her ear as the locomotive screeched to a halt. "And it will be heartwarming—if dull for lack of conflict."

Perhaps his jest didn't make the knots unravel as she stood, but it at least stilled the churning of her thoughts.

Justin and his valet exited first and then reached around to help her and Mademoiselle Ragusa alight. The wind blustered around her the moment her foot touched the platform.

Justin chuckled at her shiver. "Too brisk for you?"

Brisk? It felt as though snow ought to be swirling—not that she'd ever experienced that phenomenon. "Not at all. I'm perfectly warm."

"Liar." His laugh rang out warm and hearty, though. And when his gaze moved beyond the platform, his eyes lit still more. He raised an arm in greeting. "Thate! What are you doing here?"

Brook followed his gaze toward a man leaning against the hood of a car. Having heard of Justin's closest English friend for years, she expected the unfashionably long hair, the laissez-faire that his folded arms shouted. And the grin that made him look more the piratical rogue than the respectable earl.

She'd always thought she'd get on well with the notorious Alexander Thate. Here was a man who knew the benefits of tossing expectation to the wind and embracing one's dreams, who eschewed society's gossip. And who no doubt got away with it because of the good humor in his smile and his handsome face.

Mademoiselle Ragusa leaned close. "If these two are an example of the gentlemen to be found here, you shall have a fine time, yes?" she whispered in Monegasque.

Brook pressed her lips against a laugh as Thate pushed away from the automobile and jogged forward, hand extended. He and Justin met midway and clasped hands. She came close enough to hear the reply to Justin's question.

"I headed this way when I got your wire, and Mother insisted we pay a visit to Lady Ramsey and her daughters at Whitby Park—so naturally when Whit said someone must meet your train, I volunteered."

Then the handsome face went taut. "I'm so sorry about your father. Had there been time for me to come—"

"I know." Again the leashed pain took hold of Justin's voice. "And with Grandfather too unwell to travel and my aunts afraid to leave him . . ." His shoulders coming up, he drew in a deep breath. "But enough of sad things." He beckoned Brook forward.

Thate's eyes went wide as she approached. "Deuces, man, now it all becomes clear."

Brook looked from Thate to Justin. Did he see a resemblance to the family at Whitby Park—as Justin had insisted? The roll of Justin's eyes made her think it something else. And that glower of his when his friend turned to her made her wonder what it might be.

Thate executed a graceful bow and held out his hand to receive her fingers. Amusement winked in his eyes as he kissed them. "*Enchanté,* mademoiselle. Lord Thate at your service."

"It is a pleasure, my lord. Justin has told me much about you." She curtsied in return and gave him a warm smile.

Thate released her fingers, though the light in his eyes grew only more mischievous. "Likewise. And might I say, you have all the beauty for which the Eden family is famous."

Yet, if she weren't mistaken, the interest gleaming wasn't in *her* so much as in making Justin's brow furrow still more. No doubt he knew how protective their friend could be and enjoyed seeing him riled. A grin stole over her lips. "Thank you, my lord."

Justin all but stomped to her side and took her elbow, guiding her past his friend. "Thate, you promised."

The earl tossed his head back in laughter, though Brook couldn't think what broken promise would be so funny. Then he hurried ahead of them and opened the rear door of the car. "And *you*, Bing, said she was 'pretty.'"

Me? Brook tilted her head to look up at Justin.

He halted a step away from the door, amusement now battling the temper in his eyes, brightening them from indigo back to sapphire. "Did you just call me *Bing?*"

"Well I can hardly keep calling you Harry now, O illustrious Marquess of Abingdon."

Brook gathered up the fabric of her skirt, ready to climb into the car. "Why did he ever call you Harry? I thought that a nickname for Henry."

"It was his variation on Harlow. Thate has a remarkable knack for coming up with the most ridiculous nicknames for his friends. And," Justin added, pointing a finger at the makeshift chauffeur, "she *is* pretty."

Thate lifted a single brow. "And fire is a bit warm." Again she got the impression he said it more to irritate Justin than to compliment her, which again made her grin.

For a long moment, Justin made no reaction. Then he shook his head and gave in to a smile. "I ought to have known that having the two of you in the same country would give me nothing but headaches."

"Your own fault for choosing us as friends." Thate offered Brook a hand to help her into the car.

She settled upon the cushion that faced backward, directly behind the driver's seat, and slid over so that Justin might take the spot beside her. Mademoiselle Ragusa settled opposite, while Peters and their trunks moved to a separate carriage.

"Are we ready, then?" Thate slid into the front, behind the wheel.

Justin ran a hand over the trim. "This isn't one of yours, is it?"

"Whitby's."

"I thought so. Far too sensible for you."

As Thate navigated out of the town, conversation lulled. But once countryside surrounded them, Justin angled himself on the seat. His smile was warm and clear. "One introduction made already. I daresay you'll meet Cayton soon, Brooklet. I have a feeling he will come with me often to visit—at least so long as your cousins are there."

The engine begged for a shift and then protested when Thate ground the gears. Brook winced.

Justin arched his brows—and grinned. "Yes indeed, you ought to have seen the look in his eyes when he met your cousin. He has probably been haunting Whitby this past month."

Though she couldn't make out much of Thate's face, she saw the muscle tic in his jaw just before he said, "I daresay if he has tried it, Lady Regan sent the braggart packing."

"I didn't say Lady Regan was the one who caught his eye." Justin's grin grew, teasing out creases in his cheeks that couldn't quite be called dimples. "Though I find it fascinating you would assume so."

"Lady Melissa, then?" The edge left Thate's voice, and his next shift was smooth. "Hmm. Perhaps she could mold him into a more palatable human being."

Justin's chuckle wove through the wind. "Do you hear that, Brooklet? For your younger cousin Cayton is worth saving, but for your elder he ought to be sent packing. Methinks Thate is smitten with Lady Regan."

"Poppycock." Thate turned a bit too sharply around a corner, sending Brook sliding into Justin. "And even if I were, it would hardly matter. Everyone knows Lord Worthing will propose soon, and no young lady in her right mind would turn down a future duke."

Justin made an impressed noise. "I shall keep that in mind, Alex old friend."

"Except for you, of course. Ladies will turn *you* down by the dozen, what with that ugly mug of yours." He sent them bouncing over a rut in the road.

Brook slapped a hand to her hat to keep it from flying off in search of a new mistress. "Will you stop teasing him before he jars us from the car?"

With a laugh, Justin relented and turned the topic to automobiles. The ride smoother now, Brook settled in and let her gaze wander.

The purple-sprigged countryside surrounded them, the North Sea in sight again with every crest of a knoll. Fingers at her necklace, she twisted the two dangling pearls together, apart, together the opposite way.

The sun broke through the clouds more fully, and though its warmth was minimal, its gilding was unsurpassed. Brook drew in a long breath and watched the gold play over the heath, chasing the clouds' shadows.

So beautiful. But could it ever be home?

As the car overcame another small hill, the sea sparkled in the spreading sunshine. Justin leaned close. "There it is."

Her breath fisted in her chest, her pulse hammered. She shifted, twisted, let her fingers fall from her necklace and grip Justin's hand. And looked.

Whitby Park sprawled across the land, its central building a proud edifice of red-brown brick that seemed nearly as large as her home, the Palais Princier, in Monaco. The gardens were more expansive than anything Monaco-Ville could boast.

The grandeur she had expected. The beauty she had anticipated. But this tugging in her chest . . . Of that she didn't know what to make. She couldn't possibly remember anything from her first months of life. Yet when Thate turned the car onto the long drive, she could have sworn something clicked inside her, like a piece of a puzzle finding its place. One part of the picture that might someday reveal who she really was.

One small hint that made her wonder all the more at the blank spaces.

Five

From the car, Justin surveyed the rows of people waiting before the grand front entrance to Whitby Park, the family aligned in front and the servants behind. All stood straight as arrows. All looked taut as bows.

All wore cold cynicism under masks of welcome.

His fingers wanted to fist, but he kept them relaxed so as not to alarm Brook. If any one of them dared to insult her, dared to upset her . . . If any one of them showed her anything but kindness . . .

They wouldn't—not so long as he was there. He knew well she had only been granted this audience because Whitby wouldn't turn down the request of the Duke of Stafford's heir. But one audience was surely all it would take. Whitby would see in a glimpse what Justin had upon spotting the painting of the late Lady Whitby. The rest of the family, though?

He scanned the faces, most of them vaguely familiar. Lady Ramsey and her elder daughter, Lady Regan, he had met a time or two during the Season, though the younger girl hadn't yet debuted. The matron stood close to her brother, the tilt of her chin giving away the steel behind her gracious smile. Lady

Regan looked nearly bored, as if she had undergone this same scenario countless times. Which, likely, she had. How many pretenders had paraded through Whitby Park, hoping to charm their way into an inheritance?

Thate switched off the magneto and slid out of the car, bringing Lady Regan's smile to the surface. Justin couldn't tell if she had any interest in his friend beyond that which every female seemed to have in society's most dedicated black sheep, but her demeanor shed some light on why Thate was taken with the raven-haired beauty. The true question, though, was whether her loveliness would be soured by hatred when her cousin was legitimized and named heiress in her place.

If so, then hopefully Thate would forgive Justin for taking her to task.

The younger daughter shifted beside her sister, curiosity coloring her expression as she tried to glimpse the visitors. Whitby himself looked the least at ease. He kept his hands clasped behind his back but rocked on his heels. No smile curved his lips—his jaw was clenched too tightly.

Beside him, Brook toyed with her necklace. Twist, release, twist again. But it was the only indicator of her anxiety. Her face bore the mask learned first from Collette and then perfected under the Grimaldi tutelage. Did she realize how much the princess she looked? There was no pretending to that kind of bearing, the regal *je ne sais quoi* that made heads turn whenever she stepped onto the street.

Or perhaps heads turned because she was, as Thate so helpfully pointed out, stunning. Not that it gave his friend any excuse to flirt with her. And not that, as he had implied, her beauty had anything to do with why Justin had so long been her friend.

He gave her a little nudge toward Thate's outstretched hand. Brook let go of her necklace, drew in a long breath, and met his gaze.

Her eyes had always told him more about her thoughts than her words. Right now they said she hoped—and she feared. And that something in her was beginning to believe.

Justin smiled. When Brook believed in something, there was no stopping her. "Out you go, my lady."

She leaned toward the door but then stopped and spun back around, brows creased. "Do I have to call you Lord Abingdon now?"

He chuckled. "Try it, and I'll toss you in the drink. And if you think the air is cold, wait until you take a dip in the North Sea."

She gave him that grin that nearly stopped his heart and let Thate help her out of the car. Justin hurried out behind her and urged her forward.

Whitby took a step toward them and nodded at Justin. "My lord, welcome back to Whitby Park. I am so glad . . ." The man's face washed pale as he studied Brook's face. His hands fell to his sides, limp. "Lizzie."

Lady Ramsey rushed to Whitby, though she didn't spare a glance toward Brook. The way her hands clamped onto his arm, Justin couldn't be sure if she meant to steady him or keep him still. "Now, Ambrose . . ."

Before Justin could make the introductions, Brook eased forward, gaze tangled with Whitby's. She extended her hand and, when Whitby offered his, made a polite curtsy. "My maman called me Lizette—but since her death, I have been called by my middle name. Brook."

The marchioness released Whitby's arm, her face going even paler than his. "That voice. Lizzie." She took a step and swayed.

Whitby's face went from wonder to frustration in a heartbeat. "Mary, don't you dare—"

"Mama! Don't!" Lady Melissa reached toward her mother. To no effect. Lady Ramsey's eyes rolled back, and she crumpled with surprising grace to the ground.

Justin lurched forward, but none of the servants had budged, and Whitby waved him off. "Don't bother yourself, my lord, she is fine. Mary, do get up." He waited a moment, but her only response was a groan. To Brook he said, "She must always steal the show. We've grown accustomed to it. More or less."

Lady Regan knelt with a sigh. "You're going to ruin your new frock, Mama. Lord Thate, would you be so good as to help me get her back on her feet?"

Obviously a task his friend had no problem with, as it put him in immediate proximity to his would-be lady. Justin looked up from the flutter in time to see Lady Melissa shake her head and press her lips against a smile.

Whitby rolled his eyes. "A cup of tea and she will be right as rain. Now." He drew in a breath and tugged his waistcoat into place. "Again, welcome to Whitby Park. My lord, allow me first to offer my sincere condolences. We heard about your father yesterday, with great distress."

The mention of Father brought the clouds back again, rolling like thunder through Justin's being. Why must everyone mention it? Their condolences only made it worse. He pasted a smile into place and nodded. "He said you were an old acquaintance, when I mentioned you just before . . ."

Blast! He ought to have known better than to let his thoughts take him so near their last moments together. He had to pause to clear any telltale emotion from his throat. "It was a great shock to us all."

Whitby looked every bit as uncomfortable with the conversation. He nodded once and motioned toward the tall front doors. "You will stay here until Monday, of course. We will do our best to entertain you. A fox hunt or grouse hunting or billiards or . . . whatever it is young men do these days to fill their time."

"Oh, Ambrose, *really*. Did you not look over the list I gave you?"

They both turned to where Lady Ramsey had risen to her feet

between her elder daughter and Thate. Aside from a curl out of place, she looked no worse for her faint. Whitby blinked at her and then pivoted back to Justin. "Have you need of a footman to assist you, my lord, or is your valet with you?"

"He is, yes."

Whitby paused a moment before looking once more at Brook, and he drew in a new breath as if to brace himself. Studied her as if she might vanish like the morning mist.

Did he see any of himself in her, or just her mother? To Justin's eye, there was little resemblance. Where Brook was fair, Whitby had hair closer to his niece's raven, streaked through with silver. A broader face where hers was delicate and narrow. Brown eyes rather than green.

But the lines around the earl's mouth relaxed, and he offered her his arm. "And have you a lady's maid, my dear?"

The endearment must have loosed something inside him. His nostrils flared, and he promptly cleared his throat.

Brook tucked her fingers into the crook of his elbow and smiled. "A temporary one—my former governess is chaperoning and assisting me during the journey."

Lady Ramsey fell in on Brook's other side and motioned her daughters to follow. "Well, we shall see you have everything you need until you find a lady's maid. Deirdre has a fine hand with hair. Though yours doesn't need much work. It is lovely— exactly as Lizzie's used to be, with those curls."

Some of the pressure eased from Justin's chest. Whitby and his sister both wanted to believe her their own, which meant they would look for proof of it instead of against it. They would accept her. She would find her place.

He indulged in a quick sigh and cast a half smile Thate's way. "And where are you staying?"

"Here." He looked around with a frown. "Mother ought to be about, unless she took tea elsewhere."

Good. While the ladies fussed over Brook, he wouldn't be bored senseless. Nodding, he started after the others, shoes crunching over the carefully raked macadam.

He halted when the butler stepped forward. The man bowed and held out a folded paper that flapped in a gust of salt-tinged wind. "Pardon me, Lord Abingdon. This was delivered for you not an hour ago."

"Ah, thank you." Who would send him a telegram here? Not Cayton, certainly, being so near. Which left Grandfather—and which inspired him to open it now rather than wait for a bit of privacy. If there were more bad news, so soon after Father . . .

"Everything all right?" Thate must have had the same thought. His voice was tight.

But a quick scan elicited only minor concern. "It must be. Grandfather says he is coming to join us in Yorkshire."

Thate's scowl mirrored Justin's thoughts. "He has hardly left Ralin for two years."

"I know." He hadn't even felt able to attend the sessions this past spring—and Grandfather took his responsibilities in the House of Lords very seriously. "Maybe he is on the mend."

"I hope so." Thate's sobriety fled in the face of a mischievous grin. "And if he isn't yet, he certainly will be after one look at your Brook's angelic face. Such beauty can surely produce miraculous—"

"Oh, stop." Had they not been in company, he would have punctuated it with a shove, as they had done as boys at school.

And Thate would have shoved him right back, even as they started after the others again. "And forgo seeing that unprecedented jealousy on your face? Unthinkable."

"It is concern for her, not jealousy." If his friend so much as looked at her too long, he'd toss *him* in the drink. "And you had better watch yourself, or her cousin will overhear you singing her praises."

Thate opened his mouth but just grunted. And gave him an elbow jab too discreet to be effective.

"Adolescent." Had they not caught up with the group, Justin would have been honor bound to return the jab with increased force. He settled for swiping his hat from his head and handing it to a servant.

Their hosts had led them through the tall front door and into the great hall with its intricately patterned floor tiling and plaster reliefs of classical scenes above the paneling. Brook, having spent much of her life in the prince's palace, would not be cowed by the display of wealth—but having also spent time amid performers, she would nonetheless appreciate it.

Whitby directed them into the drawing room. Deep, rich colors took the place of the pastels that usually dominated such rooms, and reigning from the wall was the portrait that had convinced Justin this was Brook's home.

She stood now in the center of the chamber, staring at the painting of the woman who could be no one but her mother. Justin slid to her side, ready to take whatever action she might need. To support her if her knees went weak, to assure her if the doubts rushed in. To protect her if the show of acceptance from the family turned to attack.

All eyes were on her, but she seemed oblivious to that. The look on her face was the exact one she had worn when they first went to the Louvre—passionate awe. She gave a minuscule shake of her head. "She was so beautiful."

Whitby took her other side, hands again clasped behind his back. "Indeed—the most beautiful woman I had ever seen. And the kindest, with the gentlest spirit."

"You love her very much." Brook's voice was a soft echo in the room.

His larynx bobbed. "She was everything. Everything. She and our daughter, for the few short months I knew her." He pivoted to face Brook, examined her countenance yet again. "You are Lizzie's very image."

Brook's lips quirked, and a familiar light entered her eyes, the one that could keep an entire principality on its toes. "Not quite. Her nose was not so narrow, and her forehead higher. And our chins—we have very different chins. Mine is absent that crease there, below the mouth."

Leave it to Brook to point out all the differences. Justin couldn't help but chuckle. "And you'll find her spirit about as gentle as a typhoon."

Her laugh rang out like a chime. "I would warn you not to believe him, *mais alors*. He knows me too well."

Whitby and his sister exchanged a glance, Lady Ramsey lifting a hand to her chest. "She sounds so very like her, Ambrose."

"Mama." Lady Regan shook her head, though she looked more amused than anything. "After lecturing Uncle not an hour ago—"

"You didn't know her, darling." Voice soft rather than harsh, Lady Ramsey gripped her daughter's hand. "Lizzie was my dearest friend. Eighteen years has not erased her memory. The voice, the face . . ."

"The crest." Whitby's sharp gaze turned on Justin. "That was how you identified me, with an envelope with my crest on it. But you were not sure how the envelope came to be in her possession."

Justin could only look to Brook, who uttered a quick "Oh!" and let her little lace bag fall from where it had been looped over her arm. After flipping it open, she pulled out a folded sheet of yellowed paper.

She handed it to Whitby. "There is an entire box of correspondence in my trunk. Maman had it amid her collection, but something about them seemed different. I haven't read them all, not knowing what they were, but that one mentioned a baby."

"What is it, Ambrose?" Lady Ramsey asked as her daughters claimed the settee.

Justin watched the change come over Whitby's face. From unaffected to curious to certain. His eyes scanned the page, and then he lowered it to his side and focused on Brook.

"Ambrose?"

"It is only a letter, Mary. A letter I wrote to Lizzie." He spun away, raised a hand to his face, and pivoted back with a visage once again stoic. "Perhaps it is conceivable that these letters would have somehow ended up in a stranger's hands. And I have certainly seen many a young woman who bore a resemblance to my wife or my own family. But when one combines it all . . . well, there is only one thing I can say." He reached out and took Brook's hand. More, he let his lips quiver. "Welcome home."

The unmistakable sound of breaking china came from the opposite side of the room, shattering the mood as surely as it had the plate.

Six

Deirdre's face flamed hotter than a summer kitchen. She could only imagine how Beatrix felt, being the one to drop the saucer. Though it hardly mattered which of them had done it. All eyes were now on them, which was what they were to avoid at all costs.

Bile burned Deirdre's throat, and her hands shook. Never in her seven years here had she done anything to earn a reprimand from the earl when he spoke to the staff after morning prayers, but it would surely come tomorrow. And what if he dismissed her? He usually wouldn't after one infraction. But then, never before had anyone drawn such attention to themselves during what he seemed to believe was the most important reunion of his life.

"Oh, heaven above," Beatrix murmured under her breath. "I think I'll be sick."

"Hush." Deirdre wrapped the broken shards of china into her apron and curtsied low. "Begging your pardon, my lords. My ladies. So very sorry."

Oh, she should have been paying more attention to laying out the tea things and less to the conversation underway. Then she would have been able to catch the plate before it fell. But if his lordship honestly believed this girl was his daughter . . . well then, it would affect them all.

And she dared not think how Lord Pratt might react.

The marchioness sent her a scathing look, but Lord Whitby chuckled and waved a hand. "It is no matter, Deirdre. I always hated that tea service anyway."

Lady Ramsey squeaked a protest. "That was Mother's favorite pattern."

"It is hideous, Mary, and you obviously agree, since you wouldn't let me foist it on you when you married."

Her ladyship narrowed her eyes at the earl. "That doesn't meant I want to see it dashed to pieces."

"It is no tragedy." Lord Whitby moved a few steps nearer, pulling the girl along with him. He met first Beatrix's gaze, then Deirdre's. "Don't let it concern you. This is a day of celebration."

Words that soured Deirdre's stomach more than any dressing down. She nodded, curtsied again, but then darted a glance at the newcomer.

The earl had always seen through the others quickly enough, no matter how compelling their stories or appropriate their looks. What made this one different?

"Tea is ready to be poured, Lady Ramsey." Deirdre was tempted to curtsy yet again but settled for a respectful nod toward the marchioness. "I shall fetch another saucer."

The lady motioned for her daughters and started for the table. "How do you like your tea, Brook darling? Strong or weak?"

Deirdre and Beatrix hurried out of the way of the encroaching family—and the newcomer, who for some reason laughed at the simple question. "Honestly, my lady, I have rarely drunk it. The prince always served coffee, as did my maman."

Lord Harlow—or rather, Abingdon now—grinned. "I daresay you would like it best strong, Brook. Perhaps without the usual sugar and cream."

Deirdre and Beatrix slipped from the room, and her friend frowned. "She doesn't drink tea? Who in the world doesn't drink tea?"

"Not an Englishwoman, for sure and certain." Deirdre shook her head and wrapped the broken plate more tightly. With any of the other pretenders, that would have been proof enough that she lied.

"Do you think she's really the baroness?" Beatrix looked over her shoulder, though they were too far away to see the family now.

Deirdre led the way down the back hall and to the servants' stairs that would deliver them to the kitchen. Most days she didn't notice the abrupt change between the ornate and the plain, the decorative and the serviceable, but today it struck her soundly. For all they knew that nicely clad young woman would be more at home belowstairs. Like the last one, an orphan from the workhouse someone had decided to dress up.

"I think," she said quietly enough that no one would be able to overhear, "that the babe died along with her mother, sad as that is. And that the earl will be doing a terrible disservice to his niece if he allows a charlatan into the family."

"It *does* seem unfair to Lady Regan. Unless of course this girl *is* who she claims, in which case it would be unfair for her rightful inheritance to go to her cousin." Beatrix sighed and reached up to secure a lock of fair brown hair that threatened to escape her cap. "I'm glad I'm not making such decisions."

They took the stairs as quickly as they dared and nearly ran into Mrs. Doyle at the bottom. She greeted them with a tight smile. "Are they settled with their tea?"

Deirdre nodded. "Yes, ma'am."

Mrs. Doyle frowned at her balled-up apron. "What have you there?"

"Oh." Her cheeks flamed again as she revealed the broken plate. "I must hurry back up with a replacement."

With a click of her tongue, Mrs. Doyle took the pieces. "Deirdre, how unlike you. This will have to be docked from your pay, you realize."

The taste of bile returned. How much would a saucer edged in gold-leaf cost? Surely the price of a meal for the whole family in Kilkeel, if not a week's worth of meals. And she hadn't even been the one to . . . But Beatrix's family was no better off and relied as heavily on what she sent home. Deirdre dipped her head. "I understand, Mrs. Doyle."

"Deirdre, no." Beatrix put a hand on her arm, then squared her shoulders. "It was me who broke it, ma'am. She made the earl think it her, but it wasn't."

The woman's face softened, and a smile teased lines onto her face. "We shall worry with this later. Fetch another saucer, Deirdre, posthaste. Then go to the Green Room to unpack our guest's trunk."

"Yes, ma'am." Deirdre patted Beatrix's hand and slipped away.

"I daresay she won't be long considered a guest, Mrs. Doyle." Beatrix made no effort to speak softly now. "His lordship says she's his daughter."

"What? So soon?" Mrs. Doyle sounded as dismayed as Deirdre felt. Perhaps even more so, having known the late Lady Whitby.

Much as she would have liked to tarry to hear more, Deirdre didn't dare. She had only a few minutes to arrive with the new saucer while Lady Ramsey made each cup of tea. Her hands shook again by the time she reached the china cupboard.

Though she hated to take even a single moment to herself, she had to, to calm down. The last thing she needed was to drop the one replacement saucer. And praise be to heaven that

Lady Thate had taken tea in town, or they would be in a fine predicament.

Plate in hand, she hurried back through the great hall and into the drawing room.

Everyone sat round the tea table, those still without cups nibbling on biscuits. Lady Ramsey's brow was creased with thought as she tipped the pot over one of the last two teacups. "Collette Sabatini? Why does that sound familiar?"

Deirdre skirted the edge of the room as the girl—what was she supposed to call her?—smiled. "You probably saw her perform at some point, my lady. She was a legendary opera star in her day."

Not so much as a spoon clinking against china dented the silence. Deirdre paused a moment, then hurried to Lady Ramsey's side and slid the saucer into its place with a quick bob.

The newcomer didn't look cowed by the riveted attention of the other ladies. She sighed and turned to Lord Abingdon. "Did you not mention that?"

"He did." Lord Whitby took the cup from his sister and tested it. "I did not deem it worth mentioning to my sister until I knew whether you were my daughter. And, Mary, I'll thank you not to overreact."

"Overreact?" The marchioness lifted her chin. "Certainly not. But of course this is information we must guard. It could ruin your reputation before you even have one, my dear."

Deirdre started back around the perimeter of the room, but not before she saw the steel enter the blonde's eyes.

"I will do my best not to offend anyone." The girl set her cup down with nary a clatter. "But I will not deny the woman who sacrificed so much to raise me when she had no obligation to do so."

Deirdre could hardly resist peeking around to see how Lady Ramsey would respond to that. She found the woman's smile softening, but her eyes none too relenting. "Of course not, dear—in private. I only mean we need not bring up in society a relation so scandalous. We will simply emphasize your association with the Grimaldis."

Lord Abingdon choked on a laugh. "You surely realize the royal family leads the way in scandal, my lady."

The marchioness turned horrified eyes on the young woman as Deirdre nearly bumped into a chair.

"Not *me*," the girl said on a laugh of her own. "I hadn't had the chance to scandalize anyone yet, other than by rehearsing with the Ballet Russes. And ignoring all opinions on the matter, which is to be expected of a Grimaldi."

As Deirdre turned to the door, Lord Whitby snorted in amusement. Not surprising, since he had thumbed his nose at society for years. She slipped through the door, catching only one more glimpse of the family.

Enough to see that Lady Regan had sat forward, desperation in her eyes. She never was one for conflict. "Your English is good, Brook. I detect only a hint of a French accent."

Deirdre paused outside the door. If this was another case of an imposter having been schooled by someone who wanted a piece of Whitby's pie . . .

"Justin has spoken it with me since I was five, and then I had formal lessons beginning at six. Prince Albert insisted I take my lessons at the palace even when I still lived in a flat with Maman."

"Who is Justin?" Lady Ramsey's voice bespoke dread.

It sounded like one of the young men who cleared his throat. "I am. Brook has long been like a sister to me, so I pray you indulge our familiarity."

Deirdre stared at the wall, wishing she could see through the white panels. Not that watching the family would clear up any of the puzzlement.

"Are you spying, DeeDee?"

Hiram's whisper sent her a foot into the air. Barely holding back a scream of alarm, she clapped a hand over her chest and glared at him—then hurried away from the door. "I most certainly am not."

He chuckled and kept pace, balancing a few hatboxes in one arm. "So you call standing there with your ear all but pressed against the door what, exactly?"

"Curiosity." Had it been anyone else to catch her at it, she wouldn't have admitted that much. But Hiram wasn't to be fooled, and his exaggerated "Ahh" even made her grin. "You can hardly blame me. What do you think of her?"

Hiram shrugged and opened the door that would give them quickest access to the servants' stairs. "What *can* I think? I only saw her for those moments outside. She's beautiful—that's all I can say with certainty."

"I've a bad feeling about it all. I . . . Why are you carrying hatboxes?"

"Hmm?" He glanced down as if surprised to find them in his arms, when he ought to have left it to the lower manservants. "Oh. Trying to be useful. Everyone's in a tizzy." He shifted his awkward burden to the other arm. "Now, why are you uneasy? This one isn't like the others—we've no reason to think a future duke would lie to us about who she is."

"Don't we?" She frowned, though he wasn't likely to be able to see it in the dark hallway. Perhaps someday they would be able to flip a switch here for light, as in the master's part of the house. Today she would count the stairs as she always did. "Who's to say what shape the Stafford estate's in? Perhaps he fancies her but couldn't marry someone without a fortune."

"Dee." Somehow his voice combined humor with disappointment. "You never used to be so cynical. All the other maids are tittering behind their hands at how handsome our gentlemen guests are, and all you can think of are dark motives?"

His words were a fist, setting up an ache in her heart where they hit her. But she could hardly explain why handsome young lords all seemed little better than tyrants. She could hardly tell him it was easy to ascribe to one a motive she knew for a fact another had.

A chill chased up her spine. Lord Pratt would find this news most interesting when they met next week.

"Dee?"

Luckily her feet paid better attention than her mind—she stopped on the landing by rote and opened the door so he could pass through with his burdens. "I don't want to see another imposter hurt the family. Strange as it seems to feel sorry for the masters, such wealth comes with too much deception."

No one knew that better than she.

Hiram waited for her to emerge into the hall and studied her with furrowed brow. "We'll have to trust that his lordship will know if she's really his daughter."

A sigh found passage through her lips. "He thinks she is. He said as much in the drawing room."

"Well then. Our part is to welcome her."

"Oh, Hiram." Only he would try to make it so simple. But then, he would still answer to Mr. Graham and then Lord Whitby, while she and the other female servants would have to deal with the presumptuous girl when she tried to make herself mistress.

With Hiram following behind, she hurried to the Green Room—and came to an abrupt halt when she saw the girl's chaperone within. "Beg pardon."

The Frenchwoman looked up with acute relief. "Ah, *bonjour*. You can help here, *oui*? I can tie her corset and pin up her curls, but I am better with organizing books than the dresses of the *princesse*."

Princess? Doubt compounded with doubt. If they were fabricating this story, would they have chosen such a difficult one to believe? Deirdre plastered on a smile and moved to take a heavily beaded gown from the woman's hands. "Of course. You're probably exhausted from your trip—why not head to the housekeeper's parlor? Or we've a chef who would delight in speaking French with someone."

Hiram laughed and set the boxes upon the bed. "Monsieur Bisset—taking delight?"

But the woman's eyes lit. "You have a *chef de cuisine*?"

Much to the dismay of most of the servants. Temperamental as old Mrs. Wallis had been, she at least hadn't spat at them in a foreign language. "Aye, and I daresay, being French yourself, he would welcome you eagerly."

The woman paused midstep, her dark brown eyes snapping. "I am not French. I am Monegasque."

Deirdre shook out the gown, deemed it too heavy to hang, and pulled open a drawer of the armoire. "My apologies. I thought it French you were speaking."

"*Oui.*" The woman grinned. "Much like you speak English, but with an accent decidedly Irish. So if I were to call you an Englishwoman . . ."

"I see your point." She stepped back over to the trunk and pulled out another gown, equally as exquisite. And gave the woman a smile. "Or you could rest until the dressing gong. I trust Mrs. Doyle showed you your room?"

Understanding glinted in the woman's eyes. "*Oui.* Now I will remove myself from your way. *Merci beaucoup* for your help."

"You're welcome." Deirdre watched her leave, glanced at Hiram lingering in the doorway, and turned back to the armoire. "Well. This girl has lovely things, I'll grant her that."

"Would have taken a fortune to have all that commissioned. Too much a one to invest in a false story, eh?"

Deirdre folded the dress around a square of tissue and placed it on top of the first. "Hadn't you better get back belowstairs, Hiram?"

"I will. Should I move the trunk for you?"

"I wouldn't object." She indicated a spot nearer the armoire and while he hauled the laden trunk, she moved to the smaller satchel sitting atop the bed. Inside she found the usual items a lady was wont to travel with, and a book that made her snort.

"What?"

She held the tome up for Hiram to see. "*Dracula*. Our so-called baroness apparently has a taste for gothic novels."

"So do our marchioness's daughters."

"True enough." After placing the book beside the bed, she moved to the dressing table to put the brush and pins and hand-kerchief in their drawer. "I can only imagine having time to spend on such nonsense."

Hiram chuckled. "Can you imagine wearing all this fuss and bother day in and day out?"

She spun and flew his way to snatch the pale-blue silk from his hands. "If you soil that—"

"Easy, Dee, I wouldn't."

Knowing him, he had indeed checked his hands for dirt before picking it up, but that was hardly the point. If so much as a bead were lost, she would be the one held accountable. She held it against herself, away from him, with exaggerated fervor, so it came off as a jest rather than testiness.

Hiram's eyes went soft and teasing. "It's a good color for you. Do you ever wish you had such pretty things?"

When the only way to get them would be to let Lord Pratt make a mistress of her? And then to know such a frock could have paid her family's way for a month or more? Nay. She would sooner wear burlap. "Given that you just accused me of spying, I dare not say yes, lest you also accuse me of conspiring to thievery."

He chuckled, then took a long stride away. "Never. But, Dee . . . ?"

"Hmm?" She folded the beautiful blue silk, careful not to make any hard creases.

"Such lovely dresses would suit you. You've the face for them."

She snapped upright, but he was already out the door. Still, the words echoed in the room, tangling in the emerald-green bed-curtains and sticking to the paler-papered walls.

Her eyes slid closed, though it was her insides that felt heavy. Heaven help them all. She hoped he didn't mean anything by his words. Because nothing could lay down that road. Not so long as she was bound by debt to the farm.

And worse, to Lord Pratt.

Shaking the heaviness off, she turned back to the trunk and made quick work of storing the dresses. And then paused, fingers hovering over a leather-bound book. Its lack of words on the cover or spine made her think it must be some kind of journal. Should she put it out for the girl, with *Dracula*? Or store it with the other bandboxes that she'd discovered with a glance were full of correspondence?

Lifting it out, she weighed it and glanced inside, at the last pages, to see if they were dated. If the girl wrote in it regularly, she would want it out. But the last dates were from 1902—yet the hand was too mature to have been the lady's when she was so young. The words looked like French.

Slapping the cover closed again, Deirdre stood. It must be the journal of the opera singer. Which meant it might disclose who the girl actually was. If so, his lordship deserved to know. Not that Deirdre could read French to tell him anything she happened to see . . . but she knew someone who did.

Checking over her shoulder out of habit, she slid the book into the large pocket beneath her apron. If the girl asked, she would say she had put it with the other letters. But with any luck she would have it back before it was missed.

As soon as she knew whether the chit was a fraud or not.

Seven

Brook jolted awake, a cry clawing at her throat, begging for release. Her chest still heaved, her pulse still galloped. It took all her might to keep from leaping from the bed and running, so fervent was the impression that she must escape. She tried to scrabble for the dream that had found her, but so little of it made sense. Thunder. Lightning. Darkness, consuming and pursuing. And that unmistakable impression that danger poised, ready to pounce.

She squeezed her eyes shut and ran her hands over the unfamiliar blanket covering her. "*Un rêve. C'était seulement un rêve.*" Only a dream. A dream could not chase her, could not hunt her. Could not hurt her.

"Are you all right, my lady?" The soft question came from somewhere in the predawn shadows to her right. And the English words gave her pause.

Whitby Park. Brook drew in a ragged breath and pushed her errant curls out of her face. "*Oui. Je . . .*" English, she must wrap her tongue around English.

The servant stepped forward, away from the unlit fireplace. "My lady?"

"I am well." She managed to speak in the correct language, though Brook heard the French in the words more than usual. She cleared her throat and concentrated on speaking as Justin would. "Only a bad dream. Apparently *Dracula* is not wise bedtime reading."

But it hadn't been Transylvanian monsters hunting her through the darkness. A chill danced over her limbs and made her shiver.

The maid must have seen it, as she hurried to the bedside and pulled the blankets up around Brook's chin. "There now, my lady. I shall light the fire for you, and you can go back to sleep. It is only half past six."

Brook relented—for a moment, though she had no intention of succumbing to that dark dream again. Instead, she studied the face of the maid. She had seen her several times yesterday. Outside. Coming from her cousin's room before dinner. And in the drawing room at tea. "Deirdre, isn't it?"

The young woman paused halfway back to the fireplace. "Aye."

Brook nodded and nestled under the covers. Did every English morning have such a damp chill, or was it due to the mist tapping its fingers at her windowpane? "A fine Irish name—I have read some of the island's lore and remember the story of Deirdre."

The maid turned, offered a tight smile, and went back to her task. "Hard to forget such a bloody tale, I imagine. I can't think why my parents gave me a name wrapped in violence."

Brook noted the perfect profile, the creamy complexion, the rich dark hair peeking from the snow-white cap, and could well imagine why they would name her after the most beautiful woman in Irish history. But beauty had been a curse in the story, and the woman's manner wasn't one that invited compliments.

The cold compounded. And lying abed certainly wouldn't

hold it at bay. Brook tossed the covers aside and swung her legs over the edge of the mattress. Then, when Deirdre spun back to her, wondered if she had done something wrong.

Though the maid's lips smiled, her eyes had narrowed. "Can I assist you in something, my lady?"

Oh, how she missed her lady's maid. Odette knew her habits, her preferences, and had never once made her feel as if she'd committed a crime by standing up.

She took a moment to stretch, wishing for a barre. Ballet was no doubt out of question this morning, but she could surely find some exercise somewhere. "If you would help me into my corset, I can otherwise manage for now, thank you. I think I'll dress and go outside."

"At this hour?" Alarm saturated Deirdre's tone, though she cleared her throat as if to cover it.

Brook poured hot water from the pitcher into the matching basin. "Is no one else up?"

"Lord Whitby, perhaps, but the ladies never rise until after eight."

"Ah." Brook would have to learn the way this house operated and change some habits accordingly, but on other things she couldn't compromise—and wasting so much time in bed was one of them. The early morning hours were her favorite. "I'm afraid I always rise with the sun. Or," she added, looking out at the grey morn, "with the fog, it would seem."

"Of course, my lady." Perhaps most young ladies wouldn't have noticed the subtle disapproval in Deirdre's tone—but Brook had heard enough of it over the years from Prince Louis to pick it out of any voice.

And had decided long ago not to waste her life trying to please those who did not *want* to approve of her.

She chose a soft washcloth from the bottom shelf of the stand and wet it, wiped the residue of the nightmare from her face.

"Shall I choose a walking dress for you?" A walking dress, not her riding habit.

Brook turned and gave the girl, probably six or seven years her elder, her most endearing grin. "Is a ride out of the question?"

The maid paused midreach into the armoire. "If you wish to ride, give me but a moment to rouse the grooms from their breakfasts and—"

"*Non.* Never mind." Brook certainly didn't need the grooms to be put out with her. "A walk will be perfect."

Finally, a smile absent the veiled frustration. Deirdre held out a clean chemise and drawers, and Brook took them with her behind the screen. A moment later she emerged ready to slip into her corset. Silence held as Deirdre pulled the stays tight, then helped her into a walking dress of fine grey silk satin as light as the mist, which had a matching kimono coat.

"Would you like a tray of tea and toast before you venture out of doors, my lady?"

Had she offered coffee, it may have been enough to tempt her. But tea? "No thank you."

"Shall I assist with your hair, then?"

"No need, just for a walk." To prove it, Brook ran her fingers through the curls and then twisted them to her head as she walked toward the dressing table. A few pins strategically jabbed, and it was as neat a chignon as one needed for a foggy morning promenade. She fastened her pearls around her neck and turned toward the door.

Deirdre stood poker straight beside the unlit fire. Brook slid her coat on and then paused before the maid. "Thank you for your help—and I am sorry to have startled you this morning."

"It was my pleasure to assist you."

Brook let the lie slide and smiled. She then hurried from the room and toward the stairs that would lead her to the great hall and a garden exit.

She passed a horde of housemaids busy polishing and dusting in the main rooms but otherwise saw no one—which suited her well. Stepping into the cool morning, she let the fog slide over her as she walked, until she felt like nothing more than a shadow in the obscured garden.

At the moment, disappearing into the low-hanging cloud soothed her as nothing else could. All the previous evening, every single set of eyes about the place seemed trained on her. Watching, waiting for her to slip up, trying to discern who and what she was.

If only she knew, so that she could show them.

She passed the hulking forms of the shrubs, went into the flower garden. Other than the occasional birdsong, the fog dampened any noise and cocooned her in precious quiet.

Then, after exiting the gardens and wandering across the lawn until she couldn't make out so much as an outline of the house behind her, after climbing a hill, she heard sweet music—the crash of waves on shore. Brook hurried up the remaining rise and sucked in a breath at the scene before her.

Perhaps a storm raged somewhere out at sea, for the water rose and fell in a froth of whitecaps, choppy and savage. A blurry impression of white floated about the horizon, where the sun struggled to stake its claim on the day. A gull screeched and dove.

This was beauty. This could be home. More than the high ceilings and masterful plasterwork, the gleaming chandeliers. Those had evoked something in her, yes. But they hadn't beckoned like the sea.

The words she had read last night from Hosea echoed now in her mind. *"Therefore they shall be as the morning cloud and as the early dew that passeth away, as the chaff that is driven with the whirlwind out of the floor, and as the smoke out of the chimney. Yet I am the Lord thy God. . . ."*

She drew in a deep breath, pulled her coat tighter around

her. And listened for the Lord in the clap of surf, where she always heard Him best. Where He lurked from time eternal, no matter what else may change around her. *Let me not be like the mist, mon Dieu,* she prayed. *Let me not vanish into it in this strange new place.*

A horse's pounding hooves broke through the stillness mere seconds before a startled whinny brought her around. The beast reared only a few feet away, sending a spray of sandy earth in her direction.

It was a fine creature, one that spoke of wealth and a keen eye. She stepped to the side and murmured a soothing phrase in French while its master called out a harsh "Whoa!"

Her focus traveled from horse to man, and she barely held in a gasp. Obviously a man of means, the rider bespoke masculine beauty in his every line. Muscled legs, tapered waist, broad shoulders, a perfect face.

But it was the eyes, dark as jet, that made her stomach clench with the memory of the dream, that made her want to turn and run all the way to Monaco.

"Good morning." His voice was all it should be. Smooth and cultured, a rich baritone. But it made her retreat a step. As did the way his gaze swept over her. "Are you lost, Miss . . . ?"

She had the sudden urge to babble something fast and senseless in Monegasque. But it felt cowardly, so instead she lifted her chin in the way Maman had taught her. "I am not lost."

Horse calm again, the man dismounted and held the reins in one hand. The smile he gave her made unease skitter over her neck. How far had she wandered from the house? Too far, certainly, for anyone to hear her if she screamed.

But this was a gentleman. Surely it was only the nightmare, the mist, his unexpected appearance that made her uneasy. Surely she would laugh at herself once the sun broke through the clouds and she had a cup of strong coffee to bolster her.

He bowed. "Forgive me if I frightened you. Lord Pratt—at your service. You must be a guest at Whitby Park."

Brook inclined her head. "I am staying there, yes."

"One of Lady Regan or Lady Melissa's friends, perhaps? I am Whitby's cousin."

Lord Whitby hadn't mentioned any cousins in the area while they were on the topic of family during dinner. Brook lifted her brows. "Are you? I am his daughter."

"Are you?" His smile turned to a smirk. "You must be the opera singer Harlow was accompanying from the Continent."

"Abingdon. And though I was raised by a singer, I am not one myself."

"Hmm." Again his gaze swept the length of her, making her hand itch to slap him. "My apologies. How long has the earl given you to convince him? Most receive two or three days of grace, though a few have been sent packing within an hour."

Were she a cat, Brook's hackles would have risen. "I beg your pardon, my lord, but why is that any concern of yours?"

His chuckle set her teeth on edge. "I would like a more formal introduction before you leave this place."

"She isn't going anywhere." The voice came out of the fog like a lighthouse beam. Brook turned her head in its direction, but it was another moment before Lord Whitby became a silhouette and then a man.

A man with a hard expression aimed solely at the young lord. "And you, Pratt, will speak with more respect to my daughter."

Whitby stopped at her side, close enough to touch. And glowered with enough force to send the young man back to his horse.

Brook pressed her lips against a smile. With such similar glowers, he and Justin ought to get on well.

Pratt cleared his throat and bowed. "Morning, Whitby. And forgive me. There have been so many over the years."

"And yet, were she a fraud, you would have been interested in an introduction?" Her father nodded toward the way from which Pratt had come. "Get on with you."

Pratt's smile was as smooth as ice—and just as treacherous. "Of course, cousin. I know how you enjoy solitude on your morning walks. Good day." His gaze moved to Brook. It was too dark to be termed respect, but at least it was not so predatory. "And I look forward to meeting you again . . . my lady."

She made no reply, other than to shift closer to Lord Whitby. Swinging back into the saddle with a grace that normally would have earned her appreciation, Pratt nodded, gave her another too-warm smile, and turned his mount around.

Not until the horse's hoofbeats had faded away did her father let out a low sigh that sounded half like a growl. "Watch that one—he brings trouble wherever he goes. And I don't like the way he was looking at you."

Yet, now that he was gone, the morning mist seemed to glow silver. Or perhaps that was thanks to Lord Whitby. She slipped her hand through his arm. When she looked up at him, there was no stirring of supposed memory, no thought of *This is my father*. Only the recognition of a man she could like well—kind, handsome, and of the sort of disposition she had always been drawn toward.

And a lingering question that made her wonder why, in her dying moments, her mother hadn't asked Maman to see Brook safely into his arms.

Whitby looked down at her, loosing a snort of laughter. "Listen to me. Twelve hours a father again, and already I'm threatening the young men to stay away from you."

Brook smiled and let him lead her a few steps closer to the shore. "That is one man from whom I'm happy to steer clear— I didn't like the way he looked at me either. He is a cousin?"

Her father sighed. "Unfortunately, though too distant for

his tastes. I try to be patient with him, as it was through his father that I met your mother. But I have little use for those so blatantly trying to claim what is mine. He has been after your cousin Regan this past year. No doubt he'll now give his attention to you."

Brook couldn't suppress a shiver, though she tried to tell herself it was from the frigid breeze off the water and not the thought of Pratt lingering too near, too often. She also couldn't quite get used to all those *yours*. Her mother, her aunt, her cousins . . . her father.

Her gaze locked on the tossing waves, it took her a long moment to realize Whitby was studying her. She tilted her head and nodded toward the North Sea. "I have always been drawn to the ocean. Was . . . was my mother that way?"

"No." His voice went soft, filled with yearning. "The house and gardens were her domain. This—" he swept a hand out toward the sea—"you apparently inherited from me."

"Did I?" That helped—the thought that she was not just "the very image" of her mother, that she had some of him in her too. And yet. "Are you quite certain, beyond all doubt, that I am your daughter? Because if not, I do not want to prolong this, it will only make it harder. And with everyone so suspicious of my motives already . . ."

He looked into her eyes long enough that she had to wonder what he saw. "I always believed . . ." He drew in a deep breath. "From the moment you were born, I adored you. Your mother and I, we doted on you ourselves when our friends entrusted their babes to nurses. I knew you—knew how to soothe your tears, knew what would make you smile. Knew, after the accident, that you were still alive, somewhere. And I always believed that when I found you, there would be no mistake."

Something quivered inside. Not with unease. *Non*, more like a sprout unfurling its first leaf. "But there have been so many claiming they were your daughter."

"Yes." He looked out over the sea as though it were a part of him. "Beginning as soon as your mother was buried. But I knew what my babe looked like, how she acted, though no one thought I would. And as the years passed, as I realized I would likely not know my daughter by sight . . . that was when my prayers grew more fervent. Something has always made it clear that the claims were false. Information did not match up."

"Ought you not to look for that now?"

He chuckled and turned them back toward the house. "We are more alike than you think, my dear. I already have—in the time since Lord Abingdon first came to me. I found nothing to make me doubt the truth of your story. Still, I knew the true test would be meeting you." Feet still moving steadily, he looked over at her. Lips unsmiling, his eyes gleamed with certainty. "I have no doubts. And the fact that my sister agrees—well, that is miraculous enough to speak for itself."

Brook smiled and let the silence of the fog wrap around them as they crossed the wide expanse of lawn.

Once in the garden again, he cleared his throat. "I called you Little Liz when you were a babe. Even then, you looked so much like her. Which pleased me to no end."

Little Liz . . . like in that letter. His hand had penned those words to his love. She tried to picture this cynical man fawning over an infant and had to grin at the image. "That is very sweet."

"Your mother didn't think so." A corner of his mouth quirked up. "She insisted you would be your own person. She . . . she called you Brook."

"Truly?" The green life inside opened a little more. And its root shot down into the earth beneath her feet.

"Truly."

They said no more, traveling the garden path in a quiet uncannily comfortable. When they reached the house, a beam of sunshine arrowed through the mist and painted its gold upon the red brick.

A warming sign to chase away the lingering chill of that terrible dream.

"Shall we take breakfast with the others?"

She hadn't realized they had been out so long. "Am I presentable?" A quick check of her dress proved it unsoiled by her walk, if damp, and he chuckled when she lifted a hand to her hair.

"You look perfect."

She grinned and let him guide her toward the dining room, from which welcoming voices spilled. The chandelier glowed above the polished cherry table, and a cheerful fire crackled in the hearth. Her aunt and cousins and Lady Thate sat already, plates before them. Thate pulled out a chair as they entered, and Justin was still at the sideboard, selecting a rather suspicious-looking piece of . . . meat?

Her father let go her arm, and she smiled at him, then went to Justin's side. "What is that?" she asked in a whisper.

He chuckled. "Kippers—smoked fish. If you ask anyone from Yorkshire, Whitby is the only place in the world where you can get them in their right proper form."

She was saved the need to respond when Lord Thate made a noise like a wheezing animal. She looked over in time to see him lower his steaming mug and reach for a goblet of water.

"Good heavens, Bing—how do you drink that stuff?"

Brook arched a brow at Justin, who grinned and motioned toward the smaller of two carafes upon the sideboard. "Apparently the chef has an espresso machine."

"*Incroyable.*" She bypassed the plates and headed for the coffee cups.

"Drink it at your own risk, my lady. Stiff enough to stand a spoon in." Thate coughed, widened his eyes, shook his head. "I shan't sleep for a week."

An added benefit, if it fended off more of those dreams.

Her aunt chuckled and then blinked in a way that Brook suspected was a warning. "You returned just in time, Ambrose. The girls and I were discussing the need for a house party."

Whitby grunted. "The words *need* and *house party* should not be uttered in the same sentence."

Brook grinned.

Not so her aunt, who loosed a sigh bright with frustration. "Do be reasonable, Am. We must introduce Brook to the families of import, and it is far too long until next Season to wait until then. Though we must begin planning her debut now, along with Melissa's. With King George's coronation set for next summer, absolutely everyone will be in Town."

"Debut?" Her father set the larger coffee carafe down with a bit more force than was necessary. "She isn't old enough to have society foisted upon her."

"She is eighteen!"

"Nonsense. Why, she is only, what . . . four months old?" Only the small twitch at the corner of his mouth betrayed his jest.

The marchioness sighed again. "Why must you always be so absurd?"

"Because the thought of sending her straight into a Season terrifies me." He spooned an egg onto his plate, added toast, and moved over to the table. "Being every bit as beautiful as Lizzie, she'll no doubt garner a dozen proposals by the end of summer, and then I shall be forced to give her away, after just getting her back. It doesn't bear thinking about."

A rumble of thunder darkened Justin's eyes too. "Quite a valid fear, my lord. Might I suggest locking her in her chamber instead? You may have a small hope of keeping her out of trouble that way."

Brook spared him only an obligatory scowl. Of more concern was picking up a plate and considering the offerings. Justin had often told her that English sausage didn't have nearly enough spice for a Mediterranean palate, and the kippers . . . *non*. Fish was to be served fresh, not like *that*. But eggs ought to be safe, and toast with some of that delectable-looking jam.

And if all else failed, the coffee could be a meal in itself.

"Back to the topic of the house party, if you please," her aunt said.

Whitby sighed. "Why are you asking me, Mary? It is no concern of mine if you host a party when you return to London."

"Oh, but it would have to be here, Uncle Whit."

Brook turned to the table and found her younger cousin leaning forward. Taking the spot left open between Whitby and Justin, she smiled at Melissa, though the girl kept her gaze on Whitby.

He forked a bite of egg and ignored his niece.

Aunt Mary scooted forward on her chair. "She's quite right, Ambrose. The London house hasn't any ground for hunting or sport, and I don't want to impose upon Ram and his new wife so soon."

Ram, she had learned last night, was Aunt Mary's stepson, and the Marquess of Ramsey these last two years—since his father's death.

"And yet you feel no compunction in imposing upon *me*."

The words may have sounded harsh, but the tone was light. Her aunt grinned. "I seem to recall a certain brother telling me, upon my marriage, that I ought always to consider Whitby Park my home."

"Your brother was young and foolish at the time, and didn't realize you'd be forcing a house party upon him."

"So it's settled, then." Her aunt clapped her hands together, though Brook couldn't think where she'd read the permission in Whitby's response. But he made no more objection—Mary obviously knew her brother far better than Brook did. "Two weeks ought to be enough for the planning." Her aunt proceeded to tick off names that meant nothing to Brook, all those she insisted they must invite, present company included. And then, "And I suppose we must invite Lord Pratt."

Whitby, who had looked to be paying no attention until then, frowned. "Must we?"

"Indeed. And the Rushworths—they are Brook's closest relatives on Lizzie's side. I wonder if their uncle is back from India yet. Major Rushworth was always fond of Lizzie."

"Too fond," Whitby mumbled before taking a bite of toast.

"I beg your pardon?"

He gave his sister a closed-mouth grin, swallowed. "Nothing, Mary. Only I don't think he has left the subcontinent in a decade or two."

"Never mind him, then. Ram and Phoebe, of course, and her siblings."

"Oh heavens. We'll be overrun." Her father put down his cup and reached for the paper a footman held out on a silver salver.

"Oh, and Ambrose, I've noticed the servants don't seem to know how to address Brook. After prayers this morning you must officially introduce her to them as your daughter."

He sighed and unfolded the paper, amusement and frustration mingling in his expression. "Thank you, Mary. I never would have thought of that. It's a wonder the house continues to stand when you're not visiting."

"Speaking of coming and going . . ." Justin put down his fork and smiled at the group at large.

Brook's stomach knotted.

"I have the honor of meeting my grandfather's train this afternoon. We'll go directly to Cayton's so he can rest."

Her heart gave one thud. "You are leaving?"

"I will not be able to continue my overnight stay, no. But we will call on you soon. Tomorrow, or the next day at the latest."

"Which is it?" She asked the question in Monegasque—better to be rude than vulnerable—and tried to keep her tone cheerful. "Tomorrow or days from now? And when will you next be able to make the trip? For this party? In two *weeks*?"

His smile looked normal, but his eyes sparked with concern. "Please, *mon amie*, you know my grandfather's health is fragile."

Which made her feel like a selfish clod. "I know. But I . . . I need you."

"This isn't how I planned it—I'm sorry." The conflict on his face made her feel even worse. "But you will be fine. They have accepted you."

She could only swallow and reach for her coffee. He had *promised*.

That soft light in his eyes was the one that usually accompanied his reaching for her hand. But he didn't. Not here, not now, not with this particular company around them.

Which begged the question of when he ever would again.

"If you need me," he said softly, still in Monegasque, "I will come in half a moment."

She nodded. She understood that his grandfather relied on him. She understood that his responsibility was first and foremost to Stafford.

But understanding didn't keep the mist from overwhelming the sun again. Didn't change the fact that she needed him in the coming days—and he would be far away.

Eight

Justin spotted James Cayton near the train platform and told himself it would be good to see his cousin again. And more often, now that Justin had no reason to travel abroad. He told himself they could finally be friends.

But when he saw the black-haired figure making Cayton laugh, his hand curled into a fist. What in thunder was Pratt doing here? He strode forward knowing well his face reflected the question. "James!"

His cousin turned. Recognition lit his eyes—but no pleasure. "My lord."

Were it not for Pratt's smirking gaze upon him, Justin would have winced. Instead, he forced a smile. "Are we so formal, cousin?"

Cayton's smile looked every bit as strained. He motioned toward his companion. "Are you acquainted with Lord Pratt?"

Justin bit back the *unfortunately* that threatened to spring from his tongue.

Perhaps Pratt heard it anyway, given his bark of dry laughter. "We were at school together. You were, what, a year below me, Harlow? Two?"

"Two, before you were expelled." Justin tried to convince his fingers to unclench, but in vain.

Pratt had the gall to laugh again. "The headmaster had no sense of humor when it came to his daughter."

At least Cayton's grin was short-lived. Though whether from lack of amusement or the glare Justin sent him . . .

His cousin cleared his throat. "I am not certain if you've heard yet, Pratt, but my cousin is Lord Abingdon now. My uncle was recently killed in an automobile accident." Genuine grief lit his eyes.

Justin drew in a deep breath.

Pratt's smirk barely shifted. "Sorry to hear it. From what you tell me, Cay, your uncle was a man who knew how to enjoy himself. Gambling, women, and drink were his life, were they not?"

Justin's fingers curled again, and his blood went hot. Yet how was he to argue? He swallowed back the irritation and made it a point to direct his gaze to the distance, where the rhythmic puff of steam marked a locomotive's approach.

Cayton must have seen the flash of anger. He put a restraining hand on Pratt's shoulder and whispered something.

Pratt snorted and shrugged away. Took a step nearer to Justin. "I came across Whitby this morning on my ride—and the girl you brought to him. He seems convinced she is his daughter."

Brook had met Pratt already? And she had not told him? Justin pivoted slowly when he wanted to spin and lunge.

The young lord's smirk had turned to an outright sneer. "Beautiful girl, isn't she? And the fire in her eyes—that one is passionate. Tell me, my lord, how well do you know her?"

Insinuation hissed like a snake, and the answering outrage brought Justin a step closer, made his other hand clench into a matching fist.

Cayton stepped between them, eyes wide with warning. He aimed his glare at Justin, though he said, "Pratt, have a care."

Pratt's answering laugh slid over him like a shadow. "Oh, I do. I assure you. And I very much look forward to getting to know the baroness better myself. Very much indeed." He took a step backward, into the throng of people awaiting the train. "Good to see you again, Lord Abingdon. Cayton."

His cousin gave Justin an angry glare as Pratt disappeared. "Must you be always such a prude, Justin? Why can you not laugh and wave things off like any normal man?"

Were it not for the increased press of people, he may have given Cayton a shake. "And be more like *him*? No thank you. And you would do well to steer far clear of him too, James. That man is trouble."

Cayton's face went hard, his chin lifted. Rebellion gleamed hot and sure in his eyes. "You may be the next duke, but you'll not dictate to me."

Justin had to turn away, watch the approaching steam engine, and draw in a deep breath until his blood calmed. Was this what his father had been like as a young man, before he married and settled—somewhat—in Monaco? Had he chafed always against his family?

Perhaps so. But Father, at least, had never lacked for charm, making it all too easy to overlook his failings. Not so Cayton.

But they were family, and he had so little family left. Grandfather, whom they all knew was dying. Aunt Caro, his uncle Edward's widow—and also his mother's sister. Aunt Susan, Cayton's mother. Cayton himself. That was all. All the family he had left in the world. Four people, soon to be three unless Grandfather surprised all his physicians.

He shifted closer to his cousin even as the noise of the train covered the babble of the people around them. "Can we not be friends, James? Please."

Cayton kept his face toward where the engine would chuff to a halt. "Since when do you need me for a friend? You have

Thate. And now your little would-be princess is here. They have always been enough for you."

"But you are my cousin. I will be under your roof as long as Grandfather wants to stay in Yorkshire." Justin tried on a grin, though it felt strained. "And you can come with me to Whitby Park for visits. It sounded as though Lady Melissa will be in residence for some time to come."

Cayton sent him a quirked brow. The hostility had faded from his eyes, and a smile finally teased the corner of his mouth. "Are you trying to buy my friendship with the promise of fair company?"

"Will it work?"

There, a genuine laugh. "Perhaps."

The strain left Justin's smile as he turned to watch the train pull into the station, his gaze traveling its length until he found the duke's private carriage. A stride toward friendship, he hoped. The kind they had enjoyed as boys, those few times Mother had brought him to England before her death. Before James became an earl at the age of nine, when his father died. Before Uncle Edward's death meant Justin was heir apparent to the duchy, after his father. Before they grew into such different men.

"Justin." Cayton shifted closer as the *whoosh* of the train's brakes sent steam billowing out around them. "I am sorry about your father. I didn't get the message in time, but I wanted to be there. Know that."

It wouldn't have helped, not then. But knowing Cayton had *wanted* to come soothed now. "Thank you, James."

They said no more, just made their way to the end of the platform and the door that one of Grandfather's servants opened. He would travel with a whole retinue. Not because he needed anyone but his aging valet, but to keep up appearances. To make this crowd of onlookers take note and realize someone of import had arrived.

They looked. They whispered. When someone recognized the crest on the side of the car, they exclaimed.

Perhaps Father had the right idea while he'd hidden in Monaco—ignore the station, ignore the title, ignore the expectations. Be whomever he wanted to be. Justin would never have that luxury. But neither did he intend to make such a fuss wherever he went.

He drew in a long coal-dusted breath and clenched his teeth against another onslaught of emotion when Grandfather stepped down. He managed the two stairs with only the assistance of his silver-tipped cane, but the servant was there to make sure he didn't fall. His valet materialized behind him with concern etching his brows. Both of Justin's aunts soon rushed out to flank him.

The duke's clothes hung on him, evidence of another bout of too-quick weight loss. His face had gone gaunt. His hair— brown two years ago, grey two months ago—was white as the chalk cliffs.

Justin sucked in a breath to keep the pain of it from his face. "I was only gone a few weeks."

His cousin jerked a nod, his face tight with worry too. Of course it would be. Having spent most of his growing-up years at Ralin Castle after his father died, Cayton was even closer to Grandfather than Justin was. The duke was more father to him than grandfather. Did he ever resent that Justin was heir to the duchy, just because Cayton was born to the duke's daughter rather than one of his sons?

Grandfather looked up once his footing on the platform was sure, and he gave them a smile. "My boys. You both made it—good. I worried we had not given you enough notice."

"Of course we made it." Cayton leaned over to kiss his mother's cheek and grip Grandfather's free hand. "Your favorite room is ready at Azerley Hall. We can—"

"Soon." The duke's gaze went over Cayton's shoulder, to Justin. He lifted snowy brows. "We will stop at Whitby Park first, for tea. I will meet this princess of yours before I die, Justin."

He knew not whether he should smile at the mention of Brook, sigh at how Cayton bristled at being dismissed, or shake his head at the mention of Grandfather's death. He settled for a nod. "Baroness—Whitby is certain she's his daughter. She is eager to meet you as well, sir."

When the duke took a step forward, they all moved with him, a careful ballet set in time to his faltering stride. "What conveyance have we? Did you bring your new automobile, James?"

"I did," his cousin replied with a smile in his voice, "as it is large enough for us all."

Justin fell in beside Aunt Caro. With her silver-and-gold hair, her bluer-than-sapphire eyes, she was what he imagined his mother would have looked like now, had she lived. He smiled. "I accepted Whitby's offer of a carriage. Though wait until you see the Rolls-Royce that Fa—" His throat closed off. His nostrils flared.

Grandfather sent a quick look to Cayton, then focused on Justin. "I will ride with you to Whitby Park, Justin. Then we will all proceed to Azerley Hall together after tea."

Aunt Caro patted the duke's arm. "I will join you. It will give Susan time to question James on which young ladies he intends to keep in contact with now that the Season has ended."

Justin forced the pain of his father's memory back, down, away, and dredged up a grin. "I believe he has set his sights on Lady Ramsey's younger daughter, Lady Melissa."

Aunt Susan lifted her brows. "Is that so?" She tucked her hand into the crook of her son's elbow. "When did you meet her, dear? She is not out yet."

Cayton sent Justin half a glare, though its force was negated by the amusement in it. And the flush in his cheeks. "When I went with Justin to Whitby Park last month. And I accepted Lord Whitby's invitation to dinner a fortnight later."

"Well." Aunt Susan's smile was equal parts pleasure and . . . relief? "She would be an excellent match, to be sure."

The servants had cut a path for them through the crush of other passengers coming and going, through friends and family greeting or sending off one another.

Brook would be glad they were coming again so soon—or angry. A definite possibility, what with her passions reigning with Mediterranean abandon. He glanced down at his aunt Caro, over to his grandfather, to his other aunt, his cousin. All with pleasant masks over their thoughts.

So unlike the families he knew in Monte Carlo, who greeted with a shout, with a kiss—who could roar in fury one moment and with laughter the next.

His gaze drifted in Whitby Park's direction. And he found himself praying that the English rains wouldn't dim Brook's fire.

"You seem quiet, Justin." Aunt Caro spoke in a volume to match her observation as the Whitby carriage came into view. "I hope you know I have been praying for you. Every hour, every day."

"I know." Swallowing did little to relieve the lump in his throat. "I was trying to convince Father to come home. I thought the urgency was here, not there. Had I known it was our last conversation . . ."

His aunt tipped her face up to study his. "Would you have done things differently? I daresay not. It is your nature to try to hold your family together."

"And was it his to stubbornly cling to separation?"

Something shifted in her eyes, went distant and cold. "He had his reasons. I pray you do not judge him without knowing them."

"Caroline." Grandfather's tone was the one he had used on Justin and Cayton when they were children getting into mischief.

Aunt Caro pressed her lips together, her eyes now flashing.

Justin's chest went tight. He had thought that coming home, having Brook here, having nothing pulling him away anymore, would grant him a measure of peace in the wake of the turmoil.

Apparently not.

Cayton and Aunt Susan had wandered a few steps ahead, and their conversation sounded light and easy as they headed for their gleaming car. They climbed in with a wave to the rest of them as the servants loaded luggage into a carriage.

Their little party climbed into Whitby's carriage in silence. Grandfather settled on one of the facing seats, determination etching the lines in his face deeper. Justin sat beside his aunt. The door shut behind him.

Aunt Caro cleared her throat. "Susan will be pleased if James pursues Lady Melissa. I assume she is as lovely as her sister."

"She is." Justin smiled, though less at the thought of Lady Melissa than at the way Cayton flushed over her. And at the memory of Thate's scowl when he thought it Lady Regan in whom Cayton was interested. How amusing it would be if his friend and cousin ended up married to sisters.

The duke cleared his throat. "As a grandfather, I pray he chooses wisely. But as the duke, I am far more concerned with who *you* might wed, Justin. This princess turned baroness—do you intend to marry her?"

Aunt Caro hissed out a breath. "Duke!"

"Do not chide me, Caroline." Somehow, he managed to look both weary and authoritative. "The duchy has been in the Wildon family for nigh unto three hundred years. Am I an ogre for being concerned about the next generation, with ensuring an heir?"

How could Grandfather say such a thing in Aunt Caro's presence, when he knew how sensitive she had always been about her childlessness? Justin could only see his aunt's profile, but he didn't miss the way her fingers dug into the plush seat beneath her as she said, "That depends, sir, entirely upon your methods of ensuring it."

It felt as though a bare, live wire had been let loose in the carriage, sizzling and snapping. His grandfather and aunt's gazes clashed for a long moment, then Grandfather looked at Justin again. "This girl, Justin."

As if she were just a girl. As if the question were so simple. Justin wanted to look away, but he knew his grandfather expected eye contact. "I don't know, sir. When I think of the future, I can imagine no other woman at my side through the years. But I . . . She loves me, but it has long been as a brother, a friend. Her feelings have not grown as mine have, and I fear if I push her, declare myself too soon, I would ruin any chances I have."

The duke's faded brown eyes went soft. "I understand. But I would know, before I die, that you have chosen a worthy woman to assume the title of duchess. You have always spoken of this girl as you have none other, and now that she is here . . . Well, why do you think I dragged myself from the comforts of Ralin?"

Must every conversation come back to death? "You could yet recover, Grandfather. There is no need to speak of—"

"Hush, my boy." The duke leaned his head back, gripped his cane. "I am tired, and I have the peace that I leave Stafford in good hands. It is enough. I am ready, whenever the good Lord decides my time is complete."

Justin could not say the same. He was not ready to let go of his grandfather. Not so close on the heels of losing his father. His gaze now sought the window, though he looked at it rather than through it. "I remember thinking perhaps I could lure Father home for my wedding, mere minutes before . . ."

Grandfather snorted, drawing his focus back inside. "He

would not have come. You ought to have realized that after all
these years. If he did not return for his own brother's funeral,
he—"

"Why should he have?" Aunt Caro shifted, folded her arms
over her middle. Her face looked as yielding as granite, and
from this angle Justin could see her tension in the strained
muscles of her neck. "Edward never gave a thought to William.
Frankly, sir, nor did you, other than as a stopgap heir. You were
far more concerned with molding Justin into your image." She
reached over, patting Justin's hand as if the show of affection
could soften the words. Then she turned eyes on him that were
as scorching as blue flame. "Did William ever tell you?"

Something sank into Justin's stomach. It was too numb to
be called fear. "Tell me what?"

"Caroline." The duke put a world of forbidding into her
name.

"He deserves to know how much William loved him. He
needs to know—"

"He already knows that, and it's all he needs to. You will
keep your word. So long as there is breath left in my body, you
will bite your tongue." To punctuate it, Grandfather lifted his
cane and then drove it back to the floor. "Are we understood?"

Now her fingers settled over Justin's and gripped. Hard.
"Yes, sir."

The rock in Justin's stomach doubled in size. "What? You
cannot lead into a subject like that only to abandon it."

But his aunt merely sniffled and averted her face.

"Grandfather?"

The duke's hard gaze turned on him, softening only the
slightest degree. "It is nothing to worry over, Justin. A woman's
nonsense. No more."

Aunt Caro wasn't given to nonsense—she was given to faith,
had been the one to teach him to pray, to seek the Father, to

always trust in Him. And that place inside where his faith was born quivered now, warning him that whatever this truth was his aunt thought he needed to know, it was far from nonsense.

But it seemed he wouldn't learn it while his grandfather ruled the house.

Nine

Deirdre scurried behind Mrs. Doyle, her pulse quickening. "Will they stay the night, then?"

Mrs. Doyle snatched a lamp from the stand near the passageway and lit it. "For tea, they said, but I'll not be caught unawares." She spun for the stairs that would take them up to the family levels.

Deirdre tucked a stray wisp of hair into her cap, flying up the stairs after her superior. And pushing down her mounting concern. If they were going to prepare more rooms . . . if tea became an extravagant affair . . .

"I am sorry you will miss your afternoon off." Mrs. Doyle must have read her mind. "You may take it tomorrow instead, but we can't spare you today."

"Of course, ma'am." The words came out with nary a squeak. But tremors turned her stomach. Pratt would not be pleased if she missed their meeting. What was she to do though? She would just have to report next time they met that Whitby had a new heiress and ask him to translate the journal. The young lady hadn't missed it yet; surely she wouldn't in the next few days.

Lady Berkeley—that was what the earl had told them to call her.

A shudder overtook her that had little to do with the cool draft in the stairwell. "Mrs. Doyle . . . what do you think of her?"

"It isn't my place to form an opinion." The housekeeper pushed open the needed door, and they stepped into a hallway filled with opulent tapestries and ancestral paintings. "Lady Berkeley looks much like the late Lady Whitby—God rest her soul."

By rote, Deirdre crossed herself. "But . . ."

"There is no *but*, Deirdre." Mrs. Doyle's voice sounded resigned, though, not chiding. "His lordship has decided. And if I might be so bold . . ."

The older woman paused—and if she deliberately wasted time, it must be important indeed. Deirdre drew herself up, waited.

Mrs. Doyle leaned close. "This could be your chance for advancement. That Frenchwoman will be leaving tomorrow, they said. Lady Ramsey offered to help her find a maid schooled in Paris, but there is a chance she could ask you to rise to the task instead."

Deirdre's throat went dry. How was she to even try for that?

And yet . . . yet if she could. She would get to take her meals in the housekeeper's parlor with the upper staff. They would all call her O'Malley instead of Deirdre. She would no longer have to polish all the silver and dust the furniture—her sole task would be seeing to the baroness and her things. Her wage would increase dramatically.

Perhaps then she could get away from her ties to Pratt.

As if he would release her so easily, especially if she served the girl he would no doubt set his sights on. That was too much to hope.

She gathered a smile for Mrs. Doyle. "I shall do all I can, ma'am. But I daresay I oughtn't to get my hopes up, aye?"

Mrs. Doyle acknowledged that with a movement of her brow, and then she spun toward the bachelor's wing. "There is little we can do. But I would rather welcome you to my parlor than some pretentious woman from the Continent."

Well now. Even if she failed to convince her ladyship to take her on, that was something to treasure. Mrs. Doyle's respect was hard won and worth much. "I thank you for that, ma'am. Truly."

When they reached the guest rooms, they had no more time for conversation. Lord Abingdon's room was still made up—thanks be to heaven—and they set to work on the one next to his for the duke. Beatrix and the other under-maids were seeing to rooms for the dowager ladies and Lord Cayton, but sure and Mrs. Doyle would not delegate the task of a chamber for the duke himself.

They worked in efficient, precise silence and then hurried back downstairs. When she saw that the family lingered in the great hall, Deirdre slid into the shadows to wait for them to head to drawing room or parlor. The front door stood open, the line of footmen visible on the steps. His Grace must be having a difficult time exiting the carriage.

The baroness stood by Lord Whitby, her hand resting lightly upon his arm. The pretenders had tried to cling—though his lordship never allowed it for more than a few seconds. They never carried themselves as this one did, either. Fluid grace, it seemed, but with an undertone of pride.

Nothing would be the same again. Unless Lord Whitby changed his mind, this overconfident, self-assured *princess* would be the new mistress of Whitby Park.

Deirdre's gaze slid over to Lady Regan. She didn't *look* upset, but she always kept her emotions in check, always strove for peace. Lady Melissa was the one more likely to shout her opinion for all to hear, and she at least watched the newcomer closely. Perhaps she would issue a warning to her uncle.

Though just now both young ladies seemed far more concerned with the young men in attendance. Lady Melissa's gaze latched onto Lord Cayton when he entered. Lady Regan kept sending sidelong glances to Lord Thate.

Deirdre sighed. At least Pratt wouldn't care anymore who Lady Regan fancied.

Turning her eyes back to the blonde, Deirdre watched her loose his lordship's arm and step forward when Lord Abington entered with the duke. The chances of the lady wanting *her* for a maid were slim as waistlines in a famine. But she had to try. Even if she didn't like the girl, even if she hoped Lord Whitby soon saw reason and booted her out, she owed it to Mum to try.

The family exchanged words with the visitors. There was bowing and curtsying, and they all paired off. And though she was more interested in the way Lady Regan flushed when she slid her hand into the crook of Lord Thate's elbow, Deirdre focused her gaze on Lady Berkeley and Lord Abingdon.

The baroness didn't just rest her hand on his arm, she gripped it. And he didn't merely cover her fingers with his own, he clung to them. The look they exchanged—*charged* was the only word that came to mind.

By sheer force of will, Deirdre kept her eyes from narrowing. They must be more than friends, those two. And oh, but she didn't want to be the one to tell Pratt that the new heiress was already in love with another.

As they moved in the wake of the others, Deirdre caught the young lord's quiet, "Are you still angry with me?"

Lady Berkeley's chuckle was low and taut. "*Oui*. But I will overlook it for now."

He said something else, but he had shifted into the language her ladyship's maid had spoken last night. She again picked out a few words she recognized as French, but the cadence was wrong.

Whatever he said, her ladyship's face went serious. She answered in English. "My aunt has arranged for some sport—archery and croquet. Assuming the rain holds off and Lord Whitby can convince your grandfather to stay after tea, we will all have a lovely, relaxing afternoon together."

Lord Cayton and Lady Melissa partially turned around to share their enthusiasm with that plan, but Deirdre kept her gaze forward and her face clear as they passed by. What did it mean that this girl called Lord Whitby by his title, though she already greeted Lady Ramsey as Aunt Mary?

Deirdre didn't know. But she would keep her mouth shut . . . and her eyes open.

Brook shook her head, unable to think up what secrets Justin's family could be keeping from him. "The reason for the rift between your father and the rest of them, I should think. But as for what it is . . ."

She had always wondered at what had caused it. It must have been more than William's penchant for gambling. But Justin had never known, and she hadn't been well enough acquainted with his father to ever ask *him*.

Justin sighed. "Grandfather forbade her from telling me. And though I keep trying to convince myself it is likely just some old argument that makes little sense anymore, they both are—were, in Father's case—so adamant about the secret being kept."

She held tight to his arm, studying his profile as he looked out to the breaking waves of the North Sea. Sometimes it mattered less *what* a secret was than *that* it was. And right now, Justin needed his family supporting him, not adding more to his burdens. "*Ça va?*"

He sighed and squeezed her hand where it rested on his forearm, as he had done upon arriving three hours prior. "*Je ne sais pas*. It is all just . . . too much."

Laughter from the gardens drew her gaze back toward the house, where the other young people were engrossed in a game of croquet. Brook had bowed out of that particular game. And after she'd bested everyone in their impromptu archery competition, they had all made a show of thanking her for excusing herself.

Teasing . . . or were they glad to see her go, if only for a half-hour promenade? She turned to Justin again. His eyes had gone a darker blue, as they always did when he was troubled.

"It seems we both have secrets in our families. Grand-père gave me Maman's journal before I left. He said she wanted it destroyed rather than letting me see it. He said . . . he said she thought coming back here would hurt me."

Justin frowned and led her away from the frothing whitecaps, back down the hill toward the carefully structured shrubbery and the laughing couples on the lawn. "Have you read it? Does it explain why she took you away rather than delivering you to Whitby?"

"I haven't." She wanted to tug on his arm, to slow him down, to stay away a little longer. But from the house came the sound of a gong, and the croquet game came to an immediate halt. They must all get inside to dress for dinner. She contented herself with pressing upon his arm. "I promised Grand-père I wouldn't read it until I was ready to face whatever it told me. And just now . . . I feel the coward for admitting it, but it is hard enough to accept the simple facts. That he is my father, that this is my home. I want to make my own impressions, not be colored by Maman's."

"Wise." He looked down at her, a smile softening the corners of his mouth. "Curious as I know you always are, direct it now toward discovering this family of yours, not focusing on the past."

To that, she could only draw in a deep breath and tilt her head in acknowledgment. Soon they reached the indoors and parted ways. Brook tried to catch whatever glimpses she could of the house as she passed through it—a tour had been on the schedule for this afternoon, but the duke's arrival had put a halt to that plan.

She knew her way back up to the corridor that housed her and her cousins' rooms, though—and could have followed the sounds of giggling females had she not. Regan and Melissa were turning toward their doors as she topped the stairs.

Regan smiled and waved at her. "After you dress, come in with us to have your hair arranged. It will give us a chance to talk about the gentlemen."

Brook returned the smile. It had been so long since she could claim any true female friends. She had been in a strange position in Monaco—not quite a royal to rub elbows with the nobles paying court to Grand-père, but too much a one to be accepted by Maman's former ilk. Perhaps now things would be different. "Thank you. I shall."

Her smile faded, though, when she caught Melissa's low, "Regan! How in the world can you be so accepting when . . ."

Before she could hear the end of the question, their door shut. She told herself to shake it off—it was normal, after all, for them to have reservations. Slipping into her own chamber, she found Mademoiselle Ragusa holding up two of Brook's new evening dresses, tilting her head from side to side and humming a nonsense verse she had used to sing in their schoolroom. Brook closed the door behind her and gave the woman a grin. "Having trouble deciding which you will wear, mademoiselle?"

The governess laughed and held them both up to her. "I could not tie my corset tight enough. But there are so many pretty things, and all will flatter you. Which tonight?"

Brook joined her, running a hand down the pale green sleeve of one, along the violet beading of the other.

She saw only Grand-père, that indulgent smile on his face as she tried to decide between the two silks, the way he had said, "*Obtiens tous les deux.*" Get them both. Blinking against the burning in her eyes, she chose the green. It had been his favorite.

Within minutes, she had changed, slid the matching slippers onto her feet, and bade her companion a good evening. Nerves fluttered in her stomach as she made her way to the door her cousins had gone into. She had to pull in a long breath. Pray for fortification. For peace. For . . . for a connection.

At the first light rap of her knuckles upon the door, it opened inward. Melissa must have been standing there, waiting. Though her smile looked strained, she at least offered it. She motioned Brook inside, shutting the door behind her. Wariness gave way to pure feminine appreciation. "That gown! It's divine. Parisian?"

Brook smiled. Just thinking of Paris brought the smell of baking baguettes to her memory, and the sound of a lazy concertina. "*Oui.*"

Regan stepped from behind a dressing screen, her smile calmer but far more welcoming. "Your Lord Abingdon's jaw will no doubt drop to the floor." Mischief lit her eyes. "Have you an understanding? You seem so close."

"An under . . ." It took Brook a moment to process what that meant. Then she felt the heat scorch her cheeks. "Oh, no. We are only friends."

"But?" Melissa raised her brows and spun toward the bed, where an evening gown lay waiting. "You cannot be happy with that *only*. He is nearly as handsome as his cousin."

Cayton was not half so handsome as Justin. But Brook wasn't about to argue with a smitten girl. "He is like a brother to me."

"The best way for a romance to begin." Regan chuckled and motioned Brook to the seat at the dressing table. "You first, cousin. Deirdre will return in a moment."

Cousin. Brook sank onto the padded stool and smiled at Regan's reflection. They were both so beautiful, these cousins of hers, with the rich dark hair that felt like home.

Melissa had disappeared behind the screen. "I wish they were staying more than a night."

Regan shook her head and stepped to Brook's side, opening a traveling case that revealed rows of jewelry. "They will be back in a fortnight for Mama's house party."

"An eternity. And don't pretend you didn't have to stifle a groan when Thate said he would leave tomorrow as well."

Regan stifled a sigh now and pulled out a necklace dripping crystals. "It hardly matters. Thate never pays me any mind."

Toying with one of the hairpins on the tabletop, Brook met her cousin's reflected gaze. It was not so unlike the backstage dressing room at the ballet. Girls were girls. They spoke of men. They fussed and dressed and yearned. She could grin. "*Au contraire.* He grew quite testy in the car yesterday when talk turned to one of your suitors—a duke's son. I cannot recall his name."

"Lord Worthing." Melissa pronounced it with an exaggerated sigh as she reemerged. "He and your Lord Abingdon are the only two heirs to duchies between the ages of ten and fifty. Every young lady in London was in a dither when Worthing came to call on Regan."

"He is a good man." Regan fastened her necklace, her voice so even, so calm that it was clear he was, to her, nothing more than that. "Of strong faith, which is rare. Handsome. Everything a lady could want." Her hands fell to her sides, and her gaze bore right through the looking glass.

Melissa appeared at their side and slid her arm around her sister's waist. "But you have set your heart on an unfashionable young earl who will no doubt go careening into a ditch and get himself killed in one of those cars of his."

Brook winced—she couldn't help it. And thanked the Lord her cousin hadn't said it when Justin could hear and be reminded of his father's death. Better to focus on Regan and Thate. "*La vie est une fleur dont l'amour est le miel.*"

"Hmm?" Regan looked down at her, her eyes still a bit distant. "Life is a flower?"

". . . of which love is the honey. Victor Hugo." Such pretty words. But maybe they were just the stuff of novels and poems. Never had Brook seen it play out in reality. Prince Louis refused to marry, and Prince Albert . . . Grand-père had been unlucky in matters of the heart. He had divorced his first wife well before Brook's day. Then came Princess Alice. Brook well remembered his argument with her, when he moved Brook to the palace. Such accusations had surfaced then—his paramour, her paramour, problems with his son, problems with her son. They had separated.

Love, it seemed, had nothing to do with anything.

A discreet knock signaled the entrance of the maid. Brook assumed the conversation would shift, but Melissa shook her head and looked at her sister. "But can you be sure you *love* him? I like Thate, but he is hardly a responsible, dependable man to choose as a husband. If Lord Worthing proposes, you can hardly say no."

Regan loosed a long gust of breath. "If Lord Worthing hadn't come calling, everyone would consider Thate a fine catch. It isn't as though he's a pauper seeking my fortu—" She looked away, but Brook saw the flush in her cheeks.

And why would she cut herself off at the mention of a fortune? Brook glanced at Melissa in the mirror, but the younger of her cousins pressed her lips together and looked from her sister to Brook and back again.

She knew so little of this family. But they had that half-brother, Ram. He had inherited their father's titles, his estates. And from what Justin said, most money went with estates, to keep them up. So Regan would not have a fortune, aside from a dowry.

But she would have . . . had Brook not come. Excluding their mother, these two were Whitby's closest relatives, and Regan was the elder. She would have been the heiress of all that was his, aside from the title itself. And simply by showing up, Brook had stripped her of that. "Regan. I . . ."

She knew not what to say. The only words her tongue could find were Monegasque, and even they made little sense.

Regan put a warm, steady hand on Brook's shoulder. "Think nothing of it, Brook. I never put my hopes in an inheritance—Uncle Whit only just succeeded in breaking the entail that required a male heir for it all. It is worth far more to see him finally find you. To gain a cousin and friend."

It was no wonder Thate had been unable to keep his eyes off Regan all afternoon. She was far more than a lovely face. "I feel the same. When I asked Justin to help me find my family, I never imagined all this." Brook had thought that, at most, he would show her a photograph of her deceased parents. Perhaps a village in which she was born.

Deirdre took up position behind her and gathered Brook's curls.

Melissa pulled up a chair and eased to a seat upon it. "Justin. It sounds so very French. A friend of mine caught a glimpse of him during the Season, you know, and couldn't stop talking about him. So mysterious—gone most of his life on the Continent, scarcely ever making an appearance in Town."

"And nearly as handsome as his cousin?" Regan winked and leaned against the wall.

Melissa dimpled. "Nearly. Though you would probably put

Thate or Worthing at the top of the list. What say you, Deirdre? Who is the handsomest of our gentlemen friends?"

Brook expected the maid to demur, but instead she looked over at the sisters with a warm smile. "'Tis a hard matter to judge, sure enough. Though I must confess that one of the most striking men I've seen is that cousin of his lordship's—Lord Pratt."

Unease skittered up Brook's spine at the mere mention of him.

Melissa made a thoughtful hum. "He is striking. But there is something about him . . ."

"He has no heart—that's what." Regan pushed up and stepped behind Brook. "How lovely. I do wish I had curls so you could do mine like that, Deirdre. But it would take hours to use the tongs on it first."

"Your hair is beautiful, my lady. So glossy and thick. Though sure and Lady Berkeley's curls are a joy to work with too."

Brook summoned a smile, though that title still felt so odd. How long would it take for her to get used to answering to it? To seeing all these new faces? To having a father who looked at her as if she were an answer to prayer?

When Deirdre indicated she had finished, Brook rose. "Will Lord Whitby be ready, do you think? Could I find him before dinner?"

Regan sat on the stool, elegant as a queen. "He will be in the library."

"A library!" Of course a house this size would have one, but how could she have been here a complete day already without finding it? "Where is it?"

Deirdre gave her a smile thirty degrees cooler than the one she had given Regan. "I can show you the way, my lady."

"Thank you, but instruction will suffice. You are busy."

Deirdre relented without a fuss, and told her where to find

the library. With little more ado, Brook slipped out. Back to her chamber, into the attached dressing room. There, on the floor, she had already noted the bandbox that held Maman's letters . . . and theirs. Whitby and his Lizzie's. For a long moment she stared at it in the fading light.

It had been years since she'd glanced through them. She'd never much wanted to read the love notes Maman had received over the years, especially the ones from the years before Brook was born, when they were more than pleas for a meeting, always refused. When they hinted at meetings enjoyed, instead.

When Brook had started to wonder if the box of English ones were in fact to another woman altogether, when she had drawn out the one envelope with a seal to give to Justin, she had considered reading them all, more closely.

Something had stayed her.

She opened the bandbox and drew out the smaller wooden one. Held it to her middle. Now she knew the writer was not some long-gone, faceless name. He was here. Her father. And if anyone should go through these letters, it was he.

She slid out of her room, padded down the stairs, took turn after turn until she heard the snapping of a fire in a grate and smelled the perfume of books and smoke and the magic of all those tales in one place.

Whitby surged to his feet the moment she entered, as if he had been waiting for her. "Brook. Were you looking for me, or for a book?"

"You." Though now she had to turn in a circle to take in the books. Shelves upon shelves of them, floor to vaulted ceiling. "If ever you cannot find me, look here first."

Whitby chuckled and slid a step toward her. "I daresay I will already be here ahead of you. It is my favorite room in the house."

Another thing they had in common. She put on a smile—

though it felt slight and uncertain—and held out the box. "I mentioned these yesterday. The correspondence, from you to my mother. I wanted to return it."

The look that crossed his face went beyond words. As if it were the echo of a million memories, the joyous and the bittersweet. He closed the space between them and reached for the box.

His fingers were long and slender, like Brook's on a larger scale. They gripped it in one hand, traced its contours with the other. "My grandmother's box. I gave it to Lizzie thinking she would store her gloves in it, as Grandmama had." He flipped the latch, opened the lid.

Shut it again and held it out to her with flaring nostrils.

Knowing her confusion must be on her face, Brook reached for it slowly.

Her father's larynx bobbed as he swallowed. "I have the ones she wrote to me. Her words, her script, her perfume once upon them. I don't need to read my own words. You may, if you like. If you think it would help you to know us. I can give you the others, too, that she wrote."

Though she pressed the wood until it seemed her fingertips ought to dent it, reading their correspondence still seemed wrong somehow. "I do not want to pry."

But his eyes went soft, and he skimmed his hand over her wrist. Fleeting, brief, the touch of a man unaccustomed to such gestures. All the more important because of it. "I want you to. It is a daughter's privilege."

Was it also a daughter's privilege to ask questions? Because she wanted to know why her mother had had the box with her when she died. Why they were even in a carriage leaving Whitby Park in the middle of the night, on their way to York. Why, if this emotion that seemed to have drowned her father was love in its purest form, they were so disastrously separated.

One hand went to the pearls dangling from her necklace. Twisted them, let them fall, twisted the opposite way.

A knock sounded on the open door, and Brook jumped and spun. Whitby had introduced Mr. Graham and Mrs. Doyle earlier, and they both now stood in the doorway, faces pleasant but cool. The butler sketched a quick bow. "Mademoiselle Ragusa's train ticket has been purchased as you requested, my lord, and there will be one awaiting her at the port as well."

The housekeeper directed a smile to Brook. "Deirdre will be happy to serve as your lady's maid until you can find one, my lady. Or indefinitely, if you find her work satisfactory."

Though the features were still unfamiliar, she knew well the look on Mrs. Doyle's face. She had seen it often enough on the fearsome palace housekeeper's, the one who wore the keys to the Grimaldi home as if they could unlock heaven and hell themselves. It said: *My words suggest—my will commands.*

Brook told her lips to curve. She had gone head to head with her old housekeeper a time or two, but it would surely not be wise to do so with Mrs. Doyle on Brook's second day here. "I'm sure Deirdre will suit me quite well, Mrs. Doyle. I would be pleased to have her as my lady's maid."

Whitby obviously knew the look as well as Brook did. His sigh blustered forth. "You needn't agree to anything so soon, my dear. We should speak with Mary about it, see what she recommends—and you can be sure she'll have an opinion."

Mrs. Doyle stiffened.

Brook offered a conciliatory smile, though she wasn't sure who she was trying to placate. "I would welcome a maid who is already a part of Whitby Park."

"Brook—"

"*Je veux être comme l'un d'eux.*" *I want to be one of you.* She hoped her father spoke enough French to understand her meaning—and that the servants did not. Given their blinks, she was right at least on that score.

Whitby she was not sure of. Not until his lips twitched. "You are the image of your mother, my dear. But it seems your disposition you inherited from me, stubbornness and all. My apologies."

She repositioned the box of letters and returned his hint of a smile. "It serves me well."

He dismissed the servants with a nod and then studied Brook for a long moment, obviously trying to see something beyond the visible. Perhaps he managed it. The lines around his eyes softened, as did the tension in his shoulders. "Tomorrow," he said quietly, "after our guests depart, I will show you your home. And your mother's room, her things. You can have whatever you wish. I want you to be one of us too, Brook. I want you to feel that this is where you should have been all along."

She wanted it too, so very much. Wanted to walk these halls with all the abandon she had enjoyed in the prince's palace. Wanted to be welcomed and respected among the household as her cousins were. Wanted to make this man before her laugh and smile, and to know what to call him.

But those desires were much like love—pretty on paper. So very hard won in reality.

Ten

Never had the ride to Azerley Hall felt so interminable. Justin tried to watch the Yorkshire moors roll by beyond the rain-spattered windscreen, but it was no use. He kept darting glances to Grandfather, who kept ignoring him.

No, that was unfair. Grandfather was exhausted. The creases in his face had deepened, and his cane had shaken nearly violently as he made his way to the car that morning. The trip had cost him precious energy. The fact that he had been unreadable yesterday through tea, supper, and Brook's performance on the piano afterward, meant only that he did not forget his breeding even in illness. The fact that he held his silence now meant only that he was too tired to converse, not that he had something bad to say.

Still. Justin needed to know what the duke thought of her. Not that his opinion would change Justin's, but it mattered. It mattered a great deal.

"Will you relax?" Cayton leaned close to issue the order. The others seemed not to hear him over the noise of the engine. "You are taut as a bow."

"Sorry." But though he told his neck to ease, his shoulders to let go their bunching, they would not obey.

His cousin rolled his eyes. "You can call again any time you please."

Whitby had said as much when they departed, that they were always welcome. But Justin glanced again at Grandfather, and a knot tightened in his stomach. He daren't leave him. Not unless the duke improved drastically.

Cayton's gaze followed Justin's. And he nodded. His shoulders went taut too. In this, they were of the same mind.

Silence reigned again—other than the roar of the motor, the grumble of the tires over the pitted road, and the hiss of rain on glass. The air today was cool, to match the low grey clouds. And Brook, as she toured Whitby Park with her father, would be claiming she loved the rain, even as her fingers turned to ice.

Another look at the duke proved as fruitless as the first hundred. He said nothing as they covered the last miles to Cayton's home. Nor as they parked and all climbed out. Nor, even, when Aunt Susan insisted on helping him up the stairs.

Then, when they were all inside the towering great hall, he met Justin's gaze at last. "Join me in the study, if you would, Justin."

With the command, years fell away. He was back at school, getting called into the headmaster's office for putting a toad in a tutor's drawer. At the palace, being called before Prince Albert after he'd taught Brook to use a pistol when she was twelve. At Ralin, about to get a dressing down for posing a suit of armor in a too-undignified manner.

"Coming, Grandfather."

"May God have mercy on your soul," Cayton muttered as he brushed past on his way to the stairs.

Justin allowed himself only one fortifying glance at his aunts and then followed the duke's slow steps toward Cayton's study.

To the room, behind the desk, to the massive leather chair that somehow made Grandfather's weakening frame seem bigger rather than smaller.

Justin took the chair on the other side of the mahogany desk. And wished Father were there to make one of his jokes about tight laces and expectations.

Grandfather gripped the arm of the chair with one hand, held on to his cane with the other, and drilled his gaze directly into Justin's. "I did not want to mention this with your aunts present. But we have a problem."

Justin tried to straighten his spine, though it was already a ramrod. "Sir?"

"I have tried to ease you into the running of the estates. Perhaps I shouldn't have. You know we have holdings in India, Africa, Canada, and the Caribbean."

Of course he knew—and had been hinting for years that Grandfather needed to let him review the ledgers for them. Justin nodded.

The duke sighed. "Apparently my stewards there were not as trustworthy as I thought. They have been lining their pockets with Stafford money. Money I was counting on to improve the tenements. The repairs on the cottages in the village cannot be put off another year, but I don't know now how we can afford them."

The fear eased before it could slice. Those books he *did* know, better at this point than his grandfather did. "If we tighten up on our spending and cut loose a few holdings that we've no need of, we can find the money." And he had inherited a tidy sum from Father—though mentioning the fortune he had made at the tables wasn't a safe topic.

Grandfather shook his head. "I am none too sure. You will have to travel to put these issues to rights, and doing so in the style you must to make a proper impression will necessitate spending yet more." He paused, focused his gaze on the far wall and its rows of scarcely populated bookshelves, and rocked his cane back and forth. "You should marry her, my boy. Sooner rather than later. Being out of society so long, Whitby has spent little and made much. He will give her an impressive dowry, and he said he will draw up the papers to name her his heir within the week."

His throat went dry and tight. "You *asked* him?"

The duke's gaze snapped back to him. Slapped at him. "We all know how these things work. You will make his daughter a duchess. No one would expect her to come to the union empty-handed. It would be a marriage of equals, beneficial to all."

Justin clenched his teeth until he felt the tic of the muscle in his jaw.

Grandfather's eyes went dark. "Why do you look at me like that? You are fond of the girl—it is obvious. You would likely have wed her even if she were a penniless nobody, nothing but the daughter of an opera singer. You ought to be praising the Lord she is more, so that it will bring good to Stafford rather than scandal."

Justin could not convince his jaw to unclench. If he did, words would spill out that he could not in good conscience speak to the duke. Words about how he didn't want to marry for the good of Stafford. He didn't want to marry with even the thought of what money she could bring to him. If he married Brook it would be because they had always understood each other. They made each other better, stronger, more.

Because he loved her. Had always loved her, *would* always love her. And he could not cheapen that by putting a pound sign on it.

Grandfather, apparently assuming his word was, as always, law, leaned back in the chair. "Propose soon. Perhaps at this house party in a fortnight, before the rest of society meets her.

She is too beautiful to remain unattached for long, and that aunt of hers is inviting all the leading families. Nottingham's son will be there, and he's likely to switch his affections to your baroness now that she is Whitby's heir. From what I hear, he has a silver tongue and a way with the young ladies. Claim her before he can."

A stab, a twist in his gut. "Brook will not be so easily swept off her feet, Grandfather. She may sing the arias of love and romance, but she is practical and logical to a fault." When she wasn't flying off on some impulsive lark or another, anyway . . . but liberating cars and joining the ballet were a far cry from pledging her life to a stranger's.

Weren't they?

"Logic will tell her, then, to make the best match possible. And if word gets out that our estates are not in order, you will be second to Worthing. Move ahead of the rumors." Grandfather pushed himself up, slowly and obviously with pain. "You will be a good duke, Justin. A good husband. A good father. You will be all we prayed you would be. You have always made me proud."

Justin had little choice but to nod and rise too. He knew the duke meant well, meant to assure his happiness and prosperity.

But he had the wrong of it this time. Justin couldn't propose to Brook now. Not with her still settling with Whitby, not when he'd had no chance to convince her he could be more than a brother—and not with the shadow of debt over the house of Stafford. He could suffer it if the *ton* whispered that he had stationed her as Whitby's lost heiress so he could wed her and take the earl's estate. But if *she* ever thought it . . . no. He would never, never let her wonder that.

Which left him only one choice. He must put Stafford in order first. And trust that if the Lord meant Brook for his wife, she would be waiting for him once he had.

He trailed the duke out of Cayton's study, telling himself not to worry. She had always waited before. Always welcomed him to Monaco with sunshine and a kiss on each cheek. Had always made it clear he was her favorite person, aside from the prince. There was no reason to think she couldn't fall in love as he had. No reason to think another absence from her would change the bond between them, just because she was in England now.

With her family.

In a new home.

With all the nation soon to be clamoring for a peek at the princess-turned-baroness, and sure to be enamored with what they would see.

No, no reason at all to doubt.

The room felt familiar. Brook trailed a finger along the edge of a shelf as her eyes drank in the honeyed woods, the polished metals, the touches of color and play of light. It smelled of faded flowers and crisp air, of comfort.

Her mother's chamber felt familiar, but not as Whitby Park itself had when she first saw it. It stirred no imagined memories. What it brought to mind, rather, was the feel inside the sanctuary of Cathédrale Notre-Dame-Immaculée. Reverence. Sanctity. A heritage preserved with tireless care.

The dressing table still sat in the corner, no doubt as Lady Whitby left it. A hairbrush beside a bottle of perfume, at an odd angle. A necklace glinting gold as it snaked around a pot of powder. A book still sat on the bedside table, a slip of paper marking a page halfway through. *The Count of Monte Cristo.*

Brook smiled, though it faded fast. She had read the novel two years ago. It seemed her mother had never finished it.

She stifled the urge to peek into the armoire. Were she to do so, she suspected she would see a rainbow of old-fashioned gowns.

Time here had stood still.

Whitby halted by her side, regarding the room with the solemnity of the sanctuary's priest. "Mary accuses me of making it a shrine. I've never known how to explain to her that I did not keep it just so for my own benefit." He moved to a chair with a length of wispy fabric draping the arm. Gathering it in one hand, he seemed to look into the past, perhaps to the ivory shoulders it had once graced. Then he let it slide back to its place. Just so. "But when I came in here after her funeral . . . or for months after . . . I felt that—that it was not finished. There were too many questions unanswered. And you, still missing. How was I to move on? It would have been wrong."

Brook slid to the window and touched the *fleur-de-lis* pattern in the velvet drapes. She looked out but scarcely saw the maze cut into the shrubbery. Instead of the midday sun, she saw darkness. Heard thunder rumbling and felt the sizzle of lightning.

That dream had plagued her again last night.

"Are you all right, Brook?"

"Hmm?" Her hand had found her pearls again.

Her father's gaze focused upon her fingers, and a corner of his mouth turned up. "Your mother used to do that too, when she was lost in thought."

A thought that brought the burning back to her eyes. "With this necklace?"

He frowned. "That one?"

"Maman said she was wearing it that night." She touched the pearls and then lowered her hand.

Her father's face went taut. "What else did she say? Did she explain why . . . why Lizzie did not send you back to me?"

"No." Perhaps it was in the journal. She should look, for his sake if not her own. Though—she frowned—she could not

117

recall seeing it among her things since she arrived. Mademoiselle Ragusa must have slid it somewhere for safekeeping, but where? "She said only that we were in a carriage accident. That my mother took this necklace off and made her swear to keep it for me. I . . . I suppose I always assumed it was from you."

He straightened his shoulders, forcing the torment from his face, and stepped closer. Narrowing his eyes upon it, he shook his head. "I never bought her pearls. They were, at the time, more for an unwed girl than a married woman. Perhaps her family gave it to her, though. For her debut, likely."

And why would that make disappointment seep through Brook? "You do not recognize it?"

Amusement glinted now in his gaze. "Lizzie had no shortage of pretty baubles. And I took great pleasure in showering her with more. Here." He motioned Brook to the left, toward a door he opened to reveal a dressing room bursting with those gowns in every shade and hue, the leg-o'-mutton sleeves the height of fashion eighteen years before. While Brook let her eyes feast on the fabrics and colors, her father headed straight for a cabinet built into the corner and pulled open the drawers. When he waved a hand at them, she noted the harder rainbow within. Rubies and topaz and emeralds and sapphires, garnets and jet and diamonds.

More memories assaulted her. Not of this room, this mother. *Non*, now her mind went back to the little flat she had shared with Maman in Monaco-Ville before her death. She remembered playing with Collette's necklaces, earrings, and bracelets. Asking for the name of each jewel. Holding it up in chubby fingers to see how it would look on her.

And Maman would laugh that crystalline laugh, would sing the names of the gems to her. Would refuse to answer her questions of where each piece came from.

Now Brook was old enough to understand that Collette had

once accepted such gifts from wealthy patrons like Prince Louis. But she had given up such a life to be Brook's mother. To raise her with a better example.

Whitby lifted a collar necklace heavy with diamonds and emeralds. "I gave Lizzie this to celebrate our first anniversary. To match her eyes. The color of emeralds, with the light of diamonds."

Brook's heart ached for him. His tone was still so full of love. Of the pain of loss. How could he have survived so long without his Lizzie? "It's lovely."

His expression shifted, and his smile seemed lighter. "It is yours now. All of them are."

"*Non. Je ne peux pas.*" She stepped back too quickly and knocked her heels into the door, sending it into the wall with a bang.

Her father looked at her as though she had spoken in Greek instead of French. "Why can you not? *I* certainly am not going to wear them."

A breath of laughter escaped, despite herself. Still, she could not lay hold of English and spoke in French. "*Tout le mond pensera . . .*"

He lifted a brow. "What does it matter what everyone thinks? Yes, plenty will declare that you have come back solely to inherit my fortune. But *is* that why you came home?"

He asked the question with no doubt in his tone. But with discerning eyes. Eyes that had seen through imposters, eyes that had continually scanned the horizon for his lost daughter.

Brook sighed and shook her head. "But I don't want to bring scandal and gossip down upon you."

He snorted a laugh and put the necklace back, picking up a shorter string of diamonds in its stead. "I am an old favorite of the gossip-hounds. Eccentric Whitby, the recluse of North Yorkshire. According to your aunt, I have been seen haunting the abbey's ruins along with all the other ghosts, prowling the roads waiting for your mother's carriage to appear, and grabbing random blond children in the streets to see if they are my missing child." He held up the bracelet, indicated her wrist.

She stretched it out and let him fasten on the clusters of diamonds.

"Poppycock, of course. I only haunted the abbey once and couldn't tolerate the draft. I simply had to swear off it." He put on that crooked smile again and dropped his hands with a nod. "There. It suits you well. And she would be glad to know you have it. That piece has been around, I think, since the first Baroness of Berkeley."

Brook let her wrist fall to her side, let the bracelet come to a glimmering rest against her hand. The prince had given her jewels before, but she had rarely worn anything more than the pearl necklace. All she had ever wanted was her own place. Her own things. Her own identity.

She had never known what those were. "So long as you are certain. I have lived long enough on a borrowed name."

He motioned her back out of the dressing room. "Then take the one that is yours—it has been waiting for you all this time."

She stepped back into her mother's room, surrounded by her mother's things. And realized that he hadn't kept the room *just so* for himself—he had kept it for her. So that when she came home, she would find bits and pieces of the mother she had lost.

And the father who loved her enough to preserve it for her. A nod was all she could manage.

He must have spoken the language of nods well. He returned it with one of his own and led her back into the hallway, to the next door down. His room, she knew, and when he motioned her to follow, she stepped inside.

In many ways it was like the prince's chambers. That same masculine presence, the lingering scent of shaving soap, the glass case of cufflinks bright against deep colors. But here, the windows weren't open to a warm, salt-tinged Mediterranean breeze, she couldn't look out to see terra-cotta roofs lining the streets. Couldn't hear the music of shouting, laughing tourists, street performers, and bustling city life. She saw only green through the glass, heard only the muted chirping of birds.

She halted a step inside while Whitby strode directly to a chest of drawers against the far wall. Opening the third drawer, he moved aside some folded fabric and withdrew an ornate cigar box. He put the drawer to rights and was in front of her in the next moment, the box outstretched.

She knew it must be the letters from her mother. And though she still felt a little odd at the thought of reading them, it was obviously important to him that she do so. That she know their story so she could understand her own.

"Thank you." Such feeble words. But they were all she had, so she said them again as if to seal them. She offered him a smile and lifted the box. "I shall go and put them in my room. Then we can meet in the library?"

His smile was warm, the long-borne pain hidden again under fresh joy. "Perfect."

She hurried down the corridor, along another, along the maze of them until she reached the Green Room. Whitby had said they would move her to the family wing tomorrow, into the room that had always been meant to be hers. So she wasn't surprised to find Deirdre in her chamber, refolding and packing all the gowns that had only been out of her trunk for a few days. With a brief smile of acknowledgment, Brook bypassed her and went to the dressing room.

The journal had been in the bottom of her trunk. But if the mademoiselle were putting it away, she would likely store it with the letters—she knew they were her maman's, and that the book was too. It would be the logical place for them. But no leather peeked out. She didn't see it on any shelf, or in any drawer in here. Perplexed, Brook set the new collection of missives down and headed back to her bedroom. With her regular reading, perhaps? *Dracula* or *La Bible*? Both of those tomes rested on her bedside table . . . but no journal.

Deirdre cleared her throat. "Can I help you find something, my lady?"

Brook sighed. "Yes, perhaps you've seen it. I had a leather journal in my trunk, an old one. It was my maman's."

The maid's face remained blank. "A journal? I can't recall seeing it, my lady. But I shall keep an eye out for it as I repack everything."

Brook couldn't have lost it. She *knew* she had packed it, she had put it in the trunk first thing, before Odette had added her gowns. Casting her gaze around the room again, she nodded. "Thank you. It must be here somewhere. I haven't even read it yet, I . . ." She shouldn't blabber about it to the staff. Summoning a smile, she nodded Deirdre back to her task. "I'm sure you'll find it as you pack, thank you. Will you let me know when you do? I'll be in the library."

With Deirdre's quiet assurances following her out, Brook slipped into the hallway again. So much for being able to offer her father answers. Apparently they would have to wait for another day.

Eleven

Deirdre had finally managed to escape the house, and without anyone making her wait so they could walk to the village together. Not that she would have minded Hiram's company, but she needed the time to clear her head.

The rain poured down in earnest. Her half boots would be a muddy mess, and though she had donned her oiled cape and had her brolly opened above her, every time the wind gusted she got a face full of water.

And naturally, when she reached the crossroads there was a carriage bearing down, ready to slosh by and send that entire puddle upon her. She backed up, hopefully out of splashing distance.

The carriage pulled to a halt. For a moment she thought it must be someone in need of direction—then she saw the dark scowl on the man that swung open the door. Pratt. "Have you got your days confused, my lovely?" Not giving her time to answer, he jerked his head. "Get in. And make it quick."

She told herself to be grateful for the escape from the rain. Though he would likely deduct the price of cleaning up her mud from her next payment. With a glance over her shoulder to be sure no one would see, she closed her umbrella and hoisted herself up.

The interior was dim and smelled of spice and rain. Pratt tapped the ceiling to order the driver onward, never taking his eyes from her. "I expect you have an excuse for missing our rendezvous yesterday."

Her umbrella was dripping a lake onto his floor. "The Duke of Stafford came unexpectedly. I could not be spared."

"The Duke of Stafford." His glare chased away the light. "Why?"

As if she dared to interpret the mind of a duke. "On his way to Azerley Hall, he said. Thought to stop in for tea so he could meet the new baroness and Lady Melissa, whom your friend Cayton could scarcely take his eyes from."

"Is it official, then? Whitby has accepted this performer's daughter as his own?"

She nodded, not bothering to ask how he knew that much, lurking around as he always did. "Although . . . you know French, don't you, my lord?"

His answer was the arch of a dark brow.

Perhaps this wasn't such a good idea. But she had already smuggled the book out in her handbag, she might as well see it through. She drew out the leather journal. "Her ladyship had this with her. I thought . . ."

"Leave the thinking to me." He snatched it from her hands though, and flipped to the first page. The way his gaze darkened, she couldn't be sure if the words he found pleased or angered him. "This isn't the baroness's."

"The singer's. The baroness hasn't even read it yet."

There, his lips turned up.

Because she figured it would only improve his mood, she added, "I am to be her lady's maid. His lordship will announce it after prayers tomorrow."

"Moving up in the world, are we?" Yet his gaze said she was worth no more than ever. "Your instincts were good with this. And you'll be even more useful now. Earn her trust. And pay especial attention to her relations with Abingdon—I won't have him marrying her before I can so much as get a proper introduction."

She hesitated, reached halfway out. "The journal, my lord. I need it back, to return to her things. She was looking for it yesterday. If you could just take a peek to see if it verifies the story she told . . ."

That quickly, his mood turned. "My French is not so flawless that I can just glance at it. I'll read it at Delmore and return it when I am through."

Unease clawed at her, but she knew better than to argue—it would only make him more determined. She cast around for something to distract him before he decided to keep it forever. "Lady Ramsey is throwing a house party in a fortnight's time, at Whitby Park. You are to be invited."

His smile reemerged. "Good." Eden Dale was already coming into view, and Lord Pratt smacked the roof again, calling out, "Stop here!" Quiet and cold, he added to her, "Can't be seen together, can we?"

"No, of course not." If only she had her old bin of brushes and cloths so she could wipe up the mess. "So sorry for the mud, your lordship."

"I have servants to clean it." Quick as a snake, he grabbed her wrist and pulled her to his side of the carriage, pressed his mouth to hers.

More poison than kiss, more shackles than embrace. She endured it—and promised herself a thorough scrubbing when she got home.

He chuckled as he pulled away. "I saw her, you know, the other morning. She is nearly as beautiful as you." He dragged his finger down the side of her face, from temple to chin. "It will not be a hardship to marry her. And even less of one knowing you come with her."

Deirdre prayed he wouldn't detect her shudder. She said nothing. But when he let her go, she lunged for the door and exited with more speed than grace.

His laugh joined with rumbling wheels and pounding rain as the carriage rolled on again.

She had left her umbrella inside. And deemed getting wet an even trade for escaping him.

The horse was black as midnight and skittish as a phantom. Brook knew the moment she stepped into the stables and clapped her gaze upon the stallion that he would be her mount of choice. She had little use for a docile horse—when she rode, it was to give herself over to wind and earth and sky, to lay bare her soul to the Father who had crafted both beast and land across which it flew. When she rode, it was to push herself to the edge of reason and safety.

When she rode, she lived.

The stable master slurred some response to her question of the horse's name that she could scarcely understand, so thick was his accent. The groom interpreted with, "Him? Nay, milady, you don't be wanting Oscuro."

"Oscuro." She whispered the name, but not as he had done, with the dreadful British enunciation. She accented it as the Italian dictated. Oscuro, the unknown darkness.

Perhaps the horse knew his name had been said wrong all this time, for he tossed his black mane and nickered. Of course, he also reared up and pawed.

She made for his end stall.

"He ain't tame, milady!" The groom jogged to her side. "He

was bred for the races, but he wouldna tolerate a rider. Broke his trainer's leg, he did. His lordship's only keeping him to stud."

And she didn't intend to ride him today—she wasn't daft. But she would. Soon. And the start would be getting him used to her presence. She halted a bit away from his stall, out of range of hooves but close enough for him to catch her scent. "He is well groomed for being unbroken."

The man grunted. "It takes two of us to get him secured, and then we draw lots to see who risks getting bit or kicked. Stay clear of him, milady, I beg you. He'd better to have been named after the devil than darkness."

Oscuro pawed the air again, showing off his musculature and powerful frame. "He wants to run free."

"Aye, and he can never be off the tether, or he'll be over the fence and gone. Leave him be, now. We have a mare, just as handsome, same coloring—share a sire, they do, but this one's trained for the sidesaddle. Her name's Tempesta, but she's got patience to match her spirit."

Brook turned to face the groom—slowly, so as not to startle Oscuro. "I don't care for the sidesaddle. I will be riding astride."

Temper flashed in his eyes. "The young ladies always ride sidesaddle, milady. Lady Melissa is a most excellent horse-woman too. I've accompanied her many a time. Let me saddle Tempesta for you and we can go. His lordship said we ought to show you all the estate."

She tried on her sweetest smile. "I do appreciate the offer . . . what is your name?"

He heaved a sigh, but the fight didn't leave his eyes. "Francis, milady."

"Francis." He seemed immune to her grin, but she brightened it anyway. "I am happy to take the horse you recommend—though with a traditional saddle. But much as I appreciate your offer, I don't need an escort today. I'll not go far." Not *too* far.

Francis's returning smile looked about as warm as last week's unrelenting rain. "I'll fetch the horses, milady."

Horses, plural. She sighed as he strode away and then turned slowly back to Oscuro. He kicked at the stall. She nodded. "I know how you feel," she said in Monegasque. "I have not been alone for over a week, save for when I sleep, and I am about to kick something too."

She was enjoying the time with her family. Aunt Mary was welcoming, if a bit aloof, Regan sweet as could be, and Melissa's offense on her sister's behalf seemed to be fading. But Brook had not been so surrounded by people . . . ever. The prince had given her the run of the palace, and more often than he liked, she slipped out without a chaperone and took herself to ballet lessons or for a spicy *salsiccia*. Or to find Justin, if he was in Monaco.

Footsteps sounded behind her, along with a sigh she knew quite well already. "Naturally, you find the dangerous one."

Her grin, she had discovered, worked quite well on her father. She flashed it at him now. "He is the handsomest. Are you the one who gave them Italian names?"

Whitby hummed, nodded, and held out his palm. Oscuro ignored him, but given his behavior otherwise, it was surely the equivalent of a whinny of greeting from any other horse. "Not all of them, of course, but it seemed to suit him and his sister. Francis said he is saddling Tempesta for you."

"*Oui.* F—" *Father*, she almost said, but stopped herself. She had not called him such yet, and she would not now, when she was trying to wheedle him into something. "Francis said he must come with me."

Her father lifted his brow. "This is a problem?"

She splayed her hands. "Do *you* always like company on your rides?"

"I am a man." No doubt he tried to keep his expression clear—but she thought she detected amusement in it.

Now Brook planted those hands on her hips. "And I inherited your disposition."

"You'll never let me live that down."

"You'd never want me to."

Yes, definitely amusement. It made his lips twitch. "And you've only been home a week."

She flashed her grin again. "Imagine when it's been a year."

He clasped his hands behind his back, sent his gaze over her shoulder, and rocked on his heels. "An hour, and you must stay on Whitby land."

"Two hours."

His brows lifted. "But the boundary?"

"Accepted."

"Done." He held out a hand.

She shook it, unable to stifle the laugh as she did. "You are an admirable negotiator."

"Ha! You are an unabashed flatterer. Francis!"

Brook scurried to keep pace as he strode down the open space between the stalls. "He seems to think I need a sidesaddle, too, if we could correct him on that at the same time."

Her father came to an abrupt halt and turned to her with that expression of fond disbelief he had given her at least forty times in the last seven days. "You ride astride?"

"Have you ever tried to ride sidesaddle?"

A short laugh slipped out. "The prince taught you?"

"Grand-père . . . allowed it."

Whitby's eyes went to slits again. "Let me guess . . ."

"Justin taught me." A phrase she had uttered a matching forty times. "It is all his fault, really, every bit of unconventionalness . . . Is that a word?"

A snort was his only answer. He took two more steps, then halted again. Lifted a finger. "*How*, if you don't mind me asking, do you ride astride in a skirt?"

Brook kicked a leg out a bit, revealing the split that was all but invisible when she stood still.

He pressed a hand to his brow and moved onward. "My daughter is wearing trousers."

"Oh, there's no need to sound so horrified. They are not trousers exactly."

His grunt disagreed. "Your mother would kill me."

"Nonsense. She wouldn't have let a little thing like a split skirt upset her. Although now that you mention it, trousers would be far more efficient."

"Heaven help me. Next thing I know you'll be joining the suffragettes."

She tucked her hand into the crook of his arm and grinned up at him. "I'd rather learn to drive. Justin taught me a bit in his Rolls-Royce in Monaco."

"Of course he did."

"But not nearly enough. Have you learned how? You could teach me."

He sent her another look she had already learned—one that said her grin had reached the limits of its powers. For now. "I employ a chauffeur."

"So I should learn from *him*?" They reached the stall where Francis worked on another midnight-black horse. This one greeted them properly, to the point of snuffling at her father's pockets. Apparently in search of sugar, since he produced a cube of it.

"Try it and I'll lock you in your chamber as your Justin recommended. Francis—no sidesaddle for the baroness. And she has my permission to ride alone." He raised a finger and leveled it at her nose. "Two hours. On our land. Or I dig up the key—it is surely around somewhere."

"Mrs. Doyle no doubt knows where it is." And, she suspected, would happily hand it over. Brook had yet to earn more than a polite turning of the lips from her. She held out a hand for Tempesta to sniff. Getting a damp snort of approval, she rubbed the mare's ebony nose. "But about the driving."

"No."

Francis exited the stall with the sidesaddle in hand, shooting her a look that said quite simply she was not what he thought a baroness should be.

Brook focused on her father. "Another deal, then. If I can break Oscuro within two months' time, you let me learn to drive."

He was a master at the arched eyebrow, this father of hers. "You expect to convince me to let you learn one dangerous task by promising to do another?"

"He was born to race." Her tone went more serious than she'd intended. Her fingers curled into her skirt. "Some creatures have a harder time obeying the standards put before them. But if you can inspire them to, they will outdo all the rest. You must simply learn their language."

She expected him to ask if she had ever broken a horse before. She was prepared to tell him all about her favorite mount in Monaco, how she had finally ridden him over the French hills after months of work.

He didn't ask but studied her until Francis returned with a regular saddle and a stony countenance. Then he sighed. "Two months?"

"Well. Assuming I'm not forbidden from stepping out in the rain." As she had been all last week. Granted, it had been abysmally chilly, but she would have suffered it for the sake of a horse. "And then the car."

Whitby turned to face the end of the aisle again, where Oscuro still snorted and fumed. "This is certainly no life for him. If he can be trained—"

"Your lordship!" Aghast, Francis paused in his reach for the girth strap. "You've the best trainers in all Yorkshire. If they canna break him, then he canna be broken."

"Or . . ." Whitby faced her again, met her gaze. "They did not speak his language. Sometimes when we think someone should understand English, they really only know . . . French."

Brook's heart swelled, warmed.

Francis looked ready to snort along with Oscuro. "You want we should speak *French* to him?"

Another twitch of his lips, but her father didn't turn to the groom. "If you can do it, my dear, then I will not only allow you to learn to drive, I will learn with you."

She held out her hand as he had done before. "Done."

Rather than shaking, he clasped her hand in both of his and squeezed it. "Be careful. If you're not back in precisely two hours, I'll send out the hounds to find you."

"Thank you." She stretched up on her toes so she could kiss his left cheek, then his right. When she had said farewell to Justin that way a week ago, Aunt Mary had played her fainting trick again and had lectured her for a solid hour afterward.

Her father half-smiled, as if remembering the same thing. "The sea abuts our property on the east, of course. To the south, you may go so far as the copse of trees beyond the duck pond. To the west, so far as the road leading to the village, and to the north, all the way to the hedge dividing our land from Delmore."

"Delmore?"

"Pratt's estate. It's a sprawling, mazelike monstrosity that has a strange charm I think you'll enjoy seeing."

She wrinkled her nose at the name. "I'd just as soon not."

He chuckled. "Enjoy yourself. Perhaps tomorrow, if the weather holds, we can take a morning ride together."

"I can think of no better way of starting the day than with a ride."

He moved off, greeting a few of the horses with the same muted affection he gave his family. Muted, but sure. Solid.

Brook watched him step into the weak sunshine and turned to Tempesta. Francis led her out of the stall and handed Brook the reins with nary a word. He gave her the exact same flat stare her maid—whom she was apparently now to call O'Malley—had when she saw the split skirt. Silent, screaming disapproval.

And they all wondered why she needed a solitary ride.

She adjusted the stirrups and then swung up into the saddle. Its leather was supple, well worn and well cared for. She settled comfortably into it, gathered the reins, and patted the horse's neck. "*Allons-y, ma fille.*"

Go she did, at a high-stepping walk from the stables, into a trot southward with the barest of whispers, and to a full gallop when Brook gave her rein. Tempesta's hooves ate up the ground, raining clods of dirt down behind them.

Before they left the lawn, Brook reached up and unpinned her hat so she could toss it to the ground. She needed the wind to whip through her hair and blow away all the frustrations. She needed to be free, to discover, to find her place.

Find it she did, at the southeast corner, where the land rose before tumbling into the sea. The waves before her, a cliff under her, the moors rolling out behind . . . not exactly the seascape she had grown up with, but close enough. Beautiful enough. *Enough.*

For a moment after reining Tempesta to a halt, she merely closed her eyes and breathed it in. Whispered a thank-you to the Lord, and then a please. An outpouring. An in-taking. Then she slid down so her own feet could test the earth.

Were the wind not gusting off the ocean, she would have withdrawn from her pocket the two letters she had chosen to read today. One from her father, one from her mother. He had traveled a good deal, it seemed, in those days. And whenever they were apart, they would write.

Of love. Of family. Of yearning to be together again.

She had matched up the dates as best she could for the two stacks, which had taken most of one rainy afternoon . . . especially given how often she had to pause to laugh at something Regan or Melissa said as they all worked on their projects together in the upstairs salon. Reading them she was taking slowly as well. Familiarizing herself with each loop in her mother's hand, in the quick dash of her father's. Their favorite phrases, their nicknames for each other.

According to the dates, she was drawing near to the time when they would mention *her*, as in that first letter of her father's she had spotted. Though she knew already there would not be many letters for her to read for that time—they had not been apart then. She had mentioned the gap in dates as she was correlating them, and Aunt Mary had given her an indulgent smile.

"When Ambrose found out Lizzie was expecting, he could not be dragged from her side," she had said. "Not until necessity dictated it right before . . ."

Before that night. The night the carriage careened off the road and everything changed.

The wind shifted, and the warmth she had worked up on the ride went the way of the sunshine—swept away by the clouds. With a shiver, Brook pulled out her watch from her pocket. She still had time, but if the sun didn't reemerge, she would be half frozen before she reached home.

After mounting again, she set a slower pace toward the house. By the time she had found her hat and gained the stables, she was shivering. She handed the reins back over to the brooding Francis.

Coffee. She needed coffee.

"Brook!" Regan waved to her from the terrace outside the library. She sat with her sister and mother, looking positively warm in her short-sleeved afternoon dress. "Tea?"

Striding their way, Brook chafed her hands together and smiled for her cousin. "Aren't you cold out here?"

Regan laughed. "Are you jesting? It's lovely."

Aunt Mary reached for her teapot. "Strong or weak today, dear?"

She had tried both. She cared for neither. Grinning, she said, "*Caffe espresso*. Can your pot produce that? If I beg?"

Her aunt laughed and motioned toward the house. "No. But I daresay the chef's can. Ask him for some and join us."

Funny—the two times she had dared request coffee since Justin left, she had been delivered a cup of pale, watery stuff unfit for consumption. "I've been warned away from the kitchen—how, then, do I put in this request?"

"Oh, nonsense." Aunt Mary sipped at her tea, her stern gaze belying her pleasant smile. "Don't let the servants intimidate you, child, or you will never manage the house. You are mistress. Go where you will. Ask for what you want."

Mistress. Not a role that seemed hers, with Aunt Mary presiding over teas and dinner and Whitby in control of all else.

But her aunt was right. If she ever hoped to be accepted by the household, she had to earn their respect. And she wouldn't do that playing the mouse. With a smile, she nodded and made for the library door. "I shall return with *caffe*."

The door opened noiselessly, shut with a click. A rustle of newspaper from the corner proved her presence had been noted though, and her father peered over the top of the page with smiling eyes. "With twenty minutes to spare, even. All in one piece, are you?"

"So long as you are not counting hairpins. Although I would like to lodge a complaint—your air here is too cold. Might we import some Mediterranean breezes?"

He chuckled and raised the paper again. "I'll have some shipped, posthaste."

The rows of books were tempting, as was the fire in the grate. But the allure of coffee kept her feet moving through the room. She would settle into her leather chair after tea, before the dressing gong. It had become her favorite hour of the day.

The halls grew less familiar as she neared the stairs down to the kitchen. Her mother must have walked this path countless times, on her way to plan the menu with the old cook. Brook tried to picture her here, the true mistress about her duties. She would have been comfortable, in her element. Humming, perhaps. She would have smiled as she descended and the sound of laughter drifted up to her.

Brook felt like an interloper.

"Aw, come now, DeeDee. Have a cup with your lowly friends." A male voice, though Brook couldn't place it.

The answering laugh she knew, though Melissa and Regan had been the ones to draw it out before. "That's O'Malley to you, Hiram. And sure and if I do, her ladyship will return the self-same moment all covered in mud and needing my assistance."

Her cue. Clearing her throat in warning, Brook descended the last steps and turned the corner into the kitchen.

The servants all leaped to their feet or halted their work. Brook smiled at the group at large. "Don't mind me. I only need a word with Monsieur Bisset." Those about tasks resumed them. Those about their tea shifted from foot to foot without retaking their seats.

She had learned that the English took their teatime quite seriously—so she would hurry. She turned to the rotund man frowning from his place at the stove. "*Bon après-midi, monsieur. Ça va?*"

He turned back to the simmering pot. "I am busy," he answered in French.

French . . . but not quite *French*. Hadn't they said he was from Paris? Or was it only that he was *schooled* in Paris? She stuck to *français*. "And it smells delicious. I will trouble you only for a moment." Her gaze went to the beautiful, miraculous, life-promising machine in the corner. How had he come by the exact model the prince had insisted on for the palace? They weren't cheap, and she couldn't think that Whitby had bought it, given that he never drank espresso. It must be the monsieur's, and he must have spent years of savings on it. Was he simply unwilling to share with her? But if so, then why had he produced a pot when Justin was here?

Well, she would never know if she didn't ask. "I was hoping I could have a cup of espresso."

The chef spun on her, his face red. "You would have me abandon my hollandaise, the most temperamental of sauces, the one I learned from my grandmother in Provence, which she had learned from hers, to make you coffee?"

The kitchen went silent around them, but Brook merely folded her arms over her chest. The French bluster she knew well. His particular accent she did not. "Provence? I think not." More likely some corner of Quebec or another.

He sputtered and muttered, though he used no words that she could make out. And the red in his cheeks faded to white.

Blast. She hardly cared if he had lied about where he was from to secure a position as a French *chef du cuisine*. All she wanted was a cup of coffee. Why was that so much to ask?

Deirdre held her breath with the others while the baroness and the monsieur all but spat at each other in French. Apparently her ladyship had no qualms about arguing with an employee. She answered him phrase for phrase, gesture for gesture. Proclaimed something emphatic with a sweep of her arms and then pointed at the odd machine that hissed and steamed whenever the chef used it, and spurted out a coffee black as night. Other than Bisset himself, no one but Lord Abingdon had ever suffered it. Well, and the baroness. Though when a cup had been requested for her last week, the chef had not set the thing to hissing, he'd merely tossed a few grounds into a kettle.

Which her ladyship must have realized. Pure exasperation covered her face as she delivered another line of too-rapid French, ending with a *s'il vous plaît* that sounded more like command than request.

Monsieur Bisset glared. Sighed. Asked something.

"*Non.*" The baroness motioned again at the machine. "*Je veux seulement un espresso!*"

He huffed. But he nodded before he waved a hand at the stairs.

The baroness echoed his huff and spun away. "*Merci, monsieur.*" To the rest of them, she nodded. Then she stomped her way back upstairs.

"Well, I never." Mrs. Doyle smoothed a hand over her shirtwaist and looked from the stairs to the chef. "What, pray tell, was that all about?"

Monsieur Bisset barely glanced at the housekeeper—he lumbered to the machine with a kettle of water. "Coffee."

"Coffee." The housekeeper's tone was cooler than February in Kilkeel. "Her ladyship raised her voice at you over *coffee*?"

He didn't answer, not even in French. Odd—usually he greeted their questions with an unintelligible spout of nonsense. Now he cranked the coffee grinder.

Mrs. Doyle looked to Deirdre with raised brows. "O'Malley, is she always like this?"

Deirdre cleared her throat. "No, ma'am. Not that I've seen. Though she does lapse quite often into French, ma'am, and I can't be telling what she says."

"DeeDee." Hiram breathed her name like a warning.

But it was nothing but the truth, and she couldn't lie to the housekeeper. She lifted her chin.

Mrs. Doyle lifted hers too. "I do detest anyone raising their voices at one of our own. Monsieur Bisset, give the coffee to me when it is ready. I will deliver it myself."

Hiram raised his brows, but Deirdre could only shrug. She slid to her seat beside him as the chatter returned to the kitchen. But Hiram held silent, and she could think of nothing to say either.

A few minutes later the monsieur slid a cup of inky coffee onto the table before Mrs. Doyle, and everyone else fell silent again too. Silent and somber as the housekeeper fetched a larger cup, poured half the espresso into it, and filled the rest with water.

Their laughter followed her up the stairs.

Twelve

Justin pulled into the drive of Whitby Park, lined with unfamiliar carriages and cars promising strangers he didn't feel up to meeting, and knew he shouldn't have come. Never mind that Grandfather had told him to—he couldn't erase from his mind the way the duke's hand had trembled when they parted yesterday. How short of breath he had been.

Now Justin would have to paste on a smile and put aside his worry, though he would rather turn his Rolls-Royce around. Still, he followed Thate to the stables and parked.

Peters hopped out the moment Justin switched off the magneto. "I'll see to your things, my lord."

"Thank you." He slid the key into his trouser pocket as he got out and scanned the figures flocking the lawn. Given the direction of Thate's gaze, Lady Regan must be by the table. Perhaps Brook was near her.

"There you are! I thought you would never arrive."

Or perhaps she was in the stables. He pivoted, spotting her as she emerged into the sunshine, and grinned. Even though his usual reaction to her beauty made him remember Grandfather's parting remark. *"You know what you must do."*

"Hiding, Brooklet?"

She bypassed the hand he held out and greeted him as she always had, kissing him on each cheek. "*Naturellement*. She managed to get twenty people here, all to stay the week—and she has been going absolutely batty with the preparations."

He could only assume the "she" was her aunt. "Whitby allowed it?"

Her smile did his heart good. Even better was the gleam of contentment in her eyes. "I give him two days before he flees Yorkshire. And I will be there by his side—you're welcome to join us."

"You are getting on, then." He took her hand, tucked it against his arm, and led her toward the lawn. Thate awaited them with lifted brows.

"We are much alike. And Lord Thate, you can relax—for a few days at least." She flashed a grin that would likely have turned his friend to a puddle, had he not been one already over her cousin. "Lord Worthing and his sister will not be arriving until Tuesday. You have three whole days to win her, and I suggest you put them to use."

Thate grinned, too, even as he said, "I don't know what you mean, my lady. But might I say, since my oaf of a friend failed to do so, that you are looking particularly lovely today?"

It was drattedly true. She wore some blue thing that looked like a slice of the sky draping her too precisely. The nip in the air had put roses in her cheeks, and the sun—which must have shown up on order of Lady Ramsey—made her hair gleam purest gold.

No doubt every male set of eyes would be glued to her all week, and Justin wouldn't be able to rid his mind of Grandfather's warnings. Grandfather's commands.

Thate's low chuckle made Justin aware of his own scowl. "Predictable."

He lifted his brows and glanced toward the table where Thate's gaze kept wandering. "Pot and kettle."

Thate laughed, but the way Brook's brows knit made him wonder if she had not yet learned that particular idiom. She didn't seem to catch the meaning of their jest, praise be to heaven.

With a tug on his arm, she spurred him onward. "Thank heavens you're here—now I can finally get a decent cup of *espresso*."

He pulled her to a halt again, though Thate sighed when he did. "What do you mean? The chef obviously knows how to make it."

She shrugged and looked out into the distance. When her gaze grazed the collection of people on her lawn, she leaned a bit closer to his side.

He wasn't about to complain—though he wondered if she even realized she had done it. Or if she could possibly know how it made him want to catch the curl that the wind toyed with, give it the tug he always had . . . and then slide his hand to the back of her neck and lean down to touch his lips to hers.

He forced his mind back to the issue of *caffe*. "What is the problem?"

The light in her eyes dimmed. She shrugged again, a gesture so very Gallic that she might as well have broken into a rousing rendition of "La Marseillaise." "They don't like me."

Now Thate faced them, frowning along with Justin. "Who? The kitchen staff?"

"All of them." She smiled, but it was dim and forced. "The family has welcomed me, but the staff . . . It is their loyalty to my father, I think. They have seen so many pretenders over the years."

But with loyalty should have come trust—and if they distrusted *her*, then they also distrusted Whitby's recognition of her. "Unacceptable. You are their mistress, and if they cannot serve you well, they ought to be replaced. Surely your father agrees . . . Except you've not told him, or you wouldn't look away with that"—*oh so lovely*—"flush in your cheeks."

"I know I should. And I will." She forced a little smile. "After the house party."

He wanted to press the issue, but it would do no good. She had that obstinate set to her chin.

But even Thate looked concerned. He motioned them onward again but kept his focus on Brook. "Have you hired a lady's maid? Perhaps if you have someone loyal first to you . . ."

"I chose to promote the head housemaid. She has a way with hair."

Did she know how weak it sounded? She must, because she kept her gaze fastened on the ground ahead of them. "Brook."

"I thought it would help." She looked up now, and her smile went cheeky. "You ought to have seen her horror the first time I pulled out my riding habit."

He snorted a laugh at the thought. But given that she had first learned to ride astride in Justin's outgrown knee breeches, the split skirt ought to have been praised as a brilliant compromise. "I can well imagine. Have you chosen a horse yet? I hear Whitby has some of the best stock in the country."

"I have been riding a black mare named Tempesta—she is a beautiful creature, with an admirable spirit. But . . ." Her eyes gleamed so bright, he knew trouble brewed. "It is her brother I want. They say he cannot be broken and keep him on a tether at all times. His name is Oscuro."

Justin tightened his fingers around hers. Riding astride was one thing—toying with wild horses quite another. He had nearly had a fit when she'd told him last year of the prince's horse she had "helped train," and Prince Albert's quiet assurances that she had been well guarded had done little to allay the fears. "Whitby surely doesn't let you near him."

Her impish grin said otherwise. "I've already got him tolerating me in the stall. Another week and I intend to put my weight on him. If I can ride him in two months' time, my father and I will learn to drive the car together. By next spring, Lord Thate, I may be racing you at Surrey."

The woman needed to be locked in a tower somewhere. On a desert island. With no wild horses. Or racetracks. "Don't even think it."

Thate laughed. "Our friend is quite right. You would never stand a chance in that touring car of your father's. You would need a proper racing car. Perhaps a Lancia. Or a Benz."

"A Fiat," she countered. "They may not have won the Grand Prix in May, but they set the fastest lap times, *n'est pas*?"

She was mad—stark, raving mad. "Before sliding off the road and killing one of their mechanics. You are not racing, Brook. And you." Justin spun on Thate, lifting his hand from hers to give his friend a helpful shove in the arm. "Stop encouraging her. In fact, if you hope to win Lady Regan before Nottingham's son shows up, perhaps you ought to quit talk of racing altogether."

"I don't have—" He cut himself off with a huff, apparently realizing the absurdity of the claim. He pursed his lips and looked to Brook again. "I don't suppose she's mentioned me."

Brook's silver laugh chimed, making Justin's stomach tighten. "Perhaps."

"Hmm." Mouth still pursed, Thate drew to a halt a fair piece from the gathering. "My mother says no lady of quality will have me as I am."

"Well, that's ridiculous. And I think my cousin would agree." She grinned as she looked toward Lady Regan. "For all her steady ways, she is a romantic."

"She is . . . perfect." Squaring his shoulders, Thate sucked in a breath. "Excuse me, Bing. My lady. I have only three days, and I don't mean to waste another moment of them."

Justin watched his friend stride off, smiled, and was content to hold Brook on the edge of the gardens for a while longer. "He has an honest chance with her?"

Brook hummed and rested her cheek against his shoulder, making his pulse accelerate far too much. "She's in love with him. Melissa thinks it foolish, and Aunt Mary talks only of whether Lord Worthing will propose. But if Thate speaks up, she'll accept him in a heartbeat."

For a moment they said nothing more, just watched the way Thate first greeted a gentleman, how he used the conversation to shift directions, and then just happened to find himself at Lady Regan's side. Deft. Justin hadn't known he had it in him. "We ought to fashion a story to commemorate this occasion. We can call it, 'The Day Thate Conformed to Normal Social Ritual.'"

She tossed back her head in a laugh. "A bit unwieldy, that title. I prefer 'When Love Found Them.'"

His smiled. It faded, though, when a dark-clad figure caught his attention. "Pratt came, I see."

She looked his way, shuddered, and then tugged Justin toward the house. "Those are my other cousins he is talking with. The Rushworths—Lord Rushworth and Lady Catherine. My mother and their father and his brother, Henry, were first cousins. Both their parents have passed. They have only their uncle left, but he has been in India for most of their lives."

From this distance, Lady Catherine could have been Brook. Blond hair, trim figure, fashionable. Though he certainly hoped Brook never clung to Pratt's arm like that one did. "Did you meet them yet?"

"Briefly." Brook nodded toward where her father sat in a chair on the terrace, trying to disappear behind a newspaper. "Lord Rushworth said hardly a word, but his sister seemed nice enough—though Regan doesn't like her, and Regan is usually a sound judge of character." She yawned, though she tried to cover it.

Justin eyed the bench adjacent to Whitby's chair. Perhaps they could find another newspaper and follow his example. "Tired already?"

"I was up too late looking for that journal I mentioned—I've no idea where it got put, and poor O'Malley was obviously afraid I'd blame her for it. Though Odette must have moved it when she packed for me, or Mademoiselle Ragusa at some point." She shrugged, though her eyes did not lose their disturbed gleam. "And I have been having the strangest dream."

Not a good one, if the set of her mouth were any indication. "Nightmare?"

"*Oui.* The same one, over and again." Her words drifted into Monegasque. "It is very vague. A storm, fierce and frightening. Lightning, thunder, darkness . . . and always this feeling of some threat lurking." Her right fingers found her pearls, twisted.

Justin frowned. The journal would turn up, and the dreams were likely nothing—the influence of an unfamiliar home, an unknown future, unanswered questions. Still. "Every night?"

"Almost. But they will pass." She renewed her smile and removed her hand from his arm so she could sit.

Justin sat beside her, trying to ignore how cold his arm now felt.

Whitby looked up from his paper. Smiled at Brook—scowled at him. "You. You have some explaining to do, Lord Abingdon."

Perhaps he would have worried, had Brook's laugh not been so carefree. He looked from the woman beside him to her father. Was it laughter in Whitby's eyes too, or irritation? "What have I done, my lord?"

Whitby folded his paper and raised his hand, a finger up. "You taught my daughter to ride astride." He raised another finger. "To shoot a pistol." A third. "To drive an automobile." Four. "To swim." And his thumb. "To fence."

146

Brook's next laugh interrupted him, and Justin felt his mouth tug upward into a grin too.

Whitby narrowed his eyes. "What have you to say for yourself?"

Looking at her, how she sat with such confidence, how she laughed with such abandon, how she faced the world with such brilliance, there was only one thing he *could* say. "You're welcome."

Deirdre hated this time of morning. When all was still dark outside the many-paned windows of Whitby Park, when she should have had a peaceful hour to take her breakfast and go about her tasks.

It had once been her favorite time of day. Now she dreaded it, knowing she had to rush if she hoped to have Lady Berkeley's room prepared before the baroness surged out of bed. Her ladyship was up before the sun most mornings. She seldom asked for anything, but that only made it worse. She *knew* Deirdre resented her presence, and by knowing made her ashamed of it with every apologetic smile.

Sure and it was enough to spoil the whole day.

She trod silently down the hall, pausing outside the baroness's new room. Granted, it had now been hers longer than the Green Room had been, but it still felt strange to Deirdre. This was a chamber she had once cleaned with a pervasive sense of pity for his lordship. One that Beatrix wouldn't even step foot in without crossing herself. *The babe's room*, they had used to call it.

Lady Berkeley's now.

Deirdre said a silent prayer that the lady would still be abed and turned the knob. No lamplight greeted her. No soft humming came from the window seat. The baroness's wrapper was still draped on the chair—a guarantee that she was yet beneath her covers, for the girl couldn't tolerate chill air.

Deirdre loosed a breath of relief and headed for the dressing room. His lordship had been sending over jewels and hats, scarves and gloves. Anything belonging to the late Lady Whitby that had not gone absolutely out of fashion.

Still, the girl only wore that pearl necklace she had arrived in. She would slip on a bracelet or ring of the late lady's now and then, but the heavily-jeweled items remained on their velvet trays.

Deirdre flipped on the electric light once she'd closed herself in. The baroness had instructed her to have her riding habit ready this morning. A hunt was planned. Deirdre couldn't help the purse of her lips as she pulled it down. Had the woman no shame, to wear pants with all those guests around?

At least the lady would have to dress for breakfast first. She had indicated no preference for that, so Deirdre selected an ivory morning dress with rose inlays, just because she fancied it.

After gathering the necessary underthings, she turned the light back off and blinked against the darkness of the bedchamber as she stepped into it. She went stiff when she heard shifting on the bed.

By now, she knew the sounds. The muttering in French, the thrashing of limbs. The *non, non, non*. Another nightmare. For a moment, she strained forward. Little Molly'd had the worst nightmares after Da died. Deirdre had always pulled her close, smoothed her hair, whispered until her sister woke up and stopped her trembling. She could still see the fear in the wee one's big brown eyes. The same fear she had glimpsed in the baroness's one morning when she sat bolt upright after such thrashing.

But what could her ladyship have to haunt her? What had she lost to throw her into such turmoil? Nothing. All she had done was gain, gain, gain.

Deirdre spun for the fireplace. The wood had already been set, and the scullery maid would be in soon to light it, but not soon enough. She would have to do it herself, or else when the lady snapped awake in a few minutes, she would be a-shiver. Have to pull her blankets close. Chafe her hands together. Silent condemnation of Deirdre's inability to see to her needs.

Francis said Lords Abingdon and Thate had all but told her ladyship to find another lady's maid. No doubt she was waiting for an excuse to do so, and heaven help her if Deirdre would provide her with one. She already had the journal hanging over her head, though her ladyship seemed to think the Frenchwoman had misplaced it, praise be to the Lord. Still, she would ask Lord Pratt about it if she could find him alone. He had surely had time enough to translate it by now.

The first flames chased away the sulfur's bite when a scratching came at the door. Satisfied that the tinder would catch, she rose and opened it.

Beatrix stood wide-eyed in the hall. "I don't know what I'm to do, DeeDee!"

"Shh." Glancing over her shoulder to make sure the lady still slept, Deirdre stepped into the hall and eased the door closed. "What is it?"

Beatrix wrung her hands. "I was taking out the pots in the ladies' wing and went into Lady Catherine's room, but she wasn't alone. There was a *man* in her bed! Lord Whitby would—"

"Shh." Deirdre held up a hand this time to illustrate her point and leaned over. "Hush, Bea. It's a house party, what do you *think* happens?"

The younger girl's mouth fell open. "Well, not *that*. His lordship would be aghast—I know he would. And Lady Ramsey—"

"Lady Ramsey knows the ways of the world, and so long as it isn't *her* daughters disgracing themselves, she is happy to turn a blind eye."

Beatrix didn't look relieved. "But his lordship . . . You remember when he dismissed Bridey last year for getting caught with a village boy in the stables. He's no tolerance for such things under his roof, he said. And if not from us, then surely not from a lady."

"Beatrix, listen." She gripped her friend's arm and steered her back toward the exit from the family hall. "We're not going to tell his lordship. We're going to mind our own and bite our tongues and not say a word. Do you understand?"

"But—"

"It isn't our business. And if you told Lord Whitby and he confronted her, she would only say you were lying and try to get you sacked. It isn't worth it. She'll be gone when the week is."

At last, capitulation filled Beatrix's eyes. Her friend nodded.

Deirdre did too, and released her. "Now back to your duties and I to mine."

"Sorry to interrupt, Dee."

"No matter." She produced a smile and made a shooing motion that had always sent her siblings on their way. "Off with you now."

Once Beatrix had scurried along, Deirdre turned back to the baroness's door and slid inside.

"Is everything all right? I thought I heard voices." Her ladyship's voice was thick with accent, as usual when she first awoke. Sometimes her first words weren't even English, and she didn't seem to realize it until Deirdre blinked at her.

Now she smiled as warmly as she could manage. "Only Beatrix with a question, my lady. Let me get your wrapper, and then I'll fetch a cup of that coffee you like."

It didn't produce the enthusiasm she had expected. Her ladyship pulled the blankets higher. Her thank-you was low and soft and mournful. She reached up and wiped at her cheek.

Deirdre pulled the belted dressing gown from the chair and set it on the bed. The lady had closed her eyes again, but the fire's light caught on the moisture in her lashes.

Hesitating, Deirdre almost reached out. But there was no use in that. So she slipped from the room again and hurried to the kitchen.

Monsieur Bisset was in full steam, like a locomotive charging through the room, barking orders at the under cooks and assistants. Deirdre avoided whomever she could, sneaking a cup of the dark coffee and making her escape. Soon, the dumbwaiter would be coming up and down with platters of food bound for the breakfast room. The gentlemen would stir within the next hour, the ladies an hour after that.

There would be dressing for breakfast, dressing for the hunt, dressing for tea, dressing for games out of doors, dressing for dinner. She, along with the other lady's maids and valets, would be brushing this garment, pressing that, cleaning shoes and more shoes and the next pair too when they came in muddy. The guests would laugh and gossip and flirt and relax.

The staff would hustle and bustle and pray for the week to come to a quick end.

Thank heavens his lordship didn't make a habit of this sort of thing. She moved cautiously through the halls, careful not to spill a drop of the scalding liquid. When she finally gained the baroness's room again, she found her in the window seat, her wrapper on and a blanket around her. The girl stared out the window into the thick fog.

"Here we are, my lady." Perhaps the bright note felt false, but with any luck it wouldn't sound it. She held out the cup.

Lady Berkeley took it with a smile every bit as feigned. "Thank you. Would you be so good as to hand me my Bible?"

"Of course." It sat on the bedside table, as always. The gold-embossed letters read *LA BIBLE: ANCIENT ET NOUVEAU TESTAMENT*.

She picked it up, handed it over. And said, for a reason she could scarcely fathom, "It looks old."

The lady ran her fingers over the creased leather. "Justin gave it to me when I was ten—when Maman died. I understood so little of it then, but I made myself read, because he said it was important. So I read and grew and understood and believed and now . . . now these pages hold memories along with truth." Yet rather than open it, she set it on her knees and held the hot cup in both hands. Rested her head against the wall behind her. "Was it hard when you came here, O'Malley? From Ireland?"

Her hands itched for a task. Her feet strained for the door. But she held her place. "It was a blessing—I daresay one I wouldn't have received had I not had my uncle's recommendation. I send my earnings home to my family, and I know it eases them to have it. It's been hard for Mum since my da died, with the farm mortgaged as it was."

She hadn't meant to say so much, had only wanted to sound grateful. She cleared her throat. "Do you miss Monaco?"

Lady Berkeley sighed and sipped at her coffee. "My grandfather. And the weather." A smile winked out, disappeared. "But I knew I couldn't stay there forever. I was not a Grimaldi, not by blood. And there was so much unrest—the people revolted in the spring, demanding a constitution. Even as Grand-père placated them, I kept wondering if I was more like them than him—if I belonged on the streets, protesting with the crowds, or if living behind the palace walls was my place. I wanted to know who I was. So I asked Justin to help me find out, and . . ."

"And here you are. Home." How nice it must be, to go on a search for answers and find all this.

Life didn't turn out so fine for most of them.

"O'Malley." The baroness shifted, set the Bible on the seat beside her, and met Deirdre's gaze. "Please don't pretend. Your position is safe, I assure you. You needn't put on this front."

Deirdre's back went stiff. "Sure and I don't know what you mean, my lady."

"I know you don't like me—and you don't have to. I'm not . . . I'm not what you all want your baroness to be. That is mine to accept." She set the cup on its saucer, the saucer on the Bible. "But duplicity I will not."

Deirdre knew not what to say to that, what she was meant to do. Any response she could make may well explode in her face. So she stood there, held the baroness's gaze until it felt disrespectful, and then lowered hers to the floor. "Do you wish to dress yet?"

The lady stood, folded the blanket and put it back on the foot of the bed, and moved behind the screen. Deirdre handed her the shift and bloomers, the corset. Then came the dress. Her ladyship slipped it on and then stepped out, back to Deirdre, hair held up out of the way.

She made quick work of the row of the buttons, and of putting up her ladyship's hair a minute later while she sipped her coffee. Then the baroness crossed back to her window, her Bible, and dismissed Deirdre with a few quiet words.

The feeling of freedom she usually felt at the "*That is all*" didn't come as she stepped into the hall. She felt only the certainty that she should have woken the lady from her nightmare.

Maybe the morning would have gone differently if she had.

She paused at the break in the paneling that would open to the service staircase. And what would Mum say if she saw her now? Or Da, who had always called her his sunshine? She didn't feel so sunny anymore, hadn't since his death. But he would be pained to know it. He would be disappointed in seeing the resentment always a-boil inside her.

Clouds came, he had always said. Sometimes they brought rain to nourish, sometimes hail to destroy. Some years were fat, others lean.

She closed her eyes, heard his voice in her heart, so deep and sure, even as the fever consumed him. "*Crops fail, DeeDee. People die. The bad comes, to one and all. What matters . . . sure and it's what we do with it. That's what makes a man strong or weak, good or bad. Not the outside—the in.*"

The in. She pressed a hand to her ribs, where her heart beat a painful accusation. Aye, he would be disappointed in what she'd done with it. He'd look at the baroness and see a girl too long lost, not a pampered princess undeserving of all she'd been given. He'd see a hurting soul, not a pretender. But he wouldn't have made a fuss about it. He just would've said to Mum, "Bake an extra pie, Bonny-my-bonny. We've a neighbor who needs the smile."

She straightened her shoulders and pivoted on her heel, knowing what peace offering she could give. A dash down the main stairs, a turn toward the library.

A book. It couldn't make them friends, but they needn't be at odds.

Stepping into the library, she moved to the right, where his lordship kept the novels. The young ladies had been talking last night about *Jane Eyre*, and the baroness had confessed she had never read it. Lady Melissa said Lord Whitby had a copy in his collection, though, and Lady Berkeley's eyes had danced. Deirdre would find it, deliver it to her room.

The door clicked shut, and a hum as slick as darkness thrummed through the room. "Well, well. You have a taste for literature too? You are a woman of endless allure, Deirdre O'Malley."

Though she wanted to jump, to spin, to face the devil so she could read his intent, she restrained herself. Continuing to the shelf, she took a deep breath to ensure her voice came out calm and even. "Good morning, Lord Pratt. I was unaware *you* passed much time with books."

How could a laugh, quiet and short, sound so very menacing? "No. But the room I find intriguing. Has it always been Whitby's favorite spot in the house, do you think?"

His voice stayed on the other side of the chamber, muffled as if he spoke toward the opposite shelves rather than her. Good. Whatever his intent, perhaps she could go about her business without ramming into it. "I should think so." Her eyes perused the titles, alphabetized by author. The D section was before her. She needed the Bs. To the side? No—drat. She craned her neck upward, to the row of shelves well above her head. "I'm glad you found me. I need the journal back, my lord. Her ladyship has turned her room upside down looking for it. She thinks it lost."

"Let her think it so, lost in travel. I'm not finished with it."

Was his French as bad as all that? "Could you make out none of it? Whether it supports the claim she's his or not?"

"She's his daughter." His satisfied hum made her feel sick. "I hear she spends much time in here too."

Deirdre shot a look over her shoulder at him. He stood with his gaze on a row of matching tomes. Should she press the point of the journal? Much as the thought of leaving it with him made panic nip, he wouldn't budge. She strode to the wheeled ladder and pulled it to the proper shelf. "Not this time of day, if that is your hope. My lord."

"Not at all." He picked up a decorative book end, flipped it in his hands, put it back. "I seem to have gotten off on the wrong foot with her when we first met. But you are with her most of the day—tell me, what does she want in a man?"

Deirdre climbed up the first few rungs, her eyes scanning for *Brontë*. "She's mum about such things, my lord, even with her cousins. But I can tell you she reads academic texts as often as novels, in assorted languages. I've heard them discussing scientific papers a time or two, even."

No Brontë—neither Charlotte nor Emily nor Anne. She pursed her lips. They had all begun with pen names, hadn't they? His lordship must have early editions. Bell—that was it. She climbed up farther.

The ladder shook beneath her. Gasping, she gripped the sides.

"I am not interested in her reading material, my lovely. Tell me something *useful.*"

She glanced down only once at his stormy black eyes. "It *is* useful. She takes great interest in such things. And faith, she is all the time talking of her faith."

He hissed out a breath and grabbed her right ankle. "You expect me to discuss religion with her?"

The more he pulled on her leg, the tighter her throat went, so that she could barely croak out, "Horses. Automobiles. She wants to learn to drive."

Her foot slipped off the rung. He chuckled and set it back on. "Better. And?"

And his fingers went terrifyingly gentle on her ankle. She pulled it away under the guise of going up one more rung. "That is what she speaks of. Horses, cars, books."

"How very dull she would be, were it not for that alluring face, figure, and fortune."

Deirdre spotted *Jane Eyre* by Currer Bell and grabbed it. Though when she glanced down again, she saw him leaning against the ladder like a crocodile on the bank—or perhaps she had paid too much attention to Lady Melissa's reading of *Peter Pan* the other evening.

He offered a patronizing smile. "Do you really think you can climb away from me?"

Before she could form a response, he grabbed both her legs and pulled hard enough to yank her from the ladder. She tried to bite back the scream, tried to hold to the rungs with her free hand, but in vain. Before she could discern exactly how it happened, he had an arm clamped around her waist and pressed her to the bookshelf.

Struggling was no use, but she averted her face—and caught a whiff of a distinctly floral perfume. The same too-strong scent that Lady Catherine wore.

She had a feeling she knew with whom the young lady had been dallying last night.

His lips found her jaw, his other hand turned her face. Try as she might, she couldn't hold back a whimper when he kissed her, when trying to twist away accomplished nothing but him pressing her harder to the shelves.

She managed to turn her face again, at least. "Please, my lord. You promised. You promised if I gave you the information you wanted, you wouldn't—"

"DeeDee?" The door slammed open, and Hiram charged in. "I heard a scream. Did you fall? Are you . . . ?"

She squeezed her eyes shut against the horror on his face.

Pratt had the gall to laugh again. "She did, as a matter of fact, but I was fortunately here to catch her." He backed away, tweaked her chin. "Tread carefully, old girl," he murmured. Then louder, "No harm done, I think."

He whistled—*whistled*—his way out of the room.

Deirdre didn't move, didn't open her eyes as the door clicked and footsteps hurried her way.

Hiram's arms came about her. Gentle, warm. Comforting. "What happened, Dee? Did he hurt you?" His hand soothed her back where the shelf had bit, his lips settled on her hair. "Tell me."

Too soothing. Too comforting. She let her forehead rest on his shoulder one moment more, and then she eased away. "It's nothing, Hi. I fell."

Sorrow shone from the eyes usually bright with laughter. "I know you better than that, Deirdre O'Malley. He had his hands on you. He was—"

"He kissed me—that's all." She spat it out in a gush, praying he would leave it at that.

But he knew her too well. He stroked her cheek as Da had used to do, brushed his thumb over her lips as no man ever had. "'Tisn't all, Dee. It never is with men like that, who think they have the rights to whatever they want."

A shudder overtook her. She knew it. It was why she'd been hoping and praying he wanted information more than he wanted her. "He didn't hurt me."

"This time, praise the good Lord above." He leaned in, kissed her forehead. "You're too beautiful for this world. This place in it, anyway, where the fancy lords can treat you as naught but a plaything." He let his arms fall and took a step away. "You should have stayed in Ireland. Married a farmer—a big burly one that could fight off any what looked at you crossways."

"Oh, Hiram." He made a muddle of her. And she couldn't even resent him for it. "It isn't so bad. It's a good house." It's why her uncle had recommended her here, and why she always filled her letters to him with naught but the good things about it.

"It is." Determination lit Hiram's eyes—and lit panic in her stomach.

She knew *him* too well, too, and grabbed at his arm. "No. You can't be telling his lordship. It'll only make Lord Pratt angry, and he'll no doubt find a way to take it out on us." She shook him, though it barely moved his arm and certainly didn't dim his gaze. "Promise me."

"For now." He said it easily, without relenting at all.

He cupped her cheek where Pratt had pushed it and made her forget the pain. Leaned down and brushed his lips over hers so softly she couldn't remember the bruising embrace.

Then he stepped away again and held out his hand. "For now. But I'll not stand by and let him hurt you. I can't."

Deirdre stifled a sigh and slid her fingers into his. Just for a moment, until they left the library. Then she'd pull away. Then she'd put the walls back up. Because Pratt *would* hurt her, before it was over. He would have his way, whatever that way was, and she would pay the price.

But sure and she wouldn't let Hiram pay it with her.

Thirteen

Tempesta thundered into the trees, leaving Brook little choice but to laugh. The horse wasn't after the hounds, nor the fox—she was after the run, which suited Brook fine. A tug on the reins brought her down to a walk, the better to draw in a breath and watch the sunlight shaft through the reddening leaves.

In the distance, she could hear the shouts of the others. Her cousin Ram had led the way this morning, promising adventure with a wink aimed at Thate. If the whispers she had overheard in the hallway were correct, said adventure would involve sending Regan off with said young man, giving him a chance to propose.

Brook heard Regan's laugh now, sweet and too near. Thate's murmur answered, a low thrum she couldn't make out. They must have broken away from the others. And it certainly wouldn't do for them to come upon her. She urged Tempesta behind a thicket, dismounted, and murmured French nothings into the mare's ear to keep her still.

Crunching leaves, snapping twigs, snorting horses. "Are you certain you saw it come this way?" Regan's voice, breathless and excited. Who would have thought that staid Regan would be so eager on a hunt?

"I am all but sure. Through here, I think. A little farther and we shall have it cornered."

A little farther, and they would come out into the clearing by the duck pond—as perfect a spot for a proposal as any girl could dream. Brook shared her smile with her horse and rubbed Tempesta's nose. "I want them to be happy. Together," she whispered once they had moved beyond her hearing. "I want to believe it can be."

And that it could last. That death would not snatch one of them too soon, that life would not tear them apart. It was surely possible. It *had* to be possible. She could think of no examples, but if she couldn't believe it then she might as well go back to her window seat and the grey, foggy mood that had enveloped her that morning.

Non. She would not let the nightmare-induced *ennui* overtake her again. "Come, Tempesta. *Viens.*" After mounting again, she wheeled the horse around and headed back the way she had come. Which way had Justin gone? Hard to say—he and Pratt had been insulting each other all morning and were no doubt now in a heated race to nab the wily fox.

Her lips tugged up. Entertaining as it had been to listen to their repartee, she was not about to get in their way. She had joined the hunt for the riding, not the actual *hunt.*

"Good morning, cousin."

Tempesta took the last step into the clearing nearer the house, and Brook smiled a welcome for the cousin she didn't know so well. "Lady Catherine."

"Kitty, please." She sat atop one of Whitby's milder horses, her knee up against the sidesaddle, her hat at a jaunty angle. Blond curls spilled over her shoulder.

Did they look alike? They must, on the surface. Blond hair, green eyes. Her mother must have inherited it from the Rushworth side and passed it along to Brook. Though Brook never felt the same confidence in a crowd that this cousin exuded, nor did her wit lend itself to the clever-but-biting conversation Lady Catherine had apparently mastered.

Brook couldn't quite decide if she found it entertaining or off-putting.

Lady Catherine's brother sat the horse next to her. He greeted her with a nod and a quiet, "Lady Berkeley."

"Lord Rushworth." Brook hadn't formed much of an opinion on him at all. Half the time she didn't even notice when he was in the room. Tempesta fell in alongside them. "I haven't seen the fox or the hounds this direction."

Lady Catherine laughed, practiced and perfect. "Perhaps not, but Lords Pratt and Abingdon came tearing through, and that was enough to draw me." She grinned, making Brook lean toward liking her. "Though they seem to have vanished, so perhaps I ought to go back to the house and wait for Lord Worthing to arrive instead. I must say, cousin, your aunt has succeeded in gathering England's finest to come and meet you."

Brook smiled again and looped the reins lazily through her fingers. "It has been a bit overwhelming, I confess. Though I'm glad to have met you two. You live near, do you not?"

"An hour or so away, depending on the roads. It was during a visit to our parents that your mother met your father, you know." Catherine's green eyes looked sharp as flint as she scanned the area. "Mother used to tell stories of Lady Whitby's fame in London—she apparently came to our home for some quiet after her first Season. Well, I suppose she wasn't Lady Whitby then. Though even after she wed your father, the men still hounded her, it seems. Quite inspiring."

Because Catherine laughed, Brook smiled. Though she remembered too well the trouble it caused Maman to be hounded by men, and she couldn't imagine finding it amusing.

Lady Catherine leaned across the distance between their

mounts, her eyes sparkling. "Can I tell you a secret? Uncle Henry never got over her—he has been hiding in India all these years, mourning first her marriage to Whitby and then her death."

Rushworth shifted in his saddle, his brows pulling down half a degree. "Kitty. You oughtn't to gossip about Uncle."

His sister waved that off with a laugh that sounded like silver bells. "If Uncle doesn't want to be gossiped about, then he should have taken more care. Everyone knew he was in love with Elizabeth. Mother said some even whispered that they . . . But of course that's nonsense. Your mother would never betray your father, even if he *was* away so often during their first years of marriage."

Brook looked for evidence of cattiness in Catherine's tone but found none. Still, it pierced to think of people whispering so about her parents. Her father had lost enough. *Thunder roaring, lightning sizzling. Darkness all around.* Brook shook her head against the impressions of the dream. Called to mind the words she'd read in Thessalonians that morning. *"Ye are all the children of light, and the children of the day: we are not of the night, nor of darkness."*

"I'm sorry, cousin." Catherine's horse shifted and pranced, ending up nose-to-nose with Tempesta. The horses greeted each other with friendly nickers. The lady offered a smile, soft and regretful. "Cris is right, I shouldn't have brought it up. I ought to know better than to repeat anything our mother told us, God rest her soul. She was a jealous creature, and she remembered Cousin Elizabeth through that lens."

"Catherine," her brother said again.

The lady huffed out a breath and sent her gaze heavenward. "Am I not allowed to say *anything*, Cris? It's no secret that Mother was jealous!"

Rushworth pressed his lips together but said no more.

Brook conjured up a smile. "My father told me it was through Pratt's family that he met my mother."

Frustration with her brother apparently forgotten, Catherine beamed and turned her horse around again, motioning them all forward with a nod of her stylish top hat. "Oh, you'll find that the peerage is rather small, really. The late Lord Pratt was always close with both our father and uncle. The story goes that when Cousin Elizabeth came for a visit, she tired of our mother's less-than-warm company." Here she darted a look at her brother, though Rushworth made no response. "Lord Pratt came to visit Father one day and mentioned that he had a cousin about her age at Whitby Park—your aunt. So Elizabeth came here to call, she met your father, and Uncle Henry never forgave Lord Pratt for it." The last part she delivered on a laugh, tossing back her head. "Mother always said that had Henry not just got back to India when Pratt was killed, he would have been investigated for it."

Brook's brows furrowed. "Pratt's father was killed? Accidentally, you mean?"

"I'm afraid not." Rushworth's tone was several shades more somber than his sister's had been. "He was shot in a back alley of Whitby."

Catherine nodded, her eyes alight despite the serious turn of her mouth. "I was no more than two at the time, but Cris says he remembers a bit of it—the whole region was in an uproar over two such high-profile losses so close together. It was only a fortnight or so after your mother."

Brook directed Tempesta around a fallen log jutting out and then reined her in when the sound of pounding hooves and braying dogs reached her ears. A moment later the hounds tore by, Justin and Pratt hot on their heels, neither so much as noting the trio of horses still within the tree line. Brook had to smile.

Catherine sighed, her gaze on the backs of the men. "Pratt

was nine when it all happened. He still speaks, sometimes, of how he misses his father."

Despite her dislike for him, pity stirred at that. "It is no easy thing, losing one's parent so young. What of his mother?"

"She was ill for years—consumption—before passing away a year or so ago." Catherine sighed again and reached up to touch the hollow beneath her throat. "Sometimes I think he would rather let the grief drown him than be comforted by those who still love him."

"That would be Kitty." Rushworth's tone was amused . . . or perhaps mocking. Brook wasn't quite sure.

But Catherine sent him an easy, teasing glare. "I'll be Lady Pratt within the year, Crispin, mark my words." Then she grinned and turned her horse back toward the house. "Unless I toss him over for one of the future dukes available. Lady Regan seems to have thoroughly snared Worthing, but they aren't engaged yet, so there is still hope. Although I must say Lord Abingdon is every bit as handsome. Unless you've a claim to him, cousin?"

"Only of friendship." It took a bit more effort than it should have to smile back at Catherine this time. Which made little sense. Brook had long ago banished the childhood dream of finding a happily-ever-after with him, but all these questions made her realize she wasn't sure what she would actually do when he declared his intentions for some young lady . . . perhaps even one of those here.

Her cousin held out an arm through the space between them. "I am so glad you're home, Brook. It will be a delight to get to know you, to have another young lady nearby."

Brook stretched out, too, to clasp the elegant fingers in her own. Regan and Melissa would soon return to London, after all. It would be good to make other friends. "Likewise, Kitty."

Catherine smiled and nodded at Brook's wrist before releasing her. "What a lovely bracelet. Rubies, is it? And diamonds?"

"Mm." She settled her hands on the pommel again and touched a gloved finger to the gems. "It was my mother's."

"I thought it must be. Another contention of *my* mother." Catherine sent her eyes heavenward. "She was all the time claiming that Elizabeth inherited jewels that ought to have gone to Father. Though I daresay most of them are from the Brook side, not the Rushworth."

She paused as if waiting confirmation, but Brook had to shrug. "I am afraid my father doesn't remember the history of many other than the ones *he* gave her."

"Ah, it's no matter." Catherine pulled her mount to a halt and cast her gaze northward. "I think I'll have a look at Delmore while we're out here. Will either of you join me?"

"I suppose I shall." Rushworth said it on a sigh, though. "My lady?"

Brook shook her head. Though the boy-Pratt may have deserved pity, the man still made her uneasy, and she had no desire to go gawk at his home—Whitby had pointed it out once, and that was enough. "I think I'll go find my father. But I've enjoyed talking with you, Kitty. My lord."

The siblings nodded and said their farewells, and Brook aimed Tempesta back toward the stables, the thought of their neighbor irritating her more with every hoof-fall. How could Catherine be in love with him? She surely saw beyond his handsome face, saw the way he looked at all the young ladies as if they were naught but pounds sterling and playthings. He was exactly the kind of man Maman had fumed about, the kind who thought women were good for nothing but satisfying men. The kind of person who valued nothing but himself. He was an arrogant, self-absorbed reprobate, and he didn't deserve the happiness Catherine would try to bring him.

And how could a man who had a lady like her cousin waiting keep looking at Brook as he did? Irritation sizzling its way to anger, Brook dismounted at the stables and handed the reins to blank-faced Francis. It wasn't that Pratt liked her, that she knew. It was as Whitby had said that first morning—he wanted what was theirs.

A piercing whinny at the end of the aisle drew her.

She shouldn't approach Oscuro now, when her blood was high. Horses were too sensitive to mood. Still, she strode down the hay-strewn aisle until she stood before his stall.

Oscuro snorted and kicked at the door.

His leads were snapped on, anchoring him between the posts—they must be preparing to groom him. Brook stepped forward and opened the gate.

He snorted again and tried to toss his head, whinnied low and pleading.

"*Je sais*. I know." She offered her hand as she did every day. Sometimes he tried to nip. Sometimes he ignored her. Today his nostrils flared, and he turned as much as he could to look at her. She moved to his side to make it easier. "You will run soon, *mon ami*. Fast as the wind, free as the birds." Slowly, slowly she reached for his nose.

The first stroke felt like victory. The second like fate. "You will see. There are boundaries—there always are. But you can find your place within them. Learn how to live within a fence but let your spirit soar." She rubbed up his nose, down, and then along his cheek. "Your sister has learned . . . but you're not like your sister, are you? I understand that too. You can look like another and be totally different. And do you know what?"

She leaned closer, slid her other hand down his graceful neck. "That is as it should be. I don't want to make you Tempesta. I want to help you be the champion you were born to be. Fast as the wind. Free as the birds."

The hand on his nose had stilled, and he nudged it.

Sunshine scattered the last of the clouds the nightmare had gathered over her. She obliged Oscuro with another stroke.

Her father eased up beside her. She hadn't heard him approach, but his presence didn't startle her, nor did it earn any acknowledgment from the horse. "Progress." Pride colored his tone. He reached, not to try to pet the horse, but to pat her shoulder. "I thought you were on the hunt."

"I was. I spoke for a while with Lady Catherine and thought I'd come find you."

"Ah, the Rushworths." His arms went to their usual position, hands clasped behind his back. "I hear Monaco is pleasant this time of year. We could plan a little trip—that left tomorrow."

She grinned, gave Oscuro one more rub, and stepped aside for the grooms who approached with brushes and hoof pick. It must be Whitby's dislike of Henry Rushworth that made him wary of the whole family. "Perhaps in the spring. Once I have Oscuro ready for the races and have convinced you to buy a roadster."

He touched a hand to her elbow to usher her toward the exit. "Hmm. That may aid us in escaping the dreaded Season, but it doesn't help with this infernal house party."

The door came into view, and through it, the gleaming silver paint of Justin's Rolls-Royce. She grinned. "We could liberate Justin's car. Look at it, sitting there gloomy and ignored."

Whitby chuckled and led the way out into the sunshine, his eyes on the trees in the distance and the horses emerging from it. "Perhaps later. I think we had better not miss this show—there are Regan and Lord Thate."

Brook paused once the sunshine could envelope her and lifted her brows at her father. "You know."

"Ram spoke to me this morning." He nodded toward the garden where the married ladies had congregated, Aunt Mary presiding. "He fully approves the match. Mary will not."

"And you?"

His eyes smiled, though his lips only hinted at it. "He makes her laugh, shakes her from the comfortable. She reminds him there is life beyond the racetrack. They will suit well."

She linked her arm through his. "Well said."

"And well done, it seems." He nearly grinned as he watched the goings-on in the distance. Thate all but leaping from his horse at the garden's edge, reaching for Regan, and swinging her down and around.

Even from the distance, she could see Aunt Mary go still and could well imagine the wariness in her eyes as the new couple approached her. Thate gestured. Regan clasped his arm.

Whitby chuckled. "One . . . two . . . three."

Aunt Mary crumpled to the ground.

Heaving a happy sigh, he nodded. "There. All is as it should be. She will come around, and your cousin will be thrown the most obnoxiously extravagant wedding this side of Buckingham. Let us pray she does the planning at her London house and doesn't drag all the nonsense here."

Brook laughed and then turned to the driveway when a plume of dust appeared. "Our tardy guests?"

Her father nodded when a car came around the bend. "It must be. Thate acted not a moment too soon."

Though she half-expected him to lead her away in all haste, to let someone else greet the newcomers, Whitby instead lingered outside the stables amidst all the other parked cars and carriages. "You were talking with the Rushworths, then?"

"Mm. Kitty was telling me of how my mother came to meet you. Well, that she came here to call on Aunt Mary."

Brook would never tire of seeing the way his eyes went soft and warm at the mention of his Lizzie. Of the way his lips twitched. "Mary was out that day. I had seen your mother before, in London that Season—though only from a distance.

She was always surrounded by crowds of adoring beaux, and I . . . I thought it all ridiculous, honestly. All that hubbub over one lovely face."

She couldn't hold back the breath of laughter. "I am utterly shocked."

Half a grin emerged. "I had to be in Town that year, Mary was just betrothed to Ramsey. But I had no intention of playing those games. Then when I walked into the great hall as she was leaving her card . . ." His gaze went distant, awe-filled. "I was stunned. Not just because of her beauty, but because up close, without the crowds, I could so easily see that she was a woman of heart."

"And what did you do? Let her go, until the next time, when Aunt Mary was home?"

"No." He chuckled and cast his gaze to the side of the house and the maze cut into the shrubbery. "I assured her my sister would return in but a few moments and asked her to walk the maze with me to pass the time. Then pretended to get lost."

"Cunning."

He tapped a finger to his temple and, when the arriving car pulled into an open space a fair distance away, led her that direction. "I had that to my advantage, if nothing else. We strolled, talked."

"And fell in love?" It wasn't hard to picture it, not with that light in his eyes.

"It didn't take long. She and Mary became fast friends, saw each other almost every day, and I . . . I think I knew within a week, though I couldn't fathom she would feel the same. Miraculously, though . . ."

Brook patted her father's arm, even as her eyes tracked the two heads climbing from the car—one red as fire and the other dark as midnight—and the servants' carriage that followed behind, headed for the rear. "It is no miracle."

"Love is *always* a miracle. Especially in this world." He waved at all that was his—the grand house, the grounds, the extravagance. "I pray you find it someday, Brook—though *not*," he added, spinning to her with a scowl, "anytime soon. I've only just got you back. Are we clear?"

She was still laughing when the taller of the heads, the dark one, turned their way. It took only a glance to see why Thate had been worried over this future duke, and why Melissa always said his name on a wistful sigh. Lord Worthing could only be described as debonair—handsome, polished, and with a charm that all but knocked her over the moment he flashed his teeth in a grin.

"Lord Whitby! Our apologies for our late arrival." He strode their way, hand outstretched.

The other half of his *our* seemed to have disappeared, but Brook couldn't see where she'd gone. She let go her father's arm so he could shake the young man's hand. Unlike most of the other guests to greet them, he actually kept his gaze on Whitby rather than gawking at her.

"No need to apologize, my lord." Her father didn't smile now, though he looked pleasant enough. And was probably adding a silent, *The fewer the merrier.* "We are only glad you could join us at all. I am acquainted with your father, you know."

Lord Worthing's smile emerged again and nearly blinded her. He had dimples, even white teeth, and, what was more, seemed genuine in his enjoyment of life. "He speaks highly of you. He and Mother wanted to join us, but they had a few engagements yet in the Highlands they couldn't bow out of." Releasing Whitby's hand, Worthing turned the full force of his smile on her. "And this must be your daughter."

"Lady Berkeley, yes." Her father touched a supportive hand to the small of her back.

Brook held out a hand, acknowledging the skitter of pleasure that raced up her arm when Worthing took it in his and pressed his lips to her knuckles. "I've heard much about you, my lord."

He laughed as he straightened, his fingers still clasping hers. "And despite that, I hope we will be friends. I am certain you and Ella . . ."

Here he turned, and his smile gave way to a frown. "I seem to have misplaced my sister." He said it as one might say one had misplaced one's book . . . yet with obvious fondness.

Brook could see her red hair over by Regan and Thate, but she decided that might not be the wisest place to direct his gaze just then. "She must have seen a friend." Brook glanced to her father for help, but Whitby was frowning down the driveway.

He in fact patted her back and took a step away. "That appears to be a courier. Will you excuse me, my dear? My lord?"

"Of course." In proof, Lord Worthing took the fingers he still held and tucked them into the crook of his elbow, beaming down at her. "It must be my lucky day. Only here for minutes, and already I have the lady of the hour on my arm. You are every bit as lovely as I had been warned to expect, my lady . . . and perhaps a bit more besides."

The wool under her fingers was fine, worsted. The same texture as Grand-père's favorite jacket—for a moment the breeze felt warmer, the distant voices sounded Monegasque. For a moment, she was strolling through Monte Carlo, the scents of spice and salt in her nose. A princess again.

No—a pretender again.

Worthing drew her forward. "I've said something to upset you. Please, forgive me. Flattery is our language, but if it makes you uncomfortable . . . Though in my defense, it's hardly flattery when it's true."

A taste of laughter tickled her throat, though she let only a small smile escape. "I am immune to flattery, my lord—I grew up in a prince's palace."

When she glanced up, she saw his dark eyes had gone serious. And seemed to see far more of her than they ought. "You are permitted to miss it—your father will understand."

She very nearly withdrew her hand and fled—a man she had known for all of a blink had no right to see what no one else ever seemed to. But then he glanced toward the side of the house where his sister had gone, where Regan still stood with her arm woven through Thate's, and he came to an abrupt halt.

Brook sucked in a breath.

Worthing looked down at her with an arched brow and eyes filled with . . . laughter? "I seem to have missed something."

She could only stare at him. He *must* be upset at the woman he was courting attaching herself to another. And his quick stopping had shouted his surprise. Why, then, did his face reflect only amusement? Brook cleared her throat. "We just saw them come back from the hunt together. I haven't spoken to her yet . . ."

Worthing put on a lopsided smile and faced forward again, his gaze fastened on the new couple. "I deserve the credit for that, I think. I can't tell you the number of times I caught him scowling at us in London."

She could well imagine though, and had to fight back a chuckle. "Oh, Thate wouldn't scowl. Glowering, though—I have found the English to be masters of the glower."

Lord Worthing's laugh rang out free and bright. "Bested only by the Russians, I daresay. Or are they ones with proper scowls?"

Her very thought from that day in Monaco . . . which made her stomach knot up. "You've the right of it." She looked at her cousin, laughing and grinning in the distance, and then back to her companion. "You're not upset?"

Lord Worthing sighed. "Your cousin is absolutely everything I could want in a wife, were I to make a list. And I think we both hoped we would fall in love. But . . ." He motioned toward

Regan with his free hand. "We didn't. I've known for a while that the Lord had other plans for us."

Brook tugged her hand free of his arm, so she could plant it on her hip. "Why, then, were you still courting her?" Perhaps she shouldn't get irritated with a near stranger. But it was her cousin he had been toying with. Sweet, selfless Regan.

And he had the nerve to grin. "Oughtn't you to be chiding *her*, my lady, and demanding to know how she could dangle me while in love with Thate? It isn't as though I was courting anyone else at the same time. Surely *I* am the injured party here, not your cousin, who certainly looks happy with how things turned out."

The fact that he had a point did nothing to defuse the anger so quick to burn today. It must be the fault of the dream, and the restless night's sleep it had caused yet again. "You certainly don't seem injured, my lord—you seem rather happy as well."

Perhaps on another face, the arch of brow would have come off as a challenge. On him, it looked like a jest. "And now it is a crime to be glad that a young lady I care for has found the husband the Lord intended for her?"

For a moment, the irritation still simmered. But the longer she held his gaze, the weaker the fire burned. And the more amusing it all seemed. Regan was happy, Thate was happy—and it *was* due in large part to Worthing inspiring Thate to jealousy. Who knew how long it would have taken him to act otherwise? It seemed no one was displeased with how it all turned out.

With the exception of Aunt Mary, of course.

Brook relented with a gusty sigh and nodded toward the redhead hurrying their way. "I believe your sister is coming to break the bad news to you."

Lord Worthing chuckled and deftly tucked her fingers into the crook of his arm again. "Play along and I shall be forever in your debt—I can never get my fill of teasing Ella."

"Play along with what exactly?"

Rather than answer, he patted her fingers where they rested on his arm, as if she were a friend he'd known for years. "You'll get along well, I think. You'll find that she's annoyingly optimistic, but we love her anyway."

Brook directed her gaze to the distraught girl—she looked to be about seventeen—and could well imagine liking her. There was no clever cunning in her eyes, no line of artistry in her carriage. She looked all brightness and innocence.

Except for the concern in her cinnamon eyes as she rushed up. "Brice . . ."

"I know, Ella-bell." Reaching out, he slung his other arm over her shoulders, so easily he must do it often. He loosed an exaggerated sigh. "And my heart has positively rent in two. But the Lord is good, and already He has provided me the most beautiful bandage a man could ask for. This is the Baroness of Berkeley, a succor to my crushed spirits."

Ella stared at him a moment, agape, and then looked to Brook.

This must be his game, though Brook wasn't sure how, exactly, she should play along. Was she to act lovestruck? Before she could decide, Lady Ella rolled her eyes. "Sometimes I can hardly tell when you're joking."

Worthing winked at Brook. "It's a gift."

"Did you warn her that you're an unabashed flirt, and that she had better not take a word you say seriously?"

At that, Brook had to laugh. "I figured that much out for myself, my lady."

"Call me Ella, please." Dimpling, she reached across her brother to clasp the hand Brook lifted. "I hope we'll be friends. I've been absolutely dying to hear about your life in Monaco. It sounds so romantic!"

"Heaven help us—Ella, you don't need any more tales of

romance in your life. Make it out to be a bore, my lady, I beg you, or she'll be running off to the casinos."

Ella's eyes widened. "I would never! He's terrible, Lady Berkeley, ignore him. Don't believe anything he says. The only place I would ever run off to is Scotland—"

"Hear that? She's threatening to elope, and she isn't even out yet."

"Stop teasing, Brice." Ella slapped her brother in the arm, making Brook laugh. Then she looked around him again, to her. "Our mother's from Edinburgh, and we take our holiday every year at her family's lodge in the Highlands. Again, Lady Berkeley, just ignore him."

"Don't worry." She found their banter refreshing—not unlike what she and Justin so often shared. "And please, call me Brook."

Ella's smile was sunshine.

Lord Worthing's was pure mischief. "Well, if you insist, but I suspect it will make your aunt faint dead away to hear me do so. And then you'll be obliged to call me Brice, and she might never recover."

She would have laughed again, but Worthing's mirth faded as he looked at something beyond her. Her father, it seemed, though he wasn't coming their way. His jaw was clenched, his hand clutched around a piece of paper, and his course set for the house.

No, not the house—the group of hunters just dismounting on the south lawn. She hadn't noticed them come up, though now she swore she could feel Justin's eyes shooting arrows into her. That Whitby was headed his way shouldn't have made alarm race up her spine. Not until he called out for Lord Cayton as he passed.

"Oh no." Brook would have run forward, caught her father, passed him by. She would have run to Justin, gripped his hand, readied to hold him up again as she had those few short weeks ago.

But her old friend turned his face away from her and strode forward to meet her father and his cousin. Rigidity in every line. Fingers curled into fists. Posture shouting that he needed, wanted no one. The fool of a man.

Lord Worthing took her hand off his arm, let it go. But settled his fingers on her shoulder for a moment. "He's the one who brought you here, isn't he? You met in Monaco?"

She could only nod, mute.

"Everyone knows the Duke of Stafford is ill. Whatever news your father's carrying, it isn't good. Go to him. Even if he pushes you away, go. He needs you."

It was all the impetus she needed to go tearing across the lawn.

Fourteen

I *knew* I shouldn't have left." Justin pulled off his muddy boots and handed them to Peters. He needed to change. He needed to pack. He needed to leave, right now. No, yesterday.

No, he shouldn't have come at all.

His valet grasped the black leather too tightly, obviously as shaken as he and Cayton had been. "He told you to go, Your Grace. It was what he wanted."

Your Grace. "Don't. Not yet, please. Please, just . . . let me be me until we get home."

Peters turned away, toward his boot brushes. "I'm sorry, my lord."

He dragged a hand through his hair. "Don't apologize. You've done nothing wrong." Justin had, though. God had tried to warn him, and he had listened to the duke instead. Yet not, because he hadn't come with any intention of proposing to Brook.

And he'd been rewarded by seeing her laughing with who could only be Lord Worthing, her hand on his arm. Then *this*, moments later. It had been all he could do to escape the lawn before he fell to pieces, in front of her and the man he had no doubt would become her new beau.

"You were going to change, my lord."

"Right." Here he was standing in the middle of his room, shirtless, wasting precious time. He charged behind the screen and made quick work of peeling off mud-caked breeches. His trousers and shirt and waistcoat were already waiting, and the moment he stepped out in them, Peters was there, boots abandoned, to knot his tie.

I shouldn't have left. Shouldn't have come.

"Your aunts were there. He wasn't alone."

Not like Father had been. And his aunts had each other—not like him. Still. "We should leave the car here and take the train. It'll be faster."

To that, Peters nodded. "I can arrange it. You should find Lady Berkeley and your cousin to let them know."

"Yes. Thank you." He spun for the door, yanked it open, and nearly collided with the fist Cayton had poised to knock.

His cousin's face was pale, and he was still in his mud-spattered riding clothes. But at least he didn't knock on Justin's head in lieu of the door. "I was making arrangements," he said by way of greeting. "Your car will be taken to Azerley Hall, and we'll take the train. It'll be faster."

Justin nodded and stepped into the hall. "I was thinking the same. When does the next one leave for Gloucestershire?"

"Perhaps Whitby knows."

They strode together down the bachelor wing, their strides matching. "Where is he?"

"Library, I think."

They traveled the distance in silence. Would likely travel all the way home in silence, and that was fine. He needed to think.

Within a month, he had lost them both. Father and grandfather.

Voices came from the library, soft and familiar. The moment he stepped inside, Brook was there. Her arms around him, her face pressed to his shoulder. Her aunt's lips thinned in obvious disapproval, but Justin closed his eyes against it and held Brook tight. When she was flying his way across the lawn, he only wanted escape. Maybe because he knew how much he needed her, needed this.

He could crumble—she would piece him together again. He could refuse to let go, ask her to come with him—she would, despite the consequences. Which was why he knew he had to release her, though he couldn't convince his arms of it quite yet. He needed her, needed her warmth to chase away the chill inside.

Her arms tightened around him. "I'm coming with you."

"Elizabeth Brook! Ambrose, did you hear her?"

"Easy, Mary. She meant *we*."

Justin opened his eyes to find that Whitby had drawn near. He set a hand on Justin's shoulder. "I will bring her. We can be ready within the hour."

He had a feeling the offer was spontaneous, and for Brook's sake. Clearing his throat, he set her a step away. Their gazes tangled. "Not today. Come tomorrow, or Wednesday."

Temper snapped to life in her eyes. "*Non.*"

"You have guests."

Whitby snorted. "Mary has guests. No one will even notice we have gone."

Lady Ramsey huffed her disagreement. "Don't be absurd. We will end the party early, but we can hardly close the house on a minute's notice."

Brook didn't glance at her aunt, just held Justin's gaze. "I want to come with you." Of course she would. Because he was her dearest friend, the closest thing she had to a brother.

Swallowing did nothing to banish the lump in his throat. "I know. But this is what I need you to do."

Confusion swirled through her eyes. "Why?"

Because having her as a sister, a friend wasn't enough—and

he couldn't ask her for more, not when she might grant it out of pity.

He leaned down and kissed her left cheek, her right. "*S'il vous plaît, mon amie. Crois-moi.*" *Trust me.*

"Justin." She caught his hand and held it for a long moment, obviously debating whether to argue more. Then she let his fingers go.

It was what he'd wanted—it shouldn't have broken him all the more.

She nodded. "Tomorrow then. We'll be on the first train."

Not more than a day behind him, which would give him precious little time to get hold of himself. He looked to Whitby. "And when is the next one, my lord? Do you know?"

"Three o'clock."

Then they had no time to waste. He lifted his hand, wanting to settle it on her cheek or in her hair or at her waist. To hold fast to hers, as he had a month ago.

He let it drop back to his side. "I have to go. Thank you, my lord, for your hospitality. And you, Lady Ramsey."

Animosity apparently forgotten, she dropped into a curtsy. "The pleasure is ours, Duke."

A hand pressed upon him, heavy and unrelenting. Unable to utter another word, he turned and left, his silent cousin at his side. He wouldn't, apparently, have the journey home to come to grips with anything.

He was the duke. And his every step had to take that into account from now on.

Their voices a din in her ears, Brook stared at the empty doorway. He had left, just like that. Wrapped up in his own misery and unwilling to let her share it. He had deliberately pushed her away.

He needed her—Worthing was right about that—but he wouldn't let her help this time.

Her aunt's words came back into focus. "No, we *must* have the conversation, Ambrose." Aunt Mary grasped her wrist and tugged Brook around to face her. "A young lady of breeding does *not* offer to travel with a man. Surely you know that. You were raised in a palace, not a . . . a . . ."

Words must have, thankfully, failed her. Brook sighed. "You don't understand, Aunt Mary. He has always been a brother to me, my dearest friend, and he is hurting." How could she not be with him when he was hurting?

"I *do* understand, my dear."

Her father snorted. "And well you show it."

Aunt Mary shot him a glare. "But you are not children any-more, Brook. You must take your reputation into account."

"Leave her alone, Mary." Whitby settled his hand on Brook's shoulder, his arm about her back. It was the closest thing to an embrace he had given her. "There is nothing wrong with traveling with one's father to a funeral."

Lifting her hands in exasperation, Aunt Mary spun away. "You could not *possibly* have discussed it before she—"

"We didn't need to." He squeezed her shoulder. "These things are understood."

Not to all, apparently. "Ambrose—"

"She is *my* daughter, Mary. Let me worry with her. You, I believe, have a wedding to plan."

Brook leaned into him, savored the feel of his arm as it slid around her. Even so, it couldn't ease the place gone taut inside. First Justin had left her here, after promising to stay. Now he was pushing her away when he needed her most. She could fight him, fight for him, fight for what she had assumed would always be there between them.

But what good would it do if he didn't fight alongside her?

Justin stood at the window of his study, high in one of the turrets of Ralin Castle. His thumb kept rubbing at the heavy gold of the signet ring Aunt Caro had given him that morning. The seal of Stafford—the same ring that Wildon dukes had been using with their signature since the first of them, hundreds of years before.

It didn't fit. Grandfather's knuckles had swollen with age, and he'd had the thing enlarged. Now it moved all about Justin's finger, up and down, round and round. Uncomfortable. Unfamiliar. Unsuited.

What he wouldn't give to be outside on a ride through the familiar hills and dales. Instead, he stood in a somber black suit, trying to ignore the sea of people milling about below, all waiting to offer their condolences. In a matter of minutes, he would have to climb into the sedate coach, leading the procession to the chapel in town. Then another procession to the family cemetery on the far edge of the property, where they would all gather round him again.

He turned the signet around.

"Justin." Aunt Caro's voice came from the doorway, but he didn't turn around. He didn't want to see her draped in black. "We've only a few more minutes."

His nod felt stiff, his body brittle. Like if he moved too much, he could snap in two. He turned, intending to move, to slip past her. But he made the mistake of looking up and saw her in her mourning, and it made a fist form in his gut. "What was it he wouldn't let you tell me two weeks ago? About Father?"

Torment flickered over her face, the face so much like his mother's. "Now isn't the time, Justin."

She'd said then he should know, he should know how much Father had loved him—something he could use right now, when the world felt so empty. But what did it really matter? He was gone, Grandfather was gone, everyone was gone . . . or maybe it was just Justin who was. Broken. Hollow.

"Wait." Aunt Caro held up her hand, palm out. Face twisted. "I think now *is* the time, actually. I can't watch you do this, Justin. I can't let you turn into him."

His brow furrowed as he shoved his hand into his trouser pocket. "Into Father? You needn't worry about that. I'm nothing like him."

But Aunt Caro only looked all the sadder as she lowered her hands. "That's my fear. That you'll focus only on William's bad habits and not see his strengths. That you'll try to model Edward or your grandfather when . . . when you *shouldn't*. When you don't know what their single-mindedness did to this family."

Justin lowered himself to the edge of his desk, not taking his gaze off his aunt's face. He'd long known her and Uncle Edward's marriage had been rocky at best. They'd married for love, she had said once, but when she failed to produce an heir, it had soured. But aside from the mistresses he then kept, his uncle had been a decent man. Always working for the good of Stafford—that's what he remembered of him.

Aunt Caro sighed. "William . . . William wasn't your father."

She might as well have taken the medieval sword from the wall and run him through. Justin couldn't breathe, couldn't move. Couldn't believe it. If he wasn't his father's son, then it meant he had no Wildon blood in his veins, that he wasn't the rightful heir to the duchy. Well, he *was*—it was a matter of legal name at birth and little else—but he *shouldn't* be. He was only . . .

Aunt Caro's eyes slid shut. "Edward was."

The sword pulled out, but it left a gaping wound in its place. Wildon blood then . . . but suddenly that didn't matter as his mind ground into gear. "Wait. You're telling me that my mother . . . No. She wouldn't have. She was—"

"*She* was not to blame." A cynical laugh snorted from his aunt's lips, and she pressed a hand to her temple. "She was only seventeen, she had no idea, no defense—it was Edward. I knew then it was Edward, but still I was so furious, so hurt I couldn't see her pain. I couldn't see what it meant for my baby sister when she discovered she carried you. I . . . ."

She shook her head. Her lips quavered. "They wanted to keep her here through her term. Deliver the child and, if it was a boy, give him—you—to me to raise. Edward's heir. But I couldn't do it. I couldn't, not then."

He felt as heavy as the stone walls around him. "Of course you couldn't. But Mother—"

"Sweet Georgiana." Now the pain faded, and her eyes went soft. "It is just as well that I was too weak to save my sister—she never would have given you up. But my refusal forced the duke's hand. He ordered William to marry her. That way, you would be legitimate, a Wildon by name as well as blood. And assuming I never produced a son, the title would fall to your father and you after Edward. The line would be preserved."

The line. Always about the line. Justin closed his eyes and shook his head, though it did nothing to make the awful truth go away. Never once had Father hinted to Justin that he had been forced into fatherhood. Even when Justin had all but accused him of being less a man than Uncle Edward—he winced now at the thought of those words—Father had merely grinned and said how glad he was that Justin had inherited all the best traits of the family.

"But he loved her." That was a truth he couldn't question even now. "And she him."

Aunt Caro folded her hands before her. "A blessing that happened quickly. It could not erase in your father's mind the injustice we had all forced upon him, but he was a good man, Justin. He held it against us, but never you. Never your mother. He loved you both more than anything in the world."

185

Justin pushed to his feet and turned toward the window again, twisting the signet around his finger. In the silence that crept in, he sent his mind backward. Through the years, through the trips to England and home to Monaco. Trying, in retrospect, to find any flicker in Father's eyes. Any unexplained shadows.

All he could see was the way Father had drawn Mother into his arms and danced with her when a band of street performers below their window had struck up a waltz. The way they had both drawn him close—he an awkward boy of ten—to cradle the tiny form of Amalie, how they had whispered in his ear that he would be the best brother in the world. How, when his mother and sister died, Father had pulled him closer instead of pushing him away. "We *still have each other*," he had said. "We *at least have each other*."

He didn't know that he was that strong. Didn't think he could be like his father, not in the ways that mattered.

Aunt Caro touched a hand to his arm. "Don't shut us all out, Justin. Don't be like Edward, please. It would break your mother's heart. Break your father's. You're better than that, better than him."

Was he? He didn't feel it just now. He didn't feel anything, not even the promises he had stared at in his Bible last night, willing the black words to lighten his spirit. Maybe his mind knew the truth, but his heart was too raw. It had gone numb.

He pivoted, shrugging off her hand, and headed for the door and the spiral stairs beyond it.

Aunt Caro scurried behind. "Justin!"

He ignored her, hurrying past one landing, down toward the next. Maybe Brook would still be inside somewhere. Maybe he could find her and . . . and what? When she had come upon him in the library last night and wrapped her arms around him, it had taken every ounce of strength he had not to press his lips to hers and beg her to love him. Beg her to make him feel alive again.

She deserved better than that. She deserved to fall in love, not to be forced to marriage for fear of hurting him . . . and he suspected she loved him too much to say no if he asked. Just not for the right reasons. Not for the reasons he needed.

Aunt Caro sighed behind him. "Do you intend to follow the duke's instructions on where and when to travel?"

It would mean leaving almost immediately. Fixing things. Building things. Shoring up the holes inside. "I should be back by the start of the Season."

His aunt slowed his step with a hand on his elbow. "What of your Brook? Have you considered how it will hurt her if you leave her now? I thought you meant to court her. But if you leave—you could lose her."

"No." The oath whispered out, more prayer than denial. "Never. She is my very heart, Aunt Caro. *Mon âme.*" His soul.

Her smile softened, lost some of its sorrow. "You have more of William in you than you suppose."

He prayed she was right.

The silence resumed as they wound down the rest of the turret and joined Cayton and Aunt Susan in the foyer. Together, they stepped outside, into the masses.

The sun was too hot. It seemed today, of all days, England's skies ought to have been grey and low and menacing. Instead, summer had pounced on them for one last hurrah, scorching all the mourners in their dull black frocks and coats. Justin's eyes scanned the crowds, looking for the gleaming golden head that would soak in the warmth so happily.

She was there with her father, her eyes already on Justin. She didn't offer him a smile—she'd know he didn't want one. But she nodded. And it gave him strength enough to straighten his spine and head for the coach.

The services passed in a blur. The church, the graveside. The mourners passed in an even hazier one. Faces he didn't know, names he wouldn't remember. He shook hands, nodded, and even managed a strained smile now and again. Even when they called him *Duke* or *Stafford*. When those without a title of their own called him *Your Grace*.

Perspiration trickled down the back of his neck by the time the line had shrunk to a bare two dozen left to greet. That was when Brook appeared before him, on her father's arm.

Whitby shook his hand and gripped his shoulder in one strong, quick move. He said nothing, just moved on to Justin's aunts and cousin.

Brook's fingers somehow became tangled in his, though he couldn't be sure which of them had reached out. He held on and used them to pull her closer. Not as close as he would have liked. And then whispered, in Monegasque, "Say my name."

She squeezed his fingers back. "Justin Wildon." Soft J. Long U. Silent N. As it was meant to be said.

One knot of the pain loosened, and he felt his shoulders relax. "Brook. I will have to travel."

The shadows in her eyes belied the understanding nod. "I thought you might. To where?"

The names had been swirling around his head incessantly. "Canada and the Caribbean to start, so I can make it home again for Thate's wedding." His friend had looked almost apologetic as he shared his good news yesterday. "Then Africa, India."

Her eyes emptied of emotion, the way they did when she fought for composure. Her shoulders seemed to have absorbed the tension that left his. "When will you be back for good?"

His throat ached. "In time for your debut."

"Seven months." She drew herself up taller, donned the invisible cloak of the Grimaldis. "It has never been so long."

No, even when he was at school, he'd taken his holidays in Monaco. "I will be home for the wedding though. And I'll write. Tell you stories of my adventures. 'Justin Crusoe,' perhaps."

"'Around the World in Two Hundred Days.'" Her smile was but a flutter, quickly gone.

He lifted their hands and pressed his lips to her knuckles. "Pray for me?"

"Every morning. Every night. Every noon." She raised up on her toes and kissed his cheeks as she always did.

How he wished it were hello-again instead of good-bye. He gave her fingers one more squeeze. "Save your first dance for me."

"*C'est la tienne.*"

He smiled and let her move to his aunt. Someday, God willing, *she* would be his, not just a dance.

The smile faded when Pratt stepped up. Neither of them extended a hand. Pratt smirked. "No worries, old boy. I won't let her get too lonely in your absence."

Justin bit his tongue. Someday, he would level in a fist in the reprobate's nose—and enjoy every bruised knuckle he earned.

Darkness blanketed the house. It had been late when they got home from Ralin, later still by the time Brook bade her father good-night and retired. She had tried to sleep, tried to rest, tried to put aside the fear that nothing would ever be the same again between her and Justin, though she couldn't think what had caused the distance between them. Why he kept pushing her away.

She wished her mother were here, to give her advice.

Instead she had found only thunder behind her closed eyes. The lightning had flashed, the panic had nipped. The darkness had overwhelmed her.

What was it about that infernal dream? A storm, but never any other details. Just impressions, fuzzy and vague and all the more frightful for it.

She shivered and pulled her dressing gown tighter, holding the candle out before her so she wouldn't wake the house with the flip of electric switches. She had already tiptoed past Whitby's door. At her mother's, she paused. But no, if she went in there, her father might hear her. No reason to wake him.

There were other places in the house to find her mother.

Usually at the end of the corridor she turned for the stairs leading downward. Toward the outside, the dining rooms, the library. But according to her father, Mother's favorite room had always been her upstairs salon. And so Brook took the stairs going up, her candle providing scanty light in the dark stairwell.

Shadows flitted to and fro in the room she let herself into. Tree limbs swaying before moonlight, night creatures in the skies. Despite herself, she shivered again and headed directly for the oil lamp, ornate and feminine, sitting upon the well-worn desk. Once she'd lit it and its cheery yellow glow illumined her corner of the room, her shoulders relaxed.

The chair was small and dainty, woman-sized. Its padding had worn thin, evidence of how often her mother had sat just here, where she now did. Perhaps she had even brought Brook up with her when she was a babe, let her lie on the Turkish rug and coo while she attended her correspondence.

Perhaps they had been together here, before it all went to pieces.

She trailed her fingers over the embellishments carved into the edge of the desk. This, much like her Mother's bedroom, had been left unchanged aside from cleaning. She'd already poked around enough to know that the top center drawer contained pens and ink, wax, a seal. Paper was stored in the bottom right, correspondence she had saved in the left.

Brook bent down and pulled open the deep right drawer—

and realized she'd been wrong. What she had thought was a stack of paper was actually old letters.

Well, she didn't know what she would have written to Justin yet anyway. She reached for the stack and pulled them out, thumbed through.

The name Henry Rushworth was on enough of them to catch her eye, so she flipped one open at random. The handwriting was bold and bare.

Well, Lizzie, I've arrived in India, and it's hot as blazes. You would hate it, I daresay . . .

She scanned through descriptions of heat and insects, of the throngs in the marketplaces and the spice in the food. Of finding a bungalow to set up house in and locals to staff it.

I'm fortunate to have O'Malley with me—I'd never trust the locals to fix my tea.

At that, she looked up with a start. A different O'Malley, or was he related to Deirdre? She had said her uncle had recommended her here, had she not? Was this he? More scanning seemed to indicate he was Rushworth's valet . . . No, batman, he called him. The military equivalent. She read on.

You should see the fabric they make here, Lizzie. Stunning, simply stunning, with beadwork that would put Paris to shame. I've got some to send home to Mother and Rush's wife . . . would send some to you, too, if I didn't think that husband of yours would dash around the world to put a fist to my nose in thanks.

I hope you're happy there, Liz. I do. Though if ever the northern climes grow too harsh . . .

Brook shook her head and flipped to another letter. Apparently her father had reason to remember this Henry as he did. The tone may not have been that of a man trying to lure a woman away from her husband, but it was certainly that of one with regrets, and whose affections were no secret. She glanced through a few more before she came to the last one by date. Just a few months before her mother's death.

The locals have stories that would make the hair stand up on the back of your neck. Ancient curses, angry gods, marauding tigers . . . Perhaps when I'm home for leave, I'll tell you a few. I hope you'll see me, if only for tea. If he'll let you. I miss you, Liz. I know you're happy with your choice, that you'll have his babe any day now. But I miss you.

Brook touched a finger to a telltale dried water drop that smeared the last word and wondered if her father had allowed a reunion.

With a sigh, she gathered the letters to take with her to her room and stood. She had to rest, somehow or another. Tomorrow she intended to put her weight on Oscuro and see how he responded.

Perhaps a wild horse could take her mind off all the things she couldn't change . . . and the ones she wished with all her might would stay the same.

Fifteen

TWO MONTHS LATER
NOVEMBER 1910

Thunder roared. Lightning sizzled. Brook loosed a laugh from the depths of her throat that felt a little bit mad. They should ride away from the storm, back to the safety of stables and hearth. Instead, she let Oscuro gallop toward the thunderheads coming in off the sea, bringing darkness hours too early. She braced her feet in the stirrups, rose off the saddle, and leaned into him.

He soared over the fence and kept on flying. Fast as the wind. Free as a bird.

The rain greeted them in another half mile, along with the property edge. Oscuro whinnied a protest when she reined him in, but he slowed, stopped. She checked her watch. "Faster even than yesterday." He would trounce all the other horses at the races in the spring—assuming she could convince him to let someone else onto his back.

She could see Delmore from here, the sprawling maze of it. And, if her eyes and the rain didn't deceive her, the Rushworth carriage pulling away. Her lips tugged up. Would Kitty be there with her brother, trying for whatever unfathomable reason to convince Pratt to marry her? Perhaps they would stop at Whitby Park. Perhaps even stay the night.

Another crack of lightning struck to the west, thunder tripping over it for its turn. She had hoped she and her father could take their drive into Eden Dale this afternoon so she could post her letter to Brice and Ella, and another to Grand-père, but it seemed that would have to wait for tomorrow. A visit would be worth the change of plans though, if the Rushworths decided not to chance the muddy roads.

"Back we go, boy-o." She said it in her best—albeit poor—imitation of Deirdre's accent.

The horse gave an obliging shake of his head, coiled his muscles, and prepared to fly homeward again.

The storm raced them. Fat, cold raindrops struck her as the ground soaked up the torrent and turned to mud. For Oscuro's sake, she pulled up on the reins. If he slipped and fell—*non*, not on her account. Better to let the weather win and suffer the drenching.

Lights were on in her father's study, and she saw his silhouette in the window when Oscuro trotted over the lawn. Waiting, as he always did, to make sure she came safely home. Most days, he did his waiting at the stables, so he could congratulate her on the day's progress.

He wasn't quite so mad as she, though, when it came to the rain.

Another glance, this time upward, and she saw the light on in her own room, and another silhouette. Deirdre stood at the window with hands on hips, and she gave a shake of her head before she turned away. No doubt muttering in her brogue about mud and wet and cold—but she'd be drawing a hot bath and laying out a warm change of clothes.

Brook wouldn't claim her lady's maid as a friend, but they

had reached a truce. Deirdre served her well, without pretense, often displaying consideration that took her by surprise. Other than a couple cups during the fateful house party, the maid hadn't managed to secure her a decent cup of coffee, but her quiet "It isn't me, my lady, nor is it the chef" had been all the conversation on the matter Brook had the heart for.

She had been sending a few extra pound notes to the O'Malley farm every week—she hadn't told Deirdre she was doing it, nor had she mentioned it to anyone else on the staff, but her father had approved that use of her allowance. He had given her that proud look again and had patted her shoulder.

One of these days, he would give her an actual embrace in those moments when he clearly wanted to.

One of these days, she would form her lips around *Father* as she so often almost did . . . then couldn't.

She cast another look at the closed-up carriage house where the new roadster hid, and then toward the village. One of these days, she'd be able to leave a letter on the table to be posted with her father's correspondence and trust that it wouldn't still be sitting there, alone, after his had been taken.

The thunder laughed at her, mean and mocking. As it had in the dream last night.

Oscuro slowed to a walk as they crossed the drive and gave his head a shake. No sign of the Rushworth carriage, which brought a twinge of disappointment—though she could hardly blame her cousins for seeking their own hearth on such an evening. Brook patted Oscuro's neck and dismounted, her boots squishing an inch into the muck. A disgusted noise slipped from her throat, and a shiver of cold skittered up her spine. "You should experience a Mediterranean rain sometime, boy. Warm even in November, by comparison."

He nickered his agreement as she slid the reins over his head and led him toward the darkened stables.

The nicker turned to a high whinny when she stepped inside, and he pranced backward rather than follow her in. "Shh. *Calme toi*, Oscuro. *Allons-y*." She frowned at the way he sidestepped. He never exactly *liked* going back to his stall, but he hadn't behaved like this in a month.

She squinted into the darkness. Why were no lights on? "Francis? Russell?"

The strike came without warning, a blow to her shoulder that forced her to her knees. She fumbled the reins, heard the horse's fearful scream. Or maybe it was her own. Up, she had to get up—

Another blow, this one to the side of her head. Senses as muddy as the ground, she planted her hands, pulled her knees under her.

Cruel hands seized her by the back of the jacket and whipped her upward only to slam her into the wall. A heavy, putrid form pinned her there, one rough-skinned palm pressing her cheek to the splintering wood. "Where are they, missy?"

His voice rasped in her ear, and the smell of kippers and onions curdled her stomach.

"*Qui?*" Her arms were trapped, one against the wall, one between their bodies at a strange angle, his meaty hand cuffed around her wrist. English. She needed English. "Who?"

He growled and twisted her arm still higher, making her shoulder strain and pop. "Donnel be coil with me, girl, or I'll slit yer pretty throat when I'm done with ye. Where are the feral ice?"

The pain must have addled her brain—his words were mere sounds strung together, no sense behind them. "*Je ne sais quoi* . . . I don't . . ." She couldn't clear the French from her whimpering mouth. "I don't understand."

His next growl was more roar. There was a whisper of fabric, an unmistakable click, and a cold metal cylinder pressed to her temple.

Her soul cried out. A wordless prayer for help, for strength, for clarity.

Feet. It must have been the Lord, but He whispered into her ear with Justin's voice, and countless memories flooded her. Innocent tussles, fencing, boxing. So many lessons in how to move, to act, to spring. *Your feet.*

The rest of her body was pinned, but her feet were free. She slid one until it found his foot. Lift, coil, *slam.*

His scream set up a pounding in her ear, but he pulled away. Not much, but enough. It had to be enough. She jerked free of him and lunged for the doorway, back into the rain and thunder and sizzling lightning. Oscuro was still there, whinnying his warnings. She changed directions. If she could gain the saddle . . .

The mud betrayed her, and the brute grabbed her shoulder, spinning her around.

He had the gun up, pointing at her heart.

Another frantic cry from Oscuro. Hooves flew, struck. The weapon flew, too, to the left. While the man cursed the horse, she dove for the gun.

He caught her again when her fingers were only inches away, shoving her down into the mud, flipping her, pinning her legs with his knees.

Lightning flashed against the evil in his eyes—and the wicked blade he had pulled out in lieu of the gun. "The feral ice, missy— ye must knowl where they are. Ye've all her things."

"I don't . . ." She stretched, arched, writhed. Two more inches. One. ". . . know . . ." Her shoulder screamed, but she forced it farther. ". . . what you mean." *There.*

Cold metal had never felt so beautiful. She gripped it and swung, striking him in the side of the head. It won her freedom, but at the price of his rage. Something struck her face, something bit her ribs before she could get the gun between them.

He lunged away, so that her first shot found only air. Scrabbling to her knees, she cocked it again to load the next round in the chamber and took aim at his dark form in the gathering dusk.

The next flash of lightning illuminated his raised arms. Knife still in hand, but the stance of surrender.

She didn't trust it for a second.

"Careful, missy. You donnel knowl how to use it."

"Then it seems *you* ought to be careful, lest I mean to take a warning shot and send a round between your eyes by mistake." She could—her aim had always been better than Justin's, better than most of the palace guards'. If he so much as twitched the hand holding the knife . . .

No. She gripped the gun tighter, fighting the rain and the mud for purchase of the handle. She couldn't kill him. She wanted answers, and dead men never offered enough of them.

"Brook!" Her father's shout, half covered by a roll of thunder.

The brute gripped his knife and came for her. She pulled the trigger, recocked, took aim again.

But this bullet had found its mark, and he fell to the ground cradling his injured hand, screaming.

"My lady! Are you all right?" Strange hands pulled at her, igniting pain in a thousand places.

She pushed them away, elbowed and kicked.

"Stop, my lady. It is only me. Pratt. I am trying to help you."

She would sooner be left in the mud—but when his face appeared before her, he looked earnest and shaken. The rain washed the last of the fight out of her, and she let him help her to her feet and pry the revolver from her hands.

"Brook!" Her father's cry was near now.

Pain sliced through her side, her knees buckled. But the arms that caught her smelled of pipe tobacco and leather and ink, so she let them hold her. Let herself be crushed to her father's chest, even though the agony redoubled. It was worth it.

She squeezed her eyes shut tight as heaven's tears streamed down her face. "Papa."

He shuddered, wrapped his arms around her more securely. "I am here. Right here. Did he hurt you?"

A pistol shot made her jump before she could form an answer. "Pratt!"

Lord Pratt lowered the revolver as the man sagged to the ground—his hand around a second gun. Why had he not pulled it earlier?

"My apologies, my lord. I meant only to disarm him but haven't the aim of your daughter, it seems."

Brook eased away from her father, mainly so that she could press a hand to where fire ate at her side. Mud caked her everywhere, cold and slick, but this was warm. Sticky.

Her father kept one arm anchored around her. "What are you doing here, Pratt?"

Pratt wiped at the rain streaming down his face. "Some of your post was delivered to me by mistake. I thought to beat the rain—then was closer to your house than mine when it hit. Thank heavens."

That meant he left before the Rushworths. It didn't seem right. It didn't . . . he . . .

He turned to them, concern lining his face. "Were you hit, my lady?"

"Only with his fists." Did the words come out in English or French? Or perhaps Monegasque? Another peal of thunder sent the sky spinning. "Perhaps, too, with his knife."

The world tipped . . . but settled with her father's chest under her cheek and his chin in her line of vision. "Hold on, my dear. We'll get you help."

"I'll be all right, Papa." That must have been why she could never call him Father—it wasn't his name. She let her eyes slide closed when pain crashed again. "Oscuro. He saved my life."

"Oh, my Brook. Don't worry. Don't worry about a thing. Papa is here."

The kitchen door crashed open, and Deirdre nearly dropped the new cake of scented soap she had fetched from the laundry. And when she saw his lordship straggle in, soaking wet and with the baroness limp in his arms, Pratt shadowing him, drop it she did.

As the wind gusted the rain in with them, everyone in the kitchen leaped to their feet with a cacophony of questions.

Deirdre's eyes remained fixed on Lady Berkeley. And on the red stain coloring the mud on her side.

"Quiet, please!" His lordship's voice, so seldom raised, brought instant hush to the din. He wore the mask of barely held calm. "My daughter was attacked. I need O'Malley and Mrs. Doyle to come with me now. Mr. Graham, call for the physician and the constable."

The butler dashed off even before he'd finished bowing.

Deirdre stepped around Hiram to meet his lordship at the stairway. "The horse?"

"A man. The horse saved her, she said."

Mrs. Doyle pressed a hand to her chest and turned to the stairs. But before she did, Deirdre saw the look on her face. Regret . . . and determination.

"Who would dare do such a thing?"

"Those answers will have to await the constable. Jack?"

The first footman hurried around the table. "My lord."

"See Lord Pratt is shown to a room so he may dry out."

"Yes, my lord."

They were on the stairs then, hurrying up them without heed to the trail of water and mud they left behind. For a moment, Deirdre wondered who would have to scrub it all clean again.

But it didn't matter. She would do it herself if necessary, and sure and the others would feel the same. So long as death didn't visit them tonight. So long as his lordship didn't fade away again into the man he had been before she came.

There'd been laughter in the house, even with Lady Ramsey and her daughters gone back to London after the Duke of Stafford's funeral.

Under her breath she whispered a prayer for perhaps the first time since Da died. "Save her, Lord Jesus. Save her."

At the main floor, Jack led Pratt off in the direction of the bachelor's wing. Deirdre took the chance to slide around his lordship so she could hurry ahead to the baroness's room. She reached it half a minute ahead of him and Mrs. Doyle, giving her just enough time to snap open a spare sheet to lay across the coverlet.

Lord Whitby lowered his daughter's muddied form onto it with agony on his face. "Look what he's done to her. The monster."

Deirdre glanced only a moment at her face, scraped and bruised. It would hurt her, aye, but it wasn't what had knocked her into darkness. She undid the buttons on the lady's riding jacket and hissed out a breath at the bright red blood staining the side of her once-white shirt.

"Step back now, your lordship," Mrs. Doyle said, her voice calm and soothing and brooking no argument. "Let us tend her as we can. Why don't you tell us what happened?"

"I don't know." He sounded helpless. Looked it, as he sank into a chair and stared into the corner. "I saw her ride back in, dismount. The horse was skittish, but she tried to get him inside. Then . . . I don't know. The lights were out, but I thought perhaps the storm—then I heard a gunshot. And saw someone pushing her down when the lightning flashed. So I ran. Pratt reached her first and shot the man when he pulled out a second gun."

Deirdre tried to ease the jacket off the lady's shoulders. She groaned and pulled away. "Shh, now, my lady. Sure and we have to get you out of these muddy clothes."

The baroness blinked her eyes open, though they were glazed. "Deirdre?"

"Aye." She smoothed the sodden locks from her ladyship's face. "Your jacket."

The lady shifted but moaned again. "My shoulder."

Mrs. Doyle came to her aid. "The jacket is ruined anyway, we'll cut it off. And don't you fret, my lady. You won't feel a thing."

Lady Berkeley must have been clenching her teeth against the pain, given the pulse in her jaw. But she nodded and let them cut away the dark blue fabric. And, once free of it, said, "Papa?"

Lord Whitby was on his feet again in half a blink, taking Mrs. Doyle's place when she turned to fetch the basin. "I am here."

Deirdre had to give the lady credit—she nearly managed a smile.

"I see that. And in quite a state. You should go and get dry."

"Absolutely not."

"They need to help me from the rest of my habit." She swallowed and pressed a hand to her oozing side. "It isn't so bad. I think the corset must have deflected the worst of the blade."

Perhaps he believed her—or perhaps the mention of corsets did its work. Either way, Lord Whitby heaved a sigh but nodded and, after leaning down to kiss her forehead, headed for the door. "Ten minutes, and I'll be back. Is there anything I can get for you?"

Mrs. Doyle stepped forward, setting the basin on the side table where *La Bible* usually rested. "She'll want coffee, my lord. That steam-pressed concoction the chef makes."

His lordship chuckled and gripped his daughter's hand a moment.

Her attempt at a smile faded. "Oscuro?"

"Safe and well. The grooms had been knocked out and bound, but they were working themselves loose when you fainted. Francis is giving your horse an extra cup of oats for his heroics."

She nodded, swallowed, and then fastened her eyes on her father. "Is he dead? The man?"

Whitby hesitated a moment and then nodded. "I imagine the constable will want to speak with you. Tomorrow is soon enough for that though."

Deirdre tucked away a wisp of hair that had slipped from her cap and turned to the baroness's feet. She would remove the muddy boots rather than stand idle.

"No, don't put him off. I would as soon get it over with."

"We shall see."

They would see who was the more stubborn. Deirdre untied the riding boots and slipped them off as the earl finally left.

Mrs. Doyle closed the door behind him. And they got to work.

The scissors came out again to remove the ruined shirt. While Mrs. Doyle put it with the jacket pieces, Deirdre unhooked the corset and let it fall to the sides. From there, they could shift her chemise and get their first glimpse of the wound.

The baroness sucked in a fast breath but made no complaints as Mrs. Doyle sponged away the blood.

"It isn't as deep as I feared, and the bleeding is slow," the housekeeper said. "But it's long and will still require stitches."

"And let's pray this eye doesn't blacken and the scrapes heal quickly." Deirdre picked up the wet rag that had already cooled and set it gently over the swollen side of the baroness's face. "Otherwise you'll be a fine sight for your cousin's wedding next week."

Lady Berkeley lifted her uninjured arm to hold the cool cloth in place. "Aunt Mary will be furious with me."

"She couldn't be, child. You were attacked." Mrs. Doyle pressed her lips together and shook her head. Still, Deirdre caught the glint of tears in her eyes, and sure and the baroness did as well. "I cannot think why anyone would do this to you."

Deirdre's hands shook as they moved to assist her out of the split skirt. "Glad I am that Lord Pratt killed the monster."

"No." The lady's eyes slid closed. "Now I'll never know what he wanted from me."

"Leave it to the law and his lordship to figure that out, child." Mrs. Doyle held out a hand for the mud-caked skirt. "I agree with O'Malley. No one should be allowed to hurt one of our own. He got what he deserved."

The baroness didn't open her eyes, but she sniffed, and her nostrils flared. "One of your own?"

"Aye." Deirdre headed for the door when there was a knock upon it. She cracked it open, smiling when she saw Monsieur Bisset in the hall, a steaming cup in hand. His lordship couldn't have put in the order yet. But the chef had known. She took the espresso with a nod and could feel her da smiling down on her when she set it on the table. "And don't you be forgetting it, my lady."

As soon as they had her dressed again and settled in to await the doctor, Deirdre gathered the ruined habit to take down to the laundress. The split skirt possibly could be saved—and she knew that was the important part for her ladyship.

When she reached the bottom of the service stairs, those gathered in the kitchen all stood. Hiram stepped forward. "How is she?"

Deirdre nodded. "Awake again, and the bleeding has stopped."

A collective sigh filled the room, and chatter sprang up. She didn't try to make sense of all the mutters of outrage and sympathy. She headed for the laundry.

Hiram fell in beside her. "Jack said Pratt will be staying the night—I wanted you to know. He's changed already and is in the library, so keep yourself above stairs with her ladyship, Dee."

She paused in the empty, close hallway so she could look up at Hiram. "Don't be worrying for me, Hi. I know how to steer clear of the likes of him."

"I can't help it." He shoved his hands into his trouser pockets and half turned toward the kitchen. "I know he comes sniffing around after the baroness whenever he can find the excuse, but usually his lordship boots him out as soon as is decent. Tonight he invited him to stay. It could make the lout bold."

"But not so bold as to come to the baroness's room—and that's where I'll be, for sure and certain." She smiled, because she was glad he cared, even if she shouldn't be. Then she nodded toward the laundry. "I need to take care of these. I thank you for the warning, Hiram. It's good to know to mind my step."

He gave her a thoughtful little smile that seemed to say *I wonder* and spun back for the kitchen.

Deirdre sighed and shifted her muddied, bloodied burden. She would wonder too, if she dared to let herself.

Laundry deposited for a scrubbing, she headed back up without speaking to anyone else. Not all the way to the family's floor though—no, she headed for the library, checking over her shoulder often to make sure no one saw her go that way.

Ready to beard the lion, as they said, in his den. Feeling more certain with every step, she opened the door without hesitation, stepped inside, and clicked it shut behind her.

Lord Pratt stood by the fire, an arm braced on the mantel. At her entrance, he glanced up but then back to the flames. "How is she?"

"Well enough, I think." Squaring her shoulders, she marched

over to the fireplace. "Are you behind this, my lord? Did you hire him? Because I swear if you did, I'm done helping you. She could have been *killed*!"

"And you think I want that?" Temper flashing in his eyes, he straightened. "I want to marry her, you dolt, not attend her funeral. What possible good could she do me dead?"

He came a menacing step closer, but she didn't retreat. Not today.

"But your plan could have gone wrong. You could have hired him still, to scare her, then happened by at the right moment to rescue her. Play the hero, win Whitby's gratitude and her favor."

He advanced another step, glared down at her. "You think me so low. So base. So willing to flirt with death for *favor*—yet you dare come in here and accuse me of it?"

It might well be her undoing, but she lifted her chin. "Did you do it?"

For a second, he held her gaze, and the familiar devil looked back at her. Then he looked away. "No." His voice had lost its edge. "I did not hire that sot to scare the baroness so I could rescue her. Satisfied?"

She wasn't sure. She shouldn't be . . . Yet she believed him. Perhaps he had lied before, but this seemed different.

She backed up a step. "I had to ask. I don't want to see her hurt again."

"I assure you, Deirdre. Neither do I." He returned to his place by the grate, turning his face back to the flames. "Go tend your mistress."

She eased toward the door, hesitant to turn her back on him. But he seemed lost in the dance of the fire. She spun and slipped out again. As she made her way back to the baroness's chamber, though, she could scarcely make sense of it.

Was it possible he actually cared about her ladyship? No—he

hadn't mentioned feeling, just that she wouldn't do him any good dead.

She winced now, where she hadn't before. Something had to be dead inside *him*, to speak so.

Voices came from the bedchamber when she arrived, and she found Lord Whitby inside with the doctor from Eden Dale. They were both smiling and making encouraging noises, so Deirdre slipped behind them and headed for the dressing room and its attached lavatory. Much as the baroness needed it, she wouldn't feel up for the bath Deirdre had drawn. She drained the water.

Rising again, she set things to rights, taking her time. When she headed back through to the bedroom, the doctor was following Mrs. Doyle out.

The baroness seemed to be asleep.

"He gave her a bit of laudanum," his lordship said from the chair he had pulled up beside her bed. "Just enough to ease a bit of the pain so she can rest."

Deirdre crossed to the other side of the bed and pulled up another chair. "I daresay she needs it."

But it looked none too peaceful. Lady Berkeley turned her head from side to side, little restless noises coming from her lips. Then the "*Non, non, non*" Deirdre knew so well.

Lord Whitby did not. He leaned forward, brow furrowed. "Perhaps I should have let her refuse it."

"'Tisn't the laudanum, your lordship. It's the nightmare. She has it most every night." But she shouldn't have to suffer it *this* night. Deirdre sat on the bed, ran her fingers along her ladyship's face as she would have Molly's, and then caught up her hand. "*Shh* now, my lady. It's only a dream. Only a dream."

"The same one? Every night?"

She tilted her head toward Lord Whitby. "She never speaks of them—but they always look like this."

"She's never said a thing to me." And the hurt of it made

creases around his eyes. But still he took her other hand, cradled it in his. Murmured, "All is well, my little Brooklet. Hush now. Hush."

For a second it seemed she would listen. Then she gasped, her eyes flew open, and her chest heaved. "My mother—it must be. '*You have all her things*,' he said. All her things."

Now his lordship looked to Deirdre, panicked question in his eyes.

She could only shrug. "*That* must be the laudanum, my lord."

He sighed and brushed the fair curls from his daughter's forehead. "Easy, precious. Go back to sleep."

Her eyes unfocused, she shook her head. "*Non*. They always find me there. The lightning and the thunder and the night and . . ."

"Shh. They'll not find you tonight. I'm here."

"Papa." She blinked rapidly, and a measure of awareness lit her eyes. "What was I saying?"

"Nothing." He smiled and kissed her forehead. "Rest. I'm here. Rest."

Deirdre slipped from the mattress and went to the window. Arms folded across her middle, she fought back the burn of tears. Her da had done the same thing when one of them had the fever or woke up in a fright. He had looked at her and her siblings with that same light of love. Family, it seemed, crossed from abovestairs to below with few differences, at the heart of it.

She sighed and looked past the pattering rain. The thunder had moved off. The lightning had ceased. But the night was full and dark and promised to be a long one.

Sixteen

Whoever invented laudanum ought to be executed. Never in Brook's life had her head hurt so—though granted, it might not be all the fault of the drug.

She had to take the stairs slowly, largely because of the dizziness. Her legs were sore, bruised where the ruffian's knees had pressed them, but not *that* sore. Her shoulder ached from the strained muscle, but she could have ignored it. And of course, her side was so tender and raw that a corset had been out of the question, necessitating Paul Poiret dresses that didn't require one.

But it was the fuzzy head that was driving her batty.

"Lady Berkeley, what are you doing? Where is O'Malley?"

Brook gripped the banister tightly before trusting herself to look up. Mrs. Doyle was rushing up the stairs toward her, her frown not one to be ignored.

Brook ignored it anyway. "I sent her on an errand. Papa said the constable will be here in an hour, Lady Catherine's note said she will be visiting not long after that, and I need to have my wits about me."

The housekeeper pressed her lips together. And then looped

her arm through Brook's. "You should have had O'Malley help you down, my lady. We can't have you falling and hurting yourself worse."

A nearly valid point. She already looked a fright—bruised and scraped from face to foot—and they were to leave for London in three days.

There was no way she could stand beside Regan at her wedding like this. Would Aunt Mary even allow visitors for her? Brice and Ella had promised to call as soon as she made Town. And it made her stomach hurt outright to think that Justin's first view of her in two months would be when she looked like the loser of a barroom brawl.

Her hand shook against the railing as they continued down. A brawl it had been, but she hadn't been the loser. And she still couldn't think why the man had lain in wait for her.

At least she would have another story to tell Justin. "Brook Tames the Darkness" for her victory with Oscuro . . . and "The Assailant in the Stables" for last night.

"A hearty breakfast will bolster you, my lady. Chef made the eggs you like so well, a sausage so spicy it sent poor Jack running for water, and of course your coffee."

She had to swallow before she could speak. Who knew breakfast and coffee could mean so much? "Thank you, Mrs. Doyle. I will thank Monsieur Bisset later."

The grand staircase stretched on for miles, but at last her feet touched even floor, and they headed for the breakfast room at a normal pace. Or nearly normal. Almost, nearly normal.

Her father's voice floated out to meet them. "I don't care if it takes a *year*, Constable, I want this man's identity found. If I have to pay an investigator to inquire in every village and hamlet in all the empire, I will."

She halted outside the door, her brow taut. Papa had said

the constable would be here to meet with her at nine o'clock. It was only eight.

"And you may have to, your lordship—the folks in Eden Dale said they'd never seen him before, and he certainly isn't one of Whitby's usual drunks."

She stepped into the room, extracting her arm from Mrs. Doyle's. "He wasn't drunk. He smelled of kippers and onions, not alcohol, and his reflexes were as quick as mine."

The men came to a halt—all three of them. Her father with his tea halfway to his mouth, the man she presumed to be the constable with a click of his heels, and Pratt at the sideboard filling a plate with her eggs.

No one had mentioned *he* was still here. Though she supposed after saving them the night before, her father could hardly begrudge him a change of clothes and a warm bed. Something niggled there, though. What, again, had he been doing here? Some bits were so muddled . . .

"I don't know whether to scold or rejoice." Papa put down his cup and stood, motioning her in. He pulled out her usual chair. "I said we would bring him to the sitting room across from your chamber."

"And I thought to breakfast with you first." She tried to give him her usual cheeky smile, but a nasty scrape forbade it.

"Sit." He indicated her chair and then turned to the sideboard. "Eggs, sausage, and this stuff you so optimistically call coffee?"

"Yes, please. And *merci*." She sat, though it was little relief to her side, and looked to the uniformed officer. "You've no idea who he was?"

"Not yet, your ladyship. But the day is young, and we've only just started asking."

A different song, it seemed, than the one he had sung for her father. She lifted a brow and kept her back straight, trying to keep all pressure off her side. "He had a strange accent, if that helps you. He put an L on the end of some words. Donnel for don't. Coil for coy."

The constable sent a glance over her head.

Papa put her plate and cup before her. His eyes, she saw when he retook his seat, had gone thoughtful. "Bristol."

"Bristol?" Pratt echoed. He took a chair across from her with a shake of his head. "It's awfully far."

For a man out for a random robbery, perhaps. For one on a mission . . . She took a sip of the coffee, nearly sighing in bliss.

Her father ignored Pratt altogether. "So he said 'Don't be coy.' What else?"

She took another sip to clear her head. "He asked me where *they* were. I at first thought he spoke of people, but he must have meant things. Something . . ." It had made so little sense. "It sounded like *feral ice*. And he said I must have it, I had all her things."

She looked up, a blurry image surfacing of her father leaning over her, the dream still clouding her mind.

Papa must have made the same connection. "Your mother. But what among her things could anyone be looking for? And why now, when she has been gone so long?"

"I don't know." It made no more sense than it had last night, and trying to focus on it made her head hurt.

"You are yet unwell, my lady." Pratt's voice sounded concerned—anxious even. "Pushing yourself will accomplish nothing. Rest, then send word to the constable if you think of anything else."

"No. I am well enough." He ended his words with Ls. So perhaps it wasn't *feral*. Fear? But what was *fear ice*?

More coffee—that was all she needed. Though her stomach disagreed with her tongue and her head, forcing her to test the food as well. She must have missed dinner last night.

Kippers . . . so he had to have been in Whitby long enough for a meal at a pub. Perhaps he had rented a room. Maybe the constable's knocking on those doors would reveal something after all.

Fire. Not fear, fire. Fire ice. Fire and ice. Ice . . . cold? *Non.* Jewels—diamonds. The British called them *ice* sometimes, did they not?

Brook put down her fork, though the food was perfect. Diamonds . . . she had many of them, now, that had been her mother's. Bracelets, rings, necklaces.

Papa leaned back to murmur something to the constable. What was it he had said when he offered that first necklace?

"To match her eyes. The color of emeralds, with the light of diamonds."

Eyes. Fire *eyes* . . .

Written words flashed through her mind, though she couldn't be sure she remembered them correctly through the haze. She pushed away. Too slowly to be called abrupt, but still it brought the men to another halt. Brook forced a smile. "Excuse me, gentlemen. I'm afraid I'm not so well after all."

Her father all but leaped from his chair. "I'll help you back to your room."

Panic clawed at her throat. Yet it couldn't be. She would look at the letter again. Try to make sense of it. "No, Papa. You must finish your conversation here. I shall find . . ." Mrs. Doyle couldn't have gone too far. She looked to the door.

No Mrs. Doyle. But Deirdre appeared as if summoned by her very thoughts. Or, given the exasperation upon her face, by Brook's disappearance from her bedroom. "There you are, my lady! You look pale as a ghoul. Let me see you back upstairs."

"Thank you—I would appreciate it." Brook bent her knees—all the curtsy she could manage—and nodded at the men. "Pray continue, gentlemen."

213

Deirdre slid a gentle arm around her waist, careful to avoid the injured side. "I'll have someone bring your plate and coffee. You need to rest, my lady. It's quite a trauma you received, and not so many hours ago."

Brook's mind buzzed too much to argue. She gladly accepted the help up the stairs and into her room—though she declined the offer of bed in favor of a chair. And she only took the chair once she had first gone to her dressing room and tried to reach, not for the jewels, but for the box of her parents' letters.

"Your ladyship!"

Brook sighed . . . and winced. "You're right. I can't reach it. Would you be so kind?"

Mumbling in Gaelic all the while, Deirdre pulled down the box from the shelf with ease and shooed Brook back to her chair. "I can't think what's so all-fired important . . ."

Brook offered no explanation, just opened the box and pulled out the bundle of letters. She had finished reading through them all a month ago and had divided them again into his and hers, in their separate boxes. These were hers, from him.

She flipped to the bottom of the stack. The very last one by date. It had been buried in the box when she first sorted them—though the rest had been in reverse order, newest on top. She'd thought it odd, but Regan and Melissa had distracted her from dwelling on it.

Now she dwelled and unfolded the missive. Her eyes scanned over the first few paragraphs, but it wasn't there. She flipped it over. There, on the back.

I know you have jewels enough already, my love, but when I saw this, I thought of you. Of how it would look against the cream of your skin, under the fire of your eyes. You have always been my Fire Eyes.

Fire Eyes. But they weren't a *thing*, for a thief to demand. Yet he had tied them to a gift . . .

"The letters again?" Deirdre was returning from the door with her breakfast tray. She slid it onto the table by Brook's side and raised her brows at the paper. "And who's that one from?"

"My father to my mother."

"Is it? Doesn't look like his lordship's hand."

"No." It had been the first thing she had noted too, after sorting through so many of them. But the explanation for that lay in the first paragraph. "The letter says he'd hurt his hand—his valet wrote it for him."

Though now that she knew him, she couldn't imagine her father sharing such intimate thoughts with any third party. Ever. Someone else had obviously penned it though.

Another knock sent Deirdre back to the door, and Papa poked his head in the moment she opened it. "May I come in?"

"Please." He could be trusted. She had known it all along, but now she was *sure*. "I would appreciate your help."

Question in his eyes, he strode her way. She held out the letter. He took it, but without any change to that silent inquiry. "What's this?"

"I wish I knew. It was with the letters you wrote my mother, signed with your name, but not in your hand. It says you dictated it to your valet."

His gaze shot from the page to her. "I would never dictate a letter to my wife to my valet."

"I know. So then . . ."

"So then." His gaze fell to the sheet again, scanned, narrowed. "What is this gift?"

She nearly smiled at the temper in his tone—jealous, nearly twenty years later, at the thought of someone else sending a gift to his Lizzie. Did Brice ever react so? Not that she'd seen, though he looked at her warmly. And Justin . . . he was too much her brother. He guarded her fiercely, but it wasn't the same, was it? "Some kind of jewelry, obviously."

He had flipped the page, and she knew when he got to that last line by the quick breath he drew in. Knew, when he looked up, that his mind had made the same leap hers had. "Not *feral ice*. Fire Eyes."

"Yes." She moistened her lips. "I first thought it might have been ice—like diamonds. Which is what got me thinking about this letter."

"It must be one of the pieces I attributed to the Brooks or Rushworths. She—"

"Wait." Brook got slowly to her feet and walked into her dressing room, pulling out the card-paper bandbox where she'd put Mother's miscellaneous correspondence as she'd read them. Tossing it to her bed, she riffled through the contents.

It didn't take long before she lifted a few folded sheaves. "I knew I recognized that script, try as he did to disguise it. I found these letters while reading through Mother's correspondence."

Papa took the missives, and as he read, soon flushed. "That blighter." He threw the pages into the bandbox and turned abruptly. "O'Malley, find us fresh paper. We have a letter to write to one Major Henry Rushworth, in India."

Justin hadn't attended many weddings, but this one seemed exceedingly long to his way of thinking. And dull. Much as he had enjoyed the few moments before the ceremony he'd had to poke fun at Thate, who had been grinning like a lunatic, this wasn't where Justin wanted to be.

Not given the gaping absence of Brook.

His ship had been days late to port, and he was convinced it was only prayer that had allowed him to make it into the city in time for the nuptials. He'd had no time to go to his townhouse, only to send Peters for his clothes while he headed for the church. Once there, of course, it had been straight into the room with Thate and their other friends from school who would stand with him.

No one had mentioned that Brook would not be present—wasn't she to be one of the bridesmaids? He'd found Whitby in the crowd, had sent him a questioning look . . . but hadn't been able to decipher the mirroring one Whitby sent back.

The moment the interminable ceremony finally ended and the impossible crowd made its way out to greet the Earl and new Countess Thate, Justin found Brook's father. "Where is she?"

Whitby lifted a single brow. "And a cheerful hello to you too, Duke. She's at Mary's."

But . . . "Why?"

The other brow joined the first. "She wasn't well enough."

"What? Is she ill?" It would have to be serious indeed to keep her away.

Now Whitby sighed and pulled him back into the church, away from the milling nobility. "Did you not go home first, sir? She and I drove round yesterday and left a letter for you." At the shake of Justin's head, the earl nodded. "She is injured—a cut to her side that wouldn't, apparently, allow her to wear her bridesmaid's dress, and her face is a veritable rainbow of blues and greens that made my sister faint each morning for three days running."

Panic vied with pity. "That horse?" It had to be. That stubborn girl—

"No. She has Oscuro well in hand." He looked as if he were about to say more but then darted a worried look at the crowds. "I would keep the press out of it, so I'll say no more. It's all in the letter."

Letter be hanged—he'd get the story from Brook herself, and he certainly wasn't going to lollygag here when she was but a few miles away. With a nod to Whitby, he exited again and gripped Thate's shoulder.

His friend turned, that idiotic smile still in place. "There you are, Shep. I thought you'd run off to India already."

His intentions paused, he blinked. "Shep?"

"Stafford . . . Staff . . . Shepherd . . . surely you can follow the train of my thoughts by now."

A grin stole Justin's lips. "Never—mine are too logical to take the twists and turns yours do." He gazed out over the sea of people, far too many of whom watched him. "I'm going to slip away for a bit, but I'll make my way to the ball when I can."

Thate's smile went lopsided and knowing. "Any particular place you're slipping away *to*?"

As if he didn't know perfectly well. Thate must have known exactly what kinds of injuries Brook had managed to sustain, even if he hadn't taken it upon himself to enlighten Justin before the wedding. Though he supposed he would have been a bit suspicious had the man's mind been on his bride's cousin rather than his bride. "I have to see her."

Thate's smile was the exact one he'd given him in school when Justin had fallen into the pond after Thate had warned him not to trust that old log. Pure condescending glee. "Oh, I know you do. Go. Enjoy your freedom while it lasts—I daresay she'll have chains around you soon."

And if he could be as happy in them as Thate seemed to be . . . Justin grinned. "Don't make me hurt you on your wedding day, Alex."

Thate's laugh followed him down the sweeping stone steps outside the church before it got lost in the chatter of the crowd. He found the Rolls-Royce and gave the motor a crank. Slid into his seat, switched on the magneto, and turned the key.

He had the direction for Lady Ramsey's home and knew it wasn't too far from his own townhouse on Grosvenor Square, so he set off in the general direction. The sun was already setting behind the buildings of London when he found the right street and then the right number. He parked, killed the magneto, and hopped out, sparing only a moment to smile at Whitby's words. *"She and I drove over yesterday . . ."*

Which of them, he had to wonder, had been behind the wheel?

The butler opened the door to his knock. Stepping inside, Justin handed over his card and received an immediate bow.

"Good evening, Your Grace. But I am afraid the family is all out—"

"At the wedding, I know." He took a step to the right, though, when the strains of a piano—and a soprano—reached him. "I was just there, where I learned of the baroness's injuries. I needed to see for myself she is well."

The butler's eyes brightened. "Ah, you are *that* duke. Of course, Your Grace. I will let the baroness know—"

"Please, don't interrupt her playing. It's been too long since I've heard it." And what other duke would come calling? The only possible answer made his palms go damp. He handed over his hat and overcoat and let his feet point him toward her siren's song. "This way?"

"Yes, sir. Follow me."

The butler led him a short way down the hall and indicated the double French doors to what must be the music room. He glimpsed a harp near the window, an old clavichord by the shelves. With a nod of thanks he stepped inside. And saw the piano.

Her back was to him. Her hair was down—the chandelier's light shone on each spiraling strand of gold tumbling down her back, wild and free. A sight he hadn't seen in years. And which hadn't used to make him react like this.

She played with the same abandon she applied to her every other pursuit, as if it might be the last song she ever sang, the last keys her fingers would touch. He recognized the song—it was from a Puccini opera, and Collette had earned her fame belting out this particular bittersweet refrain.

Letting the music sweep through him, he eased into the room, careful to keep out of Brook's peripheral vision. The last time he had happened upon her like this had been that night in Monaco. When he had looked at her and thought how beautiful she had grown to be, how he would soon declare himself.

Swallow as he might, the lump wouldn't ease from his throat. A few more months, a few more trips, a few more continents. Things had gone well in Barbados and Canada. Not well enough that he could avoid sinking the money Father left him into improvements for the Stafford tenants in Gloucestershire, but well. Promising. If he could put things to rights as efficiently in India and Africa . . .

Brook lifted her voice in the final high, soaring note. Her fingers stilled for a measure, two, then flew over the keys in a heartrending finale. Once her voice had gone silent and her fingers still, he stepped forward, clapping.

She spun around on the bench, her eyes going bright as she sprang up. "Justin!"

Because he couldn't help it, he smiled—and because her face was mottled with bruises, that smile faded as she launched herself into his arms. He let her kiss his cheeks but knew he was scowling. It deepened when she flinched away from the hand he settled on her waist, pain flashing through her eyes.

"What happened?" He didn't mean it to come out so harsh sounding. His hands slid to her back—until he realized he felt only cloth and flesh, no rigid boning. Far too alluring. He dropped them altogether.

Her eyes flickered only briefly. "Did you not read the letter?"

"I didn't get home. I had barely enough time to reach the church. What happened?"

She sighed and rubbed a fingertip over a mostly healed scrape on her arm. "I was attacked one evening—we still don't know why, or who the man was. I took his gun and shot the knife from his hand—"

"You what?" Images assaulted him: Brook held at gunpoint. Brook with a knife at her throat. Brook, one of the few people he had left in the world, nearly killed. The fear of it swallowed him, and he dragged her to his chest again and held her close. Let the solid feel of her, the proof that she had survived her ordeal, seep into every inch.

"Justin—"

"Hush. Give me a moment." He squeezed his eyes closed and buried his face in her golden, fragrant curls.

Her arms were around him. Her breath on his neck. She even stroked a hand over the back of his head. Soothing, giving comfort, when *she* was the one who had been injured. He swallowed and forced himself to pull away, though he couldn't resist cupping her uninjured cheek as he met her gaze again. "Sorry. I can see you're all right, but the thought of it . . ." He shook his head. "You shot a knife from his hand?"

Only Brook could nod about it with a hint of a smile. "And then Papa came, and Pratt. Pratt killed the brute when he drew out a second gun."

He could only stare at her now, waiting for the words to clarify. She'd called Whitby *Papa*—that was a big step for her, and it must be a new one. But . . . "Pratt?"

The arch of her brows looked amused. "Now you sound like Brice and Ella. Pratt finds any excuse he can to call, though that was certainly the first we welcomed him."

His brain had hit another snag. "Who are Brice and Ella?"

"Sorry—Lord Worthing and his sister, Lady Ella Myerston."

Were there a seat handy, he would have sunk into it. As it was, his hand slipped from her cheek. "Lord Worthing."

He was back at Whitby Park, on the day Grandfather died. Looking across the lawn at her on his arm. Seeing the way she laughed, the way he looked down at her. "You are on a first name basis with them?" With *him*?

She spun away with a chuckle, toward a laden tea table that seemed to have everything but tea on it. A *chuckle*, as if it weren't paramount to claiming they were engaged. That, while he was an ocean away dreaming of declaring his love to her, she was forgetting he even existed.

"You'd like them," she said, insensibly. "After the house party they had gone back to Scotland to finish their holiday with their mother's family, and they all stopped again at Whitby Park for a few days' rest on their way home to Sussex."

She turned back toward him, cup of steaming black coffee in hand. "Have you seen your cousin yet? He has spent much of the fall in Town. Largely, it seems, because Melissa was here. She says she is certain he will propose soon, though Aunt Mary wants her to debut first."

When Brook extended the coffee toward him, Justin took it without thinking. But he didn't feel the heat of it on his palm. He wasn't even certain the electrified chandelier still shone. So many times he had come home from months of school or travel, had sought her out at the palace—and she had spoken to him of academic papers or dignitaries or the latest advances of the automobile.

Not weddings and debuts and cousins and friends known the empire over for their ability to make women fall at their feet. Friends she called by first name with a gleam in her eye. Friends who had looked at her as though seeing the sun for the first time.

Justin downed half the cup of coffee in a single shot. It warmed him, but not in the way he'd hoped. "You've been busy."

She paused with her hand on the gleaming silver coffee-pot and looked right into his soul. "Would you have me stand around idle?"

"No. Of course not." But he would have her not make him feel, the moment he stepped in the room, that he had become superfluous to her life. "It's good to know you've found your place. Made friends."

He must not have sounded convincing. She planted her hands on her hips and narrowed her eyes. "What choice had I? To spend my every waking hour waiting for you to deign to write a letter?"

"I wrote letters!" He held out a hand, palm up . . . though he had not written as much as he should have. Every time he put pen to paper, the only words that wanted to make their mark were *I love you. I need you.*

She rolled her eyes and spun away again. "One. One letter."

"More than one. Three, at the least. They must not have reached you."

She sighed and put a pastry on a plate, handed that to him as well. Strawberry—his favorite. But he knew well he couldn't eat a bite. Not when she looked up at him like that. "Three letters, then. In over two months. You have never written so little, *never*. You abandon me here—"

"I did not *abandon* you." He set the plate back down with a bit too much force. "I delivered you to your father!"

"Yes, and then you left. And I know . . . I *know* you had to. I know that." She pressed a hand to her forehead, holding back the curtain of curls. "But you pushed me away, Justin. You wouldn't let me in—and then silence, except for that one brief letter that might as well have been to your solicitor, for all its personal tone. And now you have the gall to stand there and be upset that I have made other friends?"

Deuces. She made him feel the fool, made Aunt Caro's warnings clang in his head. But what choice had he had? "You act as if you wrote me every day, as if *your* letters were about anything but your progress with that devil of a horse and the prattle of Lady Catherine. Where was the mention of our cousins being all but engaged? Of this . . . this *Brice* you apparently like so well?"

She stared at him as if he'd grown another head. "I only heard about our cousins when I got to London three days ago, and why are you saying Brice's name like that? Surely Thate didn't poison you against him so thoroughly—"

"By thunder, Brook, this has nothing to do with Thate and everything to do with *you*. You cannot go around calling a young man by his given name! Haven't you any idea how things are done here?"

It was a mistake. He knew it the moment the words exited his mouth. The fury that snapped in her eyes only hammered it home. "So then I should call you Duke now, after all? Is that it?"

What was wrong with her? He shook his head. "Don't be stupid. It's different for us—we were children together. But heaven help me, you better not be telling me that you feel as close to Worthing after two visits as you do to me after thirteen years, or I'll—"

"You'll what?" Her shoulders had edged back, her chin had thrust out, making the bruises shout at him. Yet somehow, she didn't look like a petulant child ready for a brawl. She looked like a princess facing down an angry mob. "Run off to another continent and not bother to write?"

"Brook, that's unfair!" He reached out, tempted to shake some sense into her—or perhaps to pull her tight and give in to the long-festering need to kiss her, to show her why he couldn't suffer another man be in her life like that. But when his hand gripped her shoulder, she hissed out a breath, her eyes went wide, and she pulled away, clutching the shoulder.

He'd hurt her. Heaven help him. "What did I do?"

She shook her head, though the denial was obviously a lie,

given the way she squeezed her eyes shut. "It's nothing. It was just wrenched, is all, and bruised."

He'd hurt her. A careless touch, and he made her wince away. Still, that was nothing. He'd done far worse in years past, he was sure, as he taught her his sports. But he'd *hurt her*. He saw it as she opened her eyes again and stared at him from too-dry eyes.

He was, it seemed, his father's son. Not Father's—Father, who could grin and sweep his lady into his arms and make her forget all the agony that had come before. Not Father, who understood that when pain came, you clung to those who mattered most, you didn't push them away.

But Edward's son. Stone-faced, coldhearted Edward's son.

Nostrils flaring, he dragged in a shaky breath. "I'm sorry. I should . . . I should go. It seems I'm still not fit for company, so I'll just . . . I'll see you in the spring." He pivoted. Eyes unfocused, he made for the general direction of the door.

"Wait!" Her long, delicate fingers caught his. Familiar. Warm. Perfect . . . But if he clung to them, it would hurt them both all the more. He wanted something she obviously didn't want to give. She hadn't been dreaming of him, hadn't been yearning for him. She couldn't have been, if she were so busy getting to know *Brice*. "Justin, you can't mean . . . When does your ship leave?"

He slid his eyes closed to keep from looking at her. Told himself not to squeeze her fingers. "Tomorrow."

"What?" Her fingers fell away. "No. You just got here, you can't possibly leave again so soon."

"I thought to have a week in Town before the wedding. I cannot help that my ship was so late." His voice sounded hollow, empty. Just as he felt. He wasn't strong enough to keep from turning to see her.

She shook her head, sending her curls swaying. "No. But you can help when you leave. Postpone a few days, Justin. Please. There are things . . ." She blinked and looked away, but one of the tears still overflowed and spilled onto her cheek. "There are things I cannot put in a letter."

"Brook." There were things he couldn't either. The truth of his father. Of his heart. "I wish I could. But I risk missing an important rendezvous if I delay my departure. I have to go."

She gripped his wrist. "I know you have responsibilities. But they cannot always take precedence over *people*."

"They are *about* people—the hundreds upon hundreds of them who rely on the Stafford estates for their well-being." It was true. Why, then, did it sound like an excuse to his own ears?

"I mean your family."

"They understand. My friends understand. Everyone else—"

"Everyone *else*?" She tossed his hand away from her and all but leaped back. "Now I am not family, not a friend?"

Why could he say nothing right to her anymore? He lifted his hand, though then he let it fall again. "That is not what I meant."

Fire snapped in her eyes. "Isn't it? It seems to me that it's *exactly* what you meant. That you can't bear the thought of not being able to do everything on your own, to control all you touch, O Mighty Duke of Stafford, and so you must push away those who make you *feel* and—"

"You have no idea what I feel!"

"*Ça c'est sûr!*"

The French sent him reeling backward—not because of her claim that that was the point, but because she had stuck with English until then, which was unprecedented when her emotions ran so high. Proof that she had built a place for herself . . . and he had no part of it.

He had ruined everything. And he didn't know what to do but turn, pray to God that He would help him mend it, and leave.

Seventeen

Brook stood where he'd left her. The threatening tears made her nose ache, and pain from holding them back scorched her side.

He'd left. He hadn't teased or cajoled or called himself a dunce. He hadn't shot back with an accusation of his own. He hadn't gathered her close again and told her why he had such shadows in his eyes.

He'd left.

A sob nearly escaped. So much she'd wanted to tell him—nightmares and jewels and lying letters in her mother's things—and now he was gone, and he was leaving tomorrow, and they would part for months with this between them, and then things would never be the same again.

Things were already not the same.

"My lady." Deirdre bustled into the room, concern in her eyes. "I heard shouting. Was that the duke?"

"Yes." But no. Yes, it had been the Duke of Stafford talking about responsibilities and trips he couldn't postpone. The Duke of Stafford, with eyes so much older than his years. But beneath him, somewhere, was *Justin*. She darted around her maid. "I have to catch him."

"But I heard his car start up."

"Then I have to go after him. I need a horse. Or the car."

"My lady." Deirdre caught her by the elbow, horror on her face. "No. You can't go out alone at night in London. Not looking as you do."

Did she mean the bruises or the clothes? Either way. Shaking her arm free, Brook charged through the doorway. "You're right. I need livery. There should be something in the laundry."

"My lady!"

This time she was the one to halt. "You can help me or you can stay out of my way, O'Malley, but I am going after him."

Indecision chased through the Irishwoman's eyes . . . then she crossed herself and flew down the corridor. "Heaven help me and may his lordship forgive me. I'll fetch the livery."

Every step seemed to take an hour, every button an age, but the clock said it was not five minutes later that Brook flew from Aunt Mary's house in borrowed Ramsey livery, a chauffeur's cap hiding her hair and shadowing her face. Papa usually helped with the car's crank, but tonight she didn't have time to find other assistance. She did it herself, ignoring the strain to her side, and leaped behind the wheel.

Thank heavens Papa had driven her to Justin's townhouse yesterday. She followed the same route now, praying he had gone home and not to the wedding ball. Surely, surely he was not so unmoved that he could feast and dance as if the world were still whole.

She took the last two turns too fast, but her galloping heart would accept nothing less. When she squealed to a stop in the rear of his driveway and saw him just exiting the carriage house, she deemed it worth it.

He spun at her ignominious entrance, light from the lamp outlining him in gold.

He wouldn't know the car. She took it out of gear and pushed open the door, tossing her cap to the seat behind her.

"Brook?" It was half disbelief, half relief in his tone.

She wasted no time on words, not quite yet. Just ran for him and didn't stop until her face was buried in his chest, her arms wrapped around him.

He hugged her back, so tightly she could feel the ache in his heart even above the one in her side.

"Gently," she muttered into his ascot.

"Sorry." His arms didn't loosen but shifted away from the sore spot. "I'm so sorry."

"I couldn't let you leave like this. I didn't mean to fight with you." She squeezed him tighter, breathed in the scent of lemon and spice. "I'm sorry, Justin. I understand your duties. I do. But why must you push me away? I need you."

He stroked a hand over her hair. Lingering . . . but sorrowful. Then he rested his head on hers. "No you don't. You've always been so strong. Independent. Look at you, flourishing in my absence."

"No." He wouldn't say that if he knew what dreams haunted her. If he'd seen the evil glint in the eyes behind the gunman. "Don't leave like this. I know you must go, but not like this."

Silence pulled her soul taut. London still made its noises, to be sure, but he made none. Made no move. He just stood there and held her and then loosed a breath that seemed to expel his every drop of energy.

"Everything has changed."

Her own thought—but hearing him say it made her shake her head and tip her face up more to look at him. "*Non*. Not everything. You are still my dearest friend."

"Am I?" He put his hands on her shoulders and urged her away. "After acting as I have?"

She gazed into his eyes and saw how dark the blues looked

in the night, how darker still with what he kept pent up inside him. "Justin . . . it doesn't matter." It couldn't.

His smile looked so sad. "Of course it matters. I've hurt you, and that's the last thing I meant to do. But I don't know how to remedy it, other than to promise you I'll try never to do it again." Now his hands dropped to his sides, and he backed up a step. "You need to go home, *mon amie*. The streets aren't safe."

Neither was home. She slid closer again, found his hand. "Not yet. We haven't talked. I don't know what adventures you've found." Squeezing her eyes shut tight, she knotted her fingers around his. "Tell me a story."

"All right." He squeezed her fingers . . . and then released them. "I believe this one is called 'The End of an Era.'"

Her throat went so tight she could only whisper her reply. "What happens?"

"I don't know yet."

She shook—not with November's cold, but with his leaving. With the changing. It seemed all she could do was try to make the parting sweet. She lifted her hands, planted them on his shoulders, and strained up.

"Go with God." She kissed his left cheek, soft and sorrowful. "Hurry back to me." She kissed his right.

But when she tried to lower back to her heels, he pulled her against him. Tangling his hand in her hair, he tilted her face back, giving her a single glimpse of his eyes—deepest blue still, and flashing. Then he touched his lips to hers. Just a touch. But it lit a spark. Then a fire, a sweeping, a diving. She clung to his shoulders and parted her lips and was lost. Utterly, beautifully lost in a sea of sensation.

He angled his head and took her deeper, making her want to dance, to sing, to fly.

Then her arms were empty and only cold air kissed her. Her eyes flew open in time to see him shove a hand through his hair.

What was that? Or rather, *why* was that? For a second, it all roiled through his eyes—question, regret, and . . . and something far warmer, far deeper. Then it was gone, locked away.

Never in her life had she felt so very cold. "Justin."

But the Duke of Stafford took another step backward, twirled the signet ring on his finger. "You need to go home. I'll have a groom follow."

No. He couldn't just run away again after that, after changing everything on her. "Justin."

He kept retreating. *"Au revoir, mon amie."*

Until I see you again. Though only the Lord above knew when that would be . . . and if she would still be his *amie.* Her stomach clenched.

"The End of an Era."

She spun and ran for the roadster, closing herself in. The car was still running—she backed up, turned, and sped onto the square before he could rouse any of the grooms. Was back to Aunt Mary's likely before one could have saddled a horse.

So very close. So very far. When she pulled back into the carriage house, she switched off the car and rested her head on the wheel for a minute. Tried to convince the breaths to come into her lungs in an orderly fashion, to exit one at a time. They seemed determined to trip and tangle.

It was cold. Her hands stung. She needed a fire. A blanket. Justin's arms.

No.

Pocketing the key, she stumbled from the car and ran toward the servant's entrance. Reached for the handle.

The door swung open before her, a man's figure looming against the lamplight within. "Elizabeth Brook Eden! Inside— *now.*"

She ought to have known her father wouldn't linger at the ball. Scarcely feeling the trudge of her feet, she slid by him.

"Into the parlor, young lady."

Of course. At home, the parlor was where he led prayers, where he doled out praise to the staff. Where, she heard, he would fire anyone to be dismissed.

She'd yet to see him do it. Perhaps the fear of it won obedience.

Or more likely their love of him.

She made her way into Aunt Mary's green and gold parlor and stopped in the middle of the room, her head too heavy to hold high.

Papa slammed shut the door behind them. "What in blazes were you thinking? Taking the car without permission is bad enough, but at night? Alone, in an unfamiliar city?"

"I know. I'm sorry."

"And running after a man? I don't care how good a man, how well you know him, some things are not *done*, Brook!"

It seemed she was forever doing things that weren't done. "I know." She couldn't lift her gaze—it felt too heavy. So all she saw were his pacing feet.

To the right, pivot, to the left.

"You could have been accosted. Hurt even worse."

She opened her mouth, but nothing came out.

"You could have been *killed*."

Her eyes slid shut.

"And by thunder, Brook, why aren't you *arguing* with me?"

The question broke her, made a strangled laugh escape her lips as tears wept from her eyes. "I'm sorry, Papa."

His feet drew near and his arms came around her, fierce and tender at once. "No crying—it isn't fair."

"I'm sorry." They were the only words she could find. She wiped at the tears and sagged against him. "He's leaving again tomorrow. And I'm a muddle. I think he's . . . in love with me."

Papa's sigh gusted along with the wind outside the windows.

"I know he is. And I strictly forbid it. You shouldn't be old enough for such things, not with all the years we've missed."

A weak smile tugged at her lips.

He led her to the sofa and sat beside her, her hands in his. His eyes searching hers. "What of you? Are you in love with him?"

Was she? She stared into the dancing flames of the hearth, felt again the heat inside her when he'd kissed her. Felt again the cold when he'd backed away. "I don't know, Papa. When I was a girl, I would dream . . . but I knew it could never be. I resigned myself to that years ago. A duke cannot marry a singer's daughter."

Papa pressed her fingers, holding them tight. "You are no longer that, though."

Her brows pulled down, her heart squeezed. "But that shouldn't be enough, should it? That now that I'm *suitable* he would . . ." She closed her eyes against the firelight and shook her head. "I love him. I've always loved him. I don't know about the romance, but I know that."

"And we all do foolish things for those we love." Papa cleared his throat, bringing her eyes open again, to latch on his pained face. "But I can't lose you again, Brook. You can't possibly know the fear that struck me when I realized you and the car were both gone."

She could imagine it. "I was selfish. I didn't think."

"Why? What happened?"

She settled into the space at his side, where she could lean into him and rest her head on his shoulder, pretending she'd done so for years. "We fought—which is nothing new, but it was different this time. I don't know why. We said things, stupid things, and then he *left*. And was leaving Town in the morning, and I couldn't let him. Not like that."

"Oh, Brook." His tone went weary. "Perhaps you *are* in love. We all say stupid things when we're in love. Argue over nothing."

"It hurts."

He snorted a laugh. "Love often hurts."

"Then why would we do it?"

He squeezed her hands, warming them. "Because it's worth it. Even when we lose them, it's worth it."

She could only sigh.

Papa planted a kiss on the top of her head. "Did you find him?"

She nodded. "He's still reeling so from his losses and now feels alone, left behind. I try to understand that, but he won't let me in. And then he kissed me, and—"

"He did *what*?" His shoulder jerked from under her. "Give me the key. I'm going over there—"

"And what?" Seeing the ire, so purely paternal, sparked life into her heart. "You'll threaten him into marrying me?"

"Hardly. I'll threaten his life if he dares to come home again."

She nearly laughed. "Papa."

"I've said it before—I'll not give you away so soon. I won't do it." He looked almost, nearly serious. And it almost, nearly made her wonder if that's what Justin wanted—to marry her.

It sent an uneasy thrill through her middle. Did she want that? Did she want a lifetime in his arms? Maybe . . . possibly. The kiss had been beyond anything she had dreamed. But what if they couldn't be in love and still be friends? Was it worth the trade?

She gripped her father's hand again. "Could we focus, please? If it isn't too much trouble?"

He pursed his lips, one of those British glowers in place. "He hurt you."

She dragged in a long breath. "Because everything's changed."

"Everything does." The offense faded from his eyes again, and that hard-won, ready-to-be-amused peace replaced it. "That's no reason to scare a decade off your father's life and break his heart with your tears. Change can be so very good."

She settled back against the couch and rested her gaze again on the crackling fire. Some change was good, yes. Coming home. Finding Papa. But what felt like a risk three months ago felt safe as a pony in contrast to this. "Sometimes. Sometimes it can tear us apart. How are we to know which is which?"

"We can't. But we can pray." He cradled her fingers between both his hands, effectively pulling her gaze back to his. His eyes shone with certainty. "And know that whatever comes, we're not alone anymore. And *that*, my dear, certainly changes everything."

Brook managed a smile, then looked again to the fire. Before, it had always been Justin beside her through the hard places. Her cold supposed-father ignoring her existence. Now she had Papa to work through the questions with her.

Her fingers found her necklace and freed it from the collar of the livery jacket so that she could toy with the dangling pearls. Questions, so many questions plaguing her.

And Justin still didn't even know what they were.

Eighteen

The sun shone through the window, the birds chorused their pleasure, and Brook dug her fingers into her palm. He would not leave the quicker if she shouted. Tempting as it was. "You cannot honestly have expected anything different, Lord Pratt."

He prowled about her mother's drawing room, a stain of shadow against the jewel-toned fabrics. Though he smiled, it could shift to a snarl at any moment. "I beg you to reconsider, my lady. I can give you all you could ask for in a husband. Independence, respect, affection. And you could stay here, in the area you've come to love so well. When we combine our estates, we will be the single greatest landowner in Yorkshire."

When? When they combined their estates?

Un. Deux. Trois. She dragged in a seething breath. "We both know it's that property you want, not me."

His gaze raked over her much as it had her first morning by the sea. At once hot and cold. Lingering and dismissive. "I assure you, my lady. I want both."

236

Had he been close enough, she would have slapped him. "Watch yourself, Pratt."

"I would rather watch you." Kitty would call the note in his voice charm—she must have been deaf to the conceit and greed. He slid around the wingback chair with the look of a panther readying to pounce. "Come, darling. Who else would overlook your eccentricities?"

She bristled when he motioned toward her trousers. She only wore them riding, and only since the split skirt was ruined with blood and mud.

"I don't much care if anyone 'overlooks my eccentricities.'" She planted her hands on her hips to prove it. "Let them think what they will. I will be who I am, and I will make no apologies. And if that means I eschew society and forgo the marriage mart . . . well, what a shame."

Something flashed in his eyes, dark and impatient. "Do you think Stafford will come home and sweep you into his arms and make you a duchess?"

Silence was the only answer she would give, along with a glare she hoped was stony and cool.

But her fingers dug deeper into her palms.

"But why would you want that?" The corners of his lips pulled up, though she wouldn't insult the word smile by calling it such. "You've the shared history, I realize. But you must have seen the man he's become. No room in his heart for anything but the duchy. He'll be like his uncle—cold, hard, unbending. A wife for the sole purpose of providing heirs, a mistress on the side whom he can dismiss at will. Safe and controlled and measurable."

He prowled closer. "Does that sound like you, my dear? Safe and controlled and measurable?"

What she wouldn't give for another six inches in height, so she could meet him eye to eye. A narrowing of them would have to suffice, and a tilt of her chin. "You know nothing of us." And given that *she* didn't know what she wanted when it came to Justin, Pratt certainly couldn't.

"I know you write to him every week. I know he hasn't written back to you even once."

A tempest crashed over her. More aimed at Justin than Pratt, but as he wasn't handy, she unleashed it where she might and slashed a hand through the air. "How could you *possibly*—"

"Have you never actually spoken to the postmaster in Eden Dale? Friendly chap. Talkative."

She drilled a hand into his shoulder, pushing him back a step. "To whom I write is *none* of your concern!"

His dark eyes snapped, and he closed his hand around her wrist. "Now who had better watch herself?"

Stupid. She should have retreated. Now when she tugged, his fingers tightened. "Release me."

Instead he raised her wrist higher and placed a kiss on her palm.

Her skin turned to ice. Kitty was due any minute, and if she came in upon this, it would break her heart. "I said—"

"I heard you." So calm, so mocking. He lowered her wrist but didn't let it go. "Or do you think to turn to Worthing? Don't put your hopes there, my darling. He may flirt with you as he does every other female, but he doesn't intend to marry you. His estates are still flush from his mother's dowry, and he enjoys the hunt far too much to settle with just one woman before he must."

Her nerves snapped. Without question, Brice flirted too much, with everyone. But she and Papa had stayed two weeks in Sussex with the Duke of Nottingham's family last month, and she had spent countless hours talking with Brice. There were moments when it wasn't just flirtation. Moments when he seemed to gaze into her very soul. Moments when she wondered if his lips would ignite the same fire Justin's had . . . and moments when she was sure they wouldn't. "You know nothing about my thoughts. Don't hazard to guess."

"I know more than you think." He finally unfurled his fingers, letting her go. Stepped to the window. "I'm not a bad option for you, Brook."

She had never given him permission to call her that—but pointing it out felt weak. "I don't need an option, Lord Pratt."

His eyes narrowed at whatever he saw out the window. "I daresay you will when Kitty is through and your reputation is slashed to ribbons." He nodded in the direction of the drive.

"You think to frighten me with *that* threat? Kitty is one of my dearest friends." Brook moved to a different window and spotted the familiar Rushworth carriage. An open one today, displaying Catherine in all her splendor. No Rush beside her, which meant no leash on her tongue. It always made for a more entertaining visit. Though it did occasionally make Brook wonder what her cousin said about *her* when she wasn't in the room.

"My cue to disappear, I think." Pratt spun and reached for the hat he had tossed to a table when he barged in fifteen minutes prior. "And if you would deny having seen me . . ."

Brook sent a pointed look toward the stables, in front of which his Benz was parked.

"Say I've been with your father the whole time."

"And why should I?"

"I saved your life—now I'm calling in the favor."

Justin would have said it with irony. Brice with mirth. Pratt delivered it with nothing but harsh sobriety as he reached the door in a full-length stride.

She shook her head and sent a glance to the painting from which her mother reigned. Forever captured in the Frederick Worth gown Brook had discovered in her wardrobe, still beautiful with its deep green fabric shot through with gold. In the painting she wore the emerald and diamond necklace Papa had first shown Brook.

And the bracelet she had worn to the hunt. The one Lady Catherine had admired. Rubies and diamonds.

Actually, Kitty always took note of whatever jewelry she wore. In part it seemed polite interest, but Brook had begun to wonder if her cousin believed those tales her mother told . . . or if, perhaps, Henry Rushworth—who had never replied to their letter—had taken something from his brother and sister-in-law and sent it to Brook's mother. It would explain the letter—and Catherine's veiled interest.

Fire eyes. Rubies? Diamonds? It seemed it ought to be one or the other. Unfortunately, that barely narrowed down her mother's collection.

Mr. Graham cleared his throat from the drawing room door. "Lady Catherine Rushworth, my lady."

Brook glanced down at her trousers. She could change first, but she still hoped to have time for a ride this afternoon. "Show her in, Mr. Graham. Thank you."

The butler bowed and disappeared.

It was scarcely half a minute later that Catherine stormed in. "Where is he?"

Brook sighed. "And a sunny good-day to you, cousin."

Lady Catherine narrowed her eyes. "I saw his car."

Brook nodded, pressing her lips together. When would Catherine see that Pratt wasn't worth her affection? That he would do nothing but hurt her? "I don't know where he might have gone." For all she knew he was cataloguing the silverware he intended to add to his estate. Though if he tried it, Mr. Graham might personally give him the heave-ho.

Worth seeing, that.

Catherine advanced with startling speed. No amusement sparked in her green eyes today, no promise of biting jests or shared laughter. Just fierceness. Desperation. "You'll not have him."

The *him* must still be Pratt. Though why Catherine thought Brook *wanted* him, she couldn't say. "On that we agree. You know I would never—"

"Don't try to placate me. I know very well he was going to propose before you leave for London, but *I* am the one he will be marrying. Make no mistake about that."

Brook almost put tongue to a flippant answer, but that glint in her cousin's eyes stilled it, made her opt for seriousness instead. "Catherine, I assure you I have no intention of marrying Pratt—or any man who is out only to get Whitby Park."

Catherine lifted her chin. "At least you have brains enough to know that's all he wants—all any man will want, once the gossips in London realize you're cut from the same cloth as Whitby."

Brook took an abrupt step back. "Why are you acting this way? I thought—"

"We were friends?" The glint in her eyes was ice, hard and deadly. "For a girl raised by a prince's mistress, you can be charmingly naïve, cousin."

Brook staggered another step back. She had spent more time with Catherine than with Regan or Melissa, had thought . . . All these months, she had ignored Papa's mutters about the Rushworths, had chalked it up to a lingering animosity toward his would-be rival for Mother's affections. "What are you saying?"

Catherine shadowed her, no light in her eyes to speak of life. No curve to her lips to say she was joking now. "I've suffered your company long enough. Listening to you go on and on about that stupid beast of yours, your ridiculous cars, your precious duke—and now Worthing to boot. But I've had enough. Your family has taken enough from mine. First the Fire Eyes, and now Pratt."

Though the glare hadn't cooled Brook's blood, the words did. She felt sculpted from ice. "The Fire Eyes?" She couldn't move. It hurt too much. "You? You were the one who hired him?"

Lady Catherine lifted her perfectly plucked brows. "Hired *whom*, darling? I can't think what in the world you're talking about."

Brook's fingers curled into her palms, finding the marks they had left from Pratt's visit. The Rushworths had been in the area that night, hadn't they? Somewhere in the muddle of memory, she remembered spotting their carriage leaving Delmore. But how, how could her cousin, her friend have a part in it? "I could have been killed, and I don't even know what these Fire Eyes are!"

Before she saw it coming, a hand connected with her cheek, and Catherine followed it with a push that sent Brook stumbling back into a chair. "How *stupid* do you think I am?"

She stood again, though slowly, ready to defend herself this time.

Her cousin spun away. "Did you honestly think it would look like a coincidence, sending your duke off as you did, to the very place they were found? You're just like your mother." She wheeled around again, looking as though she would lunge.

Brook stood prepared.

Perhaps that was why Catherine stopped and contented herself with another snarl. "You see how it ended for *her*. Don't make the same mistake, my lady."

Now it was Brook who lunged, though Catherine charged for the door. She caught her by the elbow in the threshold. "What are you talking about? What happened to my mother?"

Catherine jerked her arm free and produced a heartless smile. "How am I to know, cousin? I was not yet two when she suffered that *unfortunate* accident. But I will say this." She stepped into the hall and dragged a scathing glare down Brook's riding habit.

"Your family seems to have bad luck around horses. Perhaps you ought to take more care."

Oh, she would take care all right. She would take care to get to the bottom of whatever this Fire Eyes business was—and would assuredly *not* be intimidated by the likes of Catherine Rushworth.

Tempted to slam every door she could find, Brook stormed for the stables. And told herself the tears burning her eyes were from anger and not hurt at the betrayal.

Deirdre would have screamed, had the hand over her mouth not cut off all her air. It took her only a moment to recognize the hand, the arm, the familiar cologne. Pratt. Her panic increased when he pushed her into the empty parlor and clicked the door shut behind them.

Drawing a steadying breath in through her nose, she reminded herself that he was like any other beast, able to sense her fear. Calm was her only hope.

His fingers peeled off her mouth, and he spun her around. Eyes hard and dark as jet, he backed her into the wall and trapped her there with an arm on either side of her. "I'm done being kind." His voice came out low and deadly. "She refused me."

Deirdre's whole body shuddered. "I tried. She is willful and—"

"I know what she is." One of his hands closed around her throat. Not squeezing, but making it clear he could. His gaze burned into hers. "I have a man in your village, ready to light a torch and toss it to the O'Malley roof one night if I but give the word."

He didn't need to tighten his fingers—his words choked her, and she had to shut her eyes against the sight of him. Though then the images of her mum and siblings swam before her, from strong, near-grown Killian toiling in the fields, all the way down to little Molly. "What do you want from me? I've done all you asked." Stolen things. Told him things her ladyship would hate her for telling. She would get sacked, possibly arrested, if ever the Whitbys discovered it.

But she had risked it, because she had known his favor would turn to threat if she refused. That the wee ones would pay for it if she tried to do the noble thing.

He eased away, dropped his hand. "Nothing yet. But when I ask, I want no questions. I want obedience. Are we understood?"

Her stomach churned, and bile rose in her throat. A blank check for evil—that was what he demanded.

And she had no choice but to nod.

Justin pressed the brake longer than necessary. Waited, though the carriage had long since passed, to turn the wheel. And when turn it he did, it was with a sigh. Brook must be furious with him—no, worse than furious. Hot anger would have been banked, cooled.

She would be ice.

Eden Dale lay behind him, Whitby yet ahead, but he let the Rolls-Royce motor its way up the long, winding drive to Whitby Park. He had already done his homework. Phoned Thate . . . and Cayton . . . and Aunt Caro to be sure no one had heard conflicting information. To guarantee that, indeed, the Whitbys would be at home yet today, not already in London for the Season.

That was part of the plan. Catch her here, where she was most comfortable. Where he could more easily get her alone.

That was critical. Utterly critical to his plan. Given the beautiful spring day and the looming departure, he was hopeful he could find her out of doors. The gardens . . . the seafront . . .

anywhere he could come upon her by herself. Where he could charge right up to her, turn her around, and kiss her.

By his calculations, he may well end up with a fist to his gut or a palm slapping his cheek. But that would be fine—it would get her back to fury, take her from ice to fire. From there, it would be a matter of apology and confession.

"Please, Lord." His chest had felt so tight for months. Too many times he had relived that kiss outside his townhouse, the way she had clung to him, met him measure for measure. He could win her yet. He could. There was a fire inside her for him, and he could fan it, turn one kind of love into another.

He hoped. But then, all the letters he wrote, pouring out his heart . . . and she had never written him back. Not except that once—a letter that had made precious little sense. A collection of *still* and *again* and *yet* that appealed to a context he didn't have.

It seemed she had written others that hadn't reached him.

"Please, Lord." To think that she had instead *chosen* not to write, not to reply—no. He couldn't accept that. It would undo him.

Even if that one letter *had* mentioned plans to go to Sussex to spend a fortnight with the Duke of Nottingham's family.

He set his mouth, beat back the fear. They would bridge the gap. They must. Pick up where they'd left off, as they had always used to do. A kiss, a punch, some heated Monegasque shouting . . . then hopefully another kiss, softer words, and the months would melt away. He would—

He slammed on his brakes as he came around a bend, and coal-black forelegs pawed at the air beside him. The hooves barely missed taking a layer of paint off his door as the horse's rider pulled the beast back.

His heart wouldn't slow for an hour. "Where the devil did you come from?" He asked the question of the horse . . . then noted the hands pulling on the reins. Feminine, elegant, perfect. He took the car out of gear and leaned back in his seat.

Brook focused first on calming the horse and then lifted sparking green eyes to him. "One might ask you the same question, Duke."

Oh yes, she was angry. And he had to smile. She was hatless, and the wind had whipped many a curl free of its chignon. Her habit was a deep green, bringing out the emerald of her eyes. His smile turned to a grin. "You're wearing trousers."

She patted the horse's midnight neck. "That's what you say to me after a five-month silence? 'You're wearing trousers'? *Really?*"

He chuckled and turned sideways to better look at her. It had been six years since he'd last seen her in them. And his castoffs had never hugged her legs quite like these did. "They look good on you. Though I have a feeling your aunt disagrees."

Usually such an observation would have won him a grin, a laugh. Apparently she was in no mood to be amused today. She gathered the reins as if ready to turn the horse back into the open land.

"Brook." He reached out, though she was too far away. He needed to touch her, even if only to put her hand on his arm. But he was in his car, she on the horse. Obviously a kiss could not bridge the gap. *Lord, give me the words, please. I beg you. Help me make this right.* "I know you're angry with me."

She breathed a mirthless laugh. "Oh. Oh yes. But don't flatter yourself—you're not the one who sent me out here in a rage today."

"Who did?" At her glare, his hand fell to the door and rested on the sun-warmed metal. He sighed. And latched his gaze upon the one thing that might draw her out. "This is Oscuro?"

"*Oui.*"

The French warmed him. Let him smile. "He's magnificent." Nearly as magnificent as his rider. "You broke him."

"Never." She rubbed a hand up the stallion's neck again. "But we've reached an agreement. I let him taste freedom, so long as he does so with me on his back."

He still thought it had been foolish of her to try—but he wasn't about to say so again now. "Whatever you want to call it, you succeeded. Just as you said you would."

She lifted her chin and spun Oscuro to face the house. "Some of us believe in keeping our word."

A dagger obviously aimed at him . . . though he wasn't quite sure what he had done now, or failed to do, to deserve it. He put the car back in gear so he could keep pace when she clicked the horse into a walk. "I suppose, then, I should have made you promise to actually answer my letters."

"Your *letters*?" She drew Oscuro to a halt again and sent Justin the look she had always called the English glower. When had she picked that up? "How am I to answer what does not exist? Though I suppose I oughtn't to be surprised that you yet again chose silence when you said you would write. Even after you . . ."

After he kissed her? He took the car from gear, set the hand brake, and let himself out. "I wrote to you every other day at the start. Every week at the end, though it was disheartening never to hear back from you."

"What?" She shook her head, though her glower shifted to a frown. "I wrote to *you* every week. But never once got a letter in return."

Unease went tight inside him. Much like his chest had felt these five months when thinking of her, but more. More urgent. "You sent them first to my solicitor, for him to forward?"

"Yes! Like Thate and Cayton—I checked the direction against theirs." Her gaze went distant for a moment, then she dismounted.

Justin shook his head. "They can't all have gone astray."

"No." She shoved a few stray curls from her face and spun toward the house, then all the way around, toward the village. "Someone has been tampering with my post."

The way she said it, so calm, so sure—with dread certainty instead of outrage—tied another knot inside him. "Are the servants still unwelcoming?"

She shook her head, her eyes distant. "They have been fiercely loyal and protective since the attack."

The attack. Most of the time, he avoided thinking of that, or remembering the bruising on her face in November. He could not dwell on it if he wanted to remain sane.

He reached out again, this time able to rest a hand on her shoulder. The feel of it was familiar and sent warmth flowing through his veins.

It turned to ice when she shrugged him off.

He swallowed down the hurt. "Thate said the man's identity is still in question."

"He was using the name Fitz Jenkins, but it wasn't his real one." She turned back to the horse. "We need to talk to my father about this."

This was not how he had envisioned their reunion going. He couldn't exactly follow conversation about her attacker with a passionate embrace, but he also couldn't just follow her up to the house like this. He reached over her to put a hand on the saddle, effectively blocking her way.

When she sent him an exasperated look, he met it with a smile. "Will he let anyone else ride him?"

Her eyes glinted. Her brows lifted. "The right someone. My father has, and one of the jockeys. Though only one."

Justin inclined his head toward the Rolls-Royce. "Trade?"

She looked to the car, and the corners of her lips curled up—the exact smile she'd first worn when she spotted the car idling outside the palace in Monaco. A soothing reminder that despite new English glowers, she was still Brook. When she returned her gaze to his, challenge gleamed. "If Oscuro will allow it."

Nearly fourteen years of friendship, and he had to prove himself. But then, if he had his way, friendship would be only part of what they would have from now on.

He grinned and backed away, toward the horse's head. Holding out a hand for the beast to sniff, he stroked the other down his neck and whispered in French into his ear. "I need your help, boy. I don't want to disappoint her—you understand that, I think."

Oscuro nickered and bumped Justin's hand with his nose.

"He isn't biting you—congratulations." Brook handed him the reins and took a step toward the car.

Justin reached an arm to halt her. His hand settled on her waist. "Brook."

Rather than look at him, she stared at the car. "How did your trip go, Justin? Did you set everything in order?"

"I did." Though it gave him no pride to say so. The entire time he was away, he kept hearing Aunt Caro and Brook in his head, telling him it wasn't enough, not when he had hurt his family for it. He kept seeing his father with grief-stricken eyes, pulling him close. He kept remembering Uncle Edward, who never once looked at him with any warmth, saying, "*Focus first on Stafford, boy. People come and go, but the land stays forever.*"

God had dealt with Justin while he dealt with business. Dealt with him for trying to strengthen the outward when he should have been giving the inward to Him. He'd spent so many hours on his knees these past two months, he had memorized every stitch of the quilts over which his hands had been clasped.

All of which he'd told her already . . . none of which she knew.

"Good." Her voice came out quiet, but by no means soft.

"I prayed you would succeed. I prayed . . . I prayed you would find whatever it was you needed."

"I did." He wanted to draw her close, but she stood so stiff, so immovable. "I found that it was here all along. Which I knew, but . . . perhaps I needed the time alone with the Lord. To fully understand who I needed to be, and who I must *not* be, at all costs."

She looked up at him now, though not as she used to. No smile teased her lips, no sparkle lit her eyes. "Good."

That was all she could say? His fingers pressed against her waist, though she wouldn't come any closer. "Brook . . ."

"It is my turn now, Justin." She stepped away, and her eyes went from blank to snapping—but not with the love he'd hoped to find in them. With determination. "My turn to find some answers. They've been waiting far too long."

She opened the door of the car and slid in, scarcely smiling as she ran her hands over the wheel. So very unlike her.

All of it, so very unlike her.

He turned back to Oscuro. The horse at least proved she was still his Brook. Chasing the dangerous when a sane person would have chosen a known quantity. Never settling for the mere exceptional when the magnificent was just out of reach.

The beast let him mount, though he shifted, skittish, as Justin settled his weight in the saddle. He murmured a few French nothings, as he always did with Alabaster, and Oscuro tossed his head in seeming recognition of the words.

Brook put the Rolls-Royce in gear and, finally, shot him a look he knew well. Challenge. "I bet I can beat you there."

He lifted a brow. "You think my car is faster than your horse?"

The familiar, blessed, impish smile possessed her lips. "I think its driver is faster than his rider. Ready?"

He twisted the reins around his hands and crouched forward. "*Allons-y.*"

Nineteen

Brook had meant the ride to clarify. She had meant to come back inside with a mind cleared of Catherine's insinuations and Pratt's ill-placed proposal. She had meant to put the hurts and suspicions and outrage in their proper places before she spoke with Papa.

To her dismay, she wanted to stomp and scream and cry as much now as she had two hours ago, though it was no longer only the fault of her neighbors.

Or maybe it was.

The postmaster was talkative, Pratt said. Was he bribable? And was Pratt low enough to steal her mail to keep her from communicating with Justin?

The question made ice chase the fire in her veins.

She handed the key to the car back to Justin—and plotted how to get it from him again when she was better able to enjoy it. When the questions weren't buzzing so loudly.

He slid it absently in his pocket, his gaze still on Oscuro as Russell led him into the stables. "Magnificent. Is he ready for the races?"

"He will be by summer." She couldn't help the lift of her

head, the tilt of her chin. "Ready to admit I knew what I was doing?"

When he shot that grin at her, her stomach flipped. Which unsettled her all the more. She had hoped that by the time he returned, she would know her own mind and heart concerning him. Instead, she was more confused than ever. She wanted to kiss him again, to test her reaction . . . and yet wanted to steer far clear and force their relationship back to what it had been before.

"I never doubted you knew what you were doing," he said. "I just didn't want to see you get hurt in doing it."

"You started it." The tease slipped out. And somehow, her heart went cold in its wake instead of warmer. No, not cold. Sad. So much had changed. And communication about it had been stolen from them. Now where were they to go?

Justin chuckled and offered his arm. "I taught you to ride astride, not to break horses. To shoot at targets, not the weapon from a villain's hand."

"You gave me a taste for risk-taking."

"My lessons were hardly risks."

"They felt like it at the time." She slid her hand into the crook of his elbow. He must have kept active while he was away—his arm was firmer than before, the muscle larger.

His gaze went to her wool-clad legs. "Those I like."

The way he said it, the way he looked at her . . . he was *flirting*. Justin Wildon, Duke of Stafford, her oldest friend, was flirting with her. And she could think of nothing clever to say. Brice's words she could parry with skill, but it was different with Justin. She could think only of the inane. "I have your hat—you left it at Aunt Mary's." *That night. "The End of an Era."*

He reached up as if surprised to find it not on his head and then grinned again. "Keep it. I've given up on the thing." Then he cast a glance over his shoulder again. "Finest stallion I've seen in years. Are you studding him out? I'm considering breeding Alabaster this year—"

"And now we're going to talk about horse breeding?" She shook her head and pulled him toward the house. "Some would say a lady shouldn't discuss such things."

"Some are idiots. Will your father make all the decisions for Oscuro while you sit quietly by?"

He still knew how to make her smile, even if it faded quickly. "We'll agree to no fees until after the races, when he proves himself a champion."

"So you can gouge me? Does a lifetime of friendship not gain me a discount?"

The feigned outrage warmed some of the cold spots inside, though it didn't last. Not when her eyes fell to the bracelet on her wrist.

She had bigger matters to attend than Oscuro. "We'll see. In the autumn." Her father would be in the library. She aimed them toward that door.

Justin stepped into her path. "Brook, might we . . . have a moment first?"

His eyes were a bright sapphire today, and the April sun caught his hair and set it alight. His jaw had gotten more chiseled in his absence, his shoulders broader. Her chest went tight. "What?"

He sighed and glanced over his shoulder. Took her hands. "I was hoping . . . for some time alone with you before we join your father."

Yes, she had dreamed of this, of him, while he was away. But the other dream always overshadowed it. Thunder and lightning and darkness. "You had time."

He gave her half a smile, crooked and so very charming. "It didn't go as I planned."

"And what did you plan?"

His gaze dropped to her lips, warmed her. He eased closer, their clasped hands still between them. "Shall I show you?"

Yes! "No." Saying it made the pressure compound behind her nose and eyes, but she held his gaze. Let go his hands. "There is too much you don't know."

"You'll tell me. I'll tell you. We'll do as we've always done and—"

"No." She had to look away. Otherwise she'd forget how to speak, gazing into those familiar eyes, forget the heavy truth that had settled in her heart during her ride. A truth too-long forgotten already. "It isn't like it always was."

"No. It will be better." His voice thrummed over her nerves, and they caught fire when he feathered a hand over her cheek, into her hair. "We can make it better."

"Justin—"

His lips silenced hers, held them captive. A soft touch that promised so much more—that took her back those months to London, then forward again through the many nights she had lain awake agonizing over whether they could make each other happy or would destroy each other in trying.

Perhaps if she could relax, give herself over to the sensation again, she would know. But her mind wouldn't still. Why hadn't he listened to her? She couldn't think about this now, not clearly, not given Catherine's hissing words and the threats in Pratt's eyes.

Justin pulled away. His eyes were dark, his brow questioning. "Brooklet?"

She could only shake her head and step around him. He should have listened. Or come back yesterday, or tomorrow, or even an hour from now.

"Brook."

"You don't understand." But he would in a moment, if he followed her. Which he did, as she strode for the library door and opened it.

"Brook!"

He reached for her arm. She all but leaped into the library to avoid his fingers.

Her father looked up from behind his paper and took to his feet with a smile. "Duke! You made it home when planned, I see."

Justin sighed and pasted on a smile. "I did, yes. Forgive me for arriving without warning."

"You are always welcome here. You know that." But rather than striding forward with a hand outstretched, Papa frowned and moved toward Brook. "What is the matter, my dear?"

"It was Catherine." Neither of them could know what she referenced, so she drew in a breath and shoved the flyaway curls from her face. "She's the one who hired my attacker—she must be. She said we took the Fire Eyes from her family."

"Fire Eyes?" Justin looked from her to her father.

Papa came to an abrupt halt, thoughts whipping through his eyes. "She said that?"

Justin shifted, putting himself halfway between them. "What are the Fire Eyes?"

Her father looked to him. "We are not entirely certain—jewels, but that is all we could determine. Did she say what they were when she mentioned them?"

"No." Brook's hands curled into fists that did nothing to squeeze out the hurt in her heart. "But it links her to that man. You need to call the constable—"

"She would deny it." Sighing, Papa set aside the paper still in his hand and came over to clasp her shoulder. "And I had him looking for a connection to them when we first suspected it was Rushworth jewels."

She snapped upright, her mouth agape. But Papa had never trusted them. Not like she had.

He shook his head. "There was nothing."

"He nearly killed me, and there's nothing we can do?"

Her father looked deep into her eyes, his brow still drawn. "Tell me everything she said to you."

She did so, word for word, including the slap—at which point Justin lurched a step forward, outrage snapping in his eyes.

"She *struck* you? And you *let* her?"

Leave it to him to make it sound like her fault—and make her want to smile about it. "I assure you, had she advanced again, she would have taken a fist to her upturned nose."

Papa sighed. "Then what?"

"Then . . ." Swallowing did nothing to make the lump in her throat go away. "Then she said she was not so stupid as to think Justin's travels a coincidence, that he was in the place they originated. That I was just like my mother, and look where it led her. She intimated . . . Papa, I don't think the carriage accident was an accident. Not entirely, anyway."

There. She'd said it, that truth that had pounded her brain with every thunder of Oscuro's hooves.

Her father spun away, muttering a word she couldn't quite make out but that she suspected was a curse, given the way he seemed at a loss as to what to do with his hands. After a moment he clasped them behind his back in that way of his. "Catherine was trying to upset you. It was a fierce storm. The rain had wrought havoc on the roads. The carriage overturned. A tragic accident, nothing more."

Storm? *Thunder and lightning and darkness.*

Brook, hands shaking, sank to the edge of a chair. "No one ever mentioned that. Is that what I've been dreaming of all these months? The storm that killed her?"

Papa looked at her as if the very question would make him unravel.

Justin, when he stepped into view, instead looked at her like her sanity already had unraveled. "You were far too young to remember anything from that night."

"I know that." And she didn't need him to make her feel ridiculous. She pivoted, strode to a shelf, though all the titles upon it blurred together. "It has always been so vague. So frightening. Impressions, nothing more. But you cannot know how it has tormented me."

Justin held up his hands. "I can imagine. But focus on the facts for now. This is a serious accusation you're lobbing Lady Catherine's way. And linking it to your mother's death, which she could not *possibly* be responsible for, will do nothing to gain you believers among the constabulary."

She wasn't trying to get the constable to believe her, though—just them, the two men who mattered most. Dragging in a long breath, she fixed her gaze on her father. "What about Catherine's parents? Her father—Mother's cousin?"

He shook his head. "They were never close but never seemed at odds. His wife was jealous and contentious, but she would never have taken it so far."

"But how far *would* she have taken it? Perhaps the accident was an accident, but what sent her on that journey?" Brook splayed her hands, begging them to understand. To believe. "Why would she leave here, with me, with the letters from you? Why, when Collette arrived, did my mother tell her to take me away and not to find you? *Why?*"

Papa shook his head, the muscle in his jaw ticking. "Questions I have asked myself too long."

Justin eased forward. "The more immediate question is what Lady Catherine wants, and how far *she* will go to get it. The hint about my having traveled to these Fire Eyes' origin is little help. I was in Africa and India both, and both are rich in mines of all kinds."

Brook folded her arms over her middle. "Whatever they are, it seems my mother had them, perhaps unwittingly. It is all linked. *That* is certainly no coincidence."

For a long moment, neither man made any response. Then Justin's eyes went dark. "You didn't write to me about any of these concerns, did you?"

She shook her head, though his meaning still made her stomach churn. "I told you in November there were things I could not put in a letter."

"Good. I think we need to operate on the assumption that someone has stolen your correspondence purposefully."

"Stolen your—" Papa cursed again, louder this time. "Why have you said nothing of this to me, Brook?"

"We just realized it." Justin shoved his hands into his pockets. His shoulders had edged back. His spine had gone straight. He looked, standing there in a casual suit of clothes, perfect confidence in his every line, like a duke. "I wrote her dozens of letters, she says she got none. She sent me dozens, I received only one."

He hadn't mentioned *that*. "Which one?"

His eyes flashed. "It was dated the twenty-third of February. A week before you were set to go to Sussex." He said *Sussex* as if it were the birthplace of all annoyance.

"When we were still in London for Mary's birthday." Papa's eyes went calculating as he thought through it. "The one you posted yourself, that day we went out for a drive."

She could see the suspicions mounting in his eyes, as they had in her mind. The implications were unmistakable—she had sent other letters from London and Sussex. But they had not reached him, either.

The postmaster in Eden Dale could hardly be blamed.

She sank onto the edge of Papa's favorite chair.

Justin paced to the unlit fireplace. "Which servants travel with you?"

"My valet, Lewis. Her maid, O'Malley. Clark, who drives the carriage with them and our luggage. That's all."

Justin had turned back toward them but did not approach. "Does the maid still dislike you, Brook?"

Her father sucked in a breath. "She . . . ? Brook! What else have you not told me?"

A headache was gathering behind her eyes. "It was nothing to burden you with, Papa. The servants are all so loyal to you, it took them a while to accept that I was not out to steal all that is yours. That is all. *Je promets.*"

Her promise didn't seem to ease him any. "How long is 'a while'? How long did they not accept you after I specifically instructed them to welcome you as their mistress?"

Given the paternal fire in his eyes, he might call the servants in and dismiss each and every one of them, even though at this point they all doted on her.

Or so she thought. "Focus, Papa. We have only three suspects right now, and I daresay, whichever of them did it, it wasn't a matter of dislike. Pratt said something today about how I'd never received any letters from Justin—intimating he got the information from the postmaster."

Her father narrowed his eyes. "And what was Pratt doing here?"

She waved a hand. "Proposing. But the point is that he may have bribed—"

"*Proposing?*"

The twin responses from Justin and her father made Brook roll her eyes. "*Oui*, and I, of course, fell at his feet in adoration and said yes. Because we all know how much I like him. Again, could we please focus, gentlemen? On the possible bribery?"

Papa tugged on his waistcoat. "What kind of man proposes to a young lady without first speaking with her father?"

"The kind who knows well her father would refuse his blessing." She managed a smile for him and resisted the urge to glance at Justin. "Bribery, Papa."

"Hmph." He stalked to the window, glaring in the direction of Pratt's land. "Lewis has been with me for twenty-five years. I cannot think he would do this—he has no family to support, and I have set aside a living for him when it is time for him to retire. But . . . those years have established a friendship, and if he believed you a pretender, as those who came before . . ."

"O'Malley's family is struggling." She didn't want to say it, to admit it. Didn't want to think it could be Deirdre, with whom she'd finally established a rapport. "I've been sending extra funds, but she doesn't know that. I know little of Clark."

"I know little more—he only joined us last year. O'Malley has been here nigh unto eight." Her father nodded, staring into space. "We will look into all of them. We cannot afford to assume."

Justin was still glowering. "Have we two issues here, or one? Are Pratt and Lady Catherine working toward separate goals—he, you and she, the Fire Eyes—or are they somehow working together?"

Brook drew in a breath and leaned back into the chair. "Pratt would have no claim on any Rushworth jewels. And Kitty—Catherine." She wouldn't use the familiar name, not anymore. "She's in love with him, so she certainly would not aid him in his pursuit of Whitby Park. They must be separate."

"I agree."

Justin nodded once, then shook his head. "You always have had a knack for finding trouble, Brooklet, but this . . . Pratt is obviously not opposed to stooping low to get his way. And if Lady Catherine would really hire a man to threaten you over jewels, what would she do because of Pratt's affection for you?"

"It isn't affection—it's greed. But your point is valid." She raised a hand to rub at the muscles gone taut in her neck. So many hours spent laughing together. So many times she had listened while Catherine pined for Pratt. How could her cousin think Brook low enough to pose a threat to her relationship with him? "They may be unrelated at the core, but that does not mean that one will not exacerbate the other. Pratt thoughtfully warned me that Catherine will try to rip apart my reputation in London. I didn't believe him then, but . . ."

Papa's face finally relaxed. "We can only hope. If you complement her gossip with that horrible pink thing your aunt commissioned for your debut, we might have reason to come home again by June."

No doubt she would be ready well before then. Brook grinned. "I plan to wear the gown Grand-père sent. But have no fear, Papa—I'll not force you to too many balls."

"Your aunt will try to have us at something every night of the week."

"United, we can stand against her."

Justin had lifted a brow and seemed to squelch a grin. "Pink? You look terrible in pink."

"Thank you ever so much for noticing."

His chuckle sounded like memories, indulgent and carefree. "You've always been quick to proclaim it—I don't know why your aunt would ever dare try to put it on you. What did the prince send?"

"Oh, the loveliest gown." It seemed trivial, in light of all else they needed to talk about. And yet not, because it was a gift from her grandfather, one that proved he still thought of her, still loved her. "Pale green, with a blue overlay of beading. Wait until you see it."

Justin smirked. "Green? For a debut? Only you would dare wear something other than white or pale pink, Brooklet." Then his eyes shifted. They went softer, and that flirtatious gleam entered them again. "Don't forget you've promised me your first dance—after you open the floor with your father, of course."

"I haven't forgotten." Her smile, though, would only stretch halfway before it felt too heavy. Too false. Sighing, she met her father's gaze again. How was she supposed to worry with filling up her dance card when her mother's death still loomed over her, when mysterious jewels taunted her, when friends declared themselves enemies, when threats seemed to lurk everywhere?

Papa moved to the chair and rested a hand on her shoulder. "She has been gone this long, my dear. Much as we both need the answers, there is no urgency."

Because she must, she nodded. But she couldn't shake the feeling that in fact there *was*.

Twenty

Twilight possessed the heath by the time Justin rolled to a halt at the carriage house of Azerley Hall. He had dined with the Edens, but when Whitby issued an invitation to stay, the pressing upon his spirit said he shouldn't. He still wasn't sure if Brook had looked disappointed or relieved.

He still wasn't sure if *he* was disappointed or relieved.

He parked his car, let himself out, and trudged his way toward the front door of his cousin's house. The drive had not, as he hoped, helped him collect his thoughts. They were still awhirl with it all. Proposals from Pratt. Threats from Lady Catherine. Something called the Fire Eyes.

And she hadn't kissed him back.

"Justin."

He started at Cayton's voice. Looking up, he could barely make out his cousin's form at the edge of the garden. "James?"

"Mm. Join me? I just ordered some wine."

Out here? The evening had turned cool, but the moon held court in the heavens, and it was rare enough that his cousin actually asked for his company. Justin altered his course, thankful he had shrugged into his great coat for the drive. "Of course."

He passed through the opening in the hedge as Cayton sat at a small table, in one of two chairs. His cousin motioned toward the second. "I need to talk to you."

Justin's stomach went tight as he pulled out the cold metal seat and lowered himself into it. "Why does that not sound pleasant?"

Cayton sighed and folded his arms, shirtsleeves gleaming white over his chest in the moonlight. "You are going to London tomorrow?"

"Yes. You?"

"Soon. But I . . . I need to go to Gloucestershire first."

At that, Justin frowned. Aunt Susan was there with Aunt Caro. But they said they were traveling tomorrow too. "To Ralin? What do you need? We can phone the castle and have it sent with your mother."

A servant emerged from the house, bottle of wine and goblets on a tray. After depositing it on the table, she scurried away.

Cayton said nothing while he poured.

Justin waited. Accepted a goblet, took a sip.

His cousin's next sigh gusted forth. "I'm betrothed."

That brought Justin's spine straighter, though he had been ready to try to recline against the wrought-iron back. He smiled—halfway, until he realized that Cayton didn't. "When? I was not aware you'd seen Lady Melissa lately."

Cayton held his glass but didn't drink. Apparently he would rather stare into its burgundy depths. "I haven't seen her since last month, when I was in Town."

The frown pulled at Justin's brows again. "You have been engaged a full month and have said nothing? Someone would have mentioned—"

"No."

No . . . what? That Cayton hadn't been engaged a full month, or that he hadn't said nothing? It must be the first. "You asked her by letter?"

"No." Sounding exasperated now, Cayton looked up. The moonlight caught on the whites of his eyes. "It's not Melissa."

"It's not . . ." The words made little sense. Justin gave up on the wine. "You told me you were in love with her." And the saying of such a thing had been striking, when he read his cousin's letter over the winter—he had not thought them close enough to warrant such a confession.

"I know. I am. Or was. Or . . ." Cayton set his goblet down with a clatter of crystal upon marble—leaned forward and rested his forehead in his hands. "I'm strapped, Justin. And a second daughter's dowry isn't going to help."

"James—"

"Don't lecture me. I know you put your estate to rights, so you no doubt think I can do the same. But I can't. It's been languishing too long, and I had no idea. I thought the steward had it well in hand—he's been taking care of everything since before I was born. But when he passed away in January and I looked over everything . . ."

Now it was Justin's turn to sigh. "I was not going to lecture. I certainly cannot judge. But are you sure marriage is the answer?"

Cayton snorted. "I have no other alternatives. It seems I don't have the luck of your father."

"James—you've been gambling?"

His cousin winced. "The horse races."

A breath of laughter slipped out before he could stop it. "Perhaps you should have tried baccarat—that was Father's game." Not that Justin was actually advising . . . but his cousin knew that.

Cayton sent him a lopsided, sad smile. "Too late. I've already sworn off it all."

For a long moment, the only sound was the chirping of the frogs from the pond. Justin took another sip of the wine. "Who, then, if not Lady Melissa?"

Cayton picked his glass up again too. "Miss Adelaide Rosten."

"Rosten." Justin held his burgundy halfway to his lips. "The name sounds familiar."

"It should—she is your neighbor in Gloucestershire. Her grandfather made his fortune in the mills."

"And she is the heiress."

Cayton nodded. "She . . . she is a sweet girl. Unobtrusive. I knew her as a child, though I scarcely paid any mind to her. She has no family left."

Try as he might, Justin could not put a face to the name. "So it is official?"

"Yes. We haven't made the announcement yet, but yes. I wanted . . . Before anyone else knows, I wanted to speak with you. Mother isn't happy with me, nor is Aunt Caro. And of course, if we're all in London, the gossips will soon pick up on it all, and Miss Rosten . . . She doesn't deserve to be lambasted. If you stood with us, it would go a long way toward smoothing things over."

For Cayton, yes. No doubt it would. But for Justin? He ran a hand over his face. Brook would no doubt be furious on behalf of her cousin. One more thing between them, if he stood beside Cayton. But what choice did he have? "Have you told Lady Melissa?"

"Not yet. I will as soon as I get to London. I realize this will put you in a tight spot with your baroness. If you . . ."

"You know I will support you, James."

Cayton's shoulders sagged. "I couldn't be sure. I know you hoped it would be neat and tidy for you. Thate married to Regan, me to Melissa, you to Brook."

It would have. But he should have known better than to expect it. "Reality is rarely so tidy though, hmm?"

"Indeed. Let us pray it is simpler for you and you can win her back."

Justin had been reaching for his glass again, but that brought his arm to a halt. "Win her *back*?"

Cayton motioned in the direction of Whitby. "Melissa told me she and Worthing are always exchanging letters, that she visited him in Sussex and had nothing but happy tales to tell." He took a drink, set his glass down again. "Don't underestimate your competition, cousin. When you didn't write to her, she had to turn *somewhere*."

"I *did* write her. More frequently than I ever had before, but—it seems someone intercepted the letters."

His cousin stared at him for a long moment, brow creased. "Are you quite serious? Why the devil would anyone do that?"

Justin shook his head. "I don't know. But someone did, and caught hers to me too, before they could be posted."

"I suppose that helps, at least—that she now knows you did write."

"Yes. Maybe." He, too, looked off toward Whitby. Only darkness met him. "But knowing it cannot undo the damage. Cannot tell us all the thoughts shared and not received. Knowing there is treachery does not bridge the gap."

It just gave Brook another focus.

Cayton trailed a finger along the crystal's edge, making it sing. "You should have won her before you left. Secured an engagement, if not married her then and there."

Justin picked his glass up again, though he didn't drink. It wouldn't warm the places Brook's reception had left so cold and hopeless. "I know."

"And what about me, I ask you? No one gives any thought to *my* reputation, and the fact that it will be left in absolute tatters if I don't get the first dance from either of you."

Brook pressed her lips together against a grin as Brice splayed a hand over his heart, his face the archetype of a tragic hero. "No doubt you'll perish from the neglect, my lord."

"I shall indeed. Cruel creatures." He turned to include Melissa in his sad-eyed gaze. "First your sister dashes my heart to pieces, and now the two of you show no regard for my tender feelings."

"Careful, Worthing." Melissa angled her sweetest smile his way, though her fingers didn't pause in their embroidery. "Keep it up, and I may decide to toss Cayton over for you, out of pity. *Then* where would you be?"

"Blessed beyond measure, to have the attention of a lady so fair." He grinned as he said it . . . then sank to a seat on the couch well away from Brook's cousin. "But let no one ever accuse me of being the means of another's heartbreak. You must resist my charm, my lady, for the sake of Lord Cayton."

Brook chuckled and set aside the book she'd been reading before Brice arrived. Aunt Mary had already taken her and Melissa to the shops, spending obscene amounts of money on hats and gloves and wraps and who knew what else. Never in her life had Brook more longed for a horse, an open stretch of land, and the sea by her side. It had been nothing like shopping in Paris with Grand-père. Especially given Aunt Mary's stony silence when Brook insisted that—no, she would *not* wear the horrid pink thing to her debut—she would wear the green gown.

Brook stood and moved to the window overlooking the street, telling herself she was *not* waiting to see a Rolls-Royce hum up the drive. Her fingers found the dangling pearls. Twisted, released, twisted again. She dropped her hand when Brice leaned into the wall beside her window. Though it took effort, she mustered a smile. "Did Ella pout at being left behind in Sussex?"

He grinned. "She put up an admirable fuss, though of course it didn't budge our mother. She's got that stubborn Scotch blood, after all." His gaze went to the window, to the road she'd been *not* watching. "Have you seen him yet? Rumor says he's been back for a few days."

Nothing ever slipped by him. It could get annoying. Nodding, Brook glanced to her cousin—and was surprised to see Regan sitting beside Melissa, though Brook hadn't heard her come in. They were talking, laughing, Regan's hand resting on the barely visible bump of the child she would deliver at the end of summer. "He came to Whitby Park before we left."

"And?" Brice lifted a dark brow. "I hope you socked him right in the nose."

A laugh slipped out. "You, who wouldn't even step on that spider at Midwynd?"

"I didn't say *I* would have socked him. But I would have cheered for you, if you chose to." Despite his grin, his eyes were serious and warm. "He deserves it, after ignoring you as he's done."

"He didn't, though." She cast another glance at her cousins, who knew nothing about mail-tampering or Fire Eyes or threats. And whom she would happily keep in the dark, since their knowing would only make their mother faint. "He wrote to me, apparently. But I never got his letters, nor did he receive mine."

Brice straightened and faced the window, putting his back to her cousins. No doubt so they wouldn't see his frown. "On both ends—that is no quirk of the post."

"No."

"Brook." He reached for her hand and held it between both of his. "I've a bad feeling. I have had ever since you told me of that man in the stables, and it's only grown worse. Whatever this Fire Eyes business is about, it's dangerous."

"I don't think this had anything to do with that. More likely it was Pratt."

Brice shook his head and held her fingers tighter. "One explanation is always more likely than two. And I don't believe in coincidences—you know that."

"I know." His faith often put hers to shame. But then, he could see things so much more clearly—it was hardly fair. "Have you any insight that could actually prove helpful, instead of worrying me more?"

He held his tongue, held her gaze as thoughts marched through his eyes. His thumb stroked over her knuckles in an absent gesture—she'd seen him do the same to his mother or sister. Still, it sent a warm little tingle up her arm. Not exactly fire, not exactly hope. But perhaps it could be fanned into something. *He*, at least, wouldn't shove her away at the first possible moment.

At length, Brice nodded. "This time next week, you will be the darling of London. Use it to your advantage."

Frustration knotted in her chest, and she looked back to the window. "You are always so sure of how I will be received, but I am not. I am still so very Monegasque, and—"

"And that is still so very intriguing. You were raised by a performer, Brook, and as a princess. You don't act quite like all the other girls. You carry yourself like a ballerina. And I am in no way trying to flatter you when I say yours is the loveliest face in Town." His tone was serious, quiet, a bid to look at him again.

She did, and found his eyes dark and intent, as they had been that first day at the house party, when he'd told her to go to Justin, whether he wanted to let her or not.

"Use it," he whispered. "Enchant them. Leave them wondering, seeking more—it will mean the press will show up wherever you are."

She tried, in vain, to tug her fingers free as she loosed an exasperated sigh. "And why in the world would I—"

"Because"—all teasing left his expression, and he gripped her hand tighter, held her arm straight down to keep her still—"where the press is, there is safety. Where reporters and photographers lurk, no one will dare make a move against you."

A chill skittered up her spine. "You make the danger sound so real."

"And the knife in your side didn't? The fists that pounded your face? The gun to your head?"

Another shiver chased the first. "Point taken."

"Then take the advice as well. I don't want to see you bruised and battered again."

She was still trying to work the pent-up breath from her lungs when movement in the doorway caught her attention. Aunt Mary's butler—and behind him, Justin, whose gaze had already found her . . . and whose eyes had already narrowed.

"The Duke of Stafford, my ladies. My lord."

"Heaven help me." Brice dropped Brook's hand. "Promise you'll attend my funeral?"

She shouldn't have laughed. When she did, Justin's narrowed eyes turned to his glower.

Justin charged toward the carriage house, telling himself he was overreacting. That he ought to be glad Brook had made such good connections. Found someone to hold her hand and whisper in her ear when she thought Justin chose not to.

He wanted to rip Worthing to shreds. Feed the pieces to hungry wolves. And then, if he were feeling spiteful, burn their waste.

"Stafford!"

He stopped within a few feet of the Rolls-Royce, his hand fisted around the key. The muscle in his jaw pulsed, but he could do nothing to calm it. He turned to see the man in question coming up behind him—and it didn't escape him that the lighthearted grin that had animated his face through the entire, interminable hour they had spent in the same room was now conspicuously absent. "Can I help you, my lord?"

Worthing flashed a smile, fleeting as lightning, and motioned toward the house. "I think you misunderstood things."

Like the way he had been holding Brook's hand so tightly in his? The way their heads were bent together? The fervor in both their expressions?

A striking contrast to the way Brook had greeted *him* two days ago. "Oh, I think I understood perfectly."

"I doubt it." Worthing had the gall to smile again, longer this time. "One of us may be in love with her, but it isn't me."

Justin gripped the key until it hurt. "So you're toying with her—is that it? Flirting with her, courting her, inviting a familiarity you have no intention of seeing through?" He took a step forward.

Worthing took one back, raised his hands in exaggerated surrender—but amusement had rekindled in his eyes. "You're spoiling for a fight, aren't you? You'll not have one from me. She means the world to me, but we are only friends."

Justin snorted. "I know all about being *only friends* with Brook."

"You used to." Lowering his hands again, Worthing's face went from mirthful to serious. Condemning. "I wonder if you've forgotten all you once knew. You've hurt her. That's unforgivable, and I won't stand by and watch you break her heart."

Of all the arrogant, presumptuous . . . He stepped closer, close enough to realize they were of a height, close enough to think that Worthing's fine, straight nose could do with a knot from Justin's fist. "You have no idea—"

"I'm not talking about the missing letters."

Justin stepped back, sucked in a breath. She had told him of that? Already?

Worthing didn't so much as flinch. "You pushed her away before you ever left—effectively tossing her heart to the ground.

Then you come back and act as though *she* is to blame for not falling at your feet."

"I did not—"

"Shut up." Worthing eased half a step closer. "You weren't here. You didn't see it. You didn't see how it hurt her not to have your friendship to rely on. Yet you show up now intent on romance, as if you can charge across that half-burnt bridge and not cause even more damage. Well, I hate to tell you, but she has bigger concerns at the moment."

Justin's lip curled. "You?"

"Don't be an idiot. I'm not the one who attacked her in November—and I'm not the one set to tread on her heart." Worthing put his hands in his trouser pockets. Such a casual move, but it didn't make him look at ease. It made him look determined. "Break it, and—I warn you—you *will* have a fight on your hands. But not the kind you want."

Justin lifted his brows and folded his arms across his chest. "You're *threatening* me?"

The man smiled again. "Someone has to. And I suspect no one else would dare cross the mighty Duke of Stafford."

Expelling an incredulous breath, Justin shook his head. "I don't need to be warned."

"Good. Then we can be friends." Worthing withdrew one of his hands and held it out, as if actually expecting Justin to shake it.

He glared at him. "If you're finished, I have somewhere I need to be."

Worthing looked at his empty hand. With a shrug, he stepped back. "I know you have. What I don't know is why you're leaving it."

Arrogant, presumptuous . . . Justin turned and climbed into his car.

Friends? No. Pieces. Wolves. Waste.

273

Twenty-One

Deirdre pinned the baroness's last curl into place and then stood back, unable to keep from smiling. "There. What do you think?"

Her ladyship stood, ran gloved hands over her gown to smooth it, and looked in the mirror. Deirdre couldn't think why she sighed as she did. The gown the prince had sent fit her to perfection, the colors set off her skin and eyes, and the style was daring enough to steal the attention of everyone who would catch a glimpse of her.

"Is something the matter, my lady?"

"No." The baroness smiled, but she touched a hand to her pearl necklace, a sure tell of inner turmoil. "But I would rather be in Yorkshire. At home."

Deirdre would be too, though Beatrix hadn't been able to fathom that she would rather stay at Whitby Park than come to Town. Perhaps if she didn't know Pratt was here too . . . if she wasn't looking over her shoulder every time she stepped out of doors, wondering when he might pounce and ask something terrible of her. . . .

Then she'd have to confess that her ladyship hadn't been

herself since they'd arrived—and especially not since she'd had the duke and Lord Worthing in the parlor two days ago, then hadn't seen hide nor hair of His Grace since. Combine the baroness's melancholy with Lady Melissa's increasing rancor that Lord Cayton had yet to pay a call, and the house was in a veritable tempest.

Shaking it off, Deirdre smiled and unbuttoned the train of the gown. "You'll be the belle of every ball, my lady. No doubt you'll have all the gentlemen in love with you, and you'll have your pick of them. Though I can't imagine a better choice than the ones you already have."

The lady muttered something in French and pressed a hand to her stomach. "Nothing feels right."

At that, Deirdre's hands stilled. She rose, met her mistress's gaze. And prayed she spoke the truth when she said, "It will be."

The light in her ladyship's eyes seemed to Deirdre desperate, anxious. No doubt due to the coming evening. "O'Malley . . ." She looked away, sighed. "How is your family?"

If it was a distraction the baroness needed, Deirdre could provide. She chuckled. "Doing well, I hear. Mum said Uncle Seamus sent her a package of silk and spices last month— he's tried to take care of us since Da died, in addition to his mum. Though my stories are sure to match his when I take my holiday—rubbing elbows as I've been with dukes, handling gifts sent from princes . . ."

The baroness smiled. It wasn't as bright as usual, had none of her characteristic abandon. But somehow, she thought it would serve the lady well in the ballrooms and drawing rooms of London.

Though sure and she knew little enough about it. At the knock on the door, she stepped aside. "That'll be his lordship. It's time."

"Where *are* they?"

Brook's eyes scanned the room as surely as her cousin's did. It was crowded with people she had never met, names her aunt insisted were important ones, faces that all seemed to turn her way.

But not Justin's. And not Cayton's. In response to Melissa's hushed, furious question, Brook could only shake her head.

Papa patted her hand, which rested on his arm. "As I taught you, my dear. Trip. Run into the most ostentatiously dressed women. Step on toes, and snub anyone you can. Perhaps sneeze in a cup or two of punch, and Mary will be begging us to leave."

"Ambrose, *please*." Aunt Mary slid behind them, tugging here and there on Brook's gown. Then she paused, clasped Brook's shoulders, and gave them a squeeze. "You look stunning."

With that peace offering, she moved to Melissa.

Brook grinned up at her father, then looked over to her cousins. Melissa looked beautiful, if a bit stormy, on her brother's arm. She spotted Brice near at hand, his usual grin in place . . . but with a shadow in his eyes.

The musicians raised their bows and, of one accord, launched into the opening set.

Her father sighed. "And so it begins. We have missed our chance to run away." He turned to her, his hand extended.

She placed her fingers on his palm and smiled up at the grin hidden away in his eyes. "I'm glad to be here with you, too, Papa."

He chuckled and led her onto the dance floor.

Even above the music, she could hear bits and snips of the conversations they spun past. *Whitby . . . all these years . . . carriage accident . . . missing . . . imposter . . . princess.* They needled, but she shrugged them off and raised her chin.

She was not an imposter, but she remembered how to be a

princess. And they would have the answers to the other soon. She knew they would.

"That's my girl." Her father's eyes gleamed as he spun with her to a different corner of the floor.

All too soon, the music changed, and he delivered her back to the edge of the ballroom.

Brice waited, apology in his eyes. He nodded to her father and held out a hand. "Stafford hasn't arrived yet. Just late, no doubt, but we can't have you without a partner so soon in the night. If I might step in?"

Her lips tugged up, and she transferred her hand to his. "Selfless of you, with so many lovely young ladies about to flirt with."

"They will swoon as well later as they would now." He led her out, his smile never faltering. "You look resplendent. That gown cannot be from London."

"Paris."

"Of course." He spun her with a flourish into his arms for the waltz. "It suits you. Shall we set the tongues to wagging?"

A laugh tickled its way from her throat. "Is there any choice with you?"

"Never."

She wasn't surprised to find that he danced without flaw. Nor that he could keep up a steady stream of banter as they sidestepped the other couples. But there was no tingle tonight where his hand grazed her back or clasped hers. Instead, her gaze went to the door each time she spun to face it.

"Keep that up, and I'll never live it down—that the beautiful baroness kept searching for another when in my arms. Cruel creature."

Laughing, she turned her face back to him and returned his smile. "Perhaps you could keep my attention if you were ready to confess what you said to him the other day—"

"I'm telling you, I threatened to pulverize him. Fisticuffs, bloody noses, the whole lot."

Brice with fists raised—the picture wouldn't form. "Mm-hmm."

"Challenged him to a duel. Sabers at dawn."

"Right." Though it made her chuckle again. "Though mind your volume, *mon ami*, or that will appear in tomorrow's *Times*."

Merriment danced in his eyes. "That would be a laugh. Though I daresay your duke would not agree. And speaking of said devil." He nodded toward the door. "I had better deliver you to him before he lops off my head."

He timed it so that they reached that edge of the dance floor as the song drew to an end. Justin had worked his way to the edge of the crowd—the thunder in his brows no doubt clearing the way for him—and Brice greeted him with a bow and transferred her hand directly to his. Naturally, he grinned. "No need to thank me."

Naturally, Justin glowered. "Didn't plan to."

"You were late."

"And you were quite happy, it seems, to take my place."

She still couldn't wrap her head around Justin being jealous over her. "Gentlemen." Making sure her smile remained bright and her words quiet, Brook curtsied to Brice and tucked her hand into the crook of Justin's elbow. "We are far from alone, *n'est pas?*"

Justin grunted and took his turn leading her onto the floor. "Five minutes late."

"And the music did not wait for you." She didn't want to be irritated, not tonight, but it shivered over her skin. Or perhaps that was his touch. She wasn't sure.

Having reached a bit of open space, Justin turned her toward him and slid a hand onto her waist. He held her closer than the two-step demanded, and her pulse sped—with that irritation, or with something better? His gaze dipped down to take in her dress, and his lips tugged up. "You look . . . nice."

"Nice?" She laughed as he spun them into the dance. "As many hours as I spent getting ready, I had better look more than nice."

"Pretty, then?" His eyes gleamed.

She lifted her brows and gripped his hand. Maybe she could do this. Maybe she could slide easily from friendship to flirtation. "Your nemesis over there chose *resplendent*. Surely you can outdo that."

He smiled, the challenge turning to a simmer. "How about this." He pulled her a little closer and leaned his head toward her ear. "I have traveled the world over these last months, but nowhere, on no continent, in no country, have I ever seen anyone half so beautiful as you."

Her fingers gripped his shoulder. "Better." Wasn't it? The trip of her heart said so. But still that voice whispered in the back of her mind that he had never used to say such things, when she was just Brook Sabatini, illegitimate daughter of an opera star. He didn't used to think he could hold her close with his arms and push her away with his words.

He didn't used to try to pair fire and ice.

She didn't mean to sigh. But it built up inside and pushed its way past the music and glitter and seeped out when she spotted Melissa a few couples away, dancing with some young gentleman Brook had never seen before.

Justin followed her gaze and winced. "Was she upset?"

He must have known that Cayton had requested the first set of dances months ago. "More like furious."

"Deservedly."

"Mm. Where is he?"

He shrugged, his muscles bunching under her hand. "I haven't seen him in a few days. We are to go riding in Hyde Park tomorrow though." Looking back to her, his eyes were deep and serious. "I have to support him. I hope . . . I hope you don't blame me for it."

She glanced again at Melissa, whose laughter looked sincere rather than feigned. Missing a ball may have spoken to Cayton's character, but it need not add to the tension between *them.* "That is between our cousins, not us."

"Good." He squeezed her fingers and then looked out over the crowd. "They're all watching you. And there's a veritable sea of young men around your father and aunt, no doubt begging to be introduced. I'll have to cut a swath to claim another dance later."

Would he even bother? "Thate is in the back room, I believe. Regan said something about an airplane pilot who was coming, and now all Thate can talk about is the air race this summer." She couldn't blame Justin if he retreated that direction. Frankly, she would rather be back there too—talking of automobiles and aeronautics—than in the ballroom.

Justin grinned. "Will he take to the skies next, do you think?"

"Regan made him swear he would keep his feet firmly planted on the ground until the baby arrives. Then . . . who knows."

His eyes went wide, and his smile crooked. "Baby? I hadn't heard. I'll have to find him and torment him about his settled and predictable life." They slowed when the music hit its cadence, and the fingers against her back splayed out. "May I pay you a visit tomorrow, my lady?"

The low warmth of his tone belied the formality of his words. Not completely unfamiliar, that. And the gleam in his eyes . . . It had changed, yes, but he had always looked at her with more warmth than anyone else. Maybe it wasn't such a change. Maybe, if she gave him a chance to share his heart, he would put her fears to rest. Maybe he would kiss her again, and the sensations would swell, and she would know that no matter what had happened in her life, he would still have wanted her.

Because looking up into his sapphire eyes, she knew without a doubt that she would have come here at some point. She would have left Monaco, and where else in the world would she have gone but to him? She had always loved him. Maybe . . . maybe she had always been *in* love with him. What, then, would he have done had Brook Sabatini come knocking upon Ralin Castle's door?

She would have to find out. And it might as well be tomorrow. Pulling out a smile, she said, "I would be delighted, Duke."

Twenty-Two

Brook poured steaming black life into a cup and prayed with the first sip that it would produce miracles. Her feet were sore. Her eyes were gritty. And so many names and faces buzzed in her head that she wanted to crawl back under her covers and shut out the world.

Papa slid up next to her at the sideboard and began filling a plate—with her preferences, not his. "Now you've done it."

She took another sip of the coffee—not espresso, but at least strong—and lifted her eyes to his. His lips were twitching, so she went ahead and grinned. "What have I done this time?"

In answer, he handed her his newspaper, folded open, and indicated the table. She sat with cup and news, let him slide the plate in front of her . . . but wasn't sure how she would eat breakfast. It may have been well past noon already, but the headline made her stomach knot.

THE LOST HEIRESS OF WHITBY

"Eat." Papa dropped a kiss onto the top of her head and sat beside her. "Much as I detest being in the news, the article is not a bad one."

It felt it, though, as she read and nibbled at her toast. A reminder of the carriage accident, an explanation of how Brook had ended up in the care of Collette Sabatini in Monaco, where the opera star passed her off as the child of Prince Louis. From there it shifted, touching on the countless girls paraded through Whitby Park over the last eighteen years trying to claim her inheritance. Then it sped back to the present, summarizing her arrival home in early September, her acceptance by her family, and how the reclusive Whitby was in London for the Season with her now.

At least it didn't mention the attack in November. Nor—which, frankly, surprised her—did it mention Justin anywhere.

No, instead it reported that after opening the floor with her father last night, she was seen in the arms of Lord Worthing, with whom she danced thrice more—which was not true. She had danced only once more with Brice, once more with Justin. Her aunt had told her she could not, under any circumstances, dance more than twice with any one man unless she intended to be the subject of every gossiping tongue in London.

Apparently even obeying such rules did not guarantee avoidance of that fate.

Her eyes finally moved to the last paragraph.

In a Parisian gown of pale green silk with an exquisite overlay of blue beading, the baroness debuted in glory. As onlookers gazed upon her, many remembered the fame her mother had attained twenty years prior, and it seems only fitting that they gave to her the same name with which they had dubbed the late Elizabeth Brook and welcomed a new Baroness Beauty into their midst.

Brook lowered the paper and looked over at her father. "They called her that?"

Papa's smile was small and wistful. "They did."

Brook grinned and might have replied had the butler not cleared his throat from the doorway. "Excuse me, but the Marquess of Worthing has arrived. Shall I show him in here or . . . ?"

Brook stood even as her father did, coffee in her hand and paper in his. The food she would happily abandon. Aunt Mary employed an English cook, not a French—or French Canadian, as the case may be—chef, and her palate had not adjusted to the fare.

"Drawing room," they answered in unison.

Melissa was dragging herself down the stairs as they went by, dressed and coiffed but with eyes at only half-mast. They exchanged a grin, and her cousin fell in with them instead of heading for the breakfast room.

Brice preceded them into the room by only a few feet and spun to face them the moment they were all inside. Brook expected him to be grinning, teasing. Instead, his eyes were serious. "Have you seen it?"

"The article about our Baroness Beauty?" Papa patted her shoulder. "We did."

"No. Well, yes, that too, but did you read the rest of the paper yet, Whit?"

Her father shook his head.

Brice indicated the folded newspaper, brows arched. "May I?"

"Certainly."

Brook strained onto her toes to try to see what section he was flipping toward. Though she couldn't tell—not until he said, "Here," and handed it back.

"Engagement announcements?" Brow furrowed, Papa accepted the paper. Brook and Melissa leaned in on either side of him.

Brook sucked in a breath when her gaze snagged on familiar names. "Pratt and Lady Catherine?" On the one hand—her cousin's hand—no surprise. But *he* . . . Did that mean he had given up his hope of joining their estates?

Brice nodded. "One of the two surprises."

"What el—"

Melissa's shriek of outrage cut off her question, and she snatched the paper from her uncle's hand. "Who in blazes is Adelaide Rosten?"

Frowning, Brook looked to Brice.

"Cayton," he murmured.

Cayton—in the engagement section?

Her cousin looked ready to tear the paper to shreds. "That lying, swindling, misleading, snake-tongued, blackhearted . . ."

She had seen Melissa in quite a few storms of temper since September, but never like this. "'Hell hath no fury . . .'"

Brice grinned. "Chaucer, isn't it?"

Brook rolled her eyes.

Melissa had finished her list of adjectives, it seemed. "I'm going to kill him! I'm going to march over to his townhouse and pluck every hair from his head!"

"He's not at home," Brice helpfully supplied, hands in his pockets and half a grin still on his mouth. "I passed him on the way here—he looked as if he were going to Hyde Park."

Melissa shoved the paper back into Papa's chest. "Then so am I. And *you*"—she grabbed Brice by the arm—"are coming with me."

Amusement gave way to panic on Brice's face. "Ah . . ."

"You're going to look at me with that adoration you feign so well, and I'm going to laugh at your every ridiculous joke in sight of all London."

"Oh. Um." He looked to Brook, eyes wide, and mouthed *Help*.

Brook smiled and tucked her hand into the crook of her father's arm. "I'm sure you'd be blessed beyond measure to keep company with a lady so fair, Lord Worthing. Isn't that what you said the other day?"

Brice narrowed his eyes at her while Melissa tugged him toward the door with the strength of a bull. "You're going to let her kidnap me?"

Chuckling, she waved her fingers. "My cousin needs you."

"Your cousin's terrifying."

Melissa spun and must have given him quite the look, though Brook couldn't see her face. Brice pasted on a smile. "Terrifying . . . ly beautiful?"

Melissa yanked him out the door, giving him time for only one more pleading look.

Papa sighed. "When the anger fades, she will be heartbroken."

It was true. And though Brook had never really liked Cayton, nor his readiness to arrange trysts with Melissa behind her mother's back, she had been ready to be happy for her cousin when he proposed. Had he only been toying with her all these months? She didn't know—but she knew who would.

Perhaps he was summoned by her thoughts, for the moment she spun around, Justin stood in the doorway, question in his brows. "Where was Lady Melissa pulling Lord Fastidious?"

Brook reclaimed her hand from Papa's arm so she could fold hers over her chest. "Is *that* what you were talking about last night? Your cousin is engaged?"

He stared at her blankly for a moment and then sighed. "He said he told her."

"He lied."

"Coward." Justin pivoted, as if ready to chase after Melissa . . . then must have thought better of it. "She saw it in the paper? And that was the first she knew of it?"

Brook wanted to ask him about his cousin's motives. She wanted to ask him how he could support him. She wanted to ask him if his affections could be trusted.

She moved her arms down, over her stomach, and bit it all back. "I thought you were riding with him today."

Justin looked her way again, conflict in his eyes. "I am. James was going to fetch Miss Rosten first, though, and as I've no desire to be a third wheel . . . I thought you might join us. But that was when I thought you knew already. I understand if you would rather not. Your cousin—"

"Would not thank me if I passed up the chance to meet this Miss Rosten." Brook looked to her father, who nodded his permission. "Are you on Alabaster?"

"In a landau."

No need for her to change into her riding habit, then—which was good, since her aunt had insisted on one with a skirt, which would necessitate the dreaded sidesaddle. "I'll fetch my hat and wrap."

Justin was vaguely aware of the sun shining. Of birds flitting from tree to tree. Of the scads of people walking, riding, driving along the paths through London's largest park. He *wanted* to focus on the woman beside him, on the sweet smell of lilacs that drifted from her hair.

But Brook was focused on Cayton's landau. She had been the epitome of polite during the introductions, but now her lips were pressed together, and her fingers gripped the edge of her kimono coat. She didn't even mention the suffragettes shouting from their soapboxes as she turned a hard gaze on Justin. "Is it catching?"

He expelled a bitter breath. Miss Adelaide Rosten was not what he had expected, to say the least. "I know little about her, except that she is my neighbor in Gloucestershire. They knew each other as children."

"Tell me he met her again and fell in love and doesn't see

the obvious. Tell me *that* is why he tossed over my cousin for her."

If only he could. Ahead of them, Miss Rosten presented her profile as she looked to Cayton. She smiled, and it looked so sincere. So sweet. So . . . hopeful. But could do nothing to fill the hollow cheeks or lighten the shadows under her eyes. "She is an heiress. He is strapped."

Brook shook her head. "She is *ill*. She looks . . . she looks like Maman did at the end."

His hands tightened on the reins. "I know."

"*Mon ami.*" Her fingers landed on his arm, though they didn't stay there. "Tell me your cousin is not so low as to marry a dying woman for her money, knowing well she hasn't long to live, knowing well he can soon move on."

"I . . . don't know." He didn't want to think so. Cayton, as he confessed his engagement at Azerley Hall, had seemed honest about his reasoning, and he certainly hadn't mentioned any illness. "Perhaps it is a childhood malady that she still bears the marks of. But perhaps she is well now."

She didn't look well. But Brook didn't point it out again. "Look at how she watches him."

"She cares for him." Which raised more questions in Justin's mind. Did Miss Rosten know Cayton's reasons for proposing, or had he spoken words of love to her? Had he misled her? "Perhaps he knew of her feelings. Perhaps . . . perhaps he wanted to give her some happiness."

A delicate snort slipped from Brook's lips. "Forgive me for doubting Cayton's pure heart. Perhaps they'll be happy, though—it seems unions built on love always end miserably, so perhaps one arranged for pragmatic reasons will have better luck."

Surely she jested. "Let us hope, for Regan and Thate's sake, that you're mistaken."

The fleeting smile she managed didn't make it to her eyes. "If anyone can defy statistics, it is they."

He studied her profile, shaking his head. "When did you get so cynical on the subject of love, Baroness Beauty?"

Brook winced. "Saw that, did you?"

"It wasn't so bad." Even if it *had* exaggerated her relationship with Worthing—and even if she did dodge his question about love.

"The Lost Heiress. That's what they'll all know me as now."

Her eyes went distant, and the fingers of one hand had abandoned her kimono's hem in favor of twisting the pearls on her necklace.

He bumped his shoulder into hers. "You *are* an heiress, Brooklet. You can't expect society not to notice."

"But for most of my life I was just . . . lost." She drew in a breath and twisted the pearls the other direction. "If you hadn't found Papa for me . . ."

"Let us praise the Lord that I did, that the crest was enough."

She looked up at him, dropping her hand back to her lap. "And what if I had been a lost nobody, instead of a lost heiress?" The question turned her eyes to flame. "I would have come, Justin. I would have shown up at Ralin one day and demanded that tour you always promised. Then what would you have done?"

"I would have given you the tour." And likely drawn her into his arms and kissed her and . . . what? Even Father, who had eschewed all ducal responsibilities, claimed Justin couldn't marry her so long as she was only the illegitimate child of an opera singer. Though Grandfather had accused him of wanting to marry her even if it brought disgrace to Stafford. Which of them knew him better?

Brook shook her head and looked away. "You asked me at the funeral to say your name. Say mine."

The demand was unfair—*his* name hadn't changed, only his

title. Hers . . . "Elizabeth Brook. Sabatini or Eden, it doesn't matter. You are my Brooklet."

"I am your friend."

"You are . . ." *My heart. My soul.* "So much more."

Now anger sparked in the eyes she turned on him. "If I were still Brook Sabatini?"

"You're *not*. Why are you dwelling on hypotheticals?" He motioned to the Ramsey barouche that crossed their path, to Melissa with her chin held high and Worthing with a laugh on his lips. "Do you think *he* would be your friend if you were still Brook Sabatini?"

Her words changed to Monegasque as they rose in volume. "I think I never would have *known* him! You . . . you are the only one I could carry from one life to another. The only one who *ought* to know me and love me for my past, not just my present!"

"I do." He swallowed, held her sparking gaze. "That doesn't mean I'm not grateful for the way things *are*."

"It isn't enough." Looking away again, she pulled her kimono tighter, even though the sun was gaining in warmth. "I need to know, Justin. You are trying to change everything—I need to know why. I need to know you would have pursued me in the same way even had you discovered my father was a penniless nobody instead of the Earl of Whitby."

"Well, of course it wouldn't have been in the same way!" How could it have been? He would have had to fight his family every step of the way, would have exchanged one set of difficulties for another. He certainly wouldn't have rejected the idea of an engagement months ago in order to prove to her he wasn't after her fortune.

Brook slid to the opposite side of the bench. "Take me home. Now."

Blast. That probably hadn't sounded the way he'd meant.

"Brook—I didn't mean I wouldn't have pursued you, just that it would have been different."

How could she look so dratted beautiful even as she snorted and folded her arms over her chest. "Oh, I'm sure, Duke. You would have found some *suitable* girl to court, and I would have been . . . What? Dismissed from your life? Or would you have tried to make a mistress of me?"

His blood ignited, and he gripped the reins tight. "How could you say that? You know me better than—"

"I know it's how things are done in your family! Even your sainted Uncle Edward—"

"Don't compare me to him." His words sounded, oddly, cold rather than hot, despite the roar in his veins.

Turning her face toward him again, she lifted a brow. "And why not? You always idolized him. 'If the shoe fits . . .' as the saying goes. . . ."

He all but jerked the horses toward the nearest exit from the park. "I am not like him."

"You are exactly like him!"

"He raped my mother!" He didn't, couldn't look at her as the words, still in Monegasque, pulsed around them. His nostrils flared. "Got her with child on purpose, thinking to make Aunt Caro raise me. I am *not* like him."

"Justin." Her voice went soft, filled with sympathy that did nothing to make his fists relax around the reins. "I'm sorry. I didn't know."

"Of course you didn't know." He directed the horses back toward her aunt's, the fire only building. His words slipped back into English. "How could you? That would have required granting me ten whole minutes to speak of something other than *you*, wouldn't it? Something other than *your* problems, *your* mysteries. Oh, but this is your turn. Your time. My apologies."

291

Her fingers landed on his arm, though the touch was brief, quickly gone. "Justin . . ."

"Don't." For an eternity, he said nothing. He couldn't work any words past his clenched teeth. Couldn't dislodge those months of doubt, of wondering if she even cared or if she'd fallen for Worthing.

And now here she was, saying his feelings didn't even matter. That what he may have done if she weren't who she was outweighed what he had actually done to protect her.

He turned onto her aunt's street and forced a swallow. "I love you." The words, so long unsaid, nearly choked him. "Take your time. Decide if that's enough. And let me know when you've figured it out."

He pulled to a halt in front of Lady Ramsey's and glanced her way. She stared at him, mouth agape, incredulity shifting to irritation before his eyes. "*That* is how you choose to tell me you love me? In the middle of an argument, followed by a statement that yet again you'll retreat behind your wall?"

"When better? But if it's charm and smooth words you want, then I guess we know where your heart inclines."

"You're an imbecile." Gathering her skirt into hand, she leaped down from the landau. Stomped toward the door, but then halted at the base of the stairs and spun back to him, fury flashing in her eyes. "I'm not in love with Brice."

For a moment, hope sprouted. But she didn't follow it with anything, didn't say she *was* in love with *him*. He breathed a laugh and lifted the reins. "At the risk of sounding like an echo, my lady—that isn't enough."

He was halfway down the street by the time he heard the door's slam.

Twenty-Three

Deirdre handed the baroness the book she had fetched from her bedchamber, smiling at the yawn the lady tried to cover with a hand. "Perhaps you would adjust easier to the late nights, my lady, if you were consistent about them."

Lady Berkeley sent her a tired scowl. "You sound like Aunt Mary, O'Malley. I have been to three balls and a soiree. That is surely enough for two weeks' time."

Lady Ramsey didn't seem to think so—she and Lady Melissa had been out each and every night to something or another. Not that Deirdre could blame Lord Whitby and the baroness for staying in whenever they could finagle it.

And if the papers were any indication, her absences only increased her fame. Deirdre made no attempt to keep track of the flood of young ladies and gentlemen who swarmed the parlor and drawing room for Ladies Berkeley and Melissa. Which would be why Lord Whitby and his daughter were now hidden away here in the upstairs salon.

His lordship's paper rustled as he turned another page. "We can go home whenever you're ready, my dear. I have verified that the House of Lords cares no more for my opinion now than they ever did, so I've nothing to keep me here."

Deirdre took a seat near to the baroness's, to be at hand when next she needed something, and picked up last night's ball gown. Some clumsy oaf had stepped on the train and caused a tear, and it would take all Deirdre's skill with a needle to mend it without it being noticeable. She opened her case of thread and selected the closest match to the lavender silk.

A knock upon the open door earned a groan from the lady and brought Deirdre's gaze up. The butler stood there, silver salver in hand.

"Not more callers, Mr. Vander. I'm not at home. I've run off on safari."

The butler smiled and bowed. "A letter, my lady. Addressed to both you and his lordship."

The baroness grinned, though sure and her smiles had none of them been very bright since she returned in a huff after her drive with the duke following her debut. "In that case, thank you very much."

"And shall I tell your next callers you're on safari, Lady Berkeley?"

She chuckled as her father stood to accept the thin envelope on the tray. "I leave that to your discretion."

Deirdre threaded her needle and tied the end while his lordship picked up the letter opener from the salver and made a neat slit in the envelope. Putting it down again, he nodded his thanks and dismissal of the butler.

And frowned at the letter. "This looks suspiciously like . . . Brook, it is from Major Rushworth!"

Deirdre's hands went still even as the baroness leaped to her feet. "What does he say?"

His lordship looked up from the page with wide eyes. "That he's back in Town and will call tomorrow morning at nine o'clock. He requests a private audience with the two of us."

"Back in Town?" Deirdre realized she had spoken only when

the two looked at her. She drew in a quick breath. "Pardon me. I . . . my uncle usually travels with the major."

Lord Whitby frowned for a moment, though it quickly cleared. "Of course, I'd forgotten his batman is the one who recommended you to us. How long has it been since you've seen him, O'Malley?"

She turned her gaze back to the gown. Sure and she hadn't meant to steal the floor. "Many years, my lord. Not since I was a girl, though he is always most faithful in writing. He and my da were close, and he's done his best to see to the family since . . ."

Lord Whitby's warm smile reminded her of why Uncle Seamus had recommended his house to her. "The major is staying at the Hendon Hall Hotel, it seems. Why not take your afternoon off and see if your uncle is with him?"

"Oh." She hadn't felt such a swell of joy since Da yet lived— because seeing Uncle Seamus would be a bit like seeing her father again. Her gaze flew to the baroness. "May I, my lady?"

"Of course. Go." Her ladyship made a little shooing motion with her hands.

She didn't need to be told again. Smiling her thanks, Deirdre put needle and dress aside and dashed from the room.

She changed quickly into a matching skirt and jacket, grabbed her handbag, and fastened a hat over her chignon. Then it was down the stairs with her, and to the kitchen, where she found Lady Ramsey's housekeeper. "Pardon me, ma'am. Do you know how to get to the Hendon Hall Hotel?"

The woman pursed her lips. "They've turned Hendon Hall to a hotel, have they? Pity. But yes, I know it—it's in the north part of the city. You'll want to take the tube."

New excitement joined the flutter in her stomach. She had yet to have cause to use the underground railway. "How much?"

"Two pence is all."

"Thank you." Her grin felt as though it would split her cheeks. "Have you need of anything while I'm out, ma'am?"

The old woman returned her smile. "No. Go on with you."

Letting herself out the back door, Deirdre circled around to the street and all but skipped toward the heart of London.

And screamed when a hand closed around her mouth and tugged her into an alley, though her cry was muffled behind the fingers.

"Quiet."

Pratt. Shuddering, she nodded.

He let go her mouth and spun her around. His eyes were two black slits. "Where are you off to so merrily, my lovely?"

Why was he always there to spoil everything? She backed into the brick wall behind her. "To see my uncle is all, my lord."

"Uncle." Pratt lifted a single brow.

She swallowed and pressed her hand to the cool bricks. "Aye. My da's brother. If you'll excuse me—"

"Not so fast." He shifted when she did, to block her from making an escape back to the street. "I have missed her at every turn."

Deirdre lifted her chin. "And why should you care? You're betrothed."

"And will be married within a fortnight by special license, if Rush has anything to say about it." He put on a cold, unfeeling smile. "Which is why I must act now."

"Special license?" Deirdre felt her eyes widen. "Is Lady Catherine—"

"A liar? Most likely, but her brother believes whatever she tells him. I've a task for you, Deirdre."

For a moment she could only stare. He had gotten Lady Catherine with child and still he meant to pursue Lady Berkeley? Deirdre's breath shook when she released it. "What?"

Pratt withdrew a bundle of envelopes from his inner pocket,

secured with a feminine-looking ribbon. "It's very simple. You aren't to open them; you aren't to glance at them. You're just to put them in the bottom of Lady Berkeley's trunk, where she'll not see them. Do you understand? Under something, hidden away. And whenever you return to Yorkshire, put them away with all the correspondence she'll have collected in London."

Her hands shook as she took them and slipped them into her handbag. She pressed against the wall again when he loomed nearer. "What are they?"

He backed away a step. "No questions—or your family goes up in flames. I'm watching you, my lovely."

She shivered, closed her handbag, and said no more as he turned and strode away. It took her a long moment to push the fear down and convince her feet to move. Forward, she must go forward. She must push down the question of what he meant to do. Soon she handed over her two pennies at the tube station and climbed aboard the electric train with all the other passengers.

Pratt's black eyes kept flashing before her, sapping the joy from the experience. When she finally climbed off in north London, she had only a blurred memory of the stops and starts, the small windows, the tunnel walls hurtling by outside them.

The sunlight near to blinded her when she stepped back outside and asked a tube worker for directions to the hotel. It took her ten minutes of striding, then wandering, to find the columned exterior of what had so recently been a family's mansion.

She stood on the street and stared up at it. Once a grand home—now open to strangers to sleep and dine in for a price. Heaven help her, she hoped such a fate never befell Whitby Park. Shaking it off, she followed the walk toward the back entrance and knocked on the door.

A harried woman in a white cap and apron answered. "Yes?"

"Good day, ma'am. I've come inquiring as to whether Major Rushworth has an O'Malley with him as batman."

"And who's asking?" The voice boomed from behind her, deep and displeased.

Deirdre spun, hand splayed over her heart, and spotted who could only be the major striding her way from the garden. He was in uniform, but for the missing hat. His head gleamed bald in the sunlight, his drooping moustache accentuating his frown.

She dipped a curtsy. "Major. I'm Seamus O'Malley's niece, Deirdre. Please, did he come with you? I haven't seen him in ages."

"I should think you haven't." His scowl didn't lessen. "No one was to know we were here now. How did you learn of it?"

He looked as though he would as soon toss her into the shrubs as listen to her answer. She let her gaze fall to his boots. "I'm in service to the Baroness of Berkeley. I was there when she and Lord Whitby got your letter, and they—knowing as they do that my uncle is your batman—said I might come looking for him."

"Whitby." The major spat it out like a curse. "Naturally he would ignore the part that said to tell no one where I was staying, or that I was even in Town."

Her shoulders went tight. "Forgive me, sir. I didn't mean to step into a family quarrel. I only want to see my uncle."

The moustache twitched. "Not at the moment, you don't. Old boy is ill—he's resting now."

"Ill?" All her hope sagged within her. "Mightn't I see him, Major? Make sure he's comfortable?"

"I said he's *resting*." His nostrils flared, but then his eyes softened. A mite. "Come back around tomorrow, girl. Or the next day. We'll be in Town for the week—then it's home to India." He turned back for the garden. "Too dratted cold and rainy on this godforsaken isle."

With no other recourse, Deirdre gripped her bag in both hands and dragged her feet back the way she'd come. She'd go home. She'd put Pratt's envelopes in the baroness's trunk. And she'd wish she'd never stepped foot outside today.

Brook wished, as she paced to the far corner of the music room, that they were at home. In their library. Books surrounding her instead of instruments. She had tried to play to soothe her nerves, but soft music wouldn't come—and she couldn't very well play thunderous songs while Aunt Mary and Melissa were still abed.

She paused beside the window and looked out at the rainsoaked city. As always, her gaze sought a familiar form, a familiar car, and she chided herself for it. Justin wouldn't come any more today than he had the last fortnight. Apparently when he said she could let him know when she'd made up her mind, he meant he wouldn't grace her with his presence until she did so.

How, then? How was she to apologize for comparing him to his uncle? How was she to tell him how miserable she'd been without him? How was she to tell him that she was sure, so very sure now, that she loved him?

"Major Rushworth, my lord."

Brook turned but didn't advance. Better to stay where she was, half-hidden behind the harp, and put Justin from her thoughts before she focused on the major.

He strode in. Dressed in uniform, his skin was tan and leathery. His bald head gleamed in the chandelier's light, his moustache framed his mouth, and his brows were furrowed. He halted a few steps inside the door and glared at her father. "Whitby."

"Major." Papa had stood to greet him, though he didn't move forward to offer a hand. "Kind of you to finally reply—though a letter would have sufficed."

Major Rushworth snorted. "I think not. If I learned anything eighteen years ago, it is that letters are not secure."

Papa darted a glance her way. They had learned that truth as well. Otherwise she'd have sent one to Justin. "Did you have a safe trip from India?"

"I arrived, didn't I? And I'm eager to get back, so if we might dispense with the pleasantries—you said you found a letter I sent Lizzie in your name. What else did you find?"

Papa's expression barely flickered, but Brook could read the frustration in his stance, and in the way his hands curled. "Mysteries."

Brook edged out from behind the harp. "What are the Fire Eyes?"

They both looked at her when she spoke, but it was the major she watched. He washed pale, his eyes bulged, and his larynx bobbed as he swallowed. "Lizzie."

A corner of Papa's mouth tugged up. "We call her Brook."

"Your daughter." He shook his head, though his gaze didn't shift. He still looked at her as though she were a phantom. "She is the exact image of . . ."

Papa motioned her forward. "Not quite. Her nose is narrower, her forehead not so high. And their chins—they have very different chins."

Brook grinned at her father and stopped at his side. He *would* remember her exact words from their first meeting.

The major's nostrils flared. "But her smile. Her eyes."

It took all her will to keep from stepping half-behind her father. She could not imagine her mother ever being close to this man before her. "The Fire Eyes, Major. Not mine. What are they? And why was I nearly killed over them?"

Rushworth spun away, spitting out an expletive. "It has found you. I thought . . . with ignorance would come safety—that the curse could not strike those who didn't know about it."

"Curse." Papa's incredulity saturated his tone.

The major turned back to them with a glare worthy of the Russians. "Don't patronize me, Whitby, as if *I* am the fool. You think you can believe in your precious Lord in heaven without admitting there is another side? You think there is no power in darkness? I have felt it—I have heard it howling in the jungles while you've been safe in your mansion."

Lightning and thunder and darkness. Brook suppressed a shudder and made no objection when her father rested a hand on her back. *Children of the light. Children of the day.* "The Fire Eyes—whatever they are—carry a curse?"

His eyes found hers, and they were a roiling brown. "So goes the legend—that hatred and eventually death will follow whomever holds them. I dismissed it when I heard it. And when my every relationship crumbled to pieces, I called it man's greed, not a devil's curse. But perhaps the two are not so different." He nodded, and his gaze fell to her throat. "Your mother's pearls?"

Her fingers sought and found the familiar dangling globes. "She was wearing this necklace when she died—it was all I had of her until I came home last autumn. I always wear it."

Though the major's lips turned up, it scarcely resembled a smile. Though he laughed, it carried no mirth. "Then you have always been wearing the Fire Eyes."

She pulled her hand away, the pearls scalding her.

"What?" Papa turned a bit so they could see each other's face, his eyes wide. "That is what you sent her with that letter? The Fire Eyes are *pearls*?"

"I sent it to her. But they are not pearls." He held a hand, motioned with his fingers. "If I might see it?"

Papa seemed struck mute. So with a deep breath, Brook reached up and unhooked the necklace—stretched out her arm and let the gold and pearls drip into the major's palm.

He reached into his pocket, drew out a pen knife, and sank into a chair.

Her fingers rested on her bare neck as he fiddled with the longer of the dangling pearls. Each pulse thundered, fluttered. Try as she might, she couldn't make sense of it.

Rushworth sent a hard glare to her father and then looked down again. "I meant only to hide the Fire Eyes—that's the only reason I sent them to Lizzie. It was not . . . I knew she would never accept a gift from my hand—she had made that clear. So I wrote a letter and signed your name to it, Whitby. Sent the necklace with it. I thought she would stash it in her safe with her other jewelry, wear it once or twice, but otherwise forget about it, not even thinking to mention it to you. I knew you sent her endless gifts. I thought they would, for all intents and purposes, vanish."

Papa's nostrils flared. "What are *they*?"

The major grunted, focused on his task. "They, Whitby . . ." The tip of his knife seemed to have found purchase. A moment later, the pearl split into two perfectly even half spheres. He shook a red gem out into his palm. "Here."

He held the jewel on his outstretched palm, though it was a long moment before Papa reached for it. He frowned as he examined it. "Ruby?"

"Ruby!" Rushworth barked a laugh. "Guess again."

"Well, it certainly isn't a garnet."

"No." Brook picked it up from her father's hand and held it up to catch the sunlight shafting through the window.

Fire leaped to life within it, sending a scarlet-toned rainbow dancing on the opposite wall. "It's . . . it's a *diamond*. A red diamond."

"Two red diamonds." Rushworth held out a second one, which must have come from the other dangling pearl. "Identical. Flawless. Two carats each. Worth a fortune."

Brook accepted the second, held them up beside each other. The beauty of the stones, so pure a red, so bright with internal life, left her speechless.

Her father shook his head. "They are lovely, but rather small, aren't they? They can't be worth more than a few thousand pounds."

"Are you daft?" Rushworth motioned toward the jewels. "They are the rarest diamond in the world—only a few have ever been discovered, and the largest is only five carats. To have *two* of them—flawless, identical, and that large . . . Kings have killed for these jewels. Wise men have abandoned faith to search for them. According to Indian legend, entire villages were wiped out, burned to the ground, in the pursuit of them."

Brook lowered them, let them fall back into her palm, and then held them out. "How did you come by them, then?"

The major put his hands behind his back. "A stroke of luck— *bad* luck, I now firmly believe. They were being sold as rubies by some chap from the jungles desperate for enough money to buy food. I bought them more out of pity than anything. But when I examined them, I soon realized what I had. I asked questions—my second mistake."

Since he wouldn't take them, she closed her fingers around the diamonds. "Because then word spread that you had them."

"And everyone wanted them. The natives say the Fire Eyes were forged by the gods and given to Dakshin Ray, the tiger god. But humans stole them, and so Dakshin Ray put a curse upon them. To turn brother against brother, father against son, until chaos reigned—and then the tiger would come."

"You can't believe that." But Papa's voice was not so firm, not so strong.

Rushworth sank back down into the chair. "I didn't. But what I *did* believe were the three attempts on my life after I bought them. I thought it the craze of the locals, so I took my leave and came home. In England—sensible, staid, cool England—I knew logic would prevail."

And yet it was here, in sensible, staid, cool England, that someone had nearly killed *her* for them. Where this man's niece had declared her an enemy because she thought Brook had them. Thought they must have been among her mother's things.

And she had been right.

Brother against brother . . . apparently cousin against cousin too.

"You must have told your brother, and he his wife." She leaned into Papa's side. "That must be how Lady Catherine knew of them. They told her."

The major sneered. "No doubt raised her to think they were by rights hers, and I stole them. The moment John set eyes on the things, he wanted them. The Indians would have said the curse's fangs sank into him. I never should have brought him in. I shouldn't have told anyone about them. But I had been too long out of the country. I needed help finding a reputable jewel dealer. But a finder's fee was all I offered, not the equal partnership they claimed. Next thing I knew . . ."

He shook his head and averted his face. "They pitted us against one another. They would have torn us all apart. I did the only thing I could think to do and had this necklace made to hide them. Got rid of them."

"*Hidden* is not *rid of*." Papa took a step away from her, putting himself back in the major's line of sight. "Why not actually do it? Toss them into the sea?"

"You might as well ask why we don't destroy Rome, since people once fought over it. The history of those jewels, Whitby . . ."

"It isn't the history you wanted to preserve." Brook strode over to the side table on which he'd set the necklace. She put the diamonds back inside the shells and found they snapped together without a visible seam. Such amazing craftsmanship, all to deceive. "If that were the case, you would have donated them to a museum. Instead, you sent them to my mother knowing well you could get them back someday. And hoped that in the meantime, your brother would forget about them."

Rushworth ran a hand over his moustache but wouldn't meet her gaze. "I underestimated their potency then—I won't now. I gave them to your mother, young lady, so they are now yours. Donate them if you want, toss them in the drink if you'd prefer. But I want nothing to do with them again. I've lost enough thanks to those accursed diamonds. My brother, my best friend."

"My mother." She traced a finger along the necklace with its vicious secrets.

"Now, see here." The major rose, too fast, too close. "You can't lay the blame for that accident upon the Fire Eyes. I told John I'd sold them without his help, and I left the country. No one knew I'd sent the necklace to her, and it was so long afterward that she died . . ."

"What?" Papa stepped to her side again. "You couldn't have even boarded the boat yet when she was killed."

"Has your memory left you, Whitby? I went back in August. It was October she died."

"No, it was *August*. The nineteenth. The day you left York for Bristol."

"No." Rushworth's eyes went foggy. "It can't be. I got the telegram after I'd been back several weeks, and it said it had only just happened, after Pratt's murder . . . ."

Brooke remembered Lady Catherine's mention of Pratt's father being shot in a back alley soon after her mother's accident. *Might the two be connected?*

"I would not have . . ." The major's eyes widened. "You mean to tell me I could have gone to her funeral? Why did no one send a message while I was yet in Bristol?"

Her father drew in a long breath and heaved it back out. "I cannot answer for your brother. For my part, I could think of nothing but the loss. Lizzie dead, Brook missing. Nothing else mattered. I can scarcely even remember the trip home from London after Mr. Graham wired the news to me."

"John." Now it was his brother's name that Rushworth spat out like a curse. He passed a hand over his gleaming head. "Were he not dead, I would throttle him."

"Do you think he . . . ?" Papa's breath came too fast and then seemed to bunch up. "Could he have found out somehow that you sent them to her? Could he have threatened her—could that be why she was on the road that night?"

The major shook his head, but it didn't seem to be in answer. "I dare not say it's impossible, not at this point. Not if my niece has been asking your daughter for the diamonds."

Silence pulsed through the room for a long minute. At last Rushworth stood, tugged his jacket down, and met her father's gaze.

"I am sorry, Whitby. Much as I never liked you, I never meant to bring tragedy upon your house. I certainly never meant to hurt Lizzie."

"I know that," her father said, voice hushed.

The major's gaze shifted to Brook. "And it's then because of me that you were lost for so long. I am sorry for that too. I never wished anything but joy for Lizzie's girl."

Brook could only nod.

"I'll do what I can to set things right, though heaven knows I cannot undo the things that really matter. But I'll pay a visit to Crispin and Catherine. I documented everything, knowing I'd someday need proof the Fire Eyes were mine."

They wouldn't believe him—there was no doubt of that.

Documents could be so easily forged. But she appreciated that he wanted to try. "Thank you."

He jerked his head once in a single nod and made for the door. She thought he would charge through it without another word, but instead he paused in the threshold and turned back. "My first stop when I leave here will be my solicitor, drawing up a new document verifying they have been legally given to you. But if my niece and nephew do not cease their pestering, you may want to consider that donation, my lady. And make it very public, with cameras flashing at every turn. Where the press is—"

"There is safety. A friend of mine recently said as much."

"You have wise friends. You'll need them." His shoulders rising with his breath, he nodded once more and disappeared.

Brook turned to her father. "What now?"

Papa reached for the necklace on the table and held it up. "I don't believe in curses."

Thunder and lightning and darkness. Brook shuddered. "I do. There is a reason the Bible warns us not to dabble in such things—and it cannot be because they are fables."

He granted that with a tilt of his head. "Allow me to re-phrase—I do not believe curses can have more power than our Lord. We will pray for guidance. We will trust in Him. And . . ." He reached around her to fasten the necklace in its usual place. "Until we receive guidance from Him, we do nothing out of the ordinary. They don't know they're in this necklace, so it is, for the moment, the best place to keep them."

She touched the pearls. So many times over the years she had done so, never guessing at what lay within.

They would never feel the same to her again. "When she fled, she thought this from you. Whatever sent her to the road that night, she was wearing this because it was the most recent gift you'd given her." But it had all been a lie, and it could well have killed her. Brook shook her head. "We could give them to Catherine. Make the madness stop."

Papa's nostrils flared, and he blinked. "No. If the Rushworths are somehow responsible for her death—no. I'll not let them profit from it. It isn't right."

No, it wasn't. But then . . . so little seemed to be.

Twenty-Four

Deirdre got past the door of the Hendon Hall Hotel this time. No Major Rushworth waited in the garden to halt her, and the frazzled maid who greeted her at the door waved her in and up the back stairs.

Room six, the maid had said. She found it on the second floor easily enough and knocked. Lightly at first, though she'd been told the major was out, so she had little fear of disturbing him. When no reply came, she knocked louder.

Was that a groan from within? Her pulse increased. "Uncle Seamus? Is that you?" She pounded harder but could hear nothing else from within. "Uncle, it's DeeDee." He was in there, and the major wasn't . . . so she put her hand to the knob and turned.

It gave under her hand when she pushed. "I'm coming in."

No objection sounded, so she pushed the door open the rest of the way.

And screamed.

'Twasn't her uncle sprawled on the floor in a pool of red, that she saw in a moment. But it did nothing to keep her from screaming again, from pressing to the wall. Her knees went weak. The khaki pants, the scuffed boots, the gleam of sun on his head . . . the major. The maid had been wrong—he was here, and someone had . . . had . . .

Did he live? She couldn't imagine how, with all the blood soaking into the wooden floor beneath him. But she had heard a groan, hadn't she?

She heard it again, seconds before the pounding of feet sounded on the stairs. Not from the major—from the room to the right. Deirdre stumbled that direction and through the open doorway. "Uncle Seamus."

He lay on a cot in a stained undershirt, a sheet pulled up to his waist. Despite the years since she had last seen him, she knew him immediately—he looked like Da, but for the silver hair. "Uncle Seamus." Her knees gave out before she could lower herself gracefully to the floor, but she made it to him and gripped his hand.

No blood, praise be to the Lord.

But plenty of shouting now, from the outer room, and a flurry in her uncle's room as well. It all blurred together. A cacophony, when all she wanted was a whisper from her uncle's lips. Figures darting around her periphery, when all she wanted to see was the lifting of his eyes. "Uncle Seamus. Uncle, it's me. It's DeeDee. Are you all right? Speak to me, I beg you." She said it over and over again.

Finally he blinked.

And then hands closed over her shoulders and pulled her away. She tried to shrug them off, to slap away the arms that turned her. Her struggle stopped cold when she caught sight of the Scotland Yard uniform on the man who held her.

His eyes were icy and hard. "Are you the one who found him?"

How had the police arrived so soon? Or *was* it soon? How long had she been on her knees, gripping her uncle's hand, ignoring the buzz around her? "I . . . I came to see my uncle is all. The maid said the major was out. I . . . He's sick. Uncle Seamus is sick."

The officer's hands gripped her tighter. "Were you the one to find the major?"

She wanted home. She wanted Hiram to put an arm around her. She wanted Lord Whitby to stalk up behind her and command this man to let her go. She wanted . . . she wanted to wake up and find this nothing but a nightmare to make her thrash about on her bed the way the baroness always did.

"Miss!"

"Yes." Her eyes slid shut, and her knees felt weak again. "Yes, I found him."

"You forced the lock?"

"What?" Her eyes opened again, though they refused to focus on him. "No, sir. It was unlocked. I turned the knob, is all. I . . . I wanted to see my uncle. The major was out, she said, and I heard him groan."

His hands left her shoulders, and for a second she knew relief. Then he gripped her by the elbow instead and propelled her forward, out, into the buzz and cacophony. When he aimed her for the exit, she dug in her heels. "No! My uncle!"

"We'll see to him. You need to come with me to the station."

She nearly fell on the way down the stairs, earning her a curse from the officer—detective? He all but shoved her into the police carriage waiting outside, though then he left her in there alone for half of forever.

The other half was saved for the agonizing ride through the city.

Though when he hauled her into Scotland Yard as if she were a criminal, she began to wish the ride had lasted longer. He sat her down on a hard chair and positioned himself behind a desk. "Your name?"

"Deirdre O'Malley." Oh, how her mum would be appalled to see her here now. She twisted her fingers around each other.

"Your uncle is the batman of Major Rushworth?" The

detective—there was a little board on his desk that labeled him as Detective Cole—scribbled something onto a page.

"Aye. Seamus O'Malley."

"You're unmarried?" He glanced at her with those beady eyes again.

"Aye. I'm in domestic service."

"To whom?"

Oh, heaven help me. Would they call Lord Whitby in? But then, the major was a relation of the baroness. They would be calling on them with the news at any rate. She sucked in a breath. "Lord Whitby and his daughter, the Baroness of Berkeley."

Cole added that to his notes. "The Baroness of . . . wait." Here he paused and looked up at her with, if it were possible, even less warmth. "Baroness Beauty?"

"So she's been dubbed." She leaned forward. "Please, sir. Will they take my uncle to the hospital, do you think? Which one?"

"Liller." The detective flagged another fellow walking by in identical dress. "Ring up Lord Whitby. At . . . ?" He lifted a brow at Deirdre.

Her stomach knotted. She stuttered out Lady Ramsey's direction.

Once the second chap bustled off, Cole shot question after question at her. Did she know Major Rushworth? Had she met him before? When was the first time? How well did she know him? What did she think of him? How long since she had seen her uncle? Did she honestly expect him to believe that his lordship had granted her two afternoons off to visit an ill relative?

"He is a kind and fair employer, sir, who understands the importance of family. *Yes,* he let me off again after I was turned away yesterday! If you don't believe me—"

"Then ask me yourself."

Deirdre spun on her hard wooden chair, never so grateful to see his lordship. And the baroness had come, too, and now came to her chair and rested her hands on Deirdre's shoulders. A show of support. A touch of comfort.

Tears stung the backs of her eyes.

The detective rose, but slowly. "Lord Whitby, I presume?"

His lordship didn't stretch out a hand to shake. Rather, he folded his arms over his chest and narrowed his eyes. "I would like to know why you're interrogating my employee for visiting her uncle. Unless familial concern has been made illegal in my absence from Town, and no one thought to inform me of it."

Cole's lips pulled up in a hint of smile that dared to look mocking. "Your employee was at the scene of a murder, my lord. *First* at the scene, which more often than not denotes some involvement beyond happenstance."

The baroness's hands went lax on her shoulders. "Murder?"

The detective's eyes flicked to Lady Berkeley and swept her up and down. Judging, though Deirdre couldn't tell what verdict he came to. "Major Henry Rushworth was slain in his hotel room this afternoon."

"No!"

"It can't be." Lord Whitby stepped closer to them. He kept his gaze on the policeman. "We just saw him this morning."

"Did you now." The detective sank back into his chair, that cynical little smile back in place. "Then have a seat, my lord. I have a few questions for you as well."

Her father had lied to Scotland Yard—and Brook fully approved. He'd told them everything . . . except the small detail of the Fire Eyes. She stepped out into the sunshine and nearly stumbled back inside when a man with a pencil and pad sprang forward, another with a camera close behind.

Lovely.

She tucked a hand into her father's arm and let emotion

wash over her face. A ballerina on a stage. A princess before an angry mob.

A baroness sitting across from a detective who quite obviously had a bone to pick with the gentry. He had all but salivated at the prospect of linking her and her father to a murder. Never mind that Papa had gone to the House of Lords again today directly after Major Rushworth left them—saying he needed time to think where no real concerns would distract him. Never mind that Brook had been surrounded from ten o'clock onward by no fewer than a dozen young ladies and gentlemen. Those facts wouldn't have, Detective Cole had all but said, stopped them from hiring someone.

The reporter licked his pencil. "My lady! What are you doing at Scotland Yard? Is it true someone tried to attack you this morning after you were out riding?"

They had finally heard about that, had they? If months late . . . and a bit confused. She forced a sad, small smile to her lips when she would have preferred to storm by.

Where the press was, there was safety.

Please, Lord, help me. Help me not to crumble. Keep us safe. "No, I was not the victim of the crime today. My cousin, whom I met for the first time this morning, was murdered in his hotel room a few hours ago." She blinked several times and touched a fingertip to the corner of her eye, though no tears had gathered. They may have, had the anger not been so strong.

Another person dead. And for what? Diamonds?

Papa slipped his arm around her. Deirdre remained hidden behind them.

The reporter scratched furiously at his pad. "Your cousin?"

"My mother's cousin. Major Henry Rushworth." She looked over her shoulder at Scotland Yard and heaved a sigh she hoped was worthy of the stage. "I dare not say more. I don't want to hinder the detective's investigation. Justice *must* be done."

She had her doubts that it would be.

The camera flashed. Brook leaned into her father's side before it could flash again. A unified front, sorrow in the slope of their shoulders. Were it a dance, she would have pointed her toe, arched her back, brought her arms into a low circle to complete the picture.

"Were you brought in for . . . for questioning?" The reporter's eyes were wide.

Brook breathed a little laugh and tucked a stray curl under her hat. "No, no. We came in on our own the moment they called us. We must do anything we can to aid in the capture of my cousin's killer. We wanted to make sure the police had all the information we did, scant as it is."

Not that they had even known about the murder when they were told to come collect Deirdre . . . but her maid didn't need the attention of the press.

"Rushworth." The reporter tapped that line in his notes and looked up at her with raised brows. "He must be related to Lord Rushworth and Lady Catherine."

"Their uncle." She turned her face up toward her father. "We should pay them a visit, Papa. They will surely be even more distressed than we are."

"We will, my dear." His eyes applauded her. Then he nodded at the reporter. "If you'll excuse us."

They didn't await an answer, just continued down the stairs with a measured step. Deirdre, Brook noted when she looked up, had slipped around them while they were distracting the reporters and waited at the car. She looked awful. Her face was pale, her eyes haunted, and she clasped her hands so tightly her knuckles were white.

"I have to see my uncle," was her greeting when they joined her.

Brook reached for her hands. "Of course you do."

"We'll take you." Papa opened the door and ushered them both inside, shielding them from the camera until the door had shut.

Brook settled beside Deirdre and kept ahold of her hands, which were cold and trembling. "We can go in with you too, if you want company. I wouldn't want to be alone so soon after seeing what you did."

Deirdre's chin shook too. "Thank you. I would appreciate that." She sniffed and lowered her head. "I wish Hiram were here."

Brook squeezed her hands. She had seen them together a few times, knew they were close. "I'm sure he would want to be too."

Papa cranked the engine to life and slid into the driver's seat. Within the minute, they were pulling onto the busy streets, headed for a part of the city she had yet to see.

No one seemed inclined to talk, so Brook let her gaze drift to the window. Let the truth drift into her heart. She wanted Justin. With no front, no walls between them. She wanted to be able to rush into his arms, to kiss his cheeks, to cry on his shoulder if the tears chose to come. To tell him what the major had said that morning, what the Fire Eyes were . . . how everyone connected with them seemed to end up dead before their time.

She wanted to forget the anger, forget the questions, and just be Brook and Justin again.

Her fingers found the faux pearls and twisted them together. The irony of the long habit hit her anew, and she let her fingers fall. She needed the things gone—but Papa was right. They had to tread carefully. Too many people had already died, and if the Rushworths were responsible, they had to bring them to justice, not give them what they wanted.

For her mother. For the major.

Eventually her father pulled up in front of a large, dreary-looking building stained with soot and time. Brook reined in her thoughts and gave Deirdre's hand an encouraging squeeze. They all exited in silence, traversed the walk without a word, and only spoke once inside to learn which ward Seamus O'Malley had been taken to.

The hospital was utilitarian, the starkness unrelieved by color. Their shoes clicked loud against the tile floors. Brook and her father flanked Deirdre, and the maid darted a look her way.

"I'm so sorry for bringing this upon you."

"It isn't your doing." Brook's voice came out a whisper in the white corridor.

Deirdre shook her head. "It's because of me you were called down there. Because of me the reporters saw you leaving."

Papa sent encouragement from his gaze without the need to smile. "Circumstances that were outside your control. The only thing you did, O'Malley, was try to care for your uncle. There is no blame to be found in that."

"The detective—"

"Will keep an open, unbiased mind about it all or will find himself out of favor with his superiors." Her father's face went hard. "I have never much cared for those who use their influence amiss—but there is no guilt for this in my house, and if Cole tries to find any, I *will* use whatever force I must to see justice done. And if my influence alone doesn't suffice, we've two dukes in our corner."

"At least one of whom would be eager for an excuse to let loose his temper." Brook's lips tugged up. Justin, with his Duke of Stafford glower, would be furious indeed when he learned how Cole had interrogated her. Even with all between them, she knew that.

Papa nodded toward the door they'd been instructed to take. Inside were a row of cots filled with blanket-covered figures.

A few sat up with book or newspaper in hand, others seemed to be sleeping.

Brook touched a hand to Deirdre's back to indicate she should lead the way.

Deirdre peered at each figure they passed, until finally she sucked in a breath and came to a halt. "Uncle."

The man on the bed was pale as the moon with deep circles under his eyes, his skin wrinkled and cracked. His eyes fluttered open, though they stared up without recognition. "Who . . . ?"

His voice sounded faint, scratched. Deirdre reached for a cup of water and lifted his head to help him sip. "It's Deirdre, Uncle Seamus. I'm here in London with Lord Whitby and heard you were here as well."

"DeeDee." His eyes focused upon Deirdre's face. "All grown."

"Aye. 'Tis been too long." She settled a hand on his forehead. "You're hot as blazes. How do you feel?"

His eyes went cloudy again, and his face screwed up. "The major. Is he . . . ?"

Brook reached for her father's hand. Deirdre swallowed audibly. "Dead."

Seamus turned his face away. "I was too weak to help. All I . . . all I could do was lie there. Pretend to be dead myself."

"You're ill. Better to pretend to death than meet it in fact." Deirdre dashed at her eyes and sniffed. "Have the police been to talk to you?"

The man shook his head. "I heard . . . when they were taking me . . . something about being too far gone to have seen anything." He turned his face back to Deirdre, then beyond her. Recognition sparked when he spotted Papa. "But I did, milord. I saw him."

Papa eased forward. "Saw who, O'Malley?"

"Don't know. Young fellow. Spry—climbed . . . out window. Wore a hat. Long coat. Couldn't . . . couldn't see face, but . . ."

"Easy, uncle." Deirdre trailed her fingers over his face. "Don't tax yourself, now."

He reached up, though it looked like it took all his strength, and caught Deirdre's hand. "He took . . . papers. Solicitor."

Brook's breath tangled in her throat, and she looked up at her father. The major had said he was having papers drawn up—and who but Lord Rushworth and Lady Catherine would have a reason to take them? Who else would stand to inherit anything that was his in light of his death?

The flare of Papa's nostrils said he was thinking the same. "You heard his voice, then. Was he educated? Had he any accent?"

"I . . . Educated. He was educated." Seamus closed his eyes for a long moment, then dragged in a deep breath. "Major seemed . . . to struggle to place him."

Brook's brows pulled down. He wouldn't have struggled to place Rush—he looked just like his father's portraits. But any number of other people could have been vaguely familiar, she supposed.

Her father nodded and gave the man a tight smile. "That's very helpful, O'Malley. We'll find his solicitor and get a copy of whatever was stolen. Justice will be done. You rest now." He patted Deirdre's shoulder. "Stay with him as long as you like. But if darkness falls before you leave, don't try to take the tube—hire a hack. Here's enough for the fare."

Deirdre opened her mouth, obviously set on refusing the money Papa held out, but Brook shook her head. "Take it, O'Malley." There'd been tragedy enough for one day. They didn't need the too-lovely maid finding more in the tube tunnels.

She obeyed, slowly, and sank down onto the edge of her uncle's cot. "I don't deserve your kindness, my lord."

"Nonsense." He turned, ushering Brook along with him.

"Family is the most important thing, always. You focus on yours right now. We'll give him some peace so he can rest."

Brook cast one last look over her shoulder at the shriveled man, the broken, beautiful girl. Both with a pall of death over them.

The whole world, it seemed, had one to match.

Twenty-Five

The weight pressed upon Deirdre's shoulders until she thought she wouldn't be able to trudge her way down the hospital corridor. Last night when she finally left her uncle's side, it had been bad enough. Today, with the sun shining bright through the windows and catching on the baroness's hair, it was worse.

Perhaps, had her ladyship merely granted her more time off, it wouldn't have weighed so heavily. But she had driven her. Cheerfully so, even though Lady Ramsey had apparently insisted Lady Berkeley go out to a dinner party with them last night, and it had left her exhausted today.

Perhaps, had her uncle been as bad as yesterday, she could have shoved guilt aside and focused solely on him. But he was, praise God, much improved—and had looked at her with Da's eyes, with wise eyes, as if knowing exactly how she had treated this family that would do so much for her.

She darted a glance at the young woman beside her. There were ladies aplenty in the hospital, most of them part of some aid group or another, out to do their good deeds for nameless faces. They came in flocks, in wide-brimmed hats overflowing with lace and silk flowers, in their best morning suits and dresses.

Lady Berkeley had come in her simplest, her hat modest—her worth coming through all the louder.

A nurse passed them, and Deirdre drew in a breath and tried to smile. "Did you have a nice time last night, my lady? Was His Grace there? Or Lord Worthing, perhaps?"

Her ladyship sighed. "The duke was, surprisingly. And his cousin with Miss Rosten, which meant that *my* cousin spent the night flirting outrageously with some poor chap who's likely half blind with love now."

Deirdre smiled. "It is hard to feel sorry for her when she goes about revenge with so much energy."

Her ladyship chuckled. "It is, at that."

"And His Grace? Did you speak with him?" Though her ladyship hadn't said a word about it, she'd watched the disappointment grow each day he hadn't come. She knew that whatever they had argued about this time, the baroness regretted it.

Now all emotion drained from her countenance, the mask left in its place perfect but empty. "I did. Long enough to request he come by this morning at nine. Which, of course, he didn't."

They opened the massive front door and stepped out into a fine mist caught halfway between fog and rain. Deirdre stopped her ladyship with a hand on her arm. "My lady . . . life can be so short. You mustn't let misunderstandings get in the way of happiness. You charged through the city at night last year to keep things right between you—why do you now wait around for him to come to you?"

"Because I . . ." She looked away, but not before Deirdre saw the pain in her eyes. "Because everything has changed."

A month ago—a week ago, a day ago—she wouldn't have dared to loop her arm through the lady's. Today, she couldn't imagine doing otherwise. "He's in love with you, my lady. And you with him."

Lady Berkeley sighed. "What if it isn't enough?"

And Deirdre knew, as she gazed on this hurting girl, that she could have been *any* hurting girl—baroness or not. She knew that if Mum realized how she'd come by the money she sent, she'd toss it into the pond. Knew that she couldn't keep serving these good people knowing how she'd betrayed them. Knew she had to throw herself on their mercy and let come what may.

"My lady." A step away from the car, she drew them both to a halt. But she couldn't look into the familiar eyes or the inquisitive face. She drew in a breath that wasn't deep enough and locked her gaze on the embroidery at her ladyship's shoulder. "I need to confess. You've been so good, you and your father, especially about my uncle. But . . . but I really don't deserve it. I've done something terrible."

The shoulder sagged. "Pratt. All my post."

Of course she'd suspected, once His Grace got home and they talked. Deirdre's arm slipped from her ladyship's, down to her side. "I was only a housemaid when it began, and the money he gave me . . . they needed it, my mum and family. And it seemed harmless at first—he wanted to know which suitor Lady Regan favored, before you came home. Who was to be named Whitby's heir."

"But *stealing*?" Her ladyship stepped away. Perhaps she'd hop in her car and leave Deirdre to find her own way home—heaven knew it would serve her right. As would finding all her things tossed to the curb when she got there. "Did that seem harmless too? Did he pay you more for that?"

Deirdre winced at the bitter tone. "I couldn't get out. He turned to threats, if I tried. First that he would force me to his bed and then . . . then he threatened my family. Said he had a man in my village ready to burn the house to the ground."

"So you *come* to us!" The baroness spun to face her again, her face a combination of anger and pity. Her accent deepened, the French curling around her vowels and consonants as it did in those first moments when she awoke from the nightmare. "Did you not pause to think that we could have helped? That we could have protected them? Protected *you*?"

Had she? No. Never. Perhaps because she couldn't imagine they would go so far out of their way to help her—though they had just proven they would. Perhaps because she had never really believed that their good could win out over his evil. "I'm sorry, my lady. I know you have to dismiss me, at the least, perhaps even have me arrested for tampering with the mail. But I couldn't keep lying to you."

If he was merciful, his lordship would take action now and not wait until they got back to Whitby Park so he could make an example of her before the rest of the staff. If she were beyond lucky, he would not involve the law, in order to keep his name from the press again.

The baroness pressed the heel of her hand to her forehead, under the sloped brim of her hat.

"Well, well. Are the conspirators squabbling?"

Deirdre jolted at the voice, her gaze flying about the area until it clapped upon Detective Cole. Without allowing herself to think of the audacity of it, she stepped in front of her ladyship. "Detective. Have you come to talk to my uncle? He is awake, and he saw much of what happened yesterday."

The man tilted his lips into a patronizing smile. "Oh, I already know what happened."

"Good." She lifted her chin, even if she had to clutch her hands together to keep them from shaking. "Then you know it was an educated man what stabbed him, one he didn't know well."

A condescending chuckle joined the smile. "That doesn't much narrow it down, does it? Given that the major has been on the subcontinent for almost two decades. Which is why—" he took a step nearer, and Deirdre could see the hard light gleaming in his eyes—"I find it so very odd that *you*, niece to his batman, end up working for *them*, the house of the major's archrival."

Her back stiffened. "My uncle recommended me there—he said it was the finest house he'd seen."

The baroness stepped to her side. "And *you* are better versed in ancient gossip than I supposed, Detective, if you know of that old rivalry. But let me guess—my cousins told you."

He inclined his head.

"Did they also tell you of the argument between the major and his brother—their father?"

Such darkness . . . so like that always in Pratt's eyes. Deirdre shuddered.

The detective's eyes narrowed. "Over the diamonds. Which are by rights theirs, but which they believe *you* have. Their theory . . . Lady Berkeley . . . is that when the major tried to reclaim them, you had him killed."

Her ladyship drew herself up—but Deirdre's gaze was snagged by a new figure striding their way, fury in His Grace's every movement. She reached for the baroness's hand and gave it a little tug to get her attention.

Lady Berkeley shifted and made a quick half curtsy. "Good morning, Duke."

"My lady." The duke packed a world of feeling into the greeting, though it was the detective he speared with his glare. "Detective."

"Your Grace." Cole's face went harder, a shutter coming over the gleam in his eyes. "Excuse us, but I'm engaged in official business with the baroness."

"No you're not. You're engaged upon harassing a young lady whom your superiors have verified had absolutely no motive for arranging the death of her cousin." He jerked his head, a clear dismissal with an undertone of threat. "I suggest you return to Scotland Yard and take a look at the papers sent over by the major's solicitor."

The detective held the duke's gaze for a long moment, then glanced back to the baroness. The muscle in his jaw ticked.

His Grace moved nearer, looming over Cole. Deirdre hadn't thought the detective short, but in that moment he looked it. "And I suggest you tread carefully."

"I always do." Cole narrowed his eyes. "What exactly is your interest in all this, Your Grace?"

The duke lifted his brows. "You're a detective. Figure it out."

"Oh, I will. Rest assured."

His Grace stepped aside and made a flourishing gesture indicating the detective ought to leave. "It oughtn't to take you too long, if you know how to do your job. And do have a lovely day."

Cole stalked off toward a horse hitched at the far corner of the hospital. The duke watched him for a moment, then spun back to them. His face had gone hard as granite, and fury blazed brighter than ever in his eyes as he locked them on the baroness. "O'Malley, excuse us for a moment." He took the lady's hand and pulled her the opposite direction.

Were it anyone else looking at the baroness with such anger, Deirdre may have refused. But she wasn't about to get in the way of a man in love.

Justin's blood was a roar in his ears, his heart a thundering tempest. It had begun that morning, when he'd opened the paper to see her plastered on the front cover, with the headline of MURDER HAUNTS BARONESS BEAUTY nearly sending him into a stroke. Had her father not shown up within minutes, he would have been pounding on her door long before the nine o'clock hour she'd asked him to come. As it was, he'd spent his morning pounding on doors with Whitby instead, trying to find the solicitor that Rushworth used.

It had done little to cool his temper. Justin pulled Brook into a poor excuse for a garden at the side of the hospital and, for lack of privacy, turned to Monegasque as he spun her to face him. "Are you insane or just stupid?"

Not, perhaps, the best greeting if his aim were to keep her calm. But at the moment he had no desire for calm. He wanted a fight, and no one else in the world would give him the one he needed.

She pulled her hand free and looked as though she wanted to slap him with it. "Excuse me?" Her words were in Monegasque too.

Justin waved a hand at the world at large. "You have detectives chasing you with murder charges, a killer on the loose slaying people connected to these stupid Fire Eyes, and what do you do? You head out into the city, alone but for a maid, without ever pausing to consider for even one second that you could be next!"

He expected her to shout. Instead, she went calm—but seething. "What do you know of it? You didn't even bother to come this morning when I asked you to."

"Because your father came to *my* house at eight. I assumed you knew that and would wait for me—that while I was off pounding on solicitors' doors with him, *you* wouldn't be darting off on your own, trying to get yourself killed."

"I didn't know." Still, frustration overtook the realization in her eyes, and she pivoted away. "But how could you possibly expect me to sit idly by? It's fine and good for *you* to put yourself into the path of all this, but if I so much as take my maid to visit her uncle, I'm either stupid or insane?"

"You don't *think*. Not about consequences. You never have." He turned, too, and took a step to put himself in front of her

327

again. "You chase whatever impulse seizes you, valuing your blasted independence above common sense."

"And what if I do?" Her eyes were ablaze, green fire spitting at him. "If it's a fault, it's *mine*, and one you've long known about. If you loved me like you claimed—"

"*If?* You doubt me because I don't applaud when you run headlong into danger?"

Now the seething gave way to fuming, and she sliced a hand through the air. "For once in your life, why can't you accept the fact that perhaps a person isn't wrong just because they don't agree with you?"

He took a step back. "When have I—"

"When have you *not*? 'You'll not take the stage.' 'You'll not race.' 'You'll not get near that horse.' You always have to be giving orders, the one in control, and it drives you mad when you're not!" She surged forward, poking a finger into his shoulder. "Well, *Duke*, you're not my father. You don't get to dictate to me."

"*You're my son, Justin, not my nursemaid.*" His father's words rang in his head.

Yet again, being blamed for caring. For wanting someone to take two minutes to think about consequences, about how a decision might affect someone else. Might affect *him*. How *he* might feel if someone drove off the road or ran pell-mell into the clutches of a murderer.

He held his arms wide. "I guess that's who *I* am. Who I've always been. If it's a fault, it's one you've long known about. What, then?"

She breathed a laugh as dry as the withered flower stalk by her foot. "That would be the question, wouldn't it?"

The temper in his eyes went darker, calmer, more treacherous. Turned to ice.

No. He had already lost his father—he wasn't going to lose Brook. He *couldn't* lose Brook. Not to this Fire Eyes insanity, and not because of his own mistakes. He swallowed, breathed, sent heavenward a silent prayer. "Just tell me. Tell me what you need me to be."

"Here." She thrust her hand downward, pointing at the ground by her side. "I need you to be *here*, but you never are."

"I'm here." He stepped forward, clasping her elbows.

She wrenched free. "You're not. Even when you are, you're not, you're behind that dashed wall you've built."

She shook her head and wrapped her arms around her stomach. "You won't . . . ever since I came here, you . . ."

When she averted her face, he caught the glistening of tears in her eyes. He reached out again, but she retreated and shook her head. "I thought I loved you. That we could make it work, but . . . but we *don't*. We don't work anymore. You can't just kiss me again and set the world to rights. Maybe . . . maybe God only meant you to bring me here. Maybe friends is all we were meant to be."

The earth beneath him crumbled, opened, swallowed him into its yawning darkness. "I can't just be your friend anymore."

"I know." She held herself tighter. "I guess that means we're . . . nothing."

He couldn't move. Couldn't speak. Couldn't think. It was unfathomable. Because he needed her so much—how was it possible she could bid him farewell so easily?

Yet she did. She stood there for a moment, no tears spilling over their rims, no uncertainty shaking her. And then she turned and walked away, her arms still clutched around her stomach.

Justin could only stand there in the pathetic little garden and let his eyes slide closed. He tried to pray, but he had no words. Just a cry that came from his gut but couldn't find purchase on his tongue. And so it echoed through him, clanging and pounding. An accusation.

A desperate plea.

Twenty-Six

My lady—"

"Don't." Brook didn't even look at Deirdre as she slid into the driver's seat of the roadster. She had already cranked it and had the key in her hands. Steady, those hands. As steady as her voice. Because inside, she'd ground to a halt. Still, if not peaceful. Too still for shaking. Too still for words.

Deirdre said nothing more. Brook didn't let herself wonder what she had meant to say—no doubt it was some question about what she intended to do with the knowledge that she had acted as Pratt's spy. But Brook couldn't think about that right now either. She could only think of pressing the clutch, the accelerator, the brake. Where to turn, when to signal. How to park, and then to put one foot in front of the other to lead her inside.

She paused at the door but still couldn't look at her maid. "O'Malley, when we get inside, I want you to pack—"

"My things. I understand."

"No. Well, yes. But mine too. We're going home."

"We . . ." Wisely, she said no more.

Not in the mood to wait for a bell to be answered, Brook

pushed open the door. She bypassed the drawing room with its laughter and crowds of near-strangers and headed straight for the study, where Papa was most likely to be.

Aunt Mary was there too, leaning over his shoulder and pointing at some paper or another on the desk. They both looked up when she entered. Her aunt smiled.

Her father, when he saw her face, stood. "What is it?"

Words. The only ones she could find were French. "Can we go home, Papa? Please?"

"What?" Her aunt had obviously understood, given the outrage in her eyes, though she answered in English. "Absolutely not! You are the darling of Town, you cannot *possibly* leave before the king's coronation—"

"Of course we can." Papa's voice was low and soft, his eyes seeing far beyond hers. "Did your Justin find you?"

He tried, and failed, to pronounce it correctly. But his name still made a sob well up in that empty place, lodge in her throat. "He is not my Justin. He will never be. I . . . I want to go home."

"Of course." He came around the desk and pulled her to his chest. "My darling girl." He said no more, because he was Papa, and he understood when silence was all that could soothe.

Aunt Mary, to her credit, held her tongue, too, and didn't even faint. She just whisked by them. No doubt to go somewhere private to bemoan her niece's utter ignorance of society.

Or perhaps to get reinforcements. A minute later, when Papa drew away, Melissa was there with wide eyes. "You're leaving?"

Brook held out a hand for her cousin to grip, though she couldn't manage a smile. "I have to. I don't suppose you want to come?" She could use a friend to laugh with, to mourn with—one who may have been reserved at first but who loved her now. Who never feigned feeling just to turn on her.

But Melissa sighed. "I can't. Mama would have a fit—and I need to stay here and snag myself a husband."

"Oh, Lissa." She tugged her in for a tight embrace. "Not out of spite. Don't marry out of spite. You'll be stuck with him for all your life."

"I know." Melissa pulled away, her face somber. "I promise. But I will stay. You need your open spaces and ocean to cope, I need my crowds and laughter."

To that she could only nod. Papa, it seemed, was the only one who related to her need. So it would be just them again, and the staff who knew how she liked her coffee and sausage and to stir the fire earlier than usual in her grate.

And a maid who would sell her secrets to a land-grubbing neighbor—but she would ignore that for now. She would get home, get settled. Then talk to Papa about Deirdre.

If she were empty inside, should it not have made her feel lighter? But her legs, as she turned for the steps, felt heavy as despair.

Justin exited the House of Lords and paused a moment to look up at the grand, towering facade of the palace. For years, anytime he saw Westminster's pointed spires and gothic styling, he had dreamed of being inside its cavernous chamber, taking the seat reserved for him. Facing the throne.

A lot of good he was doing, finally there but his mind a few crucial miles away. He *wanted* to focus on the laws and debates—but he couldn't, not when Brook was still in danger . . . and had dismissed him so summarily.

His feet hitched when he caught sight of the figure leaning against a shining new Austin parked a spot away from the Rolls-Royce. Maybe Worthing was waiting for his father—Justin had noted the Duke of Nottingham chatting with a few other lords of his generation after the session ended. With any luck, the son wouldn't even notice Justin walking by. He could hope. He had, after all, spent half the night on his knees in prayer before exhaustion had claimed him. And then the other half sleeping on his hard floor. Surely that was penance enough.

Apparently not. Worthing straightened as Justin neared, that annoying grin on his face and his hands in his trouser pockets. "Stafford! Good day."

A sigh fisted in his chest. He had no fight left in him. But little patience either. "What do you want, Worthing?"

The idiot man's grin only grew. "To earn your eternal gratitude. She left Town this morning."

"What?" Justin's feet planted themselves a few feet from Worthing, refusing to go a step farther. "For Yorkshire?"

Worthing nodded. "Would have left yesterday afternoon, had it not taken so long to ready. But at first light . . ." He pulled one hand out of his pocket to illustrate his point, imitating a car driving away—complete with muted engine noises.

Had it been Thate, and news of someone else's leaving, Justin would have laughed. "She told *you* she was going though."

The grin turned patronizing. "Yes, you see, we take part in this bizarre social ritual called *conversation*. You should give it a try sometime. It's when you exchange words—at a normal volume—for the purpose of sharing information, rather than for accusation or inflicting emotional pain."

Justin's shoulders slumped. Even at that, he could muster no anger. He was too weary. "It wasn't all me. I started it, I grant that, but—"

"I know." Worthing clapped a hand to his shoulders, as if they were the best of friends. "She told me what was said, and I told *her* she was being an idiot, that you had a perfectly valid point and that you wouldn't have been so very fearful if you didn't love her so much—and had you not suffered enough losses this year. But you know Brook." He rolled his eyes and dropped his hand. "A mite stubborn, that girl."

He . . . he had *defended* him? To Brook? Justin stared at him for a long moment. "Why?"

"Is she stubborn? That is a question only the Almighty can answer. But if you mean why did I say such things to her, the answer ought to be obvious." Worthing met Justin's gaze, held it. "She's wrong. I don't know why she's so set on denying what she feels for you when it's obvious to anyone who sees her watching you, but she's wrong. You are meant for more than just getting her to England. God isn't finished with the two of you yet."

"Know that, do you?" But the words didn't come out mocking—they emerged . . . hopeful.

No smile touched Worthing's expression now. Peace, however, saturated it. "Yes. I do."

Again, Justin was reduced to staring. What stared back at him made him feel the dunce—though, granted, a relieved one. "You're really not in love with her."

Worthing chuckled and leaned into the side of his car again—at least, Justin assumed it was his. "Are you daft? I'd never survive it. If she isn't trying to bore me to death with some obscure academic work, she's trying to give me a heart attack, flying around on that wild stallion of hers."

Though he'd never expected to experience such a thing, a grin tugged at Justin's lips. In the presence of *Worthing*. "She's magnificent, isn't she?"

Worthing laughed outright this time. "That she is, and I adore her—in much the same way I adore my sister, who drives me nearly as mad." He paused and then gave a sideways nod in the direction his hand had motored. "Go after her, you imbecile. And don't relent until you have an actual conversation and have convinced her you can't live without her. Address whatever's keeping her from declaring her love for you and move on to all the happily-ever-after nonsense."

For the first time in weeks, hope sparked to life. Justin took a step toward the Rolls-Royce but then paused. "Worthing . . . I'm in your debt."

The grin reemerged. "Excellent. No doubt I'll need a favor one of these days, when I'm the one gone stupid over some young lady."

Justin smiled again and hurried to his car. Worthing followed, saying nothing while Justin cranked it and slid inside, but then he leaned toward the window. "Listen." His voice was serious again, and as low as it could be and still be heard over the engine. "My first thought, when she said she was leaving, was that it was good—she'll be away from the Rushworths, Pratt, whoever killed her cousin. But I can't shake the feeling that the danger will follow her home."

Cold dread overtook Justin's heart. Of course it would. Anyone who would kill so easily wouldn't let a few hundred miles get in his way. He nodded.

So did Worthing. "My advice would be to resolve this thing between you as quickly as her stubborn will allows—and then get ready. The tempest, I think, has only just begun."

Because the words felt like truth, Justin nodded again. And because they were a terrible omen, he sighed. "I trust you'll be in prayer."

"Without ceasing. For the both of you." He stuck a hand in, and Justin clasped it without hesitation. "Keep in touch. And if you need me, give the word."

Funny how, in that moment, this man he had thought for sure was an enemy seemed like a certain friend. "Let's pray I don't have to."

Without further ado, he backed out and joined the stream of cars and carriages. A quick stop at his townhouse to collect Peters and their things, and he'd be on his way. He'd rent rooms somewhere in Whitby, to be close by. And he'd simply wear her down with his presence. He would *be there*. Every hour, every day, knocking upon her door.

Praying, without ceasing. Until she let him in again.

Darkness cloaked the familiar heath by the time Deirdre found a moment to step outside. Still, it was earlier than it should have been. She hadn't finished unpacking for the baroness yet, but she'd been dismissed. No doubt the lady chafed at her presence.

The air had a nip to it, but it still smelled of spring in the country—a scent she had missed acutely in London. But she hadn't counted on being back so soon. And knew, now, she wouldn't be here long. The baroness would talk to his lordship soon.

Then Deirdre would find herself called forward after prayers, denounced in front of them all. Mrs. Doyle would gasp and press a hand to her mouth. Mr. Graham would rumble out a cough of outrage. Beatrix's eyes would go wide with shock.

And Hiram . . . Hiram would look at her with that profound disappointment that would shatter her heart into a million pieces.

"Escaped finally, did you, Dee?"

Her eyes slid shut against the warm, cheerful voice. She buttoned the jacket she had slipped on and sank onto the stone garden bench. "How have you been, Hi?"

He chuckled as he took the seat next to her. "It was quiet while you were gone, as expected. Though I can't say as anyone was surprised at the wire saying you were on your way back. Murder though—didn't expect that."

The image kept gnashing at her, popping up whenever she closed her eyes. The major, in a pool of his own blood, his limbs at odd angles. She shuddered. "I'm the one who found him. When I went to see Uncle Seamus."

"Oh, Dee." His arm came around her shoulders, and he pulled her to his side.

She sagged against him and wished she could stay there forever. But what was the point? She would soon be gone. Back to Kilkeel in disgrace. Then what would Mum do? "I've ruined everything, Hiram. Lord Whitby and the baroness were so kind, so supportive—but I'd tossed it all away long before that. They'll sack me soon."

Hiram's hand stroked over her hair. "What do you mean, sweetheart? You've done nothing wrong."

Sweetheart. She savored it for a moment, let it turn over in her mind. It clashed against the guilt. "I have, though. I already confessed it to the baroness. I . . . it was Pratt. He approached me in the village a year ago."

Hiram went stiff, but he held her all the tighter. "Approached you how?"

Her stomach hurt in the remembering. How she had turned down a side street to make it the quicker to the post office and had all but run into him. How, at first, she had been struck dumb by his beauty—up until then, she had only glimpsed him from afar when he prowled around Whitby Park. But he must have seen her. He knew her name, her position, her salary . . . her family's situation.

"He . . . he said he knew how my family was struggling, and he wanted to help. That I had two choices—I could either become his mistress or . . . or feed him information on who Lord Whitby would name heir."

"DeeDee." He turned a bit and wrapped his other arm around her too. Sorrow laced his tone. "Why'd you say nothing? You could have told me. Told his lordship."

She should have. That was so clear now, but at the time . . .

"It seemed so silly. I had little information to give, but he paid me well for it. But then the baroness came, and he'd grown so impatient. Threatening—which was always lurking under the surface; I knew that all along—that if I hadn't agreed, it would be trouble to find my family, not pound notes."

She fisted her hands in his shirt and pressed her forehead to his shoulder. "Now what am I to do? I'll be dismissed, possibly arrested, and my mum . . ."

"Your mum'll be fine." He pressed a kiss to her hair. "You'll be fine. His lordship won't want the attention of pressing charges, and we'll find other positions. I'll take up farming, if I must."

"Hiram." She wanted to cling to that *we*, but it wasn't right. "No. It's my trouble, my wrong. You can't be the one to pay for it."

"And you think it won't be punishment for me if you leave, if I must do without you?" He touched a hand to her face to turn it and then feathered his lips over hers. "I love you, Dee. Where you go, I go. We'll marry, and I'll help you take care of your family. I promise you."

She should refuse. But she was too selfish. Sliding an arm around his neck, she kissed him soundly, letting the joy of it scrub at the bitterness and regret. It couldn't obliterate them, but it eased their harshness. "I love you, Hiram. I'd be honored to be your wife. Though sure and I'm sorry to come to you with such trouble at my heels."

"We'll face it together." He brushed at the hair coming loose from its pins, and the moonlight gilded his smile. "Two are stronger than one, aye? We'll start looking for other positions. Together."

She nodded and rested against him again. But her mind went back inside, up the stairs, to the chamber where, if the baroness had found sleep, she was no doubt thrashing about in the throes of her nightmare.

Her ladyship couldn't escape her troubles, and heaven help her but Deirdre felt responsible for them. Bound to her through them, obligated to help. And she would, if she were given the chance.

But that seemed a very big *if*.

Twenty-Seven

From her seat at her window, Brook could hear the rumble of the Rolls-Royce as it made its way down the drive. She wouldn't look up from her book. She wouldn't. She had no need to see the silver paint, the golden head—though today the top would be up, as the rain was coming down in torrents. She had thought it would keep Justin at home, or wherever he'd been staying the past fortnight.

No such luck. Of course, if her father wouldn't keep entertaining him . . .

Her fingers curled around the edges of her book—Kant, and the German was nearly impossible. Especially when she was *not* watching the Rolls-Royce disappear over the knoll. With an exasperated breath, she tossed it to the window seat and took to her feet.

Deirdre stepped out from the dressing room. "Do you need something, my lady?" Her words were quiet and eager, as they had been each of the interminable fifteen days since they'd left the hospital in London.

Brook knew Deirdre was waiting for the proverbial shoe to drop. Waiting for Brook to tell her father, and for her father to

340

dismiss her. And several times, she had nearly confided what Deirdre had confessed. But then she would stop. Dismissing her wouldn't get the letters back or erase the secrets told. Dismissing her would mean needing to find a replacement, and that meant someone new who could be bought and bribed.

Deirdre would make no new betrayal. She might be, right now, the most trustworthy employee to be found.

Brook forced half a smile. "Nothing. Thank you. I'm going to find my father." Not meeting her gaze, Brook kept on for the door. She didn't want to dismiss her . . . but she hadn't quite forgiven. She had tried. Had prayed the words. But she was still so empty inside.

Papa was, as expected, in the library. When she entered, it wasn't just the scent of pipe tobacco and paper and leather that greeted her, though—there, too, lingered the scent of lemon and spice. *Justin.* She very nearly retreated, but then she'd be left with only her own company, and she had days ago grown annoyed with herself. "Have a pleasant chat, Papa?"

Justin had been here *hours* today. Hours.

And her father had the gall to smile over his newspaper. "I did. We were discussing the latest advancements in aeronautics. You should have joined us, my dear. You would have enjoyed it."

"Papa." She sank into her usual chair, at right angles to his. "Why will you not turn him away?"

"Because I enjoy his company." He reached for his pipe and put it between his teeth, though he didn't light it. He never did while she was in the room, after she'd once coughed. "Clever young man. I can see why you like him so well."

"*Liked.*"

"Come now, my dear, we both know you're only so miserable because you're in love. One of these days you'll relent long enough to talk to him, and it will take but a single honest, earnest conversation for you to put aside your differences." He took the pipe out again and used it to point at her. "When that day comes, I would prefer the pleasure of saying *'I knew it all along'* to the regret of saying *'I'm sorry for treating him poorly while you were at odds.'*"

"Papa."

"You cannot avoid him forever."

Why not? Why would he not go away? Back to London or Gloucestershire or India or Africa or *anywhere*—so long as it wasn't Whitby Park? She rested her elbow on the arm of the chair and then her head in her hand. "I don't want to see him. There's nothing left to say."

"I think there is." He put newspaper and pipe aside and leaned forward, resting his hand on her knee. "Brook, whenever I walk into your room, I see the same book sitting on your bedside table. What does it say to do?"

"That isn't fair." She had tried looking for comfort in *La Bible*. She had tried to find answers. But it had just been words these past weeks, never sinking deeper than her mind. "I know we are to forgive. And I will. But that doesn't mean that we can go back to the way things used to be."

"Who ever said you should?" He sat back up, shaking his head. "But God does not just instruct us to forgive—He instructs us to trust. To trust that, even though life hurts us, He will take care of us. That even if we lose the ones we love, He will sustain us through it."

Her brows knit. "*Trust* is not my problem."

"Isn't it?" He gave her knee a squeeze. "You are afraid to love, my dear. Afraid that if you do, it will only come to a miserable end. And it may—life comes with no promises. But it's worth it. It's worth the risk."

She shook her head, intending it to be a denial that she was afraid. But with each movement, her resolve shifted. "No. No, it's not worth it. How can I possibly love him when it means

342

arguing like we have been? When it means he doesn't want me to spread my wings lest I get hurt in the flight—"

"Brook, he is the one who taught you how to fly! But is it so unreasonable that he asks you to look before you leap?"

How was it that Justin could make her feel the fool even when he wasn't in the room? "What is the point, though? We will only hurt each other. Or . . . or lose each other later."

He gripped her hand, resting their clasped fingers on the book she'd left on the side table last night. "Must I quote Shakespeare at you, my dear? 'It is better to have loved and lost—'"

"No! It isn't!"

Silence greeted her outburst, and it reigned long enough to make her glance at her father's countenance. To see the patience there . . . and the sheen in his eyes. Of all the people for her to have said such a thing to . . .

His fingers tightened around hers. "Should I not have loved your mother, then? Is that what you're saying?"

"Papa . . ."

"I lost her. I lost you. And it brought me to my knees. It tormented me for years and made me shut myself off from society. But it brought me to my knees—and the Lord was there, through it all, supporting me. The Lord was there, shaping me through my loss into the man He wanted me to be."

She lowered her head, her gaze. "I didn't mean . . ."

"You did. But you don't understand, Brook. Had I run away in fear from the things she made me feel, I would not have mourned any less when she died. I would have mourned *more*. Mourned the loss of the happiness we could have had and didn't. I would have mourned what could have been and wasn't. I would have been even more miserable, I would have turned bitter, I would have been hounded not just by questions but by crippling regrets."

"But—"

"If Justin were killed today, and you had all this between you, what would it do to you?"

Her breath balled up in her chest, choked her.

He patted her hand and then leaned back. "Love is much like Oscuro, my dear. Yes, it is dangerous. You may get hurt. But the victory of the ride . . . Would you be willing to miss out on that, just because at any time he might shy at something and send you to the ground?"

And now her lips tugged up. He knew her language all too well. She sat up straighter—and then started when running steps burst into the room.

Deirdre halted halfway in, her eyes wide and her hands shaking violently as they clutched at a slip of paper. "Beg pardon. But I—it's my mum."

Brook pushed herself up even as her father did. He stepped forward, the pipe in his hand again. "What has happened?"

She was glad he had asked. Her tongue was knotted. Pratt had made good on his threats.

Deirdre must have known her thoughts. She looked her way, shook her head. "Sickness, it says. Bad. My brother, he says I need to come home. I know I oughtn't to ask—"

"Of course you ought." Brook slid up beside her father, knowing he would have said the same. "You need to go to her."

"You can make the afternoon train west if you hurry. I will send ahead to procure a steamer ticket for you."

Deirdre blinked rapidly and clutched the paper to her chest. "I'm indebted to you, your lordship."

"We've been through this, O'Malley. Family first. And give your uncle our regards—he's still there convalescing, is he not?"

"Aye. And thank you. And again, thank you." With watery eyes, Deirdre flew from the room.

Brook turned to her father. "May I drive her? She cannot walk in this weather."

"Of course." He leaned over and kissed her forehead. "But be careful of all the mud. And consider what I've said. I hate seeing you like this, Brook. You are meant to be sunshine and tempests, not dreary fog and rain."

Unable to think of any response, unable to think why it sounded like such a compliment, she could only wrap her arms around him and hold on for a long, fortifying moment. Then she ran from the room in search of Deirdre.

"But I want to come. I want to meet her, DeeDee, and if it's bad enough that they're calling you home . . ."

Tears stung at the implication, but Deirdre couldn't give them purchase yet. Couldn't let them overtake her. She swallowed the fear down and paused at the end of the servants' hall to put a hand to Hiram's face. "I know. And if I get there, and it's that bad, I'll send you word. I promise it, I will. But I couldn't take the time to explain to his lordship *why* you should come with me. We've said nothing, and now—"

"Now the train leaves so soon, and you must be on it." Because he was Hiram, he brightened. Nodded. Leaned down to press a quick kiss to her lips. "Send me word no matter what. Let me know you've got there safe, or I'll worry all the week long."

"I promise. I'll wire you before I board the ship, again when I dock, and then from Kilkeel. I promise."

"Good." He kissed her again and then jumped away from her when hurried footfalls reached them.

Deirdre recognized the step, though she heard it rarely in this part of the house, and straightened as the baroness came running down the last few steps.

Her ladyship looked relieved to have caught her. "There you are. I'll drive you, but we must hurry. The roads will be a mess."

She hadn't the time to argue, though she felt she should. Instead, she flew into her room and tossed what she hoped were suitable items into her bag, then dashed back out. The baroness no longer stood in the hall, though Hiram still did.

"She went to fetch her hat and a wrap, said to meet her at the car."

Nodding, Deirdre ran down the hall, figuring even Mrs. Doyle wouldn't chastise her for it in this case. Hiram kept pace, though she halted him at the door that would lead them out into the rain and muck. "You mustn't muddy your livery."

He looked about to argue but must've decided not to waste the time. With a heave of breath, he kissed her again and drew her in for a quick embrace. "I love you, Dee. Go with God."

"Pray for Mum. And I love you too." She held tightly to him as long as she dared and then darted out into the rain.

The baroness had beaten her out and was already driving the car from the carriage house. Deirdre climbed in, barely getting the door shut before they were off. "Thank you. Though sure and I'm sorry to leave you without warning."

Her ladyship didn't look over at her. She had scarcely touched her with a gaze these two weeks, except when it was unavoidable. "It is no great thing. You must be with your family. I know what they mean to you."

"Aye." Her throat went tight. The baroness knew the lengths Deirdre would go to in order to provide and protect. And surely hated her for it. "Ought I to bother coming back?"

The baroness sighed and shifted the gear lever. "O'Malley—Deirdre. What you did . . . were it not for the letters, it would be nothing."

"Letters . . ." There were some yet she hadn't answered for. Hadn't even thought of them in the wake of the major's death. "Forgive me, my lady. He had me plant more in your trunk, in London. I forgot about it when all . . . And when we got home, you'd finished the unpacking on your own." She clutched the handles of her bag until her fingers hurt. "I'm so sorry. I can't say it enough. I never let myself think how it would hurt you. I never thought it would so ruin things with the duke."

The lady's fingers tightened, too, on the wheel. "Can I trust you now? If Pratt comes to you again—"

"I'd go straight to you and his lordship. I swear it." Her heart thudded in her chest. Was it possible her ladyship would grant her another chance? She shouldn't. But, oh, how Deirdre prayed she would.

"Then . . ." She eased to a halt at the base of the drive, glanced both ways—and then at Deirdre. "Then come back when you're satisfied your mother is better. I'll handle my father."

"Thank you." The tears pressed again, but she blinked and cleared her throat. "That sounds so feeble. But I've no other words."

A corner of the baroness's mouth tipped up as she pulled out onto the road for Whitby. As her father's so often did. "If it's more words you're looking for, you could start with 'Hiram and I . . .' That wasn't the first I've seen you with a flush in your cheeks in his company."

They heated now, though not from embarrassment. The one joy since they returned to Yorkshire had been those moments by his side. Knowing that he knew the worst of her and loved her anyway, that he would give up all he'd worked for to be with her, and to help her family. "He's asked me to marry him. I've said yes. Though we haven't said anything to anyone yet, not knowing if . . . if we'd have to leave."

"Well." Her ladyship glanced her away again, her smile full and bright. "I'll be sure and alleviate that concern for him when I get back. Congratulations."

"Thank you, my lady." There would be new problems to figure, now that she knew they could stay at Whitby Park. God willing, children would come, and rare it was that any of the domestic help had a child underfoot.

"Don't fuss over the details yet." And when had her ladyship learned to read her so well? "We can worry over where you'll stay after you get back. For now, focus on your mum, knowing you've a good man awaiting your return."

"Aye." The worry seized her mind again. How ill must Mum be for Killian to send for her? Had they money enough for a physician? She let her eyes slide closed so she could better pray.

By the time they pulled up outside the railway station, the rain had gone from downpour to drizzle. Still, puddles splashed around the roadster's tires. And already a train puffed its steam from the tracks. She'd better hurry, in case it was hers. "Thank you again, my lady."

"Let us know how she is—we'll be praying."

Deirdre didn't know how much longer she'd be able to fend off the tears. Perhaps on the train, in the overcrowded anonymity of third class, she would indulge in a few of them. "I will. Drive safely home."

Without wasting another moment, she let herself out and dashed up to the rain-soaked platform.

Brook had waited a few minutes, studying the lightening clouds and the crowds of people, to make sure Deirdre did not come back, having missed her train. But when no raven hair reappeared after a while, she checked traffic and backed carefully out to the cobbled street.

The abbey on the hill stole her attention as she headed out of town—she'd yet to explore the ruins. Papa had never shown any interest in that particular attraction, hounded as it was by tourists.

But there would be no tourists flocking there today, she would guess. Perhaps she would walk up the hill and wander its once-hallowed chambers for a few minutes. She wouldn't linger long—Papa would be expecting her back, and she was more than a little curious to see what letters Pratt had had Deirdre put in her trunk—but she needed to pray. Earnestly, openly. Not like she'd been doing since they'd returned home.

Decision made, she found a place to park on Church Street and let herself out. The famed one hundred ninety-nine stairs loomed, and the wind blew sprinkling rain into her face. But it was warm and raw and felt like heaven's way of washing away some of the dust inside her.

She climbed quickly, having the stairs all to herself. Her legs felt a pleasant burn once she reached the top. The grass was green and bright, close cut. And the three remaining walls of the abbey towered huge and gold-grey. She squished her way through what must have once been the main doors . . . but rather than stepping into a room, she stepped instead into an unhindered view of the sea.

Yes. This was worth seeing. A skeleton of a wall, graceful arches, pointed spires, and God's creation, all together. The wind whipped the water of the harbor and tried to snatch away her hat. She closed her eyes and considered letting it. Letting the fingers of air soothe and caress.

Father God, mon Dieu. Please, I . . . Forgive me. I have been focusing only on my hurt. On my . . . my fears. Papa was right. I'm afraid of giving myself over to this. But what is it you say? Perfect love casts out fear. Cast it out of me, Lord, please. Of all the things I want to be, that is not one of them. I do not want to be a coward. I don't want . . . I don't want to miss the joys you have for me because I'm too frightened to grasp them. Purge me of the shadows, Lord, of the darkness. Fill me, please, and show me what I should do.

Warmth touched her, intense enough that her eyes flew open, expecting to see summer's sun breaking through the clouds.

But no, rain still misted over her upturned face. The heat came from within. It started in that cold, aching place surrounding her heart and seeped its way outward.

Her breath shuddered. Her knees shook. And a warm gust of wind beckoned her to look to her left.

There, perched on the base of what had once been a column, half-hidden behind the remaining column between them, he sat. With his eyes closed, his face turned to the sea, no hat to keep the misting rain from his face. And given how wet his clothes looked, he must have been there even when the rain had been torrent instead of drizzle.

Justin.

Her breath whispered out. For weeks she had avoided him—but the moment she obeyed the Lord's urging to stop and pray, there he was. And love for him nearly felled her.

She moved toward him, though he must not have heard the squishing of her shoes above the whistling of the wind. He didn't open his eyes, showed no signs of awareness. Stopping in front of him, she let the smile come. This disheveled man with the dripping hair would never be mistaken for the Duke of Stafford, even if he sat there twirling the signet round and round his finger. He was Justin. That was all.

"Haven't you the sense to go in out of the rain?" She said it lightly, still smiling.

His eyelids rose slowly, his lips parted. Disbelief filled his gaze when he looked at her, and he surged to his feet. "Brook."

His arms came around her, crushing her to his drenched, cool chest before she could protest.

She didn't want to protest. She wanted to wrap her arms around his neck and hold on until all the foolish things they'd said were washed away by the rain. "Justin. I'm sorry." Those words tasted like honey and felt like balm. She said them again. "I'm sorry, so sorry."

"But you were right. I do try to control everyone." His hands moved up her back, over her shoulders, and put enough space between them that he could frame her face.

Bright as sapphires, his eyes gleamed. She put her fingers over his. "No, *you* were right. I'm impulsive. I always have been."

He tossed her hat to the ground and rested his forehead on hers. "And much as that drives me mad with fear, I love it about you—that where I am cautious, you are bold; that where I think and never act, you charge ahead."

"But I can be careless. And you're right to think of consequences. Had your father listened to you . . . You've always been the one to take care. And *I* love that about *you*—that you consider so far ahead of where I look." She gripped his fingers as much as she could without dislodging them. Strong and familiar, long and lean, with the bold circle of gold there to proclaim what he had become.

He stroked his thumbs over her cheekbones. "*Je t'aime. Tu es mon âme. Mon cœur.*" *I love you. You are my soul. My heart.*

"Justin . . . I love you." She kept her words English, though she could hear the French in them. "And I was so very wrong. I *do* need you. I'm so much better with you than without you."

He kissed her then, his chilled lips warming against hers as his hands slid to her back again and pulled her against him. Rain from his jacket seeped through hers, but it warmed instead of cooling. This was the kiss she had dreamed of all those months he was gone—gentle but demanding, deep and slow. The kind that made her want to savor, want to strain forward, want to never leave his arms.

She slid her fingers into his hair, slick with water, and pressed close when he tried to pull away.

Smiling against her mouth, he kissed her once more but then set her back. "We've still much that needs saying."

She gripped his waterlogged lapel lest he get some foolish

idea about putting more than a few inches of space between them. "It can wait. You can come home with me, and we can talk into the night. I daresay this will be harder to achieve, though, in my father's presence."

He chuckled, his mouth hovering an infuriating breath away. "I was told that I couldn't expect to kiss you again and set the world to rights."

Oh, how she loved the way his eyes flashed darker when feeling crashed through them. "I am, on occasion, happy to be proven wrong."

"Really." Mirth sparkled in his eyes. "Not the Brook I know."

She couldn't help but chuckle. "All right, just on this *one* occasion. So you had best take advantage of it and kiss me again."

His lips brushed hers. "If I must." He pulled her closer and kissed her until her mind went muddled and her legs weak. She let her fingers trail down his neck, settling a moment at that place beneath his jaw, where she could feel how his pulse raced in time to hers. When next his lips broke away, he still held her flush against him. "I would have married you."

Her mind must still be hazy. Had he said *would have*? "Hmm?"

"Had you shown up at Ralin Castle one day, if we hadn't found your father. I would have married you." His lips trailed over her cheek, her jaw, and paused on *her* pounding pulse. "I would have agonized over it—I'll admit that—but at first I would have found some excuse to keep you close and told myself it was enough to have you near, to have your friendship. Expectation would have kept me up at night—all those centuries of dukes' voices telling me I must marry a noblewoman, and preferably a monied one, or landed."

A delicious chill raced through her. It had been too long since he'd told her a story. And never one like this. "Then what?"

He tilted her head back, kissed her throat. "At some point,

I would have been unable to deny how my feelings for you had changed. And I would have begged you to marry me. You would have put up a fuss about it though, because you distrust unions based solely on love. You would have tried to argue that a future duke couldn't marry the daughter of an opera singer. Of course, I would have pointed out the many times the Grimaldis ignored such logic."

The chuckle in her throat felt so different with his lips still resting there against her skin. "But I would have had to point out how rarely those unions ended well."

"We would be different though, you and I. We have our faith to bind us, not just our love. But that love—it's too strong to stay silent forever. You probably would have tried to do something impulsive, like leave without telling me. But I'd have been there. I'd have galloped after you on Alabaster, though she'd have a hard time keeping pace with Oscuro."

"I wouldn't have had Oscuro."

"Shh." He laughed, trailed his nose back up her neck. "Fine, then. I would have had no trouble overtaking you on whatever pathetic mount you'd found for yourself."

"Well, I wouldn't say I'd ever choose a *pathetic*—"

He pressed his lips to hers. It was, she decided, the best way to be silenced. "The important thing," he said against her mouth, "being that I caught you."

A happy sigh built in her chest. "Yes, you have."

"And you would have given up your argument. We would have been married at Ralin, setting the press and gossips abuzz, but we wouldn't have cared."

She hooked her wrists together behind his head. "And why should we? They are nothing to us."

His smile went from simmering to warm. "And then, at some point, we would have traveled to visit my cousin. On the train, no doubt, coming through Whitby. And your father would have been here, seeing off his sister and nieces, and he would have seen you and thought you his Lizzie. He would have come up to us, apologized for staring, explaining how much you looked like someone he once knew. From there, it would have been easy to piece it all together. And so, the tale called 'If Brook Were Not Eden' would still have ended with the realization that she *is*."

She loosed that happy sigh and rested her head against her arm and his shoulder. "The best yarn you've ever spun."

One of his hands moved to her head, and he wrapped a loose curl around his finger in that way he'd always done. "Brook . . . I wanted this before we were sure you were Eden. I was ready to declare myself while we were still in Monaco, but then Father's death . . . And then again, months ago, before I left for our holdings. But Grandfather told me to . . . told me to use your money to put Stafford to rights. And I couldn't do that. I never wanted you to think that it had anything to do with your fortune."

And she, foolish creature that she was, had believed just that. She stroked a hand over the back of his neck and smiled a little at the way he shivered. "That explains a lot."

"I'm sorry. I meant to protect you, but I was protecting my own pride too, by pushing you away. I should have trusted the Lord and not tried to solve it all myself. Had I listened, I wouldn't have hurt you so."

Her hand slid over his shoulder and rested against his heart. "It was my fear that hurt me, not you. But I'll not let it rule me, Justin. I want to see what the Lord has in store for us, together."

He kissed her again, featherlight. And then grinned. "I would ask you a rather important question right now, but I had better speak with your father first. I don't want to be considered the kind of man who would propose to a young lady without seeking his approval."

She laughed and shoved at him. "Justin Wildon—all those

conversations this past fortnight, and you haven't already spoken of *that*?"

"Are you daft? Had you happened by and overheard me asking such a thing, when you'd made it clear you never wanted to speak to me again, you would have challenged me to a duel—and I happen to know how good a shot you are."

Laughing again, she went up on her tiptoes to kiss him. "I suppose now I must invite you back to Whitby Park, so you can request an audience with my father . . . and then one with me."

His grin winked again. "Give me an hour to change, and I shall be there. I daresay he would have an opinion about a man showing up looking like he'd taken a plunge in the ocean too."

"Deal." She pulled away and held out a hand, to shake on it.

He took her hand, but then he raised it to his lips instead. "May I walk you back to your car, my lady?"

"I would be honored, Duke."

They traveled the steps together, quickly as they dared, and she let him steal one more kiss as he closed her into the roadster, even though other tourists were emerging from their hotels and inns now. Let them be scandalized, if they saw. She didn't care. Joy had filled the hollow inside, and she would gladly suffer hearing her father say he'd told her so.

The rain stopped as she drove out of Whitby, and she hummed a happy refrain from Mozart's "*Le Nozze di Figaro*," tapping out the beat on the wheel. For a day that began so poorly and was marred with worry for Deirdre's family, the Lord had certainly surprised her. She would pray for her maid's family—and sing praises.

Nothing could ruin the afternoon. Not the way the mud sucked at her tires with every revolution, not the clouds still rolling in off the North Sea, and not even the herd of sheep crossing the road amidst much bleating, which forced her to a halt two miles from her turn to Whitby Park. She might be unable to start again in this mud, but what did it matter? If she had to sit here until Justin came by, then it would give them something else to laugh about. She leaned back, waiting for the animals to clear the road and—

Her door was wrenched open, and a rough hand pulled her out before she could think to react. She tried to scream—surely there was a shepherd with all those sheep—but glove-covered fingers clamped down over her mouth.

"Not a sound, darling. Not unless you want to tell me here and now where the Fire Eyes are."

Pratt?

She wanted to kick, scream, something—but a sweet smell filled her nostrils, and the edges of her vision went black.

Twenty-Eight

Justin knew well he was grinning like a fool, and he didn't much mind it. Even when Mr. Graham greeted him with a raised brow. "Back so soon, Your Grace?"

He had changed into dry clothes as quickly as he could—though granted, it may have been quicker had he not kept trying to rush poor Peters, who had finally declared him hopeless and sent him out, laughing, with his tie askew. Still, by the time the Rolls-Royce chugged through the mud and ruts, an hour had indeed passed. "They're expecting me this time, Mr. Graham. Or Lady Berkeley is, anyway. I don't know about Whitby."

"Don't know what about Whitby?" Brook's father emerged from his study, his focus on a stack of post that he flipped through as he walked.

Justin's smile didn't dim. He was glad he'd had the time to get to know the earl better. Not that he would have chosen that particular reason for it, had a choice been given. "Whether Brook had told you yet that she asked me to call. We ran into each other at the abbey and finally talked."

That brought Whitby's gaze up from the letters and lit a gleam in his eye. "Did you? Good—though she certainly hasn't found me to tell me so. I actually didn't think her back yet. Did I miss her, Mr. Graham?"

The butler's brows drew together. "I am unaware of her return, my lord—though she has been known to sneak past us all before. Shall I send Beatrix up to check?"

"Yes. Please." But Whitby's brows had pulled down too, and he moved toward the door. "I should have been able to hear the car. I was listening for it. I expected her back well before now."

Justin's heart skipped a beat, though he told himself not to worry. "She must be here. She left well ahead of me—I watched her off. And had she got stuck along the road, I would have come across her."

"I'm sure she is here . . . somewhere." But the earl's step quickened as he pushed open the door and stepped outside. Justin followed him down the front steps, along the macadam of the drive. And silently echoed the curse that Whitby muttered when they saw the empty stall in the carriage house.

Her father spun, his eyes bordering on wild. "Horses. We need horses. Now. Horses!"

Justin had to jog to keep up as the earl flew toward the stables, shouting for Oscuro and Tempesta to be saddled posthaste. His heart, he was fairly certain, had stopped.

She had to be here. She had to be, because she had been nowhere between. He had been watching for her once he saw the state of the roads, half expecting to see her up to her wheel wells in mud.

Mr. Graham came huffing into the stables as the harried grooms brought the horses out. "My lord. Your Grace. Lady Berkeley is not in the house. No one has seen her since she left with O'Malley."

"I know. We're going to look for her." Whitby swung up onto Oscuro. "Mr. Graham?"

"My lord?"

"Gather the staff. Lead them in prayer. I want all work halted until my daughter is found."

Justin put his foot in the stirrup and mounted Tempesta, watching how the butler's face paled.

"*Found*, my lord?"

But the earl wasn't looking at Mr. Graham anymore. His focus had gone to the slate-grey clouds. "It's those blasted Fire Eyes—it has to be. I shouldn't have let her out of my sight until it was all resolved."

Justin nudged Tempesta forward. "We'll find her, Whit."

Whitby pressed his lips together and his heels to Oscuro's flanks.

At the crossroads they turned, without the need for discussion, toward Whitby. The horses ate up the first mile, Tempesta doing her best to keep up with Oscuro. As they closed on the second mile, Justin shouted, "Wait! I noticed ruts near here on my way over. Sheep prints, too."

They reined in to a trot until the obvious place of crossing came into view. Oscuro pranced about as Whitby studied the road. "Someone must have had to stop for them. A car, not a carriage, given the width of the ruts."

But the only tire tracks going through them were those of his Rolls-Royce, along with one set from a carriage. He nudged Tempesta forward, across the sheep prints. "Whit."

Whitby came up beside him, his gaze following Justin's. Off the road, following the two muddy tracks through the grass and to one of the copses of trees that marked the edge of pastureland. They both urged the horses to follow them, Justin's gut going tighter with every hoof fall. He knew, even before he caught sight of the bumper gleaming in the weak sunlight. Even before he saw the familiar black paint of the Eden roadster.

"No." The word tore from Whitby's throat with even more

panic than had saturated the curse. The eyes he turned on Justin were tortured. "They've taken her."

The *no* beat an echo in Justin's head, in his chest. He clenched his hands around the reins. "We'll find her. They've less than an hour on us. She is well. She's a fighter, she's bright."

But she was a fighter—and sometimes fighting could get a body killed.

Whitby turned Oscuro back to the road. "Constable. Hounds to pick up her scent. And while they're doing that, we're going to the Rushworths'. If they are back from London, then we have our answer."

They went first to see the constable, then back onto their horses and through Eden Dale, heading southward toward Azerley Hall for about half an hour before Whitby motioned Justin left at a fork, rather than right. It took another fifteen minutes before the villages and farms parted to reveal an old manor house situated well off the road. Not all that grand compared to Whitby Park or Ralin Castle, though it looked well maintained and had a stunning profusion of flower gardens.

Their approach didn't go unnoticed. They had no sooner dismounted before the front doors than Lord Rushworth emerged from the garden to the right, confusion in his brows. "Lord Whitby. Duke. What an unexpected pleasure. I was about to have tea—would you care to join me?"

Whitby looked more inclined to throttle him. "Where is she?"

The question in Rushworth's eyes only deepened. "I'm sorry—who? My sister?"

"My daughter."

Now the man's eyes went blank. "My lord, I haven't seen the baroness since I was in London. Why would I know her whereabouts now?"

Whitby's fingers had curled into a fist—a feeling Justin knew well, though now a strange calm possessed him. He put a hand on Whitby's shoulder and stepped forward. "Forgive us, my lord. We came here on a whim. We were not even expecting you to be at home. I would have thought you and your sister would stay in London throughout the Season."

Now the man's face went tight. "Kitty wanted the wedding to be here."

"Wedding." Whitby said the word as if it were actually a funeral.

And given that she had married Pratt, that comparison wasn't far off, by Justin's estimation.

A bit of color stole into Rushworth's face. "It was Sunday. There was . . . a bit of a rush."

A picture formed in Justin's mind's eye . . . and he didn't much like it. "So Pratt is back in Yorkshire too? Or did they go to the Continent for a honeymoon?" *Please, Lord . . .*

"Kitty wanted to settle at Delmore."

He exchanged a glance with Whitby. Lady Catherine—or rather, Lady Pratt—was the one blatantly pursuing the Fire Eyes. Had she filled Pratt's ears with the tales of them as well? Greedy, base, selfish, cruel-minded Pratt on the trail of price-less red diamonds?

"Wait." Rushworth raised a hand and backed up a step. "Is the baroness missing? And you think *we* have something to do with it?"

Whitby pointed a finger at the man's chest. "Your sister came to my house and demanded the Fire Eyes. She threatened my daughter. And then your uncle was murdered in his room the very day he came to tell us about them. Will you try and tell me you have nothing to do with it?"

"I swear to you, my lord—you're mistaken." Rushworth backed up another step. "Yes, Kitty was enamored with the tales our mother told of the diamonds. But we would never hurt anyone over such trifles."

Whitby advanced, seeming to tower over the younger man though he couldn't be more than an inch taller. "And your father? Will you tell me he did not threaten my wife, that fear of him did not send her into the night with our daughter when he learned Henry sent the jewels to her?"

At that, Rushworth froze. "I cannot speak to my father's actions." Slowly, his raised hands sank. "Though heaven knows he was not a gentle man. I would not put such things past him."

Justin didn't want to feel any compassion for this man, not when all fingers still pointed to his sister and Pratt as being behind their trouble. But digging up the feud from a generation past wouldn't help them now. What they needed to do was get to Delmore. "Whit."

"Right." Whitby pivoted, his face granite. "Shall we give our congratulations to the happy couple, Duke?"

Justin nodded, though he held Rushworth's gaze for a long moment. The man had to know what his sister was, had to know the kind of man she had married. He *had* to—yet he looked back at him evenly, without a flinch, without any indication that he considered the whole story of the Fire Eyes to be more than a fairy tale.

Spinning back to Tempesta, Justin let it churn around in his mind. And spoke only once they were outside the gates. "Do you believe him?"

"Not for a moment."

"Do you think him involved?"

Whitby hissed out a breath. "I don't know. He has always struck me as more a shadow than a man. But at the least, I don't think Brook is here. I know this house, these grounds, and there would be no good place to hide her."

Justin shifted in his saddle. "And Delmore? How well do you know it?"

Whitby's silence lasted three beats too long. "Not well enough."

Deirdre woke to darkness and a pounding head. A groan slipped out as she tried to sit up. Her wrists hurt, her shoulder was sore, and her mouth was parched.

"Deirdre—are you awake?"

"Lady Berkeley?" No, no, that wasn't right. Deirdre should be on her way to Kilkeel, and her ladyship should be in Yorkshire. But this dark space didn't rock as a train should. And it smelled of damp earth and mold.

"Yes. Here, I have some water."

She heard rustling, shifting, and then a hand groped at her shoulder. Deirdre reached up, and her fingers closed around a canteen. Eagerly she raised it to her lips. The water was fresh and cool, and with its touch came a few snippets of memory.

Running to the ticket counter. Being pulled to the other side of it, a gun barrel pressed to her back. Pratt.

She handed the canteen back before her shudder could spill it. "He got you too. Oh, my lady, I'm so sorry. I had no idea he—"

"This isn't your fault. He set it all up. We couldn't have known. He sent the telegram, he was lying in wait, he had his flocks ready to block the road whenever I came back."

Deirdre squeezed her eyes shut, though doing so didn't change the darkness a whit. "You shouldn't have driven me." But at least Mum wasn't ill—the one spot of good in it all. He had said so when he pressed the gun to her back.

"He said he would have taken me on my next ride, if I hadn't—and would have shot Oscuro to do so." The baroness's hands found hers and gripped them. "We are in this together, Deirdre. There is no room for regrets."

Deirdre clung to those strong fingers. "Where are we?"

"He put a hood over my head a few minutes after I roused from the chloroform, but I think we're at Delmore. Some sort of cellar?"

It made no sense. His interest had been in Whitby Park, in marrying the baroness—how would kidnapping them help him attain that? She shook her head—and immediately regretted it when the ache turned to a slicing pain. A whimper escaped, and then the baroness's arm came around her shoulders.

"I'm the one who owes *you* an apology, Deirdre." Her hand rubbed over Deirdre's shoulder. "He wants the diamonds."

She didn't know what diamonds her ladyship meant—and it didn't much matter. "Well, if you know where these diamonds are, you mustn't tell him. Sure and he'll kill us once you do. He can't let us go, not without bringing the law upon himself. He's too smart not to know that."

"I know. I know."

"He's heartless. A devil. Put nothing past him."

"I—"

Noise from the right silenced them. A clanging, a scraping, and then sudden light blinded her and made the pain slice again. Wincing, Deirdre turned her face into the baroness's shoulder and blinked until the brightness wasn't so harsh to her eyes.

"Ah, good. We're all awake." The door slammed shut, and a lamp came to a rest on a table across the room.

No—an old desk. And the room didn't have the earthen walls she had expected, but stone ones. There was even a space that must have once been a window, now filled with bricks. Not a cellar, then.

Pratt pulled the chair away from the desk. It, as opposed to everything else in here, looked solid and somewhat new. He sat and hooked an ankle over the opposite knee. The easy pose bore a marked contrast to the gun he kept pointed at them. "Now then. Ready to chat, my lady?"

Her ladyship lifted her chin and somehow managed to look regal even here, on the floor. "Oh, quite. This ought to be interesting. Do tell me, my lord, why you think *you* have any claim to the Fire Eyes."

The Fire Eyes—those she had certainly heard the baroness and Whitby discussing, though she hadn't ever heard they were diamonds.

Pratt's nasty little smile curved his lips. "I forget how little you know of family history. My father was Henry Rushworth's dearest friend."

The baroness's face shifted, though only slightly. "He is the one who introduced my mother to Aunt Mary."

"And by extension, your father—for which ol' Hank never forgave him. Leastways, not until he came home from India in need of help in peddling a few jewels. Then he was all gracious words and generous offers to whomever would help him get rid of the things." He motioned with the gun. "Even shares, he said. A third to my father, a third to his brother, a third for himself."

Deirdre rubbed at her wrists. They were chafed and red and had obviously been bound. "But that makes no sense. Why would he promise away so much of his profit, when they were in *his* possession?"

Pratt narrowed his eyes on her. "Desperation, my lovely, can make one do stupid things."

"And I suppose you have proof of this. Documentation. Evidence of a legal, binding agreement." The baroness folded her hands in her lap. Mud marred the walking dress Deirdre had chosen for her that morning.

Pratt put his second foot down and leaned forward. "I have my father's word."

"Is it worth more than his son's?"

At the fury that snapped through his eyes, Deirdre tried to squeak out a warning. When he lunged for the baroness, she tried to scrabble before her to provide a barrier. All she achieved for her efforts was another blow to her head that sent her reeling. The baroness still ended up trapped between Pratt and an old trunk. Her ladyship was bent backward at an angle that looked painful, his gun pressed to the hollow beneath her jaw.

"My father *died* for those gems! When Henry ran back to India like the coward he was, when he sent them to your mother, when he forced my father to renege on the deal he had struck with his buyer, he was *killed*. Murdered! If anyone has a right to them, it's me." He pushed her harder against the trunk. "I tried to do this the friendly way. All you had to do was marry me—then I could have searched for the jewels at Whitby Park at my leisure. So simple. But you're as stubborn and haughty as the rest of your family."

The baroness didn't shake, didn't quake, didn't waver. She smiled. "You never would have found them. Not in a million years."

"Oh, but *you* would have. You with your mother's face—the major would have told you where he'd hidden them. And he did, didn't he? He told you how he sent them to her . . . though I suspect he left out the part of how his own greed made him betray his brother and his oldest friend."

"Greed and betrayal played a crucial role in his tale, actually."

Deirdre pushed herself back up, cursing the weakness in her limbs, the pain in her skull. She needed to help—but what could she do? If she tried to knock him away, he could very well shoot the baroness.

Indeed, he pressed the gun harder into her throat. "And now he's given them to *you*. Tried to sign them over to you, ignoring the first deal he'd struck. Forgetting his own brother, his friend, and the legacy *their* children ought to be receiving."

Now the baroness's eyes slid shut. "You're the one. You're the one who killed him."

"Blood for blood—his for my father's."

Deirdre's stomach twisted so hard she had to pull her knees

to her chest to try to ease the pain. If she needed any more proof that he'd never let them out of this alive . . .

The baroness strained against him. "They are just diamonds, Pratt! I am sorry your father lost his life over them, but why would you keep the cycle of violence turning? *Why?*"

"Why?" He laughed, and the room seemed to grow darker again. "Have you any *idea* how much those 'just diamonds' are worth, you idiot woman? My father didn't die for the jewels, he died for what they would mean to us. Never again, in my lifetime or my grandchildren's, would I have to worry about whether the rents will cover the expenses. If I can afford the necessary improvements. If I need to let a footman go. And that was with a *third* of their price. Now that Kitty and I are wed, we'll have two-thirds between us—even if we give Rush his share."

"No one in his right mind would spend that much on a couple of pieces of red carbon."

Red? Deirdre eased her knees back down. Red diamonds? She'd never even heard of such things.

Pratt laughed again and pushed the baroness back harder against the trunk when she tried to twist away. "We can debate their sanity all you want, but I've a buyer already waiting, and I don't intend to share my father's fate by disappointing him. Your pieces of red carbon are destined to grace the throat of a Russian princess, my darling."

He gave the baroness another push into the trunk but then stood up.

Perhaps it was the new bit of freedom that allowed her ladyship to breathe a laugh. "No. You'll never find them unless I tell you where they are, which I will never do. That I promise you."

"Oh. My darling. I think you will. Because it's very simple. Talk, and you live. Don't, and you die."

"No matter what, I die. How stupid do you think I am, Pratt? You can't let me go after this."

His lips turned up into that evil little grin Deirdre so hated. "I didn't say I'd let you go. I said I'd let you *live*." He sent his gaze down her in a way that surely made her ladyship's skin crawl.

"More incentive to keep my lips sealed."

Deirdre winced. She was all for standing against him—but didn't her ladyship realize that antagonizing him would only make things harder?

Pratt chuckled. "It's going to be so pleasant, hearing you sing a different tune by the time we're through. Deirdre." He motioned for her to get up. With the gun.

On shaking legs, she obeyed. She tried to promise the baroness with her eyes that she would do nothing to compromise her. Prayed she understood, and that she herself would have the strength to keep that promise.

Pratt closed his fingers around her arm. "Now, as a gesture of good faith, I'm going to take your lovely little maid here for some refreshment for you. I'll let her bring in a cot, a pillow, a blanket. You're going to get a good night's sleep and consider all you have to lose by withholding from me. And then in the morning, my darling lady, you're going to talk. Are we understood?"

Given the pulsing in her ladyship's jaw, she was clenching her teeth against whatever response she wanted to make. Deirdre loosed half a relieved exhale before Pratt jerked her toward the door.

Perhaps she could get away somehow. Find help.

He tossed her through the door and pulled it shut as she fell into the wall opposite. Then, before her addled mind could recover from the jarring, he pressed her to the damp stone. "Don't get any heroic ideas, my lovely, if you even have such things in you." The barrel of the gun touched her head, directly upon the wound.

She whimpered before she could stop herself, though it only made him chuckle. "This is why I took you along with her. She will refuse me—I know that. But *you*—you're in there with her, a fellow victim of my cruelty. Get her to confide. Open up. Tell *you* where the diamonds are."

Deirdre pressed her lips shut against the *no* that threatened to spew out. Better he think she was still on his side, however reluctantly.

"Do that," he murmured into her ear, "and I'll see that your family is set up for all their miserable lives, and you'll be free to enjoy it with them. Knowing, of course, that if you ever breathe a word of this to anyone, it all disappears."

She squeezed her eyes shut. He thought her so low . . . and why wouldn't he? She had proven herself to be little more than a worm, happy to sell her own soul for a few pound notes.

Not anymore—and maybe this was how she could redeem herself. Earn *his* trust, fully, so that she could help the baroness escape with her life. It could very well cost her her own if she were caught in it . . . but it was a risk she had to take. If she were killed, the earl would see her family was cared for. And Hiram—Hiram would be proud, knowing she had done what was right.

She swallowed and bent her mind into a silent prayer. "How much?"

"Hmm?"

"How much will you give me if I help you with this?"

He chuckled and eased off her. "I thought you'd come around. Let's say . . . ten thousand pounds. That'll be enough to see your family through, won't it?"

Undoubtedly. But if he thought greed her sole motive . . . "No. I went ten *percent*. Of whatever it is you get from the Russians. Ten percent."

"Five."

"Fifteen."

Laughing again in his throat, he spun her around and pressed a kiss to her lips. It took all her willpower not to wipe it away. His eyes looked almost . . . affectionate as he tweaked her chin. "I knew I liked you. Pity you didn't accept my first offer—we would have suited well."

She lifted her chin. "Do I have my ten or don't I?"

"Fine." He took her hand and tugged her down the dim hallway. "But you're going to have to make it quick. Whitby and Stafford will be out looking for her by now."

Please, God, lead them here! Help them find us.

He stopped her at the end of the hall and motioned to a room on the right. Its windows were also bricked over, except for the transoms. But through them she could see only sky.

"You come no farther than this. I'll leave the lamp in there for now, and you can take that tray of food and water. But warn her that this is the last of my generosity. If she doesn't talk by morning, she'll have nothing." He motioned to a folded metal cot that looked as if it belonged in a military barracks. "Drag that back for her, if you want. Or if you'd rather watch her suffer through a night on the floor, tell her I changed my mind."

Deirdre nodded, kept her face neutral. And prayed she could keep up the deception until Lord Whitby came pounding upon the door.

Twenty-Nine

Justin kept his hands in his pockets to hide how they'd fisted. His feet itched, his chest ached. He needed to be *doing*, not standing here in the drawing room with Brook's mother looking down on him, all but asking with her painted eyes why they weren't out there tracking down her baby.

They'd come back only to exchange the horses and get some water for themselves. But the constable was waiting for them and insisted on a search of Brook's room before they went accusing another lord of kidnapping.

Justin paced the library while they went about it. He had wanted to follow them up, but it hadn't seemed right. He almost wished he had, though, when Whitby returned, his face a thunderhead and eyes flashing lightning. The constable followed, flipping through a stack of what looked like letters.

Justin's brows lifted. "Did you find something?"

"Lies," Whitby all but spat.

The constable sent their host a hard look. "Close as you've grown, she's still a young woman, my lord. And they all keep secrets from their fathers."

Justin watched doubt flicker through Whitby's eyes—

probably remembering all those things Brook hadn't told him. But then he straightened his shoulders and lifted his chin. "Not this, though. She would not have hidden a romance from me—especially given that she has been in love with *him* this whole time." He motioned toward Justin.

Justin's throat went dry. "Would someone please enlighten me?"

The constable motioned with the stack of folded papers. "Love letters, it seems. Dated from the time she arrived through a couple weeks ago. My French is rusty, but they seem to be from an actor. Someone she knew in Monaco. They speak of running off together."

"Nonsense." Justin strode forward and held out a hand until the constable put one of the letters into it. "I know all her friends from Monaco, and there were precious few. No young men." None, other than him. He would have known it if there had been. He would have known if she'd been in communication with anyone other than Prince Albert.

And he was shaking his head within moments of reading through the letter. "No. Whitby is right, this is a lie. Aside from the fact that I've never heard of the fellow, the writing is all wrong. This was most assuredly not written by a native French speaker."

A knock came upon the open door before the others could respond. Mr. Graham stood there, a salver in hand. "Telegram, my lord."

Whitby stepped forward to take it, trepidation in his eyes. It darkened to hurt but then blazed into anger as he read it. "No."

The constable and Justin both flanked the earl to read over his shoulder.

Forgive me, Papa STOP I do not mean to hurt you but must follow my heart STOP It is all too much STOP J is

*too cold and W not serious STOP Need someone who
understands me STOP Met the son of a friend of Maman
at train station STOP Left with him STOP Will wire when
we get to Continent*

The constable sighed. "No doubt the same man these letters
are from. Someone must have pinched her car from the station
and then dumped it."

"No." Justin balled up the paper in his hand. "No, this isn't
from her. She didn't leave from the train station—she met me
at the abbey after she dropped O'Malley off, and I watched her
drive out of town."

Whitby's mouth went firm. "Whoever sent this obviously
didn't know that. Didn't know the two of you had made up."

He was obviously the *J* in the note—and Worthing must be
W. But she never called him Worthing. She called him Brice.
He would have been a *B*.

The constable didn't look entirely convinced. He held out
a hand toward Whitby. "May I take it with me, my lord, and
the letters? I'll see what we can discover about where it originated. And in the meantime, I'll thank you two not to go off
half-cocked, accusing the neighbors of anything."

The request ate him up inside like acid, and Whitby looked
every bit as unwilling to agree. His jaw ticked for a moment
before he gave a curt nod. "For tonight, Constable. But a father
knows. A father knows when something bad has happened to
his daughter, and I'll not sit here while she is hurt or worse.
Not again. If you've no leads by the morning, the duke and I
are paying a visit to Delmore."

To his credit, the constable didn't dismiss it as an idle threat
or get in a bluster over it. He merely nodded, considering that as
he had the paper in his hands. "I've a cousin who's a groundsman at Delmore. I'll pay him a call, quietly. See if anything's

amiss on the estate. But you know as well as I that the place is a maze—if by chance she *is* there, our barging in won't help us find her. We must go about this with thought and care. And with prayer."

Praying—Justin had been praying constantly as they rode through Yorkshire. Mr. Graham had assured them the moment they stepped inside that the staff had spent the last hours on their knees. Still, he couldn't shake the feeling that they needed even more people beseeching heaven on Brook's behalf.

The constable took his leave, promising to trace the telegram posthaste and to call first thing in the morning.

As Justin watched him go, a hand settled on his spirit. And a name filtered into his mind, making him sigh. He turned to Whitby. "We need to let Worthing know. He seems to have an uncanny knack for knowing what to pray." Justin had wired him when he got to Whitby, and in the two weeks since, he'd received two letters from the man, both so very to the point that Justin had to wonder if the Lord whispered directly into his ear.

Brook's father nodded—then shook his head. "We'd have to send a letter rather than a wire, and we certainly can't use the phone. The operators could well leak it to the press. But a letter is too slow."

"No . . . wait." Ideas swirled. Motioning for Whitby to follow, he charged from the drawing room, down the hall, and into the library. Flicking on the electric lights as he entered, he headed straight for the chair Whitby had been in earlier. His newspaper still sat on the table beside it. Justin scooped it up and turned it face out.

The earl lifted a brow at the picture, weeks old, of Brook that graced the cover. "My point exactly, Duke. The merest mention of my daughter makes the front page. This insipid article is about nothing but the fact that she hadn't been to a ball in two weeks, and they wondered if she'd left Town."

"Exactly. Can you imagine if they learned she was kid-napped?" Pressure mounted in his chest, too desperate to be called excitement—but right. It had to be. "It would be in every newspaper in England. Front page. Every single person in this county and the next would see it and be on the lookout for her."

Whitby's eyes sparked. "If the article made it clear there was a sizable reward to anyone who offered solid information as to her whereabouts . . ."

Justin lifted a brow. "How well do you think Pratt can trust his servants?"

This time, a hint of a smile touched Whitby's lips as he said, "Not well enough."

Tossing the paper back to the table, Justin nodded. "Exactly. But we can't tip our hand until the constable is ready to intercept anyone coming or going from Delmore." More waiting—but waiting with purpose.

"Worthing can help us with the press. He's as much their darling as Brook—but that again leaves us with how to reach him without tipping our hand too soon."

Justin shook his head. "Let's not forget how uncanny he is. Ring him up. Say you need him to come. I daresay he'll be here by morning, with no other words needed."

Whitby's features eased a bit, and then he spun for the door. "I'll be back as soon as I reach him—you had better stay here tonight, Duke. I'll send someone for your valet."

"Thank you." Though he felt too antsy to sit, he sank down anyway, onto the seat he knew Brook favored. He ran his hands over the arms of the chair, knowing hers were the last to touch the upholstery. He reached over and rested his fingers on the book left on the side table.

La Chartreuse de Parme. She'd read it before—he remembered her talking about how a Frenchman had captured the Italian spirit. So very Brook, this book.

His eyes slid closed. "Help us find her, Lord. Please. Keep her safe until we do. Drape your protection over her, keep any harm from finding her. Please. Please."

Nothing whispered into his ear. But peace seeped into his chest, and it spread warmth into places he hadn't realized were chilled.

The lamp's oil ran out while she slept. Brook awoke to that cavernous darkness again, and with the sinking certainty that Pratt had meant the words Deirdre had relayed the day before. If she didn't cooperate, he would bring no more oil. No more water. No more food.

She sat up, the rusty metal cot squeaking underneath her. Reaching up, she touched the pearls around her neck. If he knew they were here even now . . . that yesterday, as he held a gun to her head, he had been but inches from the things he desired most . . .

What was she to do? She couldn't give them to him. He might, *might* let Deirdre go, which would mean she could fetch help, but that was a big *if*. And even if he did . . . she had a feeling that Pratt would not waste any time in teaching Brook a lesson. She would pay dearly for her impudence the moment he had the diamonds in hand.

She couldn't turn them over. That was all there was to it. She needed some other way of escape, and it would have to come from the Lord—He would have to clear the way for her.

"A fire goeth before him, and burneth up his enemies round about." The Scripture filtered into her mind—in English. Odd, given that her Bible reading was still entirely in French. Perhaps it had been in a recent sermon at the church in Eden Dale or from one of Papa's daily selections.

That must be it—she could hear it in her father's voice. Deep and strong. Authoritative. Promising.

Papa. Tears burned her eyes at the thought of him. He would be so worried. So afraid of losing her all over again, and over the same thing. And Justin, faced with losing yet another loved one in so short a time. . . .

For their sakes, Lord, have mercy. You are my champion. You are my hope. Send out that fire before us to clear the way, mon Dieu.

The rattle, the clang, and then the influx of light as Pratt came into the room. Perhaps one of these times she could be ready to dart around him, to leap out the door . . . though Deirdre had said the door at the end of the hall was locked too. She wouldn't get far enough to make it worth whatever punishment he'd dole out.

When the light shone on her, she forced a smile. "Good morning, Lord Pratt."

His smile was as dark as ever. "Good evening, Brook."

Evening? No, it couldn't be. Deirdre had seen late afternoon sunshine yesterday, she said. They couldn't have slept that long . . . or that little. It was a ploy. "Is it? And you've not brought us any tea."

"You wouldn't have drunk it if I had." He nodded toward where Deirdre was stirring on her pallet on the floor. Since Brook had the cot, she'd insisted Deirdre take the pillow and blanket. "Though perhaps your maid would have. I *am* willing to be civil, my darling. But civility must go both ways. You give me what I want, and I'll give you what you want."

She would appeal to Pratt's humanity, if he had any. Deirdre's warning rang clear in her memory though. He was a heartless devil, capable of anything. Perhaps a slight exaggeration, but . . . she had to try *something*, didn't she?

Drawing in a deep breath, she smoothed her wrinkled walking dress. If she couldn't appeal to his heart, perhaps she could appeal to his greed. "I will make you a deal. Make me one of your partners, divide it evenly with me when you sell, and I'll get them for you. You can let me go, and I'll say my car got stuck and I went out for help but got lost. No harm done."

Not that Papa or Justin would ever believe that even if she *did* want to try it—she never got lost. But anything that would get her out.

Pratt chuckled. "I'm afraid I'm not quite so stupid, darling, but good try. Let's try this instead though—you tell me where you've stashed them, and we send Deirdre in to get them. She can claim another message was waiting for her, saying her mother had recovered. Then everyone lives."

"Except that I'll be trapped here. I cannot make that deal, Pratt. You need to offer better incentive." She stood, knowing she had better move her legs while she had the light. He would no doubt take it out with him again.

She made it all of three steps before he'd come up behind her and clamped an arm around her waist.

"Now, darling, it wouldn't be so bad. I'd give you a fine room. Lovely clothes. Books. You like those, don't you?" He trailed his nose along the side of her face, from temple to cheek. "And you'd come to like me. I'd show you what a . . . generous man I can be. You wouldn't *want* to leave. I've already sent your father a note saying you've run off with a performer you knew in Monaco, and I'll let you write him from time to time. I'd have to approve the letters, of course, but he needn't think you dead."

A quaver formed in her stomach. Not so much at his words as at the way his hand slid down her hip. "You'll have to do better than that."

She'd meant it to come out strong, daring. It hadn't.

His chuckle mocked her attempt. "You seem to be under the delusion that you have room to bargain. But I'm afraid that ship has long since sailed. Now, had you told us where you'd hidden them when my rough-edged compatriot asked you in the stables—"

"You said it wasn't you!" Deirdre had apparently sat up at some point. She looked on now with horrified eyes.

Pratt's hand pressed harder against Brook's hip. "No, my lovely. I said I didn't hire him to scare her so that I could play the hero. I assure you, that was never my intent. Though I also gave the bloke strict instructions not to kill her, and he seemed to have forgotten that one. What I get for hiring riffraff, I suppose."

Brook tried to swallow, though her throat didn't want to work. She had thought it Lady Catherine . . . but they were in this together all the time, it seemed. "I didn't even know what the Fire Eyes were. How was I to—"

"You found out quickly enough, though, didn't you?" He drew away, but before she could take advantage of it, he shoved.

She landed with a crash of rusty springs back onto the cot.

He stood before her, a dark blot against the lamplight. "Sent your *duke* to India after the information. Though you must have been clever about how he was to get it back to you. I couldn't figure out any of his letters. Did you set up some kind of code?"

"*Quoi?*" He was mad. Stark, raving mad.

"No doubt you were furious when he got back—thinking he hadn't written." A chuckle rumbled out, cruel and low. "Did you think he wanted to keep it all for himself? But no—he wanted you too. That's why he brought you to England in the first place, wasn't it? Set you up as Whitby's lost heiress so he could marry you and make a fortune in the process."

Her fingers curled over the rough, rusted edge of the cot's frame.

Pratt stepped close and then closer, plunging a hand into her hair, which had long ago come loose from its chignon. "And oh, how angry *he* must have been to come back and find you all but engaged to Worthing, while he was away digging up your secrets for you. Is that why the two of you could do nothing but fight after his return? Did you not want him anymore, my darling? I can't say as I blame you. He was always a self-righteous, condescending—"

"He is *not!*"

"Ah." His hand wrapped around her hair, too tightly, and pulled her head back. "So you *do* still have feelings for him. Well, that makes this next part even more fun. Give me the diamonds, Brook, or he'll be the first one I kill."

No. Her blood froze, her fingers released their hold on the cot. He couldn't. He wouldn't. He daren't.

"Jenkins was so easy—and I was even applauded for it." He twisted her hair even tighter. "Henry—he was necessary. But Stafford . . . Stafford would be a genuine pleasure. I haven't decided yet if I'll put a bullet through his skull or a knife through his heart."

"No." Her voice, blast it, came out weak and desperate. "You can't. If you keep killing everyone connected with this, you'll get caught."

His laugh said otherwise. "Oh, but no one would know. He would get a wire saying he's needed abroad, and off he'd go. No one would think anything of it for a year or more, and by then, who would link it to me? Everyone knows the duchy comes first for him. No one would question it if he disappeared to tend it."

Releasing her abruptly, he straightened. "Your father, on the other hand—he's too much a fixture in these parts. His death will have to look like an accident. Simple enough, really. The brakes could fail in his car. Or he could be tossed from that wild horse of yours. But he will certainly be next, after the duke."

He turned, pacing toward Deirdre. "And then, if you still refuse to talk, you've an aunt. A pregnant cousin. And that fiery one that Cayton tossed over—though he's a friend, and he still loves her even though his wedding is only a fortnight away, so I had better save her for last. But then . . ." He turned back to face her. "I don't think it will take that long. Do you?"

Though she refused to shut her eyes, she wanted to. She wanted to shake, to cry, to scream—or to lunge for him and wring his neck. She wanted, *needed* to think him bluffing.

But Henry Rushworth lay in a fresh grave beside his brother. And Jenkins in a pauper's one, not far off.

Her life for theirs—that was what he was proposing. She must give him the diamonds or everyone she loved would be killed.

Lord! She wanted to believe He had some better alternative. Where, though? How? She thought—perhaps, maybe—she heard His quiet *Trust me* in the recesses of her spirit. But the fear clanged so much louder.

A weight settled beside her on the cot, and Deirdre's arm slid around her. "Don't give up, my lady," she whispered into her ear. Then, louder, "Give her time to consider, my lord."

Pratt's chuckle moved toward the door. "A few hours, and I'll leave the full lamp. But no food. No water. Not until you sing for me, my little *chanteuse*." He withdrew a leather-bound book from his jacket pocket, dropped it onto the worn surface of the desk. "Incentive—and a reminder of what we're capable of."

The click of the door a moment later sounded like canon fire to her ears.

Deirdre smoothed back Brook's hair. "He's bluffing."

"He's not. He's already killed." She stood and slid over to the desk, her eyes going wide. The journal—Maman's journal, the one she had bemoaned as lost all this time. "How did he . . . ?"

"My fault. My first crime against you." Deirdre appeared at her side, that familiar apology in her eyes. "I thought . . . I thought it would disprove your story, but I couldn't read the French."

It hardly mattered now. "My father and Justin will be working with the constable—they won't believe that note he said he sent."

Deirdre nodded. "They'll be surrounded by people, searching for you, everyone will know what they're doing. He can't make His Grace disappear."

She wanted to believe that. Wanted to hope.

But the lamp he left couldn't fend off the darkness. She clutched the journal to her chest and squeezed her eyes closed.

Thirty

Whitby Park had never been exactly boisterous whenever Justin had visited, aside from at the house party. But that morning as he made his way down the stairs, it seemed downright melancholy—which suited his mood well. Sleep hadn't come, or not for long. He had lain there praying most of the night. Eventually he had given up and had risen, switched on a lamp, and pulled out the Bible that Peters had packed for him.

He'd left a marker in the Psalms at some point or another, and that was where he'd turned. His eyes had found the ninety-seventh one:

> The Lord reigneth; let the earth rejoice; let the multi-
> tude of isles be glad thereof.
> Clouds and darkness are round about him: righ-
> teousness and judgment are the habitation of his
> throne.
> A fire goeth before him, and burneth up his enemies
> round about.
> His lightnings enlightened the world: the earth saw, and
> trembled.

The hills melted like wax at the presence of the Lord, at
the presence of the Lord of the whole earth.
The heavens declare his righteousness, and all the
people see his glory.

Testimony of the Lord's greatness, His power. Assurance
that the God of the universe was Lord of this too. Justin's part
was to trust, to tremble. To cling to the promise that they were
not of the darkness but children of light.

He paused at the base of the stairs. Breakfast room? He nearly
headed that way, but he suspected Whitby wouldn't be there.
He'd taken no dinner last night, though Mrs. Doyle and Mr.
Graham had both cajoled him. The chef claimed he couldn't
pray without cooking, and so food had been prepared.

Perhaps the staff had eaten it; Justin hadn't either and couldn't
now. He angled his feet instead for the hall that would take him
to the library.

Whitby stood by the glass doors, looking out at the early
morning sunshine. At Justin's entrance, the older man acknowledged him with a partial turn of his head. "She said, the first
time she came into this room, that if ever she went missing, I
should look for her here."

A smile bade for leave to touch Justin's lips. He let it, though
it no doubt looked as sorrowful as it felt. He moved to Whitby's
side and shoved his hands into his pockets. "We'll find her."

"We must. I already lost Lizzie to the greed for these diamonds, though she never even knew she had them. I'll not lose
Brook to them. Not again."

"We'll find her." If he said it often enough, perhaps the
doubts and fears would flee in the face of the *must*. "Then
your biggest concern will be whether or not to grant us your
blessing."

Whitby's chuckle had little mirth in it. "And yours will be

learning to tolerate your father-in-law spending months of every year at your home."

"I've rooms enough, I suppose." And it warmed him, to think that Whitby would be willing to spend part of his time in Gloucestershire.

The earl drew a deep breath in through his nose, his hands clasped behind his back. "Looking back . . . I cannot fathom how I spent all those years without her. How the hole of her absence didn't swallow me up. Finding her has made my life so full."

"I know." Justin didn't know what else to say.

And needed to say no more. Whitby breathed a shaky laugh and nodded toward the door. Or rather, toward the disheveled man striding toward it.

Any other day, seeing Worthing with his tie askew, his clothes rumpled, and his hair mussed would have inspired serious jesting. Today he settled for opening the French doors.

Worthing charged through, his eyes absent any amusement this morning. "No one opened the front door, so I made a guess. What's wrong? Something's wrong. I've had the worst feeling the whole way here—and frankly, several hours before I got your cryptic call."

Justin nodded to Whitby. "Told you he was uncanny."

Whitby sighed. "She's missing. Kidnapped, it must be. We suspect Pratt."

Justin stepped to his side. "But we have a plan."

They explained it, along with the telegram and letters that had thrown the constable, and as they did, Worthing's expression went from outrage to determination. By the time they finished their ideas concerning the press, he was nodding. "I can help with that."

"That was our hope." Justin would have said more, but Mr. Graham chose that moment to enter with the constable.

The official looked none too happy, though he made an effort to smile when introductions were made to Worthing. Still, he turned without any more small talk to Whitby. "The magistrate wouldn't order a search warrant for Delmore, my lord. I dispatched an officer to the telegraph station at the next town, and he was able to verify that a young blond woman, well dressed, sent the telegraph yesterday afternoon."

Justin folded his arms over his chest. "It couldn't have been Brook." But Pratt's new wife looked much like her—where had *she* been yesterday?

The constable inclined his head. "I don't disbelieve you, Your Grace, given what you told me of your conversation with her at the abbey. But without a warrant, we cannot do anything but pay Pratt a friendly visit—which I suggest we do. Let's go as we would to any other neighbor and ask them all to be on the lookout for her. My cousin at Delmore has promised to keep watch for anything abnormal and report it to me."

Whitby drew the constable toward the table, where a slew of paper and fountain pens had been set up. "We've another plan as well, involving the press."

The constable nodded as Whitby laid it out for him.

Worthing passed a hand through his hair—the cause of the mussing, it seemed—and stepped nearer to Justin. "You spoke to her yesterday?"

His chest tightened and he nodded. "Just before. She found me at the abbey, and we . . . It was raining. I changed into dry clothes and headed here immediately, so I could speak to Whit. I wasn't that far behind her. If only I had gone with her . . ."

"Don't." Worthing's hand gripped his shoulder.

"He wouldn't have been able to take her if I had been there."

"Or else he would have shot you and taken her anyway, and it would have been hours before Whitby knew what had happened." Worthing shook his head, his eyes intent. "Or even if it discouraged him from acting then, he would have found her another time. When she was out for one of her rides or on another drive or . . . She would have insisted on being alone at some point—you know it as well as I. And he would have been ready to pounce, whenever that was."

At least this way, they realized it almost immediately. Perhaps Worthing was right, that it was better than the alternative.

Worthing removed his hand, sighed, and focused his gaze on nothing. He had circles under his eyes and lines of weariness around them. "Evil men flourish. The righteous suffer. The Lord never promises we won't—only that He'll sustain us when the tribulation comes."

Justin shook his head. "You are uncanny. You know that, right?"

Worthing's grin made a showing—brief and muted. "She'll be glad to see you and I are friends."

"When we find her."

"We'll find her."

But the nagging fear wouldn't be banished. "I pray it's in time. He can't mean to let her go. If it's Pratt, if she knows it's him . . . he must plan to kill her once she's told him where the diamonds are."

Worthing inclined his head. "Then we pray the Lord stops her lips."

"Gentlemen." Whitby, standing by the library table, motioned them over. "We need to get this drafted for the press with all speed. And then to Delmore."

The writing went quickly, with Worthing acting as scribe. No doubt some of the papers would alter it here and there, but this would be what they sent over the wire, and this would rouse every able body to search for her.

Including, he prayed, the able bodies at Delmore.

They bolstered themselves with tea and *caffe espresso* and then headed, all of them somber-faced, outside.

Because the constable and Worthing both warned that the

roads were yet all but unpassable to anything wheeled, they opted for horses. When the grooms brought them out, Whitby handed Justin the reins for Oscuro.

It nearly choked him up. He patted the quivering midnight shoulder and stroked the beast's strong neck. "Let's go find Brook, boy. *Allons-y.*"

The horse tossed his head in what Justin chose to interpret as eager agreement.

Little conversation was exchanged along the way. But he could take some comfort in the size of their entourage, what with the constable's men and the mass of Whitby Park servants who followed behind on foot to fan out and search for any sign of their baroness.

They would find her. They must.

Unease crawled over his skin like spiders when Whitby led them down the lane marked with posts reading DELMORE. Heath gave way to pastures full of fluffy sheep only weeks away from shearing and horses grazing in their paddocks. Copses of trees, rising hills, and on the horizon a bluff that would tumble into the sea. Salt tinged the air when the breeze whistled by. The land, being so close to Whitby Park, ought to have seemed familiar.

But it didn't feel right. Didn't feel peaceful. Didn't feel lovely and welcoming, as Brook's home had from the moment he first rode up the drive to see if perhaps she belonged there.

Oscuro either sensed his discomfort or felt the oppression himself—he shied, whinnied, nearly sidestepped into Tempesta. Justin brought him back under control with a firm rein and quick French.

The constable, as they neared the carriage house, nodded toward the copse of trees behind the building and the rickety old carriage that sat in high, dried grass. "I went right round the back last night to find Antony, so I didn't notice that. But look. Ruts leading to it, and the grass is flattened. Not to mention that it looks entirely too clean for what must be an unused antique. And what cause, do you think, would he have for taking it out?"

A most excellent question—one that made those invisible spiders race over Justin's skin again.

She was here, somewhere. She had to be. *Lord, let her know we're coming. We're close. We're going to find her.*

They must have made a fairly impressive picture as they all dismounted and climbed the steps up to the door—the three gentlemen and five officers. The mighty wooden slab opened before they could even ring, and a perplexed butler stood before them.

His gaze locked on Whitby's face, which he no doubt recognized. "My lord. Do come in. Is something the matter?"

"Something is very much the matter." Whitby strode past the butler, the rest of them following in his wake. "My daughter is missing. Please fetch Lord Pratt at once, and assemble the staff. We need all available men out looking for her."

The butler's alarm seemed genuine, and he certainly wasted no time in showing them into a parlor and going to fetch Pratt. Justin exchanged a glance with Worthing. If Pratt had her at Delmore, surely *someone* on his staff knew it. But if he were any judge, it wasn't that one.

The purse of Worthing's mouth bespoke a similar thought.

Silence held until Pratt strode in a moment later, a pale-faced Lady Catherine—Lady Pratt—behind him. "Whitby." His expression turned to half a sneer when he spotted Justin. "And Stafford and Worthing. I never expected to welcome the two of *you* into my home."

"We haven't time for youth's rivalries just now, Pratt." Whitby's spine had gone straight as Stonehenge, and his face as hard. "Brook is missing."

The lady gripped her husband's arm, horror on her face. Pratt frowned. "Missing *how?*"

"Missing *missing*. She drove her maid to the train station yesterday and never returned. We found her car pushed off the road, into a copse of trees."

The constable stepped forward. "My men scoured the area thoroughly. We found no trace of her, precisely, but there *was* a set of carriage tracks leading from the area in question and heading here."

If Catherine pressed any closer to Pratt's side, it would require a tool to separate them. "You must be mistaken, sir."

The constable blinked at her. "Mud doesn't lie, my lady."

"Mud." She blinked too, with an innocence that they surely all knew was feigned. "Oh, you know, I do believe I heard the rain, now that you mention it. Although—" here she rested her head against her husband's shoulder—"I confess we've paid very little attention to the outside world. We were married on Sunday, you know."

When Pratt smiled down at her, Justin could almost believe, for half a second, that love existed there. But if it did, Pratt wouldn't have been pursuing Brook so relentlessly, so recently. His expression looked more pragmatic when he looked over to the constable. "A carriage, you say? I haven't even used one in months. I've a new car, and when the roads are impassable for it, I ride."

The constable folded his hands before him. "I noticed an old one behind the carriage house that has been out recently."

Something flashed in Pratt's eyes—a flare, quickly gone. But *there*. "That thing . . . I've given the servants use of it—you'll have to ask them."

Lifting his chin, the constable strode forward. "I'll go and see if they've gathered then, shall I?"

The lady pried herself off Pratt's side. "I'll accompany you, sir. I hate to think of my poor cousin being missing!"

Pratt watched her go, his gaze lingering on her hips. "You

know, I wasn't certain how I would take to it, but I'm finding married life to be most enjoyable."

"Our felicitations." Somehow Worthing managed to say it with a smile, yet in a tone that contained only irony. "But I'm afraid we've come to ask you to interrupt your honeymoon for a few hours. We need everyone we can muster out looking for her."

Pratt lifted a brow. "Apparently, if they've called you in from London. Can the Season continue without you, Worthing? Or did you come to Yorkshire with amorous intentions?"

Justin had never had cause to see Worthing bristle quite so much. "I came," he said with cold deliberation, "because my friends needed me. Will you join us or not?"

"This was a bad idea." Justin stepped forward, unable to stand inactive anymore. "Whitby, I'll wait outside."

Justin pushed past and made for the exit.

His host followed. "Stafford, wait."

He would rather get out of the house. Every moment he spent inside made him more ill at ease. So he didn't turn. He figured Whitby and Worthing weren't far behind, but he didn't verify that either.

He charged for the sunshine, for fresh air. And made it down the front steps before a hand on his arm stopped him.

He shook it off even as he spun. Maybe Pratt thought his expression was one of concern—but it was too dark, too hate-filled. Justin's fingers curled into his palm. "What?"

Pratt's eyes narrowed. "I'll help in the search. I must make sure Kitty is well first—she has been ill every morning this week—but then I'll join you."

He'd chased him down to say *that*? "Fine." Justin turned again.

"Duke!"

A growl formed in his throat as he slowly pivoted back. "*What?*"

Pratt had a hand extended. "I know we've never liked each other. But we can put it aside for this, can't we? A truce."

The last thing he wanted to do was put his hand in Pratt's. Those hands could well have hurt Brook. But he could hear the constable in his head, telling him not to tip their hand too much, too soon. With monumental effort, he uncurled his fingers and put his palm to Pratt's. "I will find her." Perhaps it came out more as a threat than a declaration . . . but if so, so be it.

Pratt held too hard to Justin's fingers. He had to tug to free them, and then they curled of their own will back into a fist.

Pratt smirked. "I know you'll not want to hear this from me, but have you considered the possibility that she left of her own volition?"

His fingers dug into his palm. "Excuse me?"

A lifted brow joined the smirk as Pratt shoved his hands into his pockets. "It's no secret the two of you have been at odds. What did you *think* she would do when you followed her here, hounding her steps? She probably ran away just to escape you."

Before Justin was even aware of giving his arm the command, it had pulled back, flown forward, and his fist connected with the reprobate's nose. A satisfying *crunch* met his ears, and a pleasant pain scourged his knuckles.

"Stafford!" Worthing cried, and his tone was a cross between warning, outrage, and a laugh.

Pratt staggered back, his eyes glazed. He touched a hand to the blood dripping from his nose. Then his eyes flashed hot fury, and he lunged.

Thirty-One

The sound of a gun's report brought Brook to her feet, sending the open journal to the floor. "What was that?"

Deirdre, sitting at the desk, stood more slowly. "A shot?"

"A shot." And it struck her right in the heart, bringing to life the fears Maman's words, and those she had written about Mother, had already ignited. Fire raced through her, and her legs insisted on moving. She went to the door, tried the latch. Flew to the bricked-over windows. Surely one, somewhere, was loose.

"Likely someone hunting."

"No." Her fingers bit into brick and crumbling mortar. Gripped, pushed, but they wouldn't give. "It was a pistol, not a rifle."

"You can tell that?"

Of course she could—though the sound had been distant. Still, her heart hammered, pressure seizing her head. A cloud of panic swirled around her. She slapped a hand to the brick. "Papa! Are you out there? Help!"

"My lady, if Pratt hears you screaming—"

"I don't care. Papa! Justin!" They must be out there. Why

else would someone be firing a pistol? They had found her. Or trace of her. They were there.

They were there—and a shot had been fired. By whom? She flew back to the door, pounded upon it. "Help! Let me out! Someone help!" She had to get to them. She must. They were there, so near, and bullets were flying—or one, anyway. Why had there not been a second? Had they killed Pratt? Or . . .

"Help!" She had to get to Papa. She had to tell him what that journal said, the truth of what sent Mother into the night. She *had* to. He needed, finally, those answers.

"My lady!" Deirdre tried to pull her away from the door—Brook shrugged off her hands. They landed again, and gripped her more firmly. "Stop. Please, I beg you."

"Someone will hear. Someone will come and help."

"Someone may hear, yes." Fear drenched Deirdre's tone. "And when they try to come, Pratt will kill them. And then be so furious with us . . ."

No. No. She had to get out. She *had* to, that certainty gripped her far more strongly than Deirdre ever could. She broke free and went back to pounding and screaming. She wouldn't give up . . . though her hand stung. Her throat burned. Evidence that time was passing, though it all seemed frozen to her.

Were they still there? Did they know she was?

The door pushed inward, suddenly and forcefully enough to knock her down. For one glorious second she hoped—then she looked up and saw Pratt towering over her. Blood soaked his shirt, stained his chin. He had a laceration on his cheek. And such bright hatred in his eyes that she recoiled, scrabbling back along the floor until she bumped into the cot. Was that the look that had been in his father's eyes as he and John Rushworth chased down her mother?

He whipped something at her head. She raised her arm to deflect it but gasped in pain when it hit her arm—though small, it was solid and heavy and clanged when it skidded across the floor.

"You want your precious duke? That's all you'll ever get of him!"

Justin? Resisting the urge to rub at what would surely become a welt, she pulled herself to her knees. There, glinting in the lamplight—gold. "No." Shaking too hard to stand, she crawled to it. It couldn't be—*no*. Justin would never, never take off his signet. He hadn't since his grandfather's death. It was there, always there on his right ring finger, where he could twirl it around.

The familiar lion and cross of Stafford rose from the gold. The recessed places were dark and, when she picked it up with shaking fingers, sticky. *Blood*. She closed her fist around it. "What have you done?" Did the words even make it past her dry lips?

They must have, because he laughed. "Exactly what I said I'd do. Except I didn't have to worry with hiding the body—he attacked *me*. I was defending myself, and the constable was there to see it."

He grabbed her by the hair and pulled her to her feet. "Now you'll believe me, hmm? Your father's next, my lady."

"*Non!*" She kicked him in the shins, slammed her ring-encasing fist into the laceration on his cheek.

He cursed her, but his hand loosed its hold on her curls. The moment it did, she took off for the door. He hadn't locked it behind him, hadn't even closed it all the way. She need only reach it, get through it, and then—

He slammed into her, slammed *her* into the door, slammed it closed. "Going somewhere, darling?"

Held there, pinned between the damp wooden door and him, she smelled mold and blood. Justin's blood? She squeezed her eyes shut tight. It couldn't be. He couldn't be dead. He *couldn't*. Wouldn't her soul know it if he were?

But hadn't she felt unaccountable fear at that gunshot? A sob balled up in her throat, surging upward but getting caught before it could do more than make her shudder. So much darkness. So much violence, and for what? A couple of diamonds stained red from it all? Had her arms been free, she would have reached up to rip the necklace from her throat. "You fool! You terrible, cruel fool. They're right here, you can have them. I don't care anymore! Just let me go to him. Maybe he's not dead, maybe he can be saved, maybe—"

"What is she saying?" Pratt's words came out harsh, and he pushed her harder to the door.

"It's Monegasque, my lord."

Another sob started in her stomach and convulsed its way upward, this one making it all the way past her lips. She couldn't even speak the right language. Couldn't act, couldn't escape, couldn't help Justin—and that was assuming he wasn't beyond help. She couldn't give her father the truth, couldn't keep her maid safe, couldn't break the curse that greed had wrought.

The necklace felt like hands around her throat. Pratt's hands, stained with blood. So much blood. "Justin."

"Should have learned long ago to control that temper of his. Now talk. Where are the Fire Eyes?"

"In my necklace."

He pulled her back a few inches just to slam her to the door again. "English!"

She was *trying*! But when she opened her mouth again, no words emerged at all, only a cry that snatched her breath away and made her every muscle shudder. Once open, the floodgates wouldn't be stopped. Her knees buckled, and she would have slid toward the floor if he hadn't still been holding her there.

Pratt made a disgusted noise, gripped her shoulders, and tossed her aside. Landing on the floor, she drew her knees to her chest and shut her eyes against the light from the lamp. It had no place here, with all the darkness. With the thunder of his anger. With the lightning of his hatred.

She wanted Justin. To hear his voice, whispering assurances. To feel his arms about her, promising a tomorrow worth fighting for. She wanted her father, with his dry sense of humor and fathomless understanding. She wanted home.

All she had was a bloodied ring and a tongue that wouldn't speak English long enough to make it all stop.

Hands soothed over her hair, so gentle that they must be Deirdre's. "She needs time to calm down."

As if time could reverse the damage done. Could heal him, bring him to her door.

"She has an hour—or Whitby's next. It would be easy enough for him to meet with an accident while out looking for her."

"*Non!*" She forced her limbs to uncurl, forced herself up, away from Deirdre. To her knees and then her feet. "*Non!*"

The door shut with a pistol's bang. The key in the lock ground like a bullet sliding into the chamber.

She fell onto the door again, pounding. Screaming. Even she didn't know now what words she shouted, whether they were plea or command or denial. She didn't know what she meant to do when he reentered. She should have thought. Should have found something to use as a weapon. Should have . . .

When the door pushed back, he had his gun in his hand and fury in his eyes. "Shut *up*!"

Never. Bellowing at the top of her lungs, she threw herself at him. If he shot her, she'd at least draw some blood first. Her nails bit his cheek, raked down.

A sickening thud echoed in her ears . . . in her skull. All other sound faded. The world went fuzzy and seemed to freeze, then shift. Slowly, as if she were viewing it all through morning fog, the room went sideways and the floor embraced her. Then the lamp went out.

"Wake up, my lady. Please." Deirdre had said the words so often, they had begun to sound nonsensical. The burning of the lamp was the only measure she had of passing time. She had filled it while Pratt cursed and lifted the baroness onto the cot, the only thing she could think to do to look unconcerned, when she'd *wanted* to rush over and try to rouse her.

She'd refilled it again since. That meant that at least sixteen hours had passed. More, now. A day must be done, a new one beginning. And still the baroness hadn't stirred. Hadn't wakened.

He'd come back once, when the lamp was still half full. The tempest on his face when he saw the lady was still unconscious . . . To her utter surprise, he hadn't taken it out on Deirdre. He had, instead, left her with a key to this door, though that would only give her access to the hall. She had tried every door along it, tried the key in every lock, but the only one that would open was the one she'd seen before.

He'd left food there, and water. She'd tried dribbling some onto her ladyship's lips, but that earned her no response either. She'd thought to try reading to her, but the journal was all they had, and it was in French. There had been a letter tucked into the last page though. That had been in English, and she'd read it aloud . . . then almost wished she hadn't.

It had been from them, the elder Pratt and Rushworth. To the late Lady Whitby. Claiming they'd killed her husband, saying that the body found in York the night before—a newspaper clipping was included, about a body so badly mutilated as to be unidentifiable—was him. Warning that if she didn't hand over the Fire Eyes, the baby would be next.

Deirdre's fingers went knotted as the words swam before her again. How horrified must the lady have been? A young mother getting such news, convinced, it seemed, by the horror. No wonder she had fled, thinking it the only way to save her babe.

The floor was cold and hard under Deirdre's knees, and the lamp did little to make the shadows flee. "Lord God." She had prayed more these hours than at any time in her life—other than when it was Da who had lain unresponsive on a lumpy mattress. She picked up His Grace's ring from where it had skidded under the cot and put it in the baroness's hand, curled her fingers around it. "Lord above, I beg you. Restore her. Deliver her. Give her back to her father and . . ."

She'd nearly said "His Grace." But that wasn't possible now, was it? She pressed her lips together. Pratt had said there would be no questions about killing him, that the constable had witnessed it. But no one could kill a duke without consequences, for sure and certain. Even if Pratt saw no prison term for it, there would be questions. He had to know that. It had to be what had put him in such a rage.

And what if he were taken away to answer for it? What would become of them then, with neither water nor food?

"Wake up, my lady. Come now." Deirdre rested her head against the side of the tick. Had she slept at all this night? If so, not for more than a minute here or there. "I've the key to the door. Not the outer one, only this one, but it's something. Wake up, and we can make a plan together. Lie in wait in the room by the outer door. You'll think of something, fearless as you are. But sure and you have to wake up first."

Not a whimper. Not a flinch.

Deirdre closed her eyes—jolted when her head slipped, and sure and that made her eyes fly to the lamp. Was the oil lower? She couldn't remember, now, what level it had been at. But enough remained that she could get up, walk to the end of the hall and see if new water awaited, or breakfast. Perhaps the aroma of food would stir her ladyship.

Deirdre's joints creaked when she arose, her muscles screamed. And as she walked, her feet dragged. It took all her focus to get the key into the lock and turn it. She shuffled her way down the hall.

A scratching reached her ears halfway down. She paused, the sound bringing her awake a bit more. Mice? A rat? Her pulse hammered at the thought. She lifted the lamp, though she saw no evidence of the rodent. But sure and it was the sound of claw on wood at the end of the hall.

It stopped. Then came again, louder. She squealed, though quick as a flash she clamped a hand over her mouth.

The scratching stopped. And in its place came . . . a hiss? Did rats hiss? No, wait—that was *words*! Praise be to the Almighty. Someone was at the door!

"I'm coming." Her voice came out the barest whisper, but she hoped whoever it was could hear her. Tremors possessed her by the time she reached the door. What if it was a trick? Did Pratt doubt her? Was he testing her?

It was a risk she had to take. "Is someone there?"

"Bless my soul!" came the muted reply. "I didn't hear awry, then. Who is in there? Is this the baroness?"

Someone knew! Deirdre pressed close against the door, her mouth at the crack. "Aye! I mean, not I, but I'm her maid, and she's in here too. Do you work for Pratt?"

"Much to my dismay—but I'm cousin to the constable, and he told me to be on the lookout. I was seeing to repairs outside this wing and heard the screaming. Took me all night to find the hall what corresponded. Are ye well in there?"

She splayed her fingers against the wood. "Nay. I'm well enough, but the baroness is hurt. He struck her in the head, and she's not woken for so very long. I don't know what to do."

A shuffling sound reached her, one that went away from the door and then back. "He's coming. We haven't much time. But he's joining the search this morning, ordered his horse to be ready at eight. He'll be away. Two hours' time. I'll get you out, somehow or another. Aye?"

"Aye! Aye." Two hours. She didn't know how she'd gauge it, but she knew answered prayer when it scratched. The constable's own cousin—praise be to heaven. He could help her carry the baroness out, help them sneak from the house. Then it would only be a matter of getting her the miles back to Whitby Park.

Heaven help her—how was she to do that, if her ladyship didn't awaken?

She would worry with that later. For now she rushed back to the cell, where the baroness lay as she'd left her. Golden curls tucked beside her, soiled gown half covered by the ratty blanket. Hands limp and useless at her side, with Pratt's blood still staining her nails.

The distant creak of the door echoed down the hall. Footsteps. And then a curse. "Blast it, Deirdre—why the devil is the door open?"

She spun, her fists at her sides. And took what was likely a sinful amount of pleasure in seeing the angry welts on his face, the bruises and cuts. "And what harm can it possibly do, when she hasn't so much as twitched a finger since you struck her? She needs a doctor."

"A doctor would do nothing but wave smelling salts under her nose." Apparently doubting her word, he strode to the cot. Cursed again when the truth spoke for itself. "Idiot woman, forcing my hand."

Never in her life had she been so tempted to strike a gentleman and add another mark to his once-beautiful face. She would do it, too, if the baroness didn't need her to keep his trust. But the words . . . the words came forth of their own volition. "You call *her* stupid? How did you *expect* her to react when you come barreling in here and tell her you've killed the man she loves?"

He jerked toward her, looking ready to bite. Then, with a low mutter she couldn't discern, he knelt down and pressed a finger to her ladyship's neck. "Her pulse is still strong—she cannot be too hurt. She will wake up soon, and when she does, the door had better be locked. And *you* had better be ready to get answers from her."

He stood straight again and strode for the door. Deirdre followed him out—closing the door behind her. "Sure and I will be, *if* she awakens. And what if she doesn't? Or what if you're arrested for killing the duke? Will you let us die of thirst?"

He'd left a lamp at the end of the hall. Its light outlined the hard angle of his brows. "I won't be. I did nothing but defend myself."

"But—"

"Shut up, Deirdre, or I swear I'll lay you out along with her."

Never, in the year she'd known him, had she seen his nerves so frayed, his temper so close to the surface. Perhaps, devil though he was, he hadn't been prepared for the effects of his own actions. Perhaps he staggered under the weight of his sins. Perhaps . . . perhaps he realized he'd dug himself too deep a pit.

She followed him into the other open chamber, where a new tray had taken up residence on the table.

He motioned to the bread, the cheese, the ham, the pitcher of water. "That ought to keep you alive, don't you think?"

She folded her arms over her chest. It was more than he usually brought—which meant he intended not to be back by the midday meal, she would guess. And also, praise God, that there would be plenty for both of them when the baroness awoke.

"Well then." He turned to the door.

"Wait." She didn't know what she meant to say, only that she wanted to prick at him. Needle him in whatever way she could. She lifted her chin. "If thirst doesn't kill me, boredom might, while I wait for her ladyship to flutter her lashes. Have you a book in this house of yours? One written in English?"

One she could actually read to her ladyship, that didn't speak of the horrors that had brought them here?

Pratt snorted, though not with amusement. He stood stock-still for a moment and then reached into his jacket pocket. Pulled out a newspaper, still crisply folded and bound with twine, and threw it to the floor. "Don't get the pages out of order—I'll want to read it later." Not awaiting her response, he hurried out. Though he did toss over his shoulder, "And lock the blasted door!"

Thirty-Two

Thunder roared, lightning sizzled, and darkness consumed her. Fear nipped, making a cry want to tear from her throat. But her throat wouldn't work. Brook couldn't make her body obey the command to run, flee, get away from the danger behind her.

Then the words began. Some in French—Maman's words, but in Brook's own voice as she read the pages of the journal, softly. Some in English, filling in the gaps.

Pratt and Rushworth had told Mother that Papa was dead— and that Brook was next. That's what had sent her out into the night, into the storm. Why she had the letters from Papa with her . . . and why she was wearing the pearls and gold she had thought were the last gift she would ever receive from him. When the storm raged, when the carriage tipped . . .

That was where Maman's journal had begun. With watching the accident from the distance and rushing up. Hearing the wail of a baby. The groans of a dying woman—the driver was already dead. She recorded Mother's words, her pleas to take the babe, her Elizabeth Brook, and see her to safety. Somewhere far away, she said.

She had no one left in England. Her husband was dead, and her family . . . How was she to know whom of her family she could trust, when it was a cousin who had done this to her?

In the darkness, Brook felt tears gather. How alone Mother must have felt in those last moments. Giving away her child, mourning the husband she didn't realize would soon be mourning her. Thinking her whole family turned against her.

Collette recorded her own fears too—suddenly having a child she didn't know how to care for. Fearing that whatever had sent the woman to her death would chase after her if she took the child . . . but being unable to leave the babe to the elements. She'd found nothing on the lady to offer identification—no doubt purposeful on Mother's part, if she were running away. But she took what she could for the baby. The box of letters. The necklace.

And she had devised the best plan she could come up with for seeing to the girl's future. She went to the man she'd been involved in an affair with a year before—Prince Louis of Monaco.

Prince Louis, who had never wanted to be Brook's father. Who had never loved her, never accepted her. But Grand-père had. Grand-père, always at odds with his son, had believed Maman's story. Had arranged for their care. Their flat. Had promised to provide for Brook's education.

No wonder Maman had made him promise never to tell her. To destroy the journal with the story written inside it. She no doubt feared that if Brook ever returned to England, the violence would find her as it had her mother.

And so it had.

Her fingers curled into the damp mattress, closing around something warm and hard. Metallic. Her fingertips ran over it, tracing its contours . . . slipping into it. A convulsion rippled through her. Not just Maman and Mother. Justin, too, was gone.

405

She squeezed her eyes shut against the darkness. They were all gone.

Brook tried to sit, but her head pounded too hard, and her limbs all felt so heavy. How could she feel so tired, and yet as if she hadn't moved in an eternity?

She used her fingertips to turn the large ring of gold around her finger. If Justin were here, he would prod her. Poke her if necessary, but he wouldn't let her lie about. He wouldn't let her weep away her life. He wouldn't let Pratt win. He'd tell her to get up and fight.

She didn't want to fight. It hurt. And what was the point? Pratt had already won, had avenged his father's death, had taken what mattered most. Why fight anymore over the diamonds? Why should anyone else lose their lives over the Fire Eyes?

"A fire goeth before him, and burneth up his enemies round about . . ."

"Mon Dieu." She opened her eyes again, and the lamp seemed brighter than it had before. "Are you here in this? You must be, because you promise you are. But I can't feel you now. I can't see you."

"His lightnings enlightened the world."

She shuddered. The lightning had always been there, hand in hand with the darkness. They had seemed, somehow, of the enemy, not of God. But He was the author of that story. It was from His treasury that the winds came. By His hand that night overtook day.

By His command that they died?

No. *"Ye are all the children of light, and the children of the day."*

Men made their own choices. And as some of them chose life, others chose death, chose evil. God could stop all the evil, all the violence, but if He did, He'd be rendering their choices for Him meaningless. But God did have a hand in this world.

He was the one who had brought Brook home. Back to Papa. He was the one who had led her that day to Justin, in the abbey. He had led them to reconciliation before Pratt found her.

She must praise Him for that. Papa was right. The hurt was unfathomable, the hole gaping. But it would have been even worse if they had still been at odds.

And she knew, with every fiber of her being, that Justin would tell her to buck up. To mourn later. To focus, now, on beating Pratt. Getting free, somehow. Finding justice for him . . . and gathering close what family she had left. As William had taught him.

Gritting her teeth with every contraction of muscle, she pushed herself up.

"My lady!" The door's squeak must have blended with the cot's—but Deirdre flew through it and was on her in a moment, scarcely taking time to put down the tray in her hands before pulling Brook close in a hug so exuberant it made her head throb. "You're awake! Praise be to God, you're awake!"

She pushed aside the pain and squeezed Deirdre back. "What day is it?"

"You've been out almost an entire day, and sure and you scared a decade off my life."

"Sorry." Brook pulled away and managed what she hoped was a smile. She gripped her friend's hands. "We need to get out of here. Somehow, some way. We'll lie in wait at the end of the hall if we must, and spring on him when next he comes, but—"

Deirdre's laugh, light and a bit incredulous, cut her off. She shook her head. "I knew you would come up with something like that, once you roused. But the Lord has provided. There's a groundsman what heard your shouting yesterday. He's coming back in two hours to help us."

Brook sagged in relief. "Two hours."

"Aye. Enough time to eat and for it to revive us. Here, sit at the desk. You need water right off, and then some food."

"You, too, from the looks of you. Have you slept at all?" Brook took slowly, carefully to her feet.

Deirdre steadied her and then bent for the tray. "You were sleeping enough for the both of us."

"You'll eat and then must rest. You'll need your strength."

"Aye." Deirdre slid the tray onto the desk and gave her a smile. "It's good to have you back, my lady."

Brook returned the smile and took the chair before her legs gave out. The bread smelled of heaven, and the water that Deirdre poured into a dented tin cup tasted of ambrosia. She took a slow sip, let it settle, and picked up the newspaper. "Really?"

Deirdre held out her hands, palms up. "I asked him for reading material. Mostly to irritate him, but he tossed that at me."

Tugging at the string with one hand, she reached with the other for a slice of cheese. Then she unfolded the paper.

Her own picture stared back at her. This one was from the night of her debut, but the camera had caught her in an odd moment. She was looking over her shoulder at something, no smile on her lips. Rather, concern etched her brow—had she been wondering, in that moment, where Justin was? Not a picture they would have run then, but now it suited the headline.

BARONESS BEAUTY KIDNAPPED!

A startled breath escaped and brought Deirdre to her side. She quickly read through the paragraphs. Her lungs closed off when she reached the fifth one, and she jabbed a finger at it. *In an interview given last evening, the Duke of Stafford stood with Lord Whitby and Lord Worthing and pronounced that he would match the reward . . .*

"What time?" Was it hope that fluttered, or new fear of it being dashed? "What time did Pratt come in with the ring?"

"Morning." Deirdre's fingers dug into her shoulder, but she scarcely felt it. "This had to have been after. He's alive!"

A sound came from Brook's throat that was half laugh, half cry. She pressed a hand to her mouth—the one that still had his ring slung loosely around one finger. "Pratt was lying."

Justin was alive—which meant all she had to do was get to him.

She read the rest of the article as she ate, her heart pounding with every word. The reward her father offered was substantial—and the fact that Justin had offered to match it would make it mighty tempting for anyone who had caught a glimpse of her. They'd done what they could to swing the tide. To win her allies.

She would use them.

When they finished eating, she banished a protesting Deirdre to the cot and let the words run through her mind time and again. *The Duke of Stafford.* Alive and giving quotes to the press. She stood, stretched, paced until her legs didn't feel so wooden and the tension in her neck eased a bit. She prayed and she praised and she plotted.

They would have a considerable trek ahead of them, when they got free. They had to be at Delmore, and once the groundsman got them out of the house, she could find her way home easily enough. Find the sun, find the south, and go. Pratt land would lead straight to Eden. She had only to avoid him, and she would be home.

Then she had to read the article again . . . and shake her head.

He had used the same trick on her that his father had used on her mother—and she, too, had fallen for it. Had been mourning one who hadn't been lost at all . . . but who would be concerned about losing *her*.

Well, it was time for the pattern to reach its end—and for Papa to finally have the answers he'd needed for nearly nineteen years. She retrieved the journal from the floor and made a makeshift sack for it and the canteen.

Had it been up to Justin alone, they would have been out again the moment dawn streaked the sky. But they had waited for the paper, and he was glad of that too. As he finally strode out into the cool morning air, certainty settled in his chest. They had done right. They had given her what she needed.

Even if the magistrate wouldn't budge, wouldn't let them search Delmore, they would find her. She would find a way out, find someone to help her, and they would be there when she did.

"Stafford, Whitby! Wait!"

Justin paused with one foot on the macadam and the other on the stair. Whitby was ten paces ahead of him, but he turned too.

Worthing stood at the door, motioning to the footman who had been assigned as his valet. "Tell them, Hiram."

Hiram seemed to be clinging to composure by no more than a thread as he waited for Whitby to join them. "Forgive me for not speaking sooner, my lord, but I tried to tell myself it was unrelated."

Whitby shook his head. "Speak, Hiram."

"It's Deirdre. She swore she'd wire at every stop, and she hasn't. I was worried, so yesterday afternoon when the search took me to town, I telegrammed her family. She never arrived in Kilkeel—and what's more, her mother isn't sick, they never sent her a message. Pratt must have taken her too."

Justin felt his brows pull together. His thumb moved to his ring finger to twist the signet around, but its empty state made him want to utter a few choice words. He'd worry with that later, though. "Why would Pratt take her too?"

Hiram glanced at Worthing, who gave him a helpful prod forward, his face stern. "Tell them."

The footman swallowed. "She'd been giving him information. He'd threatened her family."

Whitby pivoted away, muttered something unintelligible, and spun back to him. "Why did she not come to me?"

Hiram spread his hands. "She sees the mistake now, my lord, which is what's to the point. She won't help him in this, though he might think she will. She must be with her ladyship. She'll help her. I know my DeeDee, and she'll help her get free."

Justin wasn't so sure about that, but he didn't know the woman. Whitby, after a long moment of clenched fists and ticking jaw, nodded.

So then. Justin headed for the stables once more and nearly drew his pistol when he caught sight of the rider who trotted their way.

"Easy." Worthing stayed him with a hand on his arm. "No doubt he's keeping up appearances. Let him, for now. We'll have the noose around his neck soon enough."

There was no "soon enough" when it came to bringing down Pratt. Justin planted his feet outside the stable door, folded his arms over his chest, glared. And took no small amount of satisfaction from the bruises and gashes on Pratt's face.

And scratches—Justin hadn't scratched him.

Pratt nodded at Whitby. "I'll head toward Eden Dale, Whitby. Are we meeting back here at noon?"

Whitby shook his head. "We need you on the road toward the town, not the village. Those on foot will cover that area."

Pratt worked his jaw, no doubt hating the idea of being sent farther from his house. But he nodded. "Very well. See you in a few hours, then."

As he turned his horse and rode off, Worthing stepped close. "You didn't scratch his face."

"No."

"His wife?"

Though the idea made him want to grin, he shook his head. "I think not."

Worthing nodded. Not in general but toward his hand. "And why do you keep doing that with your thumb? Not that this is a bad time to develop a nervous tic, but . . ."

Must the man notice everything? Justin loosed his arms, stretched his fingers. "I can't find my signet. Perhaps I left it in my room in town."

But he hadn't. He couldn't remember when he'd last had it, but he'd have noticed its absence sooner if he'd left it at the hotel.

Worthing's eyes went wide. "You lost your *signet*? Are you mad? You'll have centuries of dukes haunting you—"

"It doesn't matter. Not today." He set his gaze to the north, toward where Brook had to be. "I can always have a new ring made. Just now, all that matters is finding her."

A high-pitched whinny from inside the stables underscored his point. The grooms were bringing out the horses, but they were all skittish. No doubt because Oscuro reared and bucked and pulled at his lead, his eyes flashing whites.

Whitby backed up to stand beside him and Worthing.

The groom tried to get the stallion calm with a few words that did nothing. "Sorry, milord! He let us saddle him, but then he started acting like this the moment he got free of his stall. Not fit for riding today, it seems. We'll get him put away."

"No." Whitby's voice was calm, deliberate. His eyes flashed certainty. "Don't put him away. Let him go."

The groom looked at him like he was mad. "Pardon, milord?"

"Secure the reins and let him go. Maybe he can find her where we can't."

Justin's lips tugged up. "You're using a horse as a blood-hound?"

"Have you a better suggestion? The bloodhounds couldn't find the right trail."

Too much rain, their masters had wagered, and too many trails she'd set on her many rides through the country. The dogs had chased to and fro and to again.

Justin strode to Oscuro, took the reins from the groom, and whispered to the beast in French. He calmed. Not enough that any sane man would try to ride him, but enough that he could slip the lead back over his head and pat his neck. "Go find her, boy. *Va*."

The horse didn't even need a slap to the rump to send him on his way. The moment Justin let go the reins, he took off like a sleek black bullet.

Worthing shook his head. "I do hope the idea isn't for us to keep up with him."

Brook's father motioned for the other horses. "We'd never stand a chance."

"And if he doesn't come back?"

Then Yorkshire would have a wild stallion jumping its fences and scaring its sheep. But Justin chose to believe. "He'll come back. With Brook."

He accepted the reins for Tempesta, mounted, and pointed her in the direction Oscuro had gone.

Thirty-Three

The sound of hammer on brick brought Deirdre out of sleep with a start. She flew off the cot, heart pounding as pieces of mortar crumbled and spewed out from the once-windows, hitting the floor.

The baroness was at her side in a beat, linking their arms. "Your groundsman?"

"I assumed he meant he'd return to the hall." But surely someone out to harm them, someone on Pratt's side, would use the door. She edged a bit closer, though off to the side, where the shower of brick-pieces was at a minimum. "Hello? Is that you?"

She didn't know who *you* even was, but the hammering stopped for a moment, and the same voice she'd heard earlier said, "Aye. It's me, Antony—the constable's cousin. Stand clear, it'll take only a minute."

They clutched each other the tighter, both going more and more tense as sunlight found the cracks and shone down through. Blessed, beautiful summer sunlight. First just a few spots shafting in, then a whole beam. And finally, a rough-worn but friendly face peered down at them.

He grinned. "Both awake, I see. Ready?"

The baroness's smile looked exhausted with relief. "So very."

"I've a ladder. You'll have to climb up." A moment later the face disappeared, and an old wooden ladder appeared through the space he'd made.

Deirdre rushed forward to grab it and steady it. Then she waved the baroness over. "You first, my lady. I'll hold it steady for you."

Her ladyship wobbled a few times on the way up, muttering in French as she did. No doubt frustrated at her own unsteadiness. Once her shoes disappeared through the gap, Deirdre followed. The ladder slipped when she reached the third rung, but she bit back a scream.

And hands steadied it at the top. "Quickly now. I hammer often enough out here, but not usually upon the brick. I can't be sure no one heard, but it was that or an axe to the door, and there are fewer servants out here."

Deirdre breathed a prayer and rushed up the last few rungs, exhaling in relief when strong hands grabbed her arms and pulled her out.

Their window, it seemed, had its top at ground level—the bottom being within a paved moat that seemed to line this whole side of the house. For what purpose, she couldn't discern, but the stones and bricks looked old as the hills. Part of the original structure, perhaps, from an age long-since past.

"Hurry, milady. Here." Antony grabbed up a patched jacket that had seen better days and handed it to the baroness, along with an equally battered skirt. "My wife's—she helps me in the gardens sometimes, is about your height, praise be to heaven. Put it on. And her hat, here. One for you too, miss."

"Deirdre." She took the hat and prayed its broad rim would hide her.

Her ladyship wasted no time. She slid the disguise directly over her muddied, bloodied dress—though even with the layers underneath and her sack concealed beneath it too, still she swam in it. Jamming the hat over the hair the sun was determined to catch and alight, she nodded. "Let's be off."

"Aye." Antony guided them both with a hand to each of their elbows, shooting a look over his shoulder. "There are stairs at the end there. Keep your heads down, but act like you're talking. Hopefully, if anyone sees, they'll think you're my daughter, miss, coming from town to visit."

They no sooner gained level ground than the first shout went up from the distance. It took all Deirdre's willpower not to spin to see who it belonged to, not to run for the trees.

Antony gripped her elbow the tighter. "Easy. It's Roger—he's a friend. 'Tis the chauffeur we need to be wary of, methinks, and perhaps the footmen." He half turned in the direction of the shout and let go Deirdre's arm long enough to wave. "Morning, Rog! I'll come by later, aye?"

The figure in the distance had a shovel in hand and didn't make for them. He merely raised a hand in salute and kept to his path.

Deirdre couldn't bring her breath to even out though.

Antony's fingers took her elbow again, and he guided them southward, toward a copse of trees. Five feet strode across, ten, twenty. Halfway.

"Ho, Antony!" This voice sounded harsh. "Where are you going? His lordship said no one is to leave the immediate grounds today."

Antony swallowed hard, his larynx bobbing under his kerchief. He let go their elbows again. "Stay here. Act disinterested. Don't turn around." He strode a few paces back toward the house and called out, "Just hunting truffles is all, Mr. Michaels."

Deirdre clutched at the baroness's hands, bending close. As if they were talking, laughing. Or at least, she hoped it would look like she shook from laughter and not from fear.

"His lordship ordered no truffles." Now suspicion edged the voice.

"Lord, help us," Deirdre muttered. "What do we do?"

The baroness gripped her fingers. "Hold still. A minute more."

Antony loosed a guffaw of a laugh. "He might not have, but the new lady did, and I for one don't aim to get on her bad side so soon!"

That earned him a snort from the man behind them. "Where are the hounds, then?"

"Already in the trees—though they must not have found any yet, given how quiet they are. If they don't in half an hour, we'll turn right back, sir. Better the lady's disappointment than the lord's ire, aye?"

Now a grunt. "Half an hour. Not a minute more."

Deirdre's breath whooshed out. Could they reach Lord Whitby's land in the allotted time?

Antony returned, on her ladyship's other side this time. He motioned them forward at an even, unhurried pace. "Easy now, until we reach the cover of the trees. Natural-like. And pray he don't go and see that the truffle hounds are still in their bays."

Pray she did, for that and more. All was quiet as they tromped into the tree line, at which point their guide darted a glance over his shoulder.

He nodded. "He's gone. We'd best run for it now."

They did, though within a minute her ladyship called them to a halt. "Sorry. My corset." Her breath came in short, hard gasps. She tossed the hat down and shrugged from the jacket and skirt. "You'll have to loosen it for me, Deirdre, or I'll pass out before we get more than a quarter mile."

Deirdre didn't need to be told twice. She went at the row of buttons while Antony made a show of turning his back to them.

The baroness dragged in another half breath. "What if he finds you were lying, sir? You could get in trouble for helping us."

A gnarled hand waved that away. "I've already sent my wife to our daughter in Eden Dale, first thing when my cousin spoke to me. I mean to join them there after I see you home, milady. I'll go to my cousin and tell him all I know. When Lord Pratt is behind bars, we'll decide our next step."

Deirdre tugged at the stays, loosening them until her ladyship could breathe normally and then tying a cursory bow to keep the corset up. Her fingers knew the buttons well enough to make quick work of them.

"My father's offered a reward to any who help me."

Antony nodded. "Aye, I know. It's how I talked the ladder from George."

Someone else knew of them? Deirdre's hands shook, making the last three buttons impossible. "There. Good enough."

Antony turned back toward them. "I tried to manage it on my own, but . . ."

"No matter. We'll be happy to compensate this George. And you, of course—"

"Nay, milady." Antony's shoulders straightened even as he motioned them onward again. "I'll not have it said I did right just for a bit of quid. Though if you've a position open on Whitby grounds . . ."

Her ladyship smiled as she broke into a run. "I'm certain we have, Antony. Absolutely certain of it."

They hadn't the breath for any more conversation. Sticking to the trees as much as they were able, they concentrated on covering ground.

Soon they'd be home. She'd be back in Hiram's arms, and her ladyship would be in her duke's, and her father's.

Assuming Pratt didn't find them first.

She whispered another prayer, one the baroness echoed in French.

Thundering hooves interrupted before she could say her amen. Antony halted, cursed, motioned them deeper into the line of trees.

The baroness stepped out instead, into the open. "It's Oscuro! How did he—he must have jumped the fence when they put him out or . . . No." A laugh broke free of her lips. "He's saddled! Oscuro!"

The beast bore down on them, and though her ladyship hadn't the sense of get out of his way, sure and Deirdre did.

The baroness laughed again as he shifted his course, looking as though he'd barrel right into her. Instead he circled her, nickered, and shoved his head into her side with enough force to send her back a few steps. Still laughing, she wrapped her arms about his neck and murmured something in French. Then she looked to Deirdre. "Our chariot, milady. I recognize this last stretch—on Oscuro, we'll be back on Whitby property within a minute."

"Then it'll take no more than five on foot." Deirdre stepped closer to Antony's side, though she smiled weakly. "Horses and I don't get along. But you go ahead. He'll see you safe to your da's arms. I'll take the sensible path."

"You don't know what you're missing."

"Aye, but I do. Broken limbs and a heart that gives way from fear."

Her ladyship laughed again and left the beast for a moment, long enough to come and wrap her arms about Deirdre.

And who'd have thought they'd become friends, the grand baroness with her Parisian gowns, and her, little DeeDee from belowstairs? She held her back, tight as she would little Molly. "Be careful, my lady. He's out here somewhere."

"And he'll be answering for his sins." Her ladyship pulled

away and looked to Antony. "You'll see her safely to Whitby Park?"

"Upon my honor, milady." He swept his cap from his head and held it over his heart.

The baroness nodded, a breeze toying with her loose curls. "See you soon, then."

Deirdre held her ground while the baroness swung up into the saddle. When they thundered off, Deirdre accepted the arm Antony held out.

"We'd best hurry," he said as he pulled her along toward Whitby Park with a glance over his shoulder. "Our half hour was up some time ago."

Today the wind raced them, and the sun urged them on. Brook made little use of the stirrups, which had been set for longer legs than hers, and held on with her knees. If Pratt were out supposedly helping look for her, he would, she hoped, stay near the roads. So she headed for the sea.

It crashed its greeting. Waves on shore, clouds skidding overhead as accents to the sun. After days in darkness, she soaked up the warm light with joy.

"Ye are all the children of light, and the children of the day." A promise too easily forgotten in the darkness.

The moment they crossed over to that familiar mark where they would always turn around, her heart leaped. And Oscuro put on a renewed burst of speed. He, too, knew home.

Figures appeared, mounted. For a moment she worried that it might be Pratt—but the lead horse was black. He had no black horse that she had ever seen. And given the way Oscuro shifted direction to angle for them, she let her heart leap. It must be Tempesta. No matter who rode her, it meant a friend, and a laugh tickled her throat.

The laugh turned to a shout when she caught the gleam of sunlight on a blond head. Justin. It was Justin.

An echo of a shout came her way too, woven into the rush of water and the cry of gulls overhead. He waved, but she didn't let go the reins to wave back. Better to hold on and let the stallion run faster than he ever had before.

Justin pulled ahead of whoever rode alongside him on one of the bays—Papa? Brice? Soon she could make out her beloved's form, his face.

His beautiful, strong, unmarked face. If he had indeed attacked Pratt yesterday, there was no question who the victor had been. She pulled Oscuro up to a halt and leaped from his back to cover the last few feet.

"Brook!" Justin's feet hit the ground too, and seconds later his arms were around her. "Brook. *Mon amour*. Are you hurt? If he hurt you, I'll kill him."

The laughter bubbled up again. Right then, the ache in her head meant nothing. She wrapped her arms tight around him and pulled his head down for a kiss. Quick but hard, exuberant. "I'm fine," she breathed against his mouth. "I'm home, and I'm fine. And you're fine. Pratt told me he'd killed you."

"What?" His arms tightened around her, and he buried his face in her hair. "Never."

"He had your ring."

"He has my *ring*?"

"Had. He threw it at me. It's in my pocket."

"He must have slipped it off when I shook his hand—right before I socked him in the nose." He squeezed her, and then he set her back a few inches and traced her face with his gaze. His eyes darkened. "You're bruised. He *did* hurt you. Tell me that at least it was you who put the scratches on his face."

"I would have gouged out his eyes had he not knocked me out with his pistol. What was the shot I heard? It set me to screaming, which got the attention of one of the groundsmen. He just led us out."

Justin's grin was boyish, unrepentant. "We had a bit of a scuffle. The constable fired a shot into the air."

"A bit of a scuffle?" Brice's voice brought Brook's gaze up. He dismounted, more leisurely. The usual mirth in his grin couldn't disguise the relief in it—or the circles under his eyes. "Stafford would have pounded him to a pulp." He stepped nearer and put a hand on her shoulder. "If I may, Duke."

Brook wasn't sure what exactly had changed between these two, but Justin let her go with naught but a lifted brow. Brice gave her a quick embrace. "I knew something bad was going to happen."

Stretching to her toes, she kissed his cheek. "And you came from London to help. You're a true friend, Brice."

"They couldn't have handled the press without me." With a wink, he propelled her back into Justin's arms. "Did you see our article yet?"

"It's what let me know Justin wasn't dead." And being tucked to his side was pure bliss.

Nearly as much as hearing the rumble of Justin's chuckle. "You should have seen Worthing yesterday when he arrived. Clothes wrinkled. Hair out of place."

"Extenuating circumstances."

A metallic sound cut through her laugh, one she recognized only vaguely. A shotgun being pumped. "*Non.*"

They all spun at the same time, even as Pratt stepped out of the trees. He held the weapon at the ready, pointed at the three of them. "Well, well. Look at this lovely target. I bet I could fell all three of you with the scatter shot."

Before she could even mutter a prayer, Justin and Brice had both put themselves between her and Pratt. Justin kept his hand clamped on her arm—he knew her too well, knew how she readied to elbow her way back up.

"Are you too stupid to know when you've been beaten, Pratt?" Justin's fingers squeezed a warning into her arm. Begging, that pressure, begging her to stay put. "There's no winning now."

How could a face look so shadowed in full sunlight? His eyes spewed hatred at them. "You think I didn't know this was a possibility? I'm about to disappear—and one of you is coming with me until I do, to assure my safety. Worthing? You look like you're in the mood for self-sacrifice. Spare the lovebirds another separation, hmm?"

"Don't even think about it, Brice." Brook kept her voice too quiet for Pratt to hear over the pounding surf behind them and knotted a hand in the back of his jacket to make sure he took her advice. "He could well kill you—and even if not, he'll only come back. He'll not give up on the diamonds so easily."

Brice shook his head. "You would abandon your wife, Pratt? And she with child?"

Brook's hand nearly went lax.

Pratt edged closer. "Kitty's resourceful. And she would fare better with an absent husband than an imprisoned one."

No doubt they already had a plan to rendezvous. No doubt Kitty knew every facet of his plan, had helped him devise it.

The betrayal still pierced.

Justin turned his head a fraction toward her. "I have a pistol at my back," he said in Monegasque. "Pull it out, Brooklet—you're the better shot. I'll get Worthing out of the way."

"What did you say?" Pratt stomped closer, his eyes wild and his finger twitching. "Don't try anything. A hostage would be handy, but if I have to kill you all and make a run for it, I'll do it."

Father, help us. When Justin's fingers loosened, she moved her arm to his back, slid her hand under his jacket, doing her best not to move the fabric. The pistol was at the small of his back, the grip warm under her hand.

Pratt's gaze arrowed into hers. "Step away from the baroness, gentlemen. Now."

"Dive," she whispered. "Both of you. On the count of *trois*. *Un*."

Pratt brought the butt of the shotgun to his shoulder, his lips compressed.

"*Deux*." Brook pulled the pistol free. Pratt's finger moved to the trigger. She brought the weapon up, shouting, "*Trois!*"

The men lunged to the side, but a shot ripped the air before her finger touched the trigger.

Pratt jerked. The shotgun fell. Eyes glazed, he staggered to his knees and then collapsed.

The constable stood behind him, pistol still smoking. Papa was at his side, looking ready to empty his revolver into Pratt's still form, but the constable put a hand on his arm. "I'll take care of him, my lord."

A cloud cleared from her father's eyes. He passed his gun to the constable and ran forward. Brook handed Justin's back too and met Papa in a fierce embrace. The moment his arms came about her, a cry took hold of her throat. "Papa. I'm sorry. I never wanted you to go through that again."

He held her tight, sucked in a deep breath. "You're safe. That's all that matters, my precious girl."

"She thought you were dead." She pulled away enough to look into his face. "He had Maman's journal, and that's what Mother told her. She thought you were dead, thought they would kill me next. That's why she sent me away."

Papa rested a hand on her cheek. "I would have gladly gone the rest of my life without knowing why, if it had spared you this."

She covered his hand with hers. "But I'm safe. And now we know."

"We do. And praise be to God, you are." He kissed her forehead.

Hiram ran their way, panic on his face. "Lady Berkeley! Is Deirdre with you?"

A smile tugged. "Following on foot, led by the constable's cousin. They both deserve a hero's welcome. She will be glad to see you, Hiram."

Hiram needed no more urging—he took off at a run in the direction she indicated.

The constable removed his hand from Pratt's neck and shook his head. "He's dead, which was not my goal. But Antony helped you?"

"We never would have escaped without him."

With a satisfied nod, the constable stood. "Good. Now—go home, have a meal, rest. When you're ready, I've questions."

"And I've the answers."

"When my men get here, I'll leave them to see to the body. I've a conversation to have with Lady Pratt—and no doubt a few servants to arrest."

Brook's back went stiff at mention of Catherine. She *had* to have been involved—but Pratt hadn't once mentioned her. Brook had never seen her. Other than the one time she'd demanded the Fire Eyes, she had, it seemed, kept her hands clean. It had been Pratt who hired Jenkins to attack her, Pratt who killed the major. Pratt who kidnapped her and Deirdre. A sick knot twisted in her stomach. They would have nothing to accuse Catherine of. No proof of her involvement.

She would walk free.

Papa rubbed a hand over Brook's back, no doubt feeling the tension. "Dust yourselves off, gentlemen, and let's go home. I daresay the chef has cooked enough for an army as he prayed."

Brook wouldn't let Catherine ruin her homecoming. She made herself grin at the exaggerated look on Brice's face as he brushed the sandy soil from his trousers, and then she turned to Justin, her hand in her pocket again. The gold of his ring was warm and smooth—she'd cleaned it off with some of the water earlier. As he straightened his jacket, she stepped away from her father and held it out to him.

His grin bloomed, lopsided and mischievous, to match the gleam in his eyes. "Are you proposing, my lady, with that ring?"

She grinned right back and dropped to one knee. "Will you marry me, Duke?"

Laughter rang out all around her. Justin's loudest of all as he gripped her by the arm and pulled her back to her feet. "Get up, you fool woman. And yes." He planted a kiss soundly on her lips and snatched the ring from her hand. "I most assuredly will." The gold back where it belonged, he slid an arm around her and came back for a second, slower kiss. "I'll ask you properly once we're back to Whitby Park. I've a ring in my room there too. It's a bit smaller. Has more sparkle. Was my mother's."

She nestled into his side as her father gathered the horses' reins. "Your *yes* was binding, sir—asking again would be redundant. But I'll be proud to wear your mother's ring."

Justin leaned down again, fire in his eyes.

Brice's hands appeared between them, forcing their faces apart. "I've had trauma enough for one day." He shoved his way between them, grinning all the while as he slung an arm over each of their shoulders. "Am I best man, Stafford? Or will I have to fight Thate for the honor?"

"You'll have to fight *me*, if you don't get out of my way."

"Touchy, touchy." With a wink, Brice slid his arms free and moved ahead of them as the constable called out a greeting for Antony and Deirdre, safely out of the trees. "Brook will defend me if you try to pummel me. Isn't that right, my lady?"

"Not this time." She slid her arm around Justin's waist and tilted her face up toward his. She knew it, knew every feature and expression. And loved none so well as the way he looked at her now. As if she were his yesterday, his today. His tomorrow. "*Je t'aime.*"

His smile spoke as much as his words. "And I love you. Always."

EPILOGUE

LATE AUGUST 1911

The summer sun beat down hot and glorious upon them. The North Sea wind whipped and refreshed. Justin let go of the hand he held so that he could slide his arm around her waist instead, content to stand in the sand with Brook and do nothing but watch the waves roll in.

She rested her head against his shoulder. "I'm still not sure how I shall survive for months on end without the sea at hand."

Chuckling, Justin pressed a kiss to the top of her head. "I'll keep you well distracted, Duchess. I promise. And whenever you can't suffer it anymore, we'll come back here."

"If my father will have you, after you stole his footman." She gave him a cheeky grin and walked her fingers up his chest.

It was nearly enough to ruin a man's concentration. Justin chuckled and indulged in a long, slow kiss. When he had mentioned before the honeymoon that Peters wanted to move on, out of domestic service, Whitby had been the one to suggest he take on Hiram, so that he and Deirdre could travel together whenever Justin and Brook did. A fine solution. Justin and Hiram didn't know each other well yet, but he could appreciate a man who went through each day with such good cheer.

At least when such a man didn't constantly interrupt when he wanted to kiss his wife, with cleared throats and loud *ahem*s.

He pulled away with a scowl for Worthing, who stood a few feet away, his feet in the grass rather than the sand. "Have you made it your life's work to harass us, Worthing?"

His friend grinned. "You would think so, but no. It only seems that way because there's never a moment when you're *not* sneaking off with your wife for a kiss."

"I didn't know you were here—or coming." Brook left Justin's side long enough to greet Worthing with a kiss on his cheek. "On your way to Scotland?"

"Aye, that we are," he said in a fine imitation of the Highland burr. He nodded back toward Whitby Park as Brook returned to Justin's side. "Ella and my parents are having tea with Whit, who has already convinced them to tarry here until tomorrow. He said you were greeted with a visit from Catherine upon your return yesterday."

Justin settled a hand on Brook's back in time to feel her shudder. "A lovely homecoming from our honeymoon." They had envisioned a quiet evening telling Whitby all about their trip through the Mediterranean, their visit with Prince Albert. A quiet evening at home before their planned trip this evening to Azerley Hall, to get to know the new Lady Cayton. But then Lady Pratt had glided in, all sugary smiles over the venom they knew hovered beneath. "Put a pall on the whole evening."

Worthing pressed his lips together. "Did she try to make friends again?"

"She tried. As if I'm stupid enough to fall for her tricks a second time." Brook's fingers went to her necklace, to the pearl-hidden diamonds she still wore. They needed to decide what to do with them—but had all agreed to focus first on the wedding, on getting settled in at Ralin Castle. The long, cold winter would give them time enough to discuss red diamonds and Indian curses with her father. "As if I couldn't see the hate in her eyes. She loved Pratt, unfathomable as it seems. In her eyes, we killed him. Yet another person dead because of the Fire Eyes—yet another reason for her to think they should be hers."

She was playing it smart, though, Justin had to grant her that. Gathering a horde of supporters, making herself into a celebrity. Hand-in-hand with every article about Brook had been one about Catherine—the poor, deceived fiancée and then pregnant wife, who had been used by her husband because of her connection with the jewels.

The telegraph clerk hadn't been able—or willing—to identify Catherine as the one to send that false note. But Justin knew it. He *knew* it.

Brook wrapped her arms around her middle. "This isn't over. She'll bide her time, she'll let us get comfortable and perhaps focus for now on her coming child. But she'll strike again."

Justin drew in a slow breath. "Pratt waited nineteen years to avenge his father's death—I daresay Catherine won't be quite so patient to avenge his. We can't afford to relax, to let our guards down."

Worthing shoved his hands in his pockets and stared past them, to the glimmering sea. "You should just get rid of the things. Donate them to a museum."

"Even if we did, she would still seek revenge for him." Brook's fingers fell away from the pearls. "And she would still seek the diamonds. I know she would, and probably others besides her. If we donate them, then we pass along the curse to some unwitting museum staff. Guards would end up dead in attempted thefts. Other property destroyed. Other lives ruined because of these stupid things. I can't do that. I can't make someone else pay for them."

With a sigh, Worthing looked at Brook, then at Justin. "I see your point. The poor chaps at a museum wouldn't know how to defend against this. Wouldn't know that the best way to hold the evil at bay is through prayer."

A chill possessed Justin, despite the hot summer sun. He nodded. "We know, though. We know how to fight it."

"And yet . . . you've lost so much already. Both of you. You've had so much sorrow this past year." Worthing's brow had a furrow as deep as the sea. "You deserve peace as you start your life together."

"Brice—no." Brook shook her head wildly, sending curls into the clutches of the wind. "This isn't your fight. We appreciate all the prayers you've prayed for us, all the support you have given. But your involvement ends there. Don't try to take any of this upon yourself. I won't let you."

Worthing's grin reemerged, bright if a touch sad. "But I've gotten a taste for adventure. Let me help here or I'll have to go find a mountain to scale. A horde of pirates to fight off. Maybe a sheik to challenge."

"No."

The mirth fell away. "I have to, though. The Lord has made that very clear—and *I'll* have no peace if I don't obey Him."

Justin's fingers curled over his wife's shoulder. "Worthing—"

"She wouldn't have forgotten that I was there, too, when Pratt was killed. If she blames you, she blames me. If she's made a target of you, she's made one of me." He shrugged. "Might as well make it count and tell her I have the diamonds too. Get her to focus more on me than you for a while."

Brook shook her head. "She'd never believe it. She wants them too badly to think we'd ever give them up."

Justin shook his head, too, looked off into the distance. Narrowed his eyes at the glint of sun on blond hair. "Don't look now, but I believe she's watching us as we speak. No doubt thinks we're plotting how to keep the things from her."

"Then let's make it count." Worthing swallowed and pasted on a smile. "She'll believe it if she sees it. If you give them to me now."

"Brice." No laughter laced Brook's voice.

Worthing's grin faded again. "This is what we're supposed to do."

Justin felt the breath she drew in and sucked in one to match. "You can't be sure of that."

His breath of laughter sounded more cynical than amused. "You think not? If you have an argument with it, take it up with the Almighty. Perhaps you'll convince Him where I've failed."

Only Worthing could talk so calmly about arguing with God. "You can't actually want them. If you try to sell them, if word gets out, you'll be hunted down just like Rushworth was."

"What I want is for my friends to be safe!" He shoved a hand through his hair—his tell, Justin had learned, of the deepest unrest. "She could already be carrying your child, Stafford, or if not now, then soon. What then? Why would you not take whatever safety for them I can offer, meager as it is?"

While Justin tried not to let the hope and fear of a possible coming child overwhelm him, Brook gripped the dangling pearls, the diamonds within. "It won't help. She'll still come after us."

"Yes." Worthing held out a hand. "She'll come after all of us. But if I can get her to come after me first, then you two can focus on your marriage for now. On your baby—whenever one joins you."

Brook's eyes went narrow. "Why do you keep speaking of—?"

"Call it a hunch." A wink of a grin, quickly gone. Worthing wiggled his fingers. "Let me help you. I promise I'll tread with the utmost care. With constant prayer. I'll find a way to expose her for what she is, to see she meets justice. And then I'll return the diamonds. You have my word."

Brook took her bottom lip between her teeth and then looked up into Justin's eyes. Hers were damp. "He could be right. We could . . . I could be . . ." She splayed a hand over her stomach. "I don't want to bring a child into the middle of this."

Was she saying . . . ? She couldn't be sure, it was too soon. But if she thought it possible . . . Justin exhaled shakily. "All right. All right. But we'll help you plan. We'll help you catch her."

Brook was already working at the pearls. A diamond dropped into her palm, and then, a moment later, its twin.

Justin swallowed. All the times they'd spoken of them, but this was the first he'd seen them. She held out her palm, and the sun angled down and set the jewels aflame. Could Catherine see it, from where she stood on her bluff on Delmore land? Probably not—but she would guess. She would assume.

Despite his words, Worthing stood there a long moment staring at them. He lifted his hand slowly and scooped them from hers. Held them up to catch the light . . . and perhaps the attention of their distant observer. "Hello, trouble." Lowering his hand again, he slid it and the gems into his pocket. "I had better at least be named the child's godfather for this."

Brook breathed a strained laugh and leaned into Justin's side. "Be careful, Brice."

He nodded, waved a hand at them, and turned back toward the house. "I'm going to go and tell my parents you've invited us to spend Christmas with you at Ralin Castle. It's the least you can do, after all."

"We've rooms enough, I suppose." Justin chuckled as their friend stomped back down the hill.

Brook rested her head on his shoulder. "Sometimes it still feels so unreal. One of your stories."

He thought so nearly every morning, when he awoke with her in his arms. "This one must be called 'The Life of the Duchess.' And there are many adventures yet to be spun in it—all of which have the happiest of endings."

She smiled up at him, then glanced back toward the house for which Worthing strode. "And no doubt quite a lot of excitement we would all rather do without."

"You wouldn't know what to do with a boring life. If no danger found you, you'd create some."

At that she laughed, tossing back her head so it could blend with the music of wind and surf. Then she sighed. "I suppose it's time we leave for Azerley Hall."

"Mm." He smoothed back the curl that had blown into his face, tucked it behind her ear. "Cayton's note said Adelaide is excited to get to know you better."

"And I her. Though I don't know if I have it in me to be anything but polite to Cayton. Not seeing how Melissa still mourns the loss of him."

"He at least recognizes that he made a thorough mull of everything. Perhaps there's hope for him." He pressed a kiss to the top of her head. "Shall we, then?"

He expected another sigh, another grumble about Cayton. Instead, she grinned in that way only Brook could, the way that nearly stopped his heart. And she held up the key to the Rolls-Royce that had been, a minute ago, in his pocket. "I'll drive."

There was nothing for it but to laugh and chase her down the hill.

AUTHOR'S NOTE

I often say a book has been with me for a long time . . . but
no book has been with me as long as this one. When I was
twelve, Brook's story began in what I was determined would be
my first completed novel, entitled *Golden Sunset, Silver Tear*.
I finished it a year and a half later. After nine other published
books, nineteen years, four titles, and countless rewrites, I'm
beyond ecstatic to see Brook and Justin's story in print. And
with Bethany House, the first publisher I queried about it at
the age of fourteen!

One of the first revisions I made to the story as a teen was to
change the opening setting from a fictional kingdom to Monaco,
after learning of the Grimaldis' longest monarchy in history.
Though there was obviously never a Brook in that rich family,
she fits well with the actual history. Prince Louis, who I billed as
her father, was always at odds with *his* father, Prince Albert—
largely because he refused to marry and instead kept an actress
as his mistress. Their one daughter, Charlotte, was adopted into
the Grimaldi family legally so she could be named the crown

princess, and the principality could be kept from the hands of the next nearest relative—one Kaiser Wilhelm of Germany.

The biggest change Brook and Justin underwent, though, was when I decided to change the setting of the story from the 1860s to the 1910s. The credit there belongs to my fabulous agent, Karen Ball—and the change was one of those that, once I'd thought of how to do it, earned an "Of course! How could I have missed this all these years? *This* is when Brook was supposed to have lived!" The changing times and ideas perfectly fit the spirit Brook had always had, and though it required a complete overhaul of the story, it was one I took joy in.

For those wondering about the red diamonds, let me assure you that, though the Fire Eyes are fictional, the information shared about such jewels in general is true. They really are the rarest jewel in the world, and the largest red diamond is only five carats.

On a similar note, while I set my heroine's home in a real area and descriptions of Whitby and Yorkshire are taken from research, Whitby Park and Eden Dale are fictional locations, as are the other homes mentioned.

Like any story, *The Lost Heiress* couldn't have been written without help and input. Thanks to Patrick Collins of the National Motor Museum in Brockenhurst, UK, for taking the time to answer my questions about the Rolls-Royce that later became known as the Silver Ghost—and going above and beyond by scanning pages of its manual for me! And I'm also so grateful to my English reader, Elisabeth Allen, for volunteering to read over the manuscript and make sure no Americanisms worked their way into the story. You were a real godsend, Elisabeth! I also had to tap the immense knowledge of the British Raj of my Irish-born friend, Christine Lindsay—thanks so much for patiently answering my questions about what rank Henry should have, and what Deirdre would call her parents. And of course, Wendy Chorot for reviewing all my French for me—thanks, flower!

I'm so blessed to be surrounded by encouraging family and friends, from my parents (who told me my thirteen-year-old version of this book was great) to my husband, David (who has read so many versions of it, it's amazing he hasn't gone cross-eyed). I've had priceless input on these characters over the years from critique partners (Stephanie!) and agents and editors, all of whom contributed to the story I ended up telling. And I can't begin to say how grateful I am to Charlene and the team at Bethany House for believing it was Brook's time to be published. Karen S., I still can't get over coming full circle on this after so many years since that pitch at my first conference!

The Lost Heiress has become, in my mind, a symbol of determination—a lesson in how, when we're chasing our dreams, we should never stubbornly cling to the way we think our goals need to play out . . . but we should never give up on those loves the Lord has given us. I hope you enjoyed getting to know my first heroine. Over the years her name has changed, along with her station, her home, and her family. But her spirit is still the one I envisioned when I first sat down as a preteen with a pencil, a stack of loose-leaf notebook paper, and the determination to write a book. May her story be to you just a portion of what it has been to me all these years.

Roseanna M. White pens her novels beneath her Betsy Ross flag, with her Jane Austen action figure watching over her. When not writing fiction, she's homeschooling her two small children, editing and designing, and pretending her house will clean itself. Roseanna is the author of ten historical novels and novellas, ranging from biblical fiction to American-set romances to her new British series. She makes her home in the breathtaking mountains of West Virginia. You can learn more about her and her stories at www.RoseannaMWhite.com.

More Romance From Bethany House

Entering her fourth season, Lady Miranda Hawthorne secretly longs to be bold. But she is mortified when her brother's handsome new valet accidentally mails her private thoughts to a duke she's never met—until he responds. As she tries to sort out her growing feelings for two men, it becomes clear that Miranda's heart is not the only thing at risk for the Hawthorne family.

A Noble Masquerade by Kristi Ann Hunter, HAWTHORNE HOUSE
kristiannhunter.com

After being abandoned by the man she loved, Sophie Dupont's future is in jeopardy. Wesley left her in dire straits, and she has nowhere to turn—until Captain Stephen Overtree comes looking for his wayward brother. He offers her a solution . . . but can it truly be that simple?

The Painter's Daughter by Julie Klassen, julieklassen.com

At Irish Meadows horse farm, two sisters struggle to reconcile their dreams with their father's demanding marriage expectations. Brianna longs to attend college, while Colleen is happy to marry, as long as the man meets *her* standards. Will they find the courage to follow their hearts?

Irish Meadows by Susan Anne Mason, COURAGE TO DREAM #1
susanannemason.com

You May Also Enjoy...

When a map librarian and a young congressman join forces to solve a mystery, they become entangled in secrets more perilous than they could have imagined.

Beyond All Dreams by Elizabeth Camden
elizabethcamden.com

Charlotte wants to continue working as an assistant to her father, an eminent English botanist, but he feels it is time for her to marry. Will she find a way to fulfill her dreams and her family's expectations?

Like a Flower in Bloom by Siri Mitchell
sirimitchell.com

When Miss Harriet Peabody, a shop girl with big dreams, agrees to Mr. Oliver Addleshaw's unusual business proposal, neither of them foresees the chaos their charade will cause.

After a Fashion by Jen Turano
jenturano.com

⬧BETHANYHOUSE